My Sunshine

Also by Catherine Anderson in Large Print:

Always in My Heart
Blue Skies
Bright Eyes

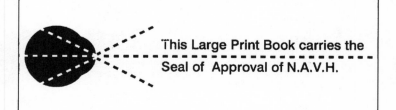

My Sunshine

Catherine Anderson

Published in 2005 by arrangement with NAL Signet, a division of Penguin Group (USA) Inc.

Wheeler Large Print Hardcover.

The text of this Large Print edition is unabridged. Other aspects of the book may vary from the original edition.

Set in 16 pt. Plantin by Ramona Watson.

Printed in the United States on permanent paper.

Library of Congress Cataloging-in-Publication Data

Anderson, Catherine (Adeline Catherine)
    My sunshine / by Catherine Anderson.
      p. cm.
    ISBN 1-59722-089-2 (lg. print : hc : alk. paper)
    1. Veterinarians — Fiction.   2. Large type books.
  I. Title.
  PS3551.N34557M9 2005
  813'.54—dc22   2005016949

This book is dedicated to Reverend James Radloff, known to his parishioners as Father Jim, a priest who has touched countless lives, including ours. As a writer, I seldom find myself at a loss for words, but sometimes feelings run too deep to be easily expressed. So I'll fall back on simplicity and merely say, "Thank you." Thank you for being such a wonderful, dedicated priest. Thank you for your friendship and guidance. Thank you for always being there. And, last but not least, thank you for all the wonderful Monday nights.

As the Founder/CEO of NAVH, the only national health agency solely devoted to those who, although not totally blind, have an eye disease which could lead to serious visual impairment, I am pleased to recognize Thorndike Press★ as one of the leading publishers in the large print field.

Founded in 1954 in San Francisco to prepare large print textbooks for partially seeing children, NAVH became the pioneer and standard setting agency in the preparation of large type.

Today, those publishers who meet our standards carry the prestigious "Seal of Approval" indicating high quality large print. We are delighted that Thorndike Press is one of the publishers whose titles meet these standards. We are also pleased to recognize the significant contribution Thorndike Press is making in this important and growing field.

Lorraine H. Marchi, L.H.D.
Founder/CEO
NAVH

★ Thorndike Press encompasses the following imprints: Thorndike, Wheeler, Walker and Large Print Press.

Acknowledgement

A wonderful lady named Virginia Son, my stepmother and good friend, was my inspiration as I wrote *My Sunshine*. Her courage and cheerful optimism became a template as I developed the character of Laura Townsend. Thank you, Virginia, for your fabulous smile and infectious laughter. You set an example for everyone who knows you by teaching all of us an invaluable lesson: how to keep going even when we can't quite remember the way or clearly see the signposts up ahead. When you read this book — and I know you'll be able to one day soon — I hope you see yourself in the story.

Prologue

Lightning flashed in the leaden sky, each brilliant burst quickly followed by a deafening clap of thunder. Rain pelted the vehicle with such force it sounded like pea gravel striking metal. Peering through the windshield, Isaiah Coulter could barely make out the houses along the tree-lined street. He dreaded the thought of making the fifty-foot sprint to the covered front porch of his parents' suburban residence. Not for the first time since this storm had started, he wished he'd thought to grab a jacket before leaving home that morning.

When he pushed open the door of the Hummer, his shirtsleeve grew instantly wet and icy, compliments of the high mountain chill that always descended on Crystal Falls, Oregon, when the autumn sunlight was obscured by clouds. Isaiah clenched his teeth, sprang from the vehicle, and broke into a run even as he slammed the door behind him.

Water streamed from his face by the time he reached the porch, and dripping shanks of dark brown hair were plastered to his forehead. Swearing under his breath, he raked back the strands with rain-slicked fingers and slapped uselessly at his soaked shirt.

"Mom?" he yelled as he opened the front door. "It's me, Isaiah!"

As he wiped his feet on the entryway rug, Isaiah scanned the tidy living area, barely registering any details because the furniture and decorations were so familiar. On the longest wall, the faces of his brothers and sister as well as his own stared back at him from countless framed photographs, a pictorial record of their lives from infancy to adulthood. The delicious smells of warm apple pie and freshly brewed coffee greeted him as he moved farther into the room.

"In the kitchen, dear heart!" Mary Coulter called.

Following his nose and the sound of her voice, Isaiah stepped into the archway. Standing at the kitchen counter, his mother flashed him a welcoming smile. Her plump cheeks rosy, her dark hair lying in loose curls around her face, she was, in Isaiah's eyes, just as beautiful at almost sixty as she had been twenty years ago.

"How's my best girl?" he asked.

"Hmph," she responded with a shake of her head. "And isn't that a fine kettle of fish? The handsomest of all my sons, and you're still single."

Isaiah knew very well that he wasn't the handsomest pup in her litter. In truth, he and his brothers were all carbon copies of their dad and looked pretty much the same. As for his being single, he liked it that way. Veterinary medicine was a demanding field, leaving him little time for personal relationships. Someday, when his life grew less hectic, he might consider settling down, but for now he needed to stay focused on his career.

"Ah, Mom," he replied in a whiny baritone, his stock response when Mary needled him about getting married.

"Don't you 'ah, Mom' me. Just look at you, Isaiah Joel, drenched to the skin and blue around the lips. You need someone with good sense to look after you." She tossed him a hand towel. "Mop up as best you can before you make puddles on my floor." She glanced at his boots. "If you've tracked in horse dung, I'll snatch you bald-headed."

Catching the towel in one fist, Isaiah blotted his face and dried the back of his neck. "My boots got pressure-washed coming across the lawn, and I wiped them dry on the rug. As for my lips being blue, that's because it's colder than a well digger's ass out there."

"Your lips are blue because it's October and you aren't wearing a coat. A man with your IQ should know better."

"I know better. I just forgot."

"You'd forget your head if it weren't attached. Absentminded, I guess, always thinking deep thoughts and oblivious to everything else."

"It was sunny when I left the house this morning."

"Grab your father's sweatshirt there on the back of the chair and put it on. You'll catch your death, sitting around in that wet thing you're wearing."

Isaiah did feel cold. He quickly divested himself of the wet garment, plucked a plastic shopping sack from the cloth bag holder hanging on a hook by the kitchen door, and stuffed the shirt inside. A moment later, as he drew his dad's sweatshirt over his head, his mother clucked her tongue, saying, "Your ribs are showing, Isaiah Joel. I swear, a high wind would blow you away."

Isaiah knew very well he wasn't that thin. "Ah, Mom."

Accustomed to Mary's scolding, Isaiah bent to kiss her cheek before taking a chair at the round oak table in one corner of the kitchen. "Man, that pie sure does smell good."

"Made it especially for you." Mary took two pie plates from the cupboard and set herself to the task of cutting the dessert. "It's not often anymore that I know ahead of time when you're coming over."

"If apple pie is my reward, I'll start calling in advance. It's my favorite."

Mary smiled. "Yes, I know. I'm your mother, remember."

"Thanks for making me a pie, Mom. That was sweet of you." Isaiah settled back on the chair. "Where's Pop?"

Mary released a shrill little sigh, conveying with a lift of her shoulders that her trials were many as Harv Coulter's wife. "He set out early this morning to meet Zeke at Natalie's supper club. Something's gone haywire with the refrigeration system, I think. After that, he was heading out to the Lazy J to help Hank and Jake mend fence line. His back has been giving him fits all week, but do you think he'll take it easy?"

"He enjoys helping at the ranch, Mom. Just because he's retired doesn't mean he has to stop living."

13

"I know." Mary released another sigh. "And Jake and Hank really do need the help right now. With Molly expecting again, and Carly trying to care for a baby so soon after eye surgery, both your brothers are spread mighty thin."

Isaiah had been so busy that he'd nearly forgotten his sister-in-law's corneal surgery. "How's Carly doing?"

"Good." Mary beamed a glad smile as she licked a bit of pie filling from her fingertip. "She can see, at any rate. The major problem right now is retraining her thing-amajig."

"Her visual cortex," Isaiah offered.

"There you go," she agreed with a nod. "All those medical terms go in one of my ears and out the other. Hank called last night. He bought some red duct tape and lined the edges of all the steps so Carly can tell where one ends and another starts. She almost fell on the front porch yesterday when she was carrying Hank Junior."

Isaiah winced. "No wonder Hank's taping the steps."

"He says it helped." Mary opened another cupboard to get some coffee mugs. "With no depth perception, she can't see the stair treads clearly."

Enjoying the warmth that still radiated

from the oven, Isaiah sighed and flexed his shoulders. It was strange, he thought, how quickly he could always relax in his mother's kitchen. He guessed it was because the room was a reflection of the woman herself: small, colorful, busy, and full of love.

The fact that Mary Coulter loved her children was in evidence everywhere he looked. All available surfaces were crowded with plaster handprints, school portraits, art projects gone yellow with age, and silly stuff that he or his siblings had given her over the years, including a knick-knack shelf filled with some old-fashioned power-pole insulators that Isaiah and his twin brother, Tucker, had carted home one long-ago day. Now it appeared that Mary had begun to collect grandchild keepsakes. Jake's son's baby booties were pinned to the ruffled white curtains at the window, and the front of the refrigerator was hidden by his crayon creations, all of which were nothing but scribbles.

Normally Isaiah disliked clutter, but somehow his mom made it work. The crowded walls and splashes of color were not only pleasing to the eye but also oddly soothing. The tension that had knotted his shoulders all day eased away as he rocked back in the chair. He observed his mother with a faint smile. Even her apron took him back through the years, a white frilly thing with embroidery on the pockets that she'd worn for as long as he could remember.

As always, she chattered nonstop as she worked, launching into a story about some neighbor's granddaughter as she drew a half-gallon of vanilla ice cream from the freezer and rifled through a drawer, looking for the scoop. Isaiah listened with only half an ear, his mind on a cow he'd treated that morning.

"Anyway," Mary said as she advanced on the table, "the reason I asked you to stop by is because I have an idea I want to run by you."

Isaiah accepted the plate his mother slid toward him. "An idea about what?" he asked as he forked up a chunk of juicy fruit and flaky golden crust that dripped with melting ice cream.

"Not what, *who*," Mary corrected. After filling two mugs with piping-hot coffee, she returned to the table and took a seat across from him. "It's about Laura, the young woman I've been telling you about."

Isaiah didn't recall his mother's saying anything about someone named Laura.

He sent her a bewildered look.

Mary huffed in exasperation. "Haven't you been listening?"

Isaiah swallowed and nodded. "Mostly."

"Mostly?"

He lowered his fork back to the plate. "I'm sorry, Mom. I guess I'm a little distracted."

"What is it this time?" Mary asked resignedly. "Not another rat fatality, I hope."

Isaiah winced at the reminder. Two months ago, a new tech had prepped some lady's pet rat for abdominal surgery. After shaving the rodent's belly, she'd tried to vacuum up the fur and accidentally sucked up the rat as well. Isaiah had been left to explain the rat's unexpected demise to its owner. It hadn't been one his finest moments as a veterinarian.

"No, not a rat, thank God. A cow this time. Uterine infection. I've done three flushes and hit her with every antibiotic there is. If this next round doesn't work, I'll have to put her down. The farmer's a young guy with a growing family. He can't afford to lose her."

Mary reached across the table to push a tendril of hair from Isaiah's eyes. "Oh, sweetie, you worry me so."

Isaiah caught her wrist to kiss her fingertips. "I'm fine, Mom. Just busy, that's all."

"You're not fine," she insisted. "Just look at you."

Isaiah glanced down. "What's wrong with me?"

"You've lost weight, for starters, and your hair is so long it's almost to your collar. And where on earth did you find that shirt you were wearing? It looked like you slept in it."

Isaiah shrugged. "It just looked bad because it was wet."

"Wet, my foot — it was wrinkled."

"I forgot to take it from the dryer, that's all. I shook it out."

Mary rolled her blue eyes toward the ceiling. "And your weight? You can't be eating right. What did you have for breakfast?"

Isaiah tried to recall and couldn't. "Yogurt, probably."

"Probably?"

"A dog got run over, Mom. I was in surgery at six forty-five."

"So you ate no breakfast." Mary nodded sagely. "And lunch? Please tell me you had something."

He'd wolfed down a package of Twinkies and a bag of Cheese Nips between ranch calls. "I ate while I was driving." He glanced guiltily at his hands, hoping his fingers weren't stained yellow. "I'm doing fine. Really."

"Ha. If ever a man needed a wife to look after him, it's you."

"Are we back to that again?" Isaiah chuckled. "Let up on me, Mom. Like getting married would solve everything? It's a new generation. Young women today don't stay at home and look after their husbands. They have demanding careers of their own, and that's just as it should be."

"There must be a few old-fashioned girls left out there."

If so, Isaiah hadn't encountered any. Not that he'd been looking. "Maybe so," he settled for saying, then glanced at his watch. "About that idea you wanted to discuss. If we're going to talk, we need to get cracking. I have to be back at the clinic by three."

Mary took a sip of her coffee. "Do you remember my neighbor, Etta Parks?"

"The old lady two doors down?" A fleeting image of a pretty, silver-haired woman passed through Isaiah's mind. "Yeah, I remember her."

Mary smiled. "Laura is her granddaughter. She's a lovely, sweet girl. Almost every day she comes by to see Etta while she's out walking the dogs."

"Dogs? How many does she have?"

"Oh, they're not actually hers." Mary's blue eyes went misty. "That's one of the ways Laura supplements her disability income, by walking people's dogs or caring for them while the owners are on vacation. I think she does other things as well, housework and ironing and such. But it's her knack with animals that made me think of you."

Isaiah realized that his mother was working her way up to something. He glanced at his watch again. "I'm sorry. I'm not following. A disability income, did you say?"

Mary filled in the blanks, explaining how Etta's granddaughter had gone swimming with friends five years before and hit her head on a rock when she dove into the river. "It left her with brain damage of some kind," she explained.

Isaiah dimly recalled hearing about that. For a while the young woman had been comatose and not expected to live, if he remembered correctly.

"When Laura awakened after the accident," his mother went on, "her whole life had been destroyed. I can't remember now what she did for a living — a scientist of some kind, I think. Very good income, lots of travel. Then, in a twinkling, it was all taken from her. Now she lives in an apartment over someone's garage and walks dogs to earn money."

"That's a shame," Isaiah said. And he meant it with all his heart. "I'm just not sure what any of this has to do with me."

The corners of Mary's mouth tightened. "Laura is such a pretty girl, and sweet as can be. Her life would be so much fuller if she had a regular job and could meet people her own age."

Isaiah shifted uneasily on the chair. "I suppose that's true, Mom, but practically speaking, what kind of work can a woman with brain damage do?"

"Well, you see, that's just the thing." Mary leaned slightly forward, her expression suddenly earnest. "She's absolutely wonderful with dogs, Isaiah. It occurred to me the other day that she might make an excellent kennel keeper."

"Whoa." Isaiah held up a hand. "You're not suggesting what I think you are. A kennel keeper at our clinic?" He shook his head emphatically. "Tucker and I are running a veterinary hospital, Mother, not a charity organization. We can't hire someone with brain damage."

"But, dear heart, Laura's brain damage isn't that bad. I never even knew something was wrong until Etta mentioned it."

"No, absolutely not. I'm sorry, Mom, I really am. I'd like to help her out, but there's just no way. Remember the rat? A perfectly normal woman pulled that stunt. Tucker and I have worked hard to get where we are. Our reputations as vets are on the line. We're responsible for the well-being of people's pets and farm animals. We can't have a mentally handicapped woman working at our clinic."

Mary pursed her lips. Isaiah knew that look. She'd used it on him a fair thousand times when he was a kid. "If you'll remember, your father and I loaned you boys the start-up capital you needed to open that clinic."

Isaiah pinched the bridge of his nose. That was true. The debt had been repaid in full, but that was beside the point. "I know we owe you a lot, Mom."

Mary nodded. "And it's not often I ask a favor."

Why, Isaiah wondered, was it so difficult for him to tell his mother no? He was thirty-three years old and hadn't lived at home since he started college. He guessed it was because his parents had always come through for him without fail when he needed them, and he felt obligated to do the same for them. "That's true. You seldom ask me for anything."

"Well, I'm asking now," she said softly. "I honestly believe Laura can do the work, Isaiah, and I know for a fact that you have trouble finding good kennel keepers."

Isaiah couldn't argue that point. Hosing dog poop down kennel drains wasn't a glamorous job.

"It seems to me the least you can do," Mary went on, "is interview her for the position." She spread her hands in appeal. "If you decide she isn't capable of doing the work, fine. I know you have a kind heart, and I'll trust your judgment. But won't you at least give her a chance?"

Isaiah knew when he was licked. "I'll have to talk with Tucker first. We're partners, remember. We don't make decisions like that independently."

Mary arched a sable eyebrow. "Have Tucker call me if he has any objections. I'll handle him."

Isaiah had no doubt that his mother would do just that.

Chapter One

Sweat filmed Laura Townsend's palms as she parked her old red Mazda in front of the Crystal Falls Animal Clinic. *A real job.* Since her phone conversation with Mary Coulter last night, those three words had danced repeatedly through her mind. She was thrilled at the prospect of working in an official capacity again, but she was also terrified. What if Isaiah Coulter actually hired her, and then she made some awful mistake?

After slipping the car keys into her purse, Laura sat for a moment, staring through the streaked windshield at the veterinary clinic, which faced a busy two-lane highway at the far north end of town. A sprawling brick structure with a wing at each end, it was frontally divided by a tall, wide bay with tinted floor-to-ceiling windows that overlooked a landscaped grass median bordered on both sides by walkways and parking slots. The pinkish color of desert sand, the building was striking, with several tiled rooflines that peaked and sloped together.

At the back of the clinic, a large, un-paved parking area peppered with barnlike structures, fenced enclosures, and ponderosa pines created a rural backdrop that suited the sparsely populated surroundings. The largest of the outbuildings bore a sign that sported the silhouette of a horse and the words EQUINE CENTER. It took Laura a second to sound out the words and to recall what they meant. No small operation, this, but a full-scale hospital for both large and small animals.

Did she really want to work in a place like this? More important, could she handle the responsibility? She was fairly happy as things were. A little lonely, maybe — okay, a *lot* lonely — but she managed to keep busy with her odd jobs and hobbies, and overall her life was far better now than the doctors and therapists had predicted five years ago. As long as she remained calm, she could speak fairly well, and she was finally able to watch television and movies, which she greatly enjoyed. Recently she'd even improved enough to listen to books on tape and could understand practically all the words. Why turn her world topsy-turvy by taking a job that might overwhelm her? Once she got a taste of something more, would she ever again be satisfied with her life as it was now?

Greatly tempted to drive away, Laura continued to stare at the clinic. What if kennel keepers were required to administer medication, and she misread a label? Or what if she had to take temperatures when the animals were sick? She had no idea if she could read a thermometer. *Don't set yourself up for failure.* That motto, drilled into her at rehab, had saved her a lot of grief over the last five years.

But she *wanted* this job. It would be so wonderful to work with other people again — to possibly even make friends close to her own age. She craved more human contact — a chance to talk and laugh with others, maybe even enjoy an occasional night out with the girls. She would never have those pleasures in her life if she always played it safe. Change involved a certain amount of risk, and taking chances took courage. It all boiled down to one question: Was she a coward?

Laura wrenched open the driver door and forced herself to exit the vehicle. *One step at a time.* Why worry about worst-case scenarios before she even got the job? During the interview she would be completely forthright with Isaiah Coulter about her disability. If he still wanted to hire her, she'd be delighted. If not, she would accept it, go home, and be happy with things as they were.

As Laura approached the clinic, she took measured breaths and forced the tension from her body. When she got in there, she wanted to put her best foot forward, not babble like an idiot and make a fool of herself. Aphasia, her type of brain damage, did not mix well with agitation. The last therapist had best explained it by likening Laura's brain to a complicated electrical panel, and agitation to a mental wrench that blew all the circuits. Staying calm was as vital as breathing to someone like her.

To that end, Laura tried to talk herself down, something she'd done repeatedly since her conversation with Mary Coulter last night. *It's just a dumb job, a dead-end position most people wouldn't even want.* Somehow, though, the words failed to comfort her as she grasped the handle of the door and pushed it open. She wasn't like most people, not anymore, and this might be her only chance to rejoin the workforce and lead a halfway normal life.

Laura stopped just inside the doorway. The spacious lobby was crammed with customers, several waiting in line at the U-shaped front desk, others seated in a divided waiting area to her right, one section for people with dogs, the other for those with cats. The drone of human voices was interspersed with the shrill barks of nervous canines and the terrified meows of felines imprisoned in pet carriers.

Four harried receptionists manned the counter, while two others bustled back and forth behind them, pulling files, plucking printouts from machines, and answering phones. Laura got a jumbled impression of pristine white walls, attractive cedar accents, a vaulted wood ceiling, and the faint, pleasing scent of lemony disinfectant.

She had never imagined that a veterinary clinic would be this busy — or so interesting. She studied a dachshund in a bright yellow raincoat, then turned her attention to a small brown-and-white dog in a siren-red pet stroller. Recently she had watched a newscast about the billions of dollars Americans spent annually on their pets, but she'd never realized until now just how frivolous some of those expenditures were. She could scarcely believe her eyes when she saw a Chihuahua in a colorful wool poncho and a miniature sombrero. *Amazing.* And people thought *she* was strange?

Concerned about the time, she glanced at her watch, an old-fashioned clock-face timepiece with dots instead of numbers. Numbers tended to confuse her because she sometimes saw them upside down or backward. It was two dots shy of four thirty. Normally ten minutes would have given her plenty of leeway, but the lines at the desk were three and four deep and didn't appear to be moving quickly. She hated to wait her turn and risk being late for her appointment, but unless she crowded to the front, she saw no alternative.

Good manners won out, and she took her place behind a man in dusty jeans, a red windbreaker, and a greasy yellow ball cap.

Shoulders aching from long hours in surgery, Isaiah hunkered down in front of a cage to check on a patient just coming out from under general anesthesia, a six-month-old chocolate Lab that had gotten its right rear leg tangled in barbed wire. By the time the owner found the dog, the leg had been damaged beyond repair, and Isaiah had had no choice but to amputate. The operation had gone well, but the pup had lost a great deal of blood and was weak despite a lifesaving transfusion from its sire.

"Hey, Hershey." Isaiah opened the cage door to check the dog's gum color. "Oh, yeah, you're doing great. Before you know it you'll be back on your feet and feeling fine."

The Labrador whined and nudged Isaiah's wrist with a dry nose. A firm believer that a little TLC was as important after surgery as pain management and good medical care, Isaiah stayed for a moment to scratch the animal's ears.

It was sad to see a dog so young lose a leg, but Isaiah knew from experience that canines were amazingly resilient. If this pup recovered — and all indications were positive — the missing limb probably wouldn't slow him down.

"You've got a lot of great years ahead of you, Hershey," Isaiah whispered. The realization helped to ease the ache in his shoulders. *Another success.* Over time, Isaiah had learned to appreciate the successes, because, like any doctor, he also had many failures. "A lot of great years."

Just then Isaiah heard someone enter the room behind him. Because of the hour, he guessed without looking that it was Belinda, the technician who had assisted him in surgery all afternoon. She opened the fridge. An instant later a soft spewing sound told him she'd just pulled the tab on a soft-drink can.

"You thirsty?" she asked. "All we've got is diet orange, but it's wet."

"No, thanks." What Isaiah needed was a hearty meal. He'd had a bagel for breakfast early that morning and hadn't had a chance to eat since. It was now half past six. "I think I'll wrap it up and get out of here." He pushed to his feet and gave her a weary smile. "You do the same. You put in one hell of a day."

A brunette with regular features, pretty brown eyes, and a great figure, Belinda laughed softly. "In the six months since I've been here, when haven't we put in a hell of a day?"

"Point taken." Isaiah rubbed the back of his neck. "Tucker and I need to bring in a couple of partners."

"Good idea. Unfortunately that won't help us out tonight." She flashed him a saucy grin. "Got any plans for dinner? I make a mean spaghetti sauce, and I've got a fabulous merlot I've been saving for a special occasion."

This wasn't the first time Belinda had invited Isaiah over for a cozy supper, and he

31

was running out of polite excuses. Meeting her hopeful gaze, he decided it was time to level with her. "You're an attractive lady, Belinda."

"Glad you noticed."

"Oh, I've noticed." Not wishing to hurt her feelings, Isaiah injected more enthusiasm into that rejoinder than he actually felt. The truth was, he worked too hard and slept too little nowadays to feel much interest in the opposite sex. "But for purely selfish reasons, I'm not going to act on it. You're a valuable member of my team here at the clinic. I can't risk losing you over a workplace romance gone sour."

She set the soda can on the counter and shrugged out of her blue smock. Underneath, she wore a tight green sweater that showcased ample breasts. "We have so much in common: a keen interest in veterinary medicine, a love of animals, and a mutual desire to excel at what we do. What's to say it'll ever go sour?"

Isaiah chuckled. "Murphy's Law." He crossed the room, clasped her shoulder, and gave her what he hoped was a regretful smile. "Let's keep it professional. All right? You're a fabulous tech, one of the best we've had."

"I'll take that as a compliment, even

though you haven't been in business all that long."

"Going on three years — long enough to know a great technician when I see one. We can't afford to lose you."

Her eyes went misty. The corners of her mouth quivered as she said, "Spaghetti and professional conversation, then. We both have to eat."

"I'm done in," he replied. "Maybe another time. Tonight the spaghetti will come out of a can — if I can muster the energy to hunt up the can opener."

"You don't know what you're missing," she called as he left the room.

Isaiah didn't bother with a reply. He'd been polite, hadn't minced words. There was nothing more to say. Maybe Belinda was one of those women who had trouble taking no for an answer — or maybe he was sending her mixed signals. That was possible, he supposed. He admired her professional skills and enjoyed her quick wit and sense of humor. Unfortunately, liking a woman and wanting an intimate relationship with her were two different things.

Belinda was attractive, but he felt no spark, no zing. Not that it came as a surprise. The clinic was so busy that even

Tucker, who had taken their brother Hank's place as the Coulter family lothario, had backed off on dating recently. Neither he nor Isaiah had the time or energy for much of a social life.

Isaiah opened his office door, stepped inside, and stopped dead. A blonde was straightening the framed diplomas on the wall behind his desk. He gave her slender backside a slow once-over. She wore a loose, bulky white sweater that somehow managed to accentuate the narrow expanse of her shoulders and the trimness of her waist. As his gaze dipped lower, his recent certainty that he was too preoccupied and exhausted to feel physical attraction went out the proverbial window. Snug blue jeans cupped a delightfully well rounded posterior and showcased a pair of shapely legs that begged for a much longer look.

Because it was so late, Isaiah assumed she worked for the janitorial service that came in each evening after the clinic closed. "Hi, there."

She jumped as if he'd jabbed her with an electric prod and whirled to face him. "Oh!" She splayed a slender, fine-boned hand at the base of her throat. "I'm sorry — for touching your things. They were — hanging crooked."

She spoke in a slow, halting way that Isaiah blamed on nervousness. "I hope you dust them while you're at it. Half the time they forget, and Val, our office manager, goes ballistic when she finds cobwebs."

A bewildered look came over her face. And a very pretty face it was, an almost perfect oval with large hazel eyes lined with thick, sooty lashes, delicate features, and a full, lush mouth. Her hair was the color of expensive cognac, streaked with wisps of lighter blond, and was cut in a collar-length, every-which-way style.

Isaiah felt sure he had never seen the lady before. He would have remembered. No big surprise. The cleaning company was continuously training new people, mostly college students in sore need of extra cash. This woman looked older than that, but not by much, late twenties at a guess. He wondered if she was studying for her master's degree.

"No need to stop what you were doing," he told her. "I'm not here to work. I just have to grab a couple of things." As he leaned around the door to get his jacket, he added, "Can you make sure to empty my trash? They've forgotten to dump it a few times."

"Your trash?"

The confusion in her voice caught Isaiah back just as he started to tug his jacket from the hook. Hand hovering over the leather, he gave her another long study. "You are one of the cleaning crew, right?" When she only gaped at him, he lowered his arm. "No, I guess not." He ventured an inquisitive smile. "So, who are you, then?"

"My name is —" She broke off, flicked the tip of her tongue over her lower lip, and then stared at him with what could only be mounting dismay. "My name is —" She thrust a hand into her hair and took three deep breaths. "Oh, *God,* just give me a second."

"No problem." Relaxing his weight against the door to push it closed, he crossed his arms and offered her another smile. "Maybe we should move on to how I can help you and come back to the name business later."

Some of the rigidity left her body. She pressed a fingertip against her temple, closed her eyes, and slowly exhaled. "I'm L-Laura Townsend."

Isaiah's stomach dropped. *Laura Townsend, the four-thirty interview.* The memory punched into his mind like a hard fist. He'd been doing an exploratory on a shepherd with a lacerated bowel when

Gloria, one of the secretaries, had paged him on the intercom. "Tell Gloria to have Ms. Townsend wait in my office," he had told one of the techs, and then the chocolate Lab had come in with a mangled leg, and he had completely forgotten about it.

All the starch went out of Isaiah's spine. He let his head fall back against the door and almost groaned. "I am so sorry." He straightened and glanced at his watch. Two hours — she'd been waiting for over two hours. He would have been climbing the walls. "This is inexcusable." He hurriedly explained about the emergencies that had come in. "Things got so crazy, I totally forgot you were here."

"It's okay." Her lovely eyes went dark with concern. "Did the dogs both live?"

Once again, Isaiah noticed how slowly and deliberately she formed her sentences. *Brain damage.* It all made sense now — her flustered reaction when he startled her, then the confusion about her name. "The shepherd swallowed a piece of glass," he replied. "Fortunately his owners suspected that he had, and the moment he started to act sick, they brought him in. The damage wasn't as bad as it could have been. I think he'll pull through."

She looked relieved to hear that, which

told him more about her than she could possibly know.

"What about the Lab?" she asked. "Will he live, too?"

"He'll make it, but he wasn't quite so lucky. The leg couldn't be saved."

"Oh, no." A distant look entered her eyes. "The poor thing. How will he walk?"

"Dogs are amazing creatures. They do very well on only three legs. In a few weeks he'll be back out chasing field mice and squirrels." Isaiah pushed erect. "Enough about that. I can't believe I left you waiting all this time. You must think I'm the rudest person alive."

She hugged her waist and shook her head. "Saving two dogs was much more im-portant than the meeting with me."

She said *important* as though it were two separate words. "The least I could have done was send someone to tell you I was tied up."

"It was better that I waited." Her mouth turned up sweetly at the corners. Her smile lent her lovely countenance a glow that made him feel as if the sun had just broken through on an overcast day. "It gave me a chance to hear all the stuff going on out there." She inclined her head toward the door. "It gets very busy here — hurt animals and upset people. I don't think I'm right for the job, after all."

Isaiah was still struggling with the fact that *this* was Laura Townsend. Granted, his mother had told him she was pretty, but he'd learned from hard experience that Mary Coulter's taste in women seldom jived with his own. There had also been the brain-damage thing. Maybe it had been bad of him — okay, no maybe to it; it had been *really* bad of him — but he had envisioned a dumpy, shuffling individual with a vacuous expression and a bottom lip perpetually shiny with drool. He hadn't been prepared for hazel eyes bright with intelligence, a body that could stop traffic, or a face to break a man's heart.

When she moved past him to get her coat, he snapped back to the moment. "You're leaving?"

Smiling, she tugged the pink jacket from a hook. As she drew it on, she nodded. "I think it's best." She drew her purse from where it had been hanging beneath the coat. "You need someone who's quick on her feet, not someone like me, who gets rattled and forgets her name."

As she started for the door, Isaiah made a snap decision. "I need someone who loves animals." Even as he spoke, he had to wonder what he was doing. "Working in the back, you seldom have to deal with emergencies."

"No?"

"By the time a dog or cat is put in a kennel, the worst is usually over. The job mostly involves washing down cages, changing bedding, and refilling food and water dishes. The only confusion in the kennels is usually generated by the animals themselves. The dogs tend to bark a lot, trying to get attention. The noise is so bad you can barely hear yourself think. The cats meow almost as much, probably for the same reason."

She gave him a wondering look. "And that's all there is to it?" She pushed at her hair. The golden wisps drifted back into place like strands of silk. "I wouldn't have to give out meds or take temps?"

Isaiah noted that she shortened both long words in that sentence. Words with more than two syllables were clearly difficult for her to pronounce.

"No medications, no taking temperatures," he assured her. "My mom says you're absolutely fabulous with dogs. Is that true?"

Still smiling, she wrinkled her nose, a gesture he felt sure was meant to convey humility, but instead only made her look cute as a button. "I like them a lot." She lifted her narrow shoulders in a slight shrug. "They don't care how well I can talk, only how my voice sounds."

Isaiah didn't care how well she could talk, either. She managed to communicate. That was all that mattered. "Do you like cats?"

"Yes. Not as much as dogs, but I like them."

Isaiah crossed his arms. Before he could offer the lady a job, there was a lot more about her that he needed to know, but he was well on his way to believing that his mother was right: Laura Townsend might have what it took to be a great kennel keeper. "If I apologize profusely for making you wait, ingratiate myself, and beg a lot, will you stay and let me interview you for the job? If I let you leave without at least talking to you, my mom will have my head."

A dimple flashed in her cheek. "Your mom is a sweet lady. She won't be mad. Just tell her you don't think I'm right for the job."

"That isn't precisely true. I think you may be perfect for the job."

"You do?"

He gestured at the castered chair in front of his desk. "Please, Laura, have a seat. Maybe you're right, and you aren't suited for the work. Neither of us will ever know if you won't stay and discuss the particulars with me."

She glanced hesitantly at the chair. Isaiah saw that she was sorely tempted, which told him she wanted the job a lot more than she was letting on.

"Just to talk," he assured her, and then settled the matter by grasping her elbow to lead her toward the desk. After pressing her down onto the chair, he circled to sit across from her. She hugged the coat close as if she were chilled.

Isaiah rocked back in his chair and rested a booted foot on his opposite knee. "Kennel work requires three things: a love of animals, a kind heart, and a strong stomach. On a glamour scale of one to ten, it's about a negative one." He saw a tiny frown pleat her brow and wondered if he might be talking too fast. Relaxing more deeply into the leather cushions, he made a conscious effort to slow down. "The worst part of the job is having to clean up a lot of smelly messes," he went on. "We occasionally board healthy animals, but mostly they're either sick or recovering from surgery."

She clasped her hands on her lap, the clench of her fingers so tight that her knuckles went pale. "Did your mom tell you I have brain damage, Dr. Coulter?"

"Isaiah," he corrected, "and, yes, she mentioned it. A swimming accident, I believe she said."

She nodded. "Five years ago. It left me with aphasia." Her cheek dimpled in a fleeting smile. "I can finally say it. For a long time I couldn't."

Isaiah subscribed to a few medical journals to keep abreast of the advances made in treatments for humans. Canines had many of the same ailments, and the same medications often helped them. As a result, he had recently read an article about aphasia, which affected approximately a million Americans to varying degrees, their numbers growing at an alarming rate of about eighty thousand annually. Some people became afflicted because of strokes, others due to head injuries that damaged the left lobe of the brain.

"Ah," he said. "Aphasia affects language, doesn't it?" Isaiah also knew what aphasia did not affect — a person's intelligence. Victims were essentially trapped in their own bodies, the damage to the left lobe interfering with normal brain signals. Many people had weakness on the right side of the body. In severe cases, sufferers were unable to speak and understood very little or nothing of what was said to them. Laura Townsend was fortunate in that regard. "You seem to speak quite well."

"I couldn't at first." She looked him directly in the eye. "And I still have problems."

Now that he knew what kind of brain damage she had, Isaiah better understood why.

"Even if I'm thinking the right word," she went on, "I can say the wrong one — and sometimes when I get nervous, even words that should be easy, like my name, just won't come to me."

Little wonder his mother's heart went out to this young woman. She was beautiful and obviously very bright. One had only to look into her eyes to see that. Yet she'd been reduced to this — applying for a menial job that many people wouldn't even want. Even sadder was the undeniable fact that neither he nor any other vet would normally consider hiring her.

The realization made him feel small. How many people like Laura lived in or around Crystal Falls — people the world ignored and had left behind? Her brain injury clearly wasn't so severe that she had nothing to contribute. All she needed was for someone to give her a break.

He hated to embarrass her by asking personal questions. When he tried to imagine how he might feel if he were in her shoes, he almost cringed. But there were some things he had to know before he offered her a job.

"Are you able to read, Laura?"

"On a good day." She shrugged, the gesture implying that there were worse things. "About a third-grade level the last time I was tested."

He tugged on his earlobe. "And on a bad day?"

"The letters jump around." She pushed at her hair again, a gesture he was coming to suspect was a nervous habit. "My per-periph—" She broke off and lifted her hands in defeat.

"Your peripheral vision?" he supplied.

She nodded. "It's messed up, worse some days than others. I can still read the words in the middle — if they're short."

Isaiah jotted a note on a Post-It pad, ripped off the top sheet, and handed it to her. "Can you read that?"

She stared down at the writing for a full two seconds. "This isn't a good day," she said with an airy laugh that was just a little shaky. "When I get nervous, it's always worse."

A strange, achy sensation filled Isaiah's throat. Being tested on her reading ability obviously unsettled her. "It's not a pass-or-fail thing. Just take your time. Give it your best shot."

Her delicate brows scrunched together over the bridge of her nose. "You spelled out the numbers."

"We do that here to avoid mistakes. I had a one mistaken for a seven once. Luckily the result wasn't disastrous. Now it's our policy to write the number and also spell it out."

She looked relieved. "That's good. That you spell them out, I mean. Numbers are tricky for me. Sometimes I see them upside down or backward." She hunched over the note, frowned again, and haltingly read the words aloud. "Three — cups — dry — food, two —" She broke off and looked up. "There's an X all by itself."

"It's an abbreviation for 'times,' in this case, two times daily. I use it a lot in chart instructions."

"Oh." She nodded. "Two times daily. I see."

She laid the paper on the desk and smoothed the tacky edge with trembling fingertips. Watching her, Isaiah found himself wanting to pat her hand. "You managed that very nicely. Can you remember from now on what an X stands for?"

"I think so."

"Do you have difficulty counting?"

"I lose track without my beans."

He'd been almost convinced that she could do the work. Now she'd thrown him a curveball. "Without your *what?*"

"Beans." She fished in a pocket of her coat and held out her hand. Several dried kidney beans rested on her outstretched palm. "It's — a trick — from rehab. I carry twenty with me. That way, when I have to count, I don't lose track."

"What if you have to count to over twenty?"

She put the beans back in her pocket. "I'm in deep doo-doo."

He gave a startled laugh, pleased on the one hand that she could joke about it, but sad for her as well. "What did you do for a living before your accident, Laura? My mom couldn't recall."

She puffed air into her cheeks. "Why does that matter? I can't do it now."

Isaiah acknowledged the point with a nod. "True, and it doesn't really matter. I'm just curious."

"I, um, did — studies — before they built roads." She pressed her lips together and swallowed. "To see if traffic would hurt the plants and ani-mals." She gestured helplessly again. Her eyes darkened with frustration. "I was an env-envi—" She went back to clasping her hands, the tendons in her neck growing distended as she struggled to speak. Finally she released a taut breath, squeezed her eyes closed, and shook her head.

Isaiah realized that he was leaning forward in the chair, his muscles knotted, his teeth clenched. *God.* He wanted to help her get the words out, only he couldn't. "An environmental scientist?" he offered.

Her sooty lashes fluttered open. "Yes. I w-worked all over the N-Northwest."

She'd once done environmental-impact studies, and now she had to carry beans in her pocket in order to count? He had taken tons of biology courses while studying to become a vet and had a fair idea of what it took to become an environmental scientist. What courage it must have taken for her to pick up the shattered pieces of her life and build a new one. In a very real way, she was a phoenix that had risen from the ashes.

Gazing across the desk at her, Isaiah

reached a decision guaranteed to please his mother. "Being a kennel keeper won't be nearly as exciting as doing environmental-impact studies."

"I don't care about excite-ment. I'd just like a normal job again. I miss working with people and having friends."

Searching her expression, Isaiah could almost taste her yearning. "If a job is all you want, you're in luck. Judging by what I've seen so far, there's no reason you shouldn't be able to handle this one just fine."

"There isn't?"

She sounded so incredulous that Isaiah chuckled. "No, there isn't. You may need a little extra training before we let you take a shift by yourself, but that's a simple enough thing to arrange."

For an instant she looked at him as if he'd just offered her the moon. Then her expression clouded. "What if I make a bad mistake?"

"You'll be monitored closely during the training period. If you make a mistake, and I stress the 'if,' the person training you will catch it. At the end of two weeks we'll do a performance review. If you're going to have problems doing the work, it should be apparent by then." Isaiah lowered his foot to the floor and swiveled on his chair to face the desk. "It's only ten dollars an hour to start, and we can't offer you full-time. Veterinary clinics require an inordinate number of employees in order to cover all the shifts and give everyone enough time off."

Laura had never really thought about the behind-the-scenes operation of an animal clinic, but she supposed it would be similar to a hospital, with inpatients requiring constant care or observation.

"The animals are left alone here from about six in the evening — sometimes later, depending on when Tucker and I leave — until nine, when a night-shift person arrives," he went on. "Then they're left alone again from two in the morning until six. But aside from those brief periods, we've got to have someone here seven days a week. As a result, we have the usual full-time employees who work the same days all week — office personnel, technicians, and tech assistants — plus a number of part-time people who work rotating shifts. Kennel keepers fall into that group."

She nodded, an indication to Isaiah that she was following him.

"For a kennel keeper, it works out to about twenty hours a week, I think."

"Part-time is better for me," she assured him. "I can't work too much without losing part of my assist-ance."

"There, you see? This may turn out to be the perfect job for you."

Her cheeks flushed with pleasure, and a gleam of excitement lighted her eyes. "Maybe so," she agreed.

"In addition to the position being only part-time, you'll also have two bosses, my-self and my brother Tucker." Isaiah ges-tured toward the door. "Our building is laid out like a plus sign. We have the lobby at the front and a kennel at the rear, which serve both the north and south wings. Tucker conducts his practice in the north section; I conduct mine in the south, and we share the front office and the kennels. I have techs and assistants who work pri-marily with me. Tucker does as well. But the office and kennel people work for both of us."

"I see."

"Will it bother you, having two bosses?"

She considered the question for a mo-ment and then shook her head. "I don't think so."

"Does that mean you'll take the job?"

She gave him a questioning look. "If your brother is going to be my boss, too, won't he want to meet me?"

Isaiah almost said that their mother would snatch Tucker bald-headed if he threw a wrench in the fan blades, but he settled for, "We're not quite that formal around here. Tucker and I trust each other's judgment. If I think you're the lady for the job, he won't quibble with my decision. And I do. Think you're the lady for the job, I mean."

She beamed another smile, revealing small, perfectly straight teeth. "Well, in that case, yes, I'd like to give it a try."

Isaiah had a feeling that *try* had been her motto for the last five years. Only a positive, do-or-die attitude had gotten her where she was today. He opened a drawer and drew out an application form. "How does this sound? We'll get you trained and see how you're doing in two weeks. If you've had problems doing the work, I'll let you go then, no hard feelings. If you're doing fine, we'll give it another two weeks, just to be sure, and then we'll make it permanent."

"That sounds good."

Isaiah asked the usual questions, getting her full name, her birth date, and her last place of employment. Because of her disability, her responses took a little longer than normal. By the time he got down to the withholding section, his stomach was snarling with hunger, and his hands were getting shaky. He hurriedly jotted down her Social Security number and returned the card to her.

"That about covers it," he said, rocking back in the chair. "How soon can you start training?"

"I can come in mornings now. Later in the day will be harder. I do odd jobs. I don't want to quit any of them until I know this job will last. I need the money."

Isaiah tossed his pen on the desk blotter. "For the time being, training in the morning will work fine. If all goes well, we'll readdress your hours when the thirty days are up. Once you become a permanent member of the team, you'll be required to work the night shift about one week a month. It's from nine until two in the morning. We rotate our kennel people. That way no one gets stuck on night shift all the time. Will that pose a problem?"

She shook her head. "Nights are fine."

His stomach growled again, so loudly this time that her gaze dropped to his midsection. Embarrassed, he flattened a hand over his diaphragm. "I'm sorry. I haven't eaten since six this morning."

Her eyebrows lifted. "That isn't good for you."

"So my mother tells me." He smiled sheepishly. "When I get busy, I'm a little absentminded, I'm afraid."

Her eyes danced with amusement. "I noticed."

He had to laugh. "I really am sorry about that." He bumped his temple with the heel of his hand. "I can't believe I forgot you were waiting in here."

"I'm the queen of forget-ting. Don't feel bad." She nibbled her lower lip. "What's his name?"

Isaiah gave her a blank look. "Pardon?"

"The brown Lab that lost his leg."

"Ah. His name is Hershey, after the chocolate bar."

"Hershey," she repeated softly. "Maybe I'll get to meet him."

Isaiah would have offered to introduce her to the dog right then, but he was starving and needed to get something in his stomach fast. "That depends on when you can start training." He put the application in the center drawer. "He'll be here only a couple of days."

"As long as I have after-noons free for my other jobs, I can start right away."

"Tomorrow?"

She thought about it for a moment, then nodded. Urgency to eat driving him, Isaiah rose and circled the desk to grab his jacket. "Can you come in at six? They start pretty early in the kennels."

"Six will be fine."

As he slipped on his coat, he said, "I'll leave a note for Susan Strong, the gal who'll be opening up in the morning. If I'm not here, she'll get you all lined up."

Laura retrieved her purse from the floor and slung the strap over her shoulder as she stood up. "Thank you. I'm very glad for this chance. I can't promise I won't make mistakes, but I'll try my best."

"Your best is all anyone can expect."

She nodded and turned to the door. At the last second, she hesitated and glanced back at him. "One thing."

"What's that?"

She swallowed hard and stood there for a moment, turning the doorknob back and forth. Her eyes sparkled with pride as she met his gaze. "I need to know that you'll tell me if I'm not doing the work well enough. I don't want the job unless I'm really good at it."

"I'll tell you," he promised.

She nodded, said good night, and let herself out. Isaiah stared somberly at the closed door after she left, wondering if he'd be able to follow through on that promise. Laura Townsend had touched him in a way few people ever had. If she wasn't able to do the work and he had to fire her, it would be one of the hardest things he'd ever done in his professional career.

Chapter Two

As Laura drove to the clinic the next morning, an eerie predawn gloom blanketed the northbound bypass. When she reached the outskirts of town, she saw that a faint crescent moon still shone in the blue-gray sky, its bottom tip reaching so low it seemed to touch the tops of the ponderosa pines that crowded the banks along each side of the road.

Steering with her left hand, Laura took careful sips from a spillproof mug that she'd filled with coffee before leaving her garage apartment. Each time the bitter brew washed over her tongue, she grimaced. She'd been running late and hadn't bothered to use her beans to keep track of the scoops she'd put in the filter basket. The result was the equivalent of Mississippi mud. Always the optimist, she consoled herself with the thought that one cup would do her this morning. In order to wake up, she normally needed at least two.

Just as Laura set aside the mug and reached to turn on the radio, her cell phone rang. She groped in her purse, found the device, and flipped it open. "Morning, Gram."

"How did you know it was me?" Etta Parks asked.

Laura checked to make sure the oversize mug hadn't tipped sideways in the cup holder. "You said you would call this morning to make sure I got up on time."

"Which you did!" Etta noted cheerfully. "It's good to know you've finally mastered that darned alarm clock."

"Not really." The alarm clock Etta referred to had been one of Laura's Christmas gifts from her mother last year, a digital gadget that was too complicated for her to set or read. "As soon as Mom and Dad moved, I stuck it in a drawer. I'm using my old windup again."

Etta gave a raspy laugh, compliments of a smoking habit that had spanned over forty years. "Uh-oh. Do I detect a trace of rebellion in your voice?"

"No. I think Mom's right. I'll never get better unless I work at it. But I need to choose my battles."

"And be practical. If you learn to set a digital alarm with all the bells and whistles, how will it improve your quality of life?"

"Good point."

Etta sighed. "Don't feel too bad about the alarm clock. The instant your mother left town, I got rid of that horrid bedspread she gave me."

"The green one?"

"I called it the Rambo spread. It was supposed to be a floral pattern, but it looked like camouflage."

"What'll you tell Mom when she comes back for a visit?"

"That I wore a hole in it having hot sex with all my lovers."

Laura gave a horrified laugh. "You are *so* bad."

"Not nearly as bad as Marsha thinks I am." Etta sighed. "If only I were having that much fun. It's so nice having them down in Florida. She calls me once a week, and we have a nice little chat. She asks questions, I tell her what she wants to hear, and she never gets in a dither."

As much as Laura loved her mother, she knew exactly what her grandmother meant. Marsha Townsend was a wonderful woman, but she had a tendency to micromanage other people's lives. Laura didn't miss all the hovering, and if she never had to take another brain-enhancement herbal supplement, it would be too soon. Her mom still sent her bottles of pills — all the old standbys and anything new that promised to work a miracle — but now Laura could just toss them in the trash.

The click of Etta's cigarette lighter came over the line. "So how are you this morning? Still nervous about the job?"

"Very," Laura confessed. "I'm afraid I'll mess up."

"Sweetheart, you're so good with animals. You're going to be the best kennel keeper they've ever had. Trust me on this. Sweet old grannies know about these things."

Laura's sweet old granny slept in lacy teddies, one a mind-boggling hot pink. She'd also dated four different men in the last six months, all of them over a decade younger than she was.

"There's going to be a lot for me to learn," Laura reminded her.

"You can handle it."

"I hope so." Laura tucked the phone under her chin so she could take another sip of coffee. The sun had risen higher in the sky, and the light coming at an angle through the trees dappled the blue-gray highway with splashes of gold and shadow. "It'll be fun to have a real job again."

"I'm so happy for you, honey."

"I'm happy for me, too. I just hope it all works out."

"It will. No son of Mary Coulter's can be anything but wonderful. She is such a lovely person. What do you think of Isaiah, by the way? We were so busy talking about the job last night that you never said much about him."

An image of Isaiah's dark, chiseled features flashed in Laura's mind. On a handsomeness scale of one to ten, he was clear off the chart, one of the most attractive men she had ever seen. "Well, I can say his name. That's a big plus. 'Aphasia' and 'Isaiah' are sort of alike."

"And that's it?" Etta asked incredulously. "You can say his name?"

"He's nice," Laura expounded.

"*Nice?* Oh, come on. I've seen that young man. Only from a distance, mind you, but even then he packed a wallop. Made me wish I were fifty years younger."

"He's my *boss*, Gram."

"Meaning what, exactly?"

"No drooling allowed."

"So you *do* think he's cute."

Cute was not the word Laura would have chosen to describe Isaiah Coulter. Rumpled sable hair, a devastating grin that was impossible to resist, and sizzling sky-blue eyes that made her skin tingle every time he looked at her. It had been a very long time since she had felt even mildly attracted to a member of the opposite sex — over five years, in fact — and even then her heart hadn't thudded against her ribs like a hard rubber ball bouncing down ladder rungs.

"He's a *vet,* Gram. He prob'ly makes more money in a month than I do in a year."

"Pro-ba-bly," Etta corrected. "And what does his annual gross have to do with anything?"

"He's way out of my —" Laura broke off, unable to recall the word she wanted to use.

"League," Etta supplied. "And that's pure nonsense. You're an intelligent, beautiful young woman. You have a lot to offer any man, Isaiah Coulter included."

"Right." Laura could no longer even say *intelligent* without her tongue getting tied into knots. Men like Isaiah wanted female companions who challenged them intellectually, women who were smart, beautiful, and successful in their own fields. What was her field — cleaning toilets? "Put it out of your head, Gram. It won't happen."

The moment Laura said the words, the hair at the nape of her neck started to prickle. She remembered how surprised she'd been the night before last, when Mary Coulter had called her about a job possibility at her sons' clinic. Then she recalled Isaiah's words to her yesterday: *If I let you leave without at least talking to you, my mom will have my head.* He'd obviously been pressured into giving her an interview.

"Oh, Gram," Laura murmured shakily.

"What?" Etta asked innocently — a little too innocently for Laura's peace of mind.

"Are you and Mary hoping that Isaiah and I might —" Laura broke off, her tongue suddenly as dry as cotton.

To Etta's credit, she didn't prevaricate. "And why not? He's handsome, successful, single, and needs a wife. He just hasn't met the right lady yet. Who's to say you aren't exactly the kind of girl he's been looking for?"

"Oh, *Gram.* I was so glad to get this ch-chance, and now I f-find out it's a sch-scheme you and Mary hatched?"

"Laura, sweetie, calm down. You're starting to stammer."

"How could you *do* this?"

"Do what? Laura, listen to me. This is a great opportunity for you, and it'll benefit Isaiah, too. He and Tucker have a terrible time keeping good help in the kennels, and you'll be wonderful at the job. Mary and I are just hoping that something more may come of it. That's all."

Laura wondered if Isaiah realized that his mother and her grandmother were trying their hands at matchmaking. *Oh, God.* Of *course* he realized. He wasn't dumb. She was the one who'd taken forever to catch on. How would she ever face him?

"I n-need to go," Laura said tautly.

"Sweetheart, don't be this way. You want the job. That's all that really matters. The rest is . . . well, a wait-and-see kind of thing. Maybe he'll never look twice at you. If so, you've still got the job."

Laura had a very bad feeling that Isaiah had already looked twice at her and thought she was pathetic. He'd probably realized all along what his mother was up to and had played along only to please the woman. No big deal, from his perspective. If Laura was foolish enough to harbor any hope that he might be interested in her, he could quickly disabuse her of the notion by ignoring her. In the meantime, he'd be doing a good turn, giving a handicapped person a chance at gainful employment.

Laura's cheeks stung with embarrassment and no small amount of anger. She didn't want to hang up on her grand-mother, but she was too upset to continue the conversation. It felt as if a noose had tightened around her throat.

"It's not as if Isaiah knows anything about it," Etta went on. "That part is just between Mary and me — and now you, of course. There's really no reason for you to be —"

Laura ended the call. Then she pulled over to the side of the road, turned off the car engine, and stared blindly out the windshield. So much for her wonderful new job. She closed her eyes, her sense of disappointment so crushing it was hard for her to breathe. After the interview with Isaiah, she'd left the clinic walking on clouds, believing that he'd hired her on her own merit. It hurt — oh, how it hurt — to realize that hadn't been the case.

She could not, under any circumstances, accept the position now. She hadn't clawed her way, inch by inch, toward a partial re-covery to accept Isaiah Coulter's charity. She needed to make her way in the world without any special concessions. Otherwise all her struggles had been for nothing.

Three hours later, Isaiah was turning off onto a rutted dirt road to make his weekly call at a local dairy farm when his cell phone rang. Jerked from his distracted perusal of the snowcapped Cascades on the horizon, he sighed and tugged the silver communication device from his belt. "Isaiah here."

"Hi, sweetie."

"Hi, Mom." Isaiah had expected it to be someone from the clinic. His mother seldom telephoned during the day because he was always too busy to talk. "How are you this morning? Is everything okay with you and Dad?"

"Oh, Isaiah, I'm so upset. I've made an awful mistake, and now I don't know what to do."

Isaiah frowned in concern. The dairy barns were just around the curve, so he pulled the vehicle over onto the grassy shoulder of the road, shifted into park, and cut the engine. "Anything I can help with?"

"Oh, dear, I hope so."

Boomer, the dairy farmer's tricolored Australian shepherd, careened around the curve just then, gave a glad bark, and leveled out into a run to reach the Hummer. Tied up on the phone, Isaiah couldn't greet the Aussie as he normally did, so he quickly grabbed a dog biscuit from the sack he kept on the passenger seat and thrust it out the open driver-side window. The strategy worked. Instead of jumping at the door and scratching the paint, Boomer took a running leap to snatch the treat from Isaiah's hand. For good measure, Isaiah tossed out two more biscuits to keep the dog occupied.

"You know I'll help if I can, Mom. What's the trouble?"

Mary made a mewling sound. "It's about Laura Townsend."

Isaiah's attention sharpened. "Yeah, what about her?"

"Oh, Isaiah, you're not going to be happy about this. First, let me just say that I really, really believed she would be a fabulous kennel keeper. You know I'd never have recommended her otherwise."

Isaiah cocked an eyebrow. "Of course you wouldn't. That goes without saying. The clinic is my and Tucker's livelihood."

"Exactly, and I'm sure Laura would have been a fabulous asset to both of you."

"Would have been? I'm not following." He glanced at his watch. "She's at the clinic as we speak. This is her first day of training."

"No," Mary said faintly. "I'm afraid she's not there. Oh, Isaiah, I'm so upset I could cry. She's such a sweet girl. I never in a million years meant for her to know."

"Know what?"

Mary moaned. Isaiah began to get a very bad feeling, which only grew more pronounced when his mother added, "Oh, how I wish I didn't have to tell you. You're always so unreasonable about this sort of thing."

Isaiah narrowed his eyes. The only times he could recall being remotely unreasonable with his mother had been when she tried to set him up with women. "You didn't."

"I meant well."

"You *didn't.* With Laura, Mom?" Isaiah pictured Laura's oval face and large, expressive eyes. She'd been so hesitant during the interview last night, then so grateful for the job. "What the hell were you thinking?"

"Now, now. I don't blame you for being angry, Isaiah, but don't curse at me."

His eyes narrowed even more. "Don't play the mother card. You know very well I wasn't cursing at you. Out with it, Mom. Why isn't Laura at the clinic, training?"

"Because she found out," Mary wailed.

Isaiah pinched the bridge of his nose. "Found out what, exactly?" he asked, even though he feared that he already knew.

"That it was a matchmaking scheme. Oh, Isaiah, we meant no harm. You have to know that. She would have been a great kennel keeper. I'm convinced of that. If something more had come from the two of you working together, we couldn't see the harm."

" *'We'*? Don't tell me Dad was in on this."

"No. *No!* You know how your father is. If you choose to stay single forever, he figures that's your business."

Isaiah tossed Boomer another biscuit. "Maybe you should take a page out of his book. Define *'we,'* Mother. Is Bethany involved?"

"Goodness, no. Your sister is so busy with Little Sly, Chastity Ann, and the riding academy that I hardly ever talk to her anymore."

"Molly?" Isaiah pictured his brother Jake's amber-haired wife conspiring with his mother over coffee.

"Molly has morning sickness. I don't get to talk to her very often anymore, either."

Isaiah couldn't believe that Hank's wife, Carly, was involved. She'd only just recently had eye surgery. That left only Natalie, Zeke's wife, and she wasn't the busybody type. "Who, then?"

"Etta, my neighbor, Laura's grand-mother."

Isaiah let his head fall back against the seat and closed his eyes. "I'm running late for a farm call, Mom. Spit out the rest."

"Laura and Etta were talking early this morning. Somehow Etta let it slip to Laura that we'd hatched this plan to get the two of you together. Laura got really upset, hung up on her grandmother, and never showed up at the clinic."

"You're sure she isn't there?"

"I called to see. Val says she didn't come in."

Isaiah released a weary breath. "Okay, let me get this straight. Laura came in for the interview yesterday, completely unaware that her interfering grandmother and *my* interfering mother were plotting to marry her off to her new boss. Now that she knows, she no longer wants the job and didn't show up for training. Do I have it right so far?"

"Yes. That pretty much covers it."

"And you expect me to somehow clean up your mess?"

"She's such a sweetheart, Isaiah, and she was so excited about the job. It just breaks my heart to think that everything is ruined for her now."

"How the hell can I fix that?" Isaiah bumped the steering wheel with the heel of his hand. "If she doesn't want the job, she doesn't want the job."

"I was just thinking she might change her mind if you . . . well, you know . . . dropped by to talk with her."

"And say what, Mom? That she shouldn't be upset or feel humiliated? That you and her grandmother are harmless busybodies, and we shouldn't pay you any mind? I have it. Why don't I tell her I'd never in this lifetime be interested in her, so it's not really a problem?"

"I don't blame you for being angry."

"That's good, because I am angry, and justifiably so." Isaiah envisioned Laura's face again and clenched his teeth. "Laura really *wanted* the job, Mom. It was important to her. And you know what else?"

"No, what?" Mary asked thinly.

"I think you're absolutely right. She would have been a damned good kennel keeper. Now, because of you, she's decided to pass on the opportunity. That's a shame. It's not just any vet who'll hire her, you know."

"Oh, Isaiah, I feel so awful."

"Good. You should. The next time you get an itch to interfere in my life, remember how bad you feel right now. Matchmaking never pays, and it's always, *always* a bad idea."

"Does this mean you won't go talk to Laura?"

"Give me one good reason why I should."

Long silence. Finally Mary replied, "Because she's a sweet, wonderful girl, and you're a good man."

Isaiah held out the phone, glared at it for several long seconds, and then broke the connection. *Damn.* Would his mother never learn? The last time she'd pulled this stunt, he'd found himself sitting across the supper table from a woman with three chins and a hopeful look in her eyes.

He didn't need or want his mother's help to find a wife. News bulletin: He didn't even *want* a wife. More important, when and if he ever decided to find one, he wanted to do his own looking. Why couldn't she get that through her head?

A deep gray gloaming heralded the end of another busy day as Isaiah mounted the exterior stairway to Laura Townsend's residence, the top story of a two-level garage that had been converted into an apartment. From the outside it didn't look like much, a white clapboard rectangle with blue trim and a small porch. But, living on a fixed income as she did, she probably couldn't afford anything nicer.

Isaiah knew firsthand how costly housing was nowadays. A run-of-the-mill one-bedroom apartment ran from seven to eight hundred a month. He and Tucker had paid twice that for the town house that they'd shared for over two years. Now, thank God, they both had their own homes. Isaiah had found a piece of land out on Old Mill Road near Zeke's place and built a log house. Tucker had purchased an old farmhouse on a large acreage on the other side of town. Their days of paying rent were over.

When Isaiah reached the landing, he stopped for a moment to admire the porch decorations. Planter boxes filled with trailing greenery lined the deck rails. Within the sphere of illumination cast by the porch light, two large terra-cotta pots filled with ivy flanked a dark blue door that sported an ornate brass knocker. Under the eave, safe from rain, an old rocker held a trio of stuffed toys — a bear wearing a satin vest and cummerbund, a yarn-haired doll in a pinafore that he guessed was a Raggedy Ann, and a pig in patched denim overalls. The effect was homey and welcoming.

Isaiah straightened his shoulders and dragged in a bracing breath before rapping his knuckles on the door. From inside he heard the clatter of metal followed by fast footsteps. He stepped back just as Laura opened the portal. She looked nonplussed and charmingly tousled, her hair in an attractive stir around her lovely face. Her eyes went wide when she recognized him.

"Isaiah," she said. And then her face turned scarlet.

He tugged on his ear and shifted his weight from one foot to the other. "Hi, Laura. Can we talk?"

With the back of her wrist, she brushed a streak of what looked like flour from her cheek. Then she retreated a step to allow him entry. The instant he stepped over the threshold, his senses were bombarded, first with color — bright throw rugs, colorfully draped furniture, artfully arranged pillows — then with delicious smells — pumpkin and cinnamon, roasted meat, and fresh coffee.

His stomach growled. He could only hope Laura didn't hear the rumble, for in that moment he wasn't sure what appealed to his senses more, the smells or the woman. She wore a red gingham bib apron over a red knit top and snug blue jeans. As he trailed his gaze downward, he noticed that her feet were bare. Normally he wasn't into feet, but hers were small, delicately made, and oddly cute, the tips of her toes as pink as rose petals.

Pushing the door closed behind him, Isaiah found himself at a loss for words. He settled for, "It would seem that my mom and your grandmother have been up to mischief."

Laura's face reddened even more. She rubbed her palms over the front of the checkered apron. "I'm sorry about that. I didn't know. Really, I didn't."

Isaiah took a quick breath and plunged in. "It's not your place to apologize." He tucked his hands under the hem of his old leather jacket to rest them on his hips. "It was undoubtedly my mother who came up with the idea. She has a history."

"Oh," she said softly.

Isaiah rubbed his jaw. "Normally I can just shrug it off. She'll invite me over for dinner or throw a party, and when I arrive there's some lady she wants me to meet. It's uncomfortable, but no real harm is done. This is the first time she's ever gone this far. I'm as embarrassed as a cougar chased off by a ground squirrel."

Her lovely hazel eyes filled with incredulity. "You?" she said softly.

"Wouldn't you be embarrassed? It's not like she's done this only once. She's a repeat offender, continually trying to find me a wife." He glanced down at himself. "Is there something so wrong with me that she doesn't think I can find one on my own?"

She gave a startled laugh. Then she caught her lower lip between her teeth, studied him for a time, and shook her head. "There's nothing wrong with you that I can see."

Isaiah could see nothing wrong with her, either. No acne, no double chin, no irritating personality quirks. For once his mother had chosen someone who was actually appealing. And wasn't that just his luck? What went for Belinda went for every female employee at the clinic: No workplace romances. It was a hard-and-fast rule, instituted before he and Tucker had opened their practice. If Laura came to work for him — and he sincerely hoped she would — she would be strictly off-limits.

She gestured toward the kitchen. "I was about to eat, and I always make way too much. Would you like to talk over supper?"

Isaiah was starving, and the smells drifting to his nose were almost too tempting to resist. "Oh, no, I shouldn't. You weren't expecting a guest, and you probably have plans for the leftovers."

"No." She shook her head and smiled. "I can't change the amounts in the cookbook to make less of something. Counting is one thing, real math another. I have trouble with divide and subtract."

Most people would have said *division and subtraction.* It occurred to Isaiah that she constantly had to choose her words to avoid stammering.

She lifted her hands in mock appeal. "*Please* save me from having to eat the same food all week."

"No man can resist an invitation like that," he said with a grin. "I'd love to talk over supper."

She gestured to a coat tree next to the door. "Take off your jacket and come on in. I only have a little left to do."

As she turned toward the adjoining kitchen, Isaiah trailed his gaze over the small living area. Overstuffed furniture draped with slipcovers vied for space with mismatched end tables, a battered old trunk that served as a coffee table, and a hodgepodge of knickknacks, wall hangings, and stuff sitting on the floor in all the corners. Everywhere he looked, his eye was caught by something — a wreath made out of what looked like hay and bedecked with ribbons and flowers, little hand-painted plaques, braided rugs, vases of all shapes and colors, and family photographs, which particularly piqued his curiosity. Were her parents still together? Did she have siblings, and if so, how many?

He shrugged out of his jacket, hung it up, and slowly followed her, pleased to note that her decorating scheme included animals, a gold-framed painting of a dog, a plaque depicting a trio of kittens at play, and all kinds of critter figurines. Her love of animals was clearly genuine, a trait that would serve her well in a veterinary clinic.

Her kitchen, open to the living area, continued the warm, country feeling. A hickory hutch and china cabinet displayed a mismatched collection of blue-and-white dishes. A writing desk along the wall was surrounded by practical yet decorative stuff — a hanging shelf full of cookbooks, a teacup rack, a cottage-scene calendar, and a clock with a rooster painted on the face.

Without being directed, Isaiah sat at an odd-looking dining table, which was small, rectangular, and had drawers under the top lip. None of the four chairs matched.

"Yard sales," she explained as she filled two goblets with dark red wine. "I moved out on my own only six months ago. My folks gave me a few things. The rest I picked up here and there. That's an old pastry table. The drawers held rolling pins."

"Ah." Isaiah's gaze went to the adjacent wall, which had been covered halfway up with synthetic rock capped by a thick, shelflike ledge to hold baskets and more doodads. "I should hire you to decorate my house. It's as empty as a beggar's pocket."

"I couldn't take money. I'm not that good."

Isaiah thought she was. He liked the warm, cozy feeling she had created. Somehow she'd transformed a small, rectangular living space into a home with character and appeal.

As she set down the glass of wine, she inclined her head at a basket of fruit at the center of the table. "If you're hungry, help yourself. It'll be a few more minutes."

While she returned to the stove, Isaiah took her up on the offer, selecting a big red apple, rubbing it on his shirt, and then taking a crunchy bite. She put on mittens, opened the oven, and withdrew a blue-speckled baking pan. When she removed the domed lid, the smells that wafted across the room almost made him groan.

"I hope you like roast."

"I *love* roast."

She smiled, plucked the meat from the pan to put it on a waiting platter, and then began spooning carrots and potatoes into a serving bowl. As she busied herself making gravy from the meat drippings, she glanced over her shoulder. "And pumpkin tarts. Do you like those?"

"I like pumpkin pie."

"Good. These are little pumpkin pies. I made oodles, and they're never as good after I freeze them."

Isaiah settled back to munch on the apple, sip the wine, and enjoy watching her work. She did everything with an economy of movement, indicating that she not only knew her way around a kitchen, but also enjoyed cooking.

When she'd set the table and put out the food, he stared incredulously at the side dishes, which included fluffy homemade biscuits. "My God, this is a feast."

She dimpled her cheek as she unfolded a dark blue napkin and spread it over her lap. "Crazy, huh? I ate frozen dinners for a while, but that gets old. Now I cook and freeze what I can't eat. My food bill is huge, and my freezer is crammed. I take stuff to Gram and the people on my street, but I can give away only so much."

Isaiah started to dig in. Then he noticed that she'd folded her slender hands and bent her head. He quickly followed suit, feeling like a dunderhead. At home his family always blessed the food at mealtime, but he'd fallen out of the habit.

"Dear Lord," she said softly, "thank you for this nice day, and thank you for blessing us with plenty. Amen."

"Amen," he mumbled.

She glanced up. "I'll let you slice the meat."

Great. His father always did that. Reminding himself that he was a surgeon and could surely handle carving a roast, Isaiah drew the platter toward him. While he applied himself to the task, she dipped some food onto her plate and buttered a biscuit.

When they had both served themselves, she said, "I'm sorry I didn't show up at the clinic this morning. After talking to Gram, I just couldn't."

Isaiah searched her beautiful eyes. "I'm not clear on why, Laura. My mom and your grandmother were trying to set us up, and we found them out. I admit that it could be an uncomfortable situation if we allowed it to be, but why should we? Let's just laugh it off and continue as planned."

"I only wanted the job if you thought I'd be good at it," she said. "For someone like me, that's very im-portant."

"I *do* think you'll be good at it."

She flicked him a dubious look. "You're a smart man. You say your mom has done this before. I think you knew all along and were only being kind. There's nothing wrong with that, mind you. But I can't take a job I didn't get on my own merit."

So that was it. Isaiah rested his fork on the edge of the plate and leaned back in the chair, which creaked in protest under his shifting weight. "I'm a busy man, Laura. Smart, maybe, but hopelessly absent-minded, too. I have way too much on my mind to keep track of my mother's match-making schemes. Maybe I *should* have known, but I honestly didn't."

She still looked unconvinced.

"Okay," he said. "You want the actual truth?"

She nodded.

"I never suspected a matchmaking scheme because my mother told me you had brain damage. I pictured a shuffling, overweight lady with blank eyes, a lax mouth, and drool on her chin." He paused to let that sink in. "Mom has tried to set me up a number of times, but never with anyone like that."

Stomach knotted and hands clenched into fists under the table, Isaiah waited for her reaction, half-afraid she might be hurt and burst into tears. Instead her mouth quirked at the corners, and then she giggled. *"Drool?"*

Relieved, Isaiah grinned. "Bad of me, right? I shouldn't stereotype people, but that's honestly what I expected. When I saw you in my office and realized who you were, I was so surprised — pleasantly so — that I never gave my mother's motives a thought."

"On my *chin?*"

He couldn't help but chuckle. "I'm sorry."

"Not all people with brain damage are like that," she informed him.

"Intellectually, I knew that," he confessed, "but I wasn't wearing my thinking hat or trying to call up clinical images the afternoon she told me about you. I was worried about a sick cow."

She tipped her head questioningly. "If

you thought my brain damage was that bad, why did you agree to meet with me?"

Isaiah picked up his wineglass. "Because my mom seldom asks me for a favor. To make her happy, I said I'd interview you. I honestly didn't believe you'd be able to do the work. But once I met you, I changed my mind."

She dabbed at the corners of her mouth with her napkin. "After I got hurt, not being able to talk was only part of the problem. My right arm and leg were almost useless, and I had motor problems." A faraway look entered her eyes. "When I wasn't in rehab, my parents had to look after me. When I started to get better and could do some things for myself, I swore I'd get well and never need help again."

Isaiah nodded. "Becoming self-reliant wasn't easy for you, in other words."

"No." Her gaze flicked to his and held. "I had to take it one day at a time. I'm as well now as I'll ever be." She gestured at their surroundings. "For this to work, I have to make it on my own. No special favors, not from my parents, not from you, not from any-one. It's no good, other-wise. I'd only be kidding myself. Do you understand?"

Isaiah understood better than she knew.

His sister, Bethany, had expressed similar concerns after the barrel-racing accident that had paralyzed her from the waist down. *I need to do it by myself,* she had cried whenever anyone tried to help her. It had been frustrating for everyone in the family. But in the end, her stubbornness had paid off. She'd become self-sufficient, and now she was happily married to a wonderful man and had a normal life.

"I do understand," Isaiah replied. "No special favors, Laura. If I didn't sincerely believe you could do the work, I wouldn't be here. We desperately need good kennel people. They quit almost as fast as we can train them. I think you'll do a great job, and I believe you'll stay, not because you'll have no other opportunities along the way, but because you'll really like the animals."

She searched his face for a long moment. "All right then," she finally said. "If that's really why you gave me the job, I'll be there in the morning."

"That's really why."

She didn't prompt him to offer her more reassurance. Taking him at his word, she simply resumed eating her meal. Isaiah released a pent-up breath, took a sip of merlot, and reclaimed his fork.

After taking a few bites, he had to compliment her on the food. "The only time I get to eat like this is when I go home for dinner."

"What do you eat the rest of the time?"

"Restaurant fare, TV dinners." He shrugged. "Sometimes nothing at all. When I get home late, I'm generally too tired to dig something out of the freezer and nuke it. I'd rather go to bed hungry."

She shook her head. "You should keep things on hand — cheese, fruit, stuff like that. At least then you could grab something quick and easy."

Isaiah shrugged. "I would, but half the time I forget to go shopping."

She pushed the platter of meat toward him. "Have some more roast and taters. You're too thin."

Taters. There it was again, her avoidance of words with more than two syllables. Little wonder she talked slowly. It would be difficult enough to learn to speak all over again without constantly having to choose words that were easy to say.

By the time the meal was over, Isaiah had devoured three large helpings of meat and vegetables, four buttered biscuits, a generous serving of salad, and five little pumpkin pies topped with whipped cream. He was so stuffed that he groaned when he rose from the table.

"You don't have to help clean up," she protested as he began scraping plates.

"Sure I do." He glanced up and winked. "After a meal like that, helping with the dishes is the least I can do."

They fell into a comfortable silence as they worked. Then the phone rang. Isaiah continued loading the dishwasher while Laura took the call. When she returned to the kitchen, she said, "That was Gram."

"My mother's partner in crime?"

She rolled her eyes and nodded. "I'd like to stay mad at her for a while, but she makes it hard."

"More like impossible, if she's anything like my mom." Isaiah ran a plate under the faucet before sticking it in the rack. " 'I'm so sorry, Isaiah,' " he mimicked in a high-pitched voice. " 'Please, please, *please* forgive me. I'll never do it again.' After about six phone calls, I finally caved."

"Do you think she'll keep her promise?"

"To never do it again, you mean?" Isaiah considered the question. "Heck, no." He flashed a quick grin. "But at least her taste has improved."

Laura bent to put away the roasting pan. "Right. No drool on my chin."

It goes a lot farther than that, Isaiah

thought as he surveyed her attractive backside, but he refrained from saying so. He had accomplished what he'd set out to do. Laura had agreed to take the job at the clinic. They had established a friendship of sorts. He didn't want to mess that up by telling her she was the most attractive woman he'd met in a very long time. It wasn't an appropriate thing for an employer to say. Hell, it wasn't even an appropriate thing for an employer to *think.*

Chapter Three

The following morning, as Laura parked her Mazda behind the clinic, she whispered scolding lectures to herself. "You're only a kennel keeper — a lady who'll be hosing dog poop down the drains. If you blow this chance and get fired over a silly crush on your boss, you'll be sorry."

And it *was* a silly crush. Isaiah Coulter was a handsome, accomplished, and very successful man who could have his pick of women. He'd never look twice at someone like her.

Schooling her expression, Laura entered the building and found herself in a room lined from floor to ceiling with boxes of surgical supplies. She traversed the pathway to a gray door and was promptly greeted by a cacophony of mournful wails when she opened it. The kennels, she realized, and from that moment forward she forgot all about Isaiah Coulter.

Dogs. Looking up the center aisle, she saw all different kinds, purebreds and mutts, large ones and small ones. The only

89

things any of them seemed to have in common were their limitless joy at seeing her and their frantic attempts to get her attention.

"Oh, you poor baby," Laura whispered as she knelt in front of a rottweiler's cage. A tube protruded from a wide bandage around the canine's belly, and an IV was taped to its front leg. "What happened to you?" she asked softly, thrusting her fingers through the wire mesh to touch his broad muzzle. The dog nudged her fingers and whined. "Oh, yes, I *know.* It's so awful. Here you are, sick and hurting, and your people have left you all alone."

Laura knew exactly how that felt. After her accident she'd been hospitalized and then eventually transported to a rehab center. Her friends had come to see her at first, but over time they'd shown up less and less, uncomfortable in her presence because she could no longer talk. Her family had visited her as often as they could, of course, but after several weeks, the demands of day-to-day living had kept them away a good deal of the time. Even now Laura could remember her sense of abandonment. Unable to communicate, walk, read, or watch television, she'd been isolated in her misery, the hours of each day stretching endlessly before her. Blocks of painful physical therapy had been her only relief from the boredom and loneliness.

Looking into the rottweiler's bewildered brown eyes, she remembered her own bewilderment during that time and the helpless rage that had often come over her in waves. Trapped and forgotten, that was how she'd felt, exactly like this dog.

In that moment, a sense of purpose filled her. *This is where I belong,* she thought. *I can help, really help these poor animals, because I understand how they feel in a way no one else can.* It was the loveliest sensation, a huge, exhilarating rush. For five long years she'd been searching for her place in a world that had been turned upside down. Now she'd finally found something important that she could do. These animals truly needed her.

Laura moved up the aisle, stopping to pet a spaniel with a cast on its front leg, a poodle with a shaved butt that seemed otherwise fine, and a black Lab with a bandaged paw and what looked like a plastic lamp shade buckled around its neck. She would have visited each and every cage if not for the sudden appearance of a stout blonde at the end of the aisle. As Laura pushed to her feet, she took in the other woman's shoulder-length hair, kindly blue eyes, and masculine features set in a square face.

"You Laura?" the woman asked, her tone clipped and unfriendly.

"Yes. I was just saying hello to the dogs."

"You shouldn't poke your hands through the wire until you've been briefed. You looking to get bitten?"

Laura tucked the offending hand into a hip pocket of her jeans. "No, I was just —"

"A couple of these dogs are mean. To clean their cages, you'll have to use the loop."

Laura had no idea what a loop was. She glanced into the sad eyes of an Irish setter. She had never been wary of strange dogs, least of all pathetic creatures like these. As she walked up the aisle, she yearned to stop at each gate. Tomorrow, she vowed, she would come thirty minutes early so she could give each animal a little one-on-one.

"I'm not late, am I?" she asked.

"No." The blonde opened a cage. Drawing a syringe from the front pocket of her blue smock, she petted the collie within the enclosure, and then bent to grab the animal by its scruff. As she gave the injection, she said, "You're a little early, in fact. I'm Susan Strong. I'll be training you."

Laura held out her hand as the other woman straightened. "I'm pleased to meet you, Susan."

Instead of smiling, Susan merely tightened her mouth. At the right corner a pinpoint dimple popped up, so low that it was almost on her chin. "You like dogs?"

"Oh, yes, very much."

"Good thing." She finally shook Laura's hand and then gestured at the cages. "We have 'em in spades. They come and they go." She gave Laura a scowling look. "Sort of like kennel keepers. Mucking around in shit and puke gets old real fast. If you don't have the stomach for it, save me a lot of trouble and quit right now. It's a lot of work to train someone."

Laura straightened her shoulders. She couldn't honestly say she liked the smell of poop, but she did have a strong stomach. She was also convinced that she'd finally found her niche.

"If I can do the work here, I'll never quit," she replied.

Susan snorted, a loud, up-both-nostrils snort that made her meaning clear. "Heard it before. And just for the record, any idiot can do the work."

Laura didn't normally discuss her affliction with strangers, but in this case it seemed smart on two counts. Susan needed to know about Laura's handicap. She also had a chip on her shoulder that needed to be knocked off.

"That's good news. I'm an id-iot."

Susan gave her a sharp look.

Laura moistened her lips. "Brain damage. I dove off into the river near the falls. Most times it's safe, but there'd been a drought that year, and I hit my head on a rock."

"Holy Toledo." A thoughtful look came into Susan's eyes. "I remember that. It happened a few years back, didn't it?"

"Five," Laura confirmed.

Susan nodded. "For a while they thought you might die. You were in a coma, weren't you?"

"Yes, for about three weeks. I woke up with aphasia, damage to the left lobe of my brain."

"Bummer."

"I had to learn to talk all over again," Laura went on. "You'll notice that I speak slowly. I also have trouble keeping up if people talk too fast or use long words." She gestured at the cages around them. "As for this job, I'm very lucky to get it." She met Susan's gaze. "If I can do the work, I won't be quitting."

Susan finally smiled, and it transformed her face, making her look more like a plump angel than a Marine Corps drill sergeant. "You'll be able to handle the work."

Isaiah leaned his head to one side so the technician-cum-anesthesiologist could dab the sweat from his brow. In the middle of an abdominal surgery he had blood to the top of his surgical gloves, and Belinda, his assistant, was frantically searching for a clamp. Just then a door at the rear of the room swung open. Isaiah glanced up to see Susan Strong entering the chamber. He gave the stocky blonde a "stay put" look, then returned his attention to his patient.

When the artery was clamped, he met Susan's questioning gaze. "How's Laura Townsend doing?"

"So far, so good," Susan replied. "You know the boxer with the attitude problem? When she opened the gate to his kennel I about had a heart attack, but all he did was lick her to death."

Isaiah chuckled. "Has a way with dogs, does she?"

"Big-time. Even that nasty little Pomeranian likes her."

"We need someone good with animals back there," Isaiah observed.

"Amen. Her biggest problem will be caring too much," Susan predicted. "I don't know how she'll handle it the first time she gets a 'dead dog walking' order."

Isaiah hated to put down an animal himself, but he had long since come to accept it as a necessary evil. When nothing more could be done to ease an animal's suffering, euthanasia was the only merciful option.

"You think she'll be able to handle the work?"

Susan planted her hands on her broad hips. Under the gruff exterior she was a marshmallow, one of the kindest and most caring people Isaiah knew. "My money says she'll do fine," she replied. "Been a nasty morning. Puke, shit out the yang, and a hemorrhage to top it all off."

"A hemorrhage?"

"The little red cocker miscarried."

"That really old dog?" the anesthesiologist asked.

"That's the one," Susan confirmed. "It's sad that she lost her puppies, but she'll be better off. Tucker had to spay her. People who keep breeding animals when they get that old are crazy. I just don't get it."

"They're not crazy," Belinda inserted. "They're just mercenary. If the cocker had whelped seven pups, they would have sold for four hundred dollars apiece, possibly more."

"More." James Masterson, a tall, stocky twenty-year-old with brown hair and baby-blue eyes who'd begun training as a tech assistant a year ago, drew a blanket from the warmer. "My mom paid six hundred for a cocker last month. Run the numbers on that, why don't you?" He grinned and winked at Belinda. "Two litters a year would put a serious dent in my rent."

"Mine, too." Belinda pursed her lips. "Seven puppies. My God, that'd be forty-two hundred dollars! Maybe I'll move where I can have a dog and become a breeder."

"I'd never breed an old dog," James said, "but I can't see any harm in breeding a young, healthy one. If nothing else, it'd help to cover the vet bills."

"I'm just glad the little cocker's whelping days are over," Susan said. "If her owners want to continue making money on the side selling puppies, they'll have to buy another bitch."

"How did Laura handle all the blood?" Isaiah asked.

Susan shrugged. "I think she panicked a little at first."

"Doesn't everyone?" Angela chimed in. "How'd she do once she calmed down?"

"Better than most trainees. When I needed help, she jumped right in and did what I told her."

Isaiah was pleased to hear that. "I had her figured for a gutsy lady. Nobody could come through what she has without having plenty of backbone."

"Who's this you're talking about?" Belinda asked as she handed Isaiah the stapler.

"Laura Townsend." Isaiah quickly closed up. "Susan's training her for the kennels."

"Oh. I didn't know Val hired anybody." Belinda drew the paper pad closed over the contaminated surgical implements. "That's good news. We never have enough kennel people."

"Actually, Val didn't hire her," Isaiah corrected. "I did."

Belinda raised her eyebrows. "*You?* I thought Val handled all that."

"Normally she does." Isaiah stripped off the surgical gloves and deposited them in a waste container. "Laura's a friend of the family. My mom recommended her."

"Ah." Belinda stepped over to the sink to rinse the implements before putting them in the sterilizer. "Have you known her long?"

"No, just met her." Isaiah recalled Laura's expressive eyes and smiled slightly. "You're all going to like her. She's a sweetheart. Right, Susan?"

Susan shrugged. "So far I like her fine. She talks kind of slow, and every once in a while she looks at me like I'm speaking Greek. But otherwise I can barely tell there's anything wrong with her."

Belinda turned from the faucet. "There's something wrong with her?"

"Aphasia," Isaiah replied, deciding on the spot that it would be easier for Laura if all her coworkers knew about her disability from the start. "It's a form of brain damage that affects language and math skills."

Belinda gave him a wondering look. "You hired someone who can't talk or do math?"

"It isn't that bad," Isaiah countered. "She speaks slowly, like Susan says, and she gets confused if you throw long words at her. But otherwise she does fine. As a favor to me, I'd appreciate it if all of you would make a special effort to help her settle in."

Belinda lifted her shoulders in a shrug. "Sure. I'll help her out any way I can."

Her first morning of training was over, and Laura felt as if her bones had turned to water. She had never shied away from work, but this job taxed her mentally as well as physically. There was so much to remember. She'd met at least a half dozen people, Tucker, her other boss, included. Oh, how disconcerting that had been. She'd known that he would resemble Isaiah. They were twins, after all. But she'd never expected them to be so identical at a glance, both tall, dark, muscular, and too handsome for words.

She'd been cleaning a cage, and he had appeared out of nowhere to jot something on the dog's chart. "Hello!" she'd said. "How are you this morning, Isaiah?"

He'd given her a long look and then smiled. "I'm not Isaiah; I'm Tucker. You must be Laura."

Laura's face had gone instantly hot. They were slightly different when you really *looked.* Tucker was just a little heavier, and there was a sharpness to his gaze that was absent in Isaiah's, an edge that said, *I'm here, I'm paying attention, and nothing gets past me.*

"Yes, Laura, I'm Laura," she'd said.

He had thrust out a big brown hand. "Good to meet you, and welcome to the clinic. Our mother has only good things to say about you."

In between the lines, Laura had heard, *I'll still be watching you closely. Don't think I won't. As far as I'm concerned, the jury is still out.*

As unnerving as that had been, Laura respected it. An employer who didn't demand excellence didn't get it. Tucker Coulter would be fair. She sensed that in him. But he'd also put her on notice that he wouldn't overlook anything, either.

"I'll do my best to do a good job," she'd said.

He had given her another long look, a straight-into-the-eye look. Then his expression had softened. "I'm sure you will, Laura. If you have any questions, don't hesitate to ask someone. We've got a great team here at the clinic. Everyone is always willing to lend someone else a helping hand."

Everyone had been the key word in that sentence. There were so *many* people, all of Tucker's team as well as Isaiah's. Just keeping their names straight would be a challenge. In addition to that, she'd had to learn the layout of the clinic and where everything was stored. Her eyes ached from staring at chart instructions, and her head hurt from information overload.

But, oh, it was a wonderful kind of tired.

101

After sinking down to sit on the concrete floor of a kennel stall, Laura closed her eyes, leaned her head against the cement-block wall behind her, and began petting Marcus, a boxer who'd convinced everyone that he was a vicious killer. It felt nice to sit for a moment on the cool, slightly damp cement and stroke his coarse fur.

She was going to be *good* at this job, she thought with a shiver of delight. She'd had a few bad moments this morning, but overall her first day had gone well. She'd managed to make sense of the charts and follow all the instructions. More important, she'd kept her head and had been able to help save the life of an old cocker spaniel. That had been so rewarding, like working in the ER.

Laura opened her eyes to look down at her blue smock. It was smeared with blood and other stuff she preferred not to identify, but she still hated to take it off. *A uniform.* She didn't have a name badge yet, but Susan said she would get one tomorrow. Then she'd look just like everyone else. She guessed it was silly, but looking like everyone else was important to her.

"Good grief, what're you doing?"

Startled, Laura glanced up to see a pretty brunette outside the wire-mesh gate.

"I'm just sitting with Marcus for a while."

The woman rested her shoulder against the wire and smiled. "Susan said you'd made friends with him. That's amazing. My name is Belinda, by the way."

"I'm pleased to meet you."

When Laura started to get up, the tech waved her back down. "Don't bother." She hunkered to get on Laura's eye level. "We aren't formal around here."

Laura resumed stroking Marcus's head where it rested on her thigh. "Have you worked here long?"

"Only about six months. But around here that makes me a veteran. Only two techs have been here longer than I have now, and they work in Tucker's wing."

Laura stilled her hand on the boxer's head. "I have trouble with long words. Your name will be hard for me."

"Would Lindy work better?"

Laura nodded. "Much better."

"Just call me Lindy, then. I won't mind. It's a family nickname, and I'm used to it." Belinda stuck a finger through the wire and wiggled it, earning herself a low growl from Marcus. "God, he's nasty. I'm surprised you're not missing an arm."

The tension eased from Laura's body. Glancing down at the dog, she said, "He isn't as mean as he acts. All bark and no bite. He's just afraid, I think."

"Got him all figured out, do you?" Belinda shook her head. "With those teeth, what does he have to be afraid of?"

Laura could have named several things. Marcus had an infection, requiring twice-daily injections of antibiotic, and because he looked mean, all the techs went to extraordinary lengths to protect themselves from him. A loop, Laura now knew, was a retractable cable noose at the end of a long pole. The user could ensnare a dog's head, tighten the loop, and hold even a large animal like Marcus immobile while someone else moved in on him. Naturally Marcus was fearful. No one here petted him. Instead they ganged up on him, one person choking him while someone else stuck him with needles.

"It's hard for dogs to understand why they're here," Laura said softly, her mind swimming with unpleasant memories. "Their people leave them all alone, and strangers do mean things to them."

Belinda regarded Marcus thoughtfully. "Yeah, I guess maybe you're right. When I treat dogs, I think of it as helping them, but from their perspective I suppose it does seem mean sometimes." Her mouth curved into a smile. "Very insightful, Laura. No wonder Isaiah is convinced you'll be a great kennel keeper."

"I hope he's right."

Belinda pushed to her feet. "You'll do fine."

"I'm going to try. This seems like a great place to work."

"A fabulous place, actually. I love it. Mostly I work with Isaiah. He's a great boss." She shrugged and grinned. "The scenery isn't bad, either."

Laura wondered what she meant. Her bewilderment must have shown in her expression, because Belinda laughed.

"Isaiah," she explained. "Talk about easy on the eyes. Isn't he gorgeous?"

Heat gathered in Laura's cheeks. "He's all right, I guess."

"All right?" Belinda laughed again. "Hey, it's just us girls, honey. We can get down and dirty."

"Okay," Laura relented. "He's a little better than all right."

"Tucker isn't bad, either," Belinda confided. "Of course, they're twins, so that goes without saying." She thumped the heel of her hand against her temple. "What am I thinking? You've probably known Tucker a heck of a lot longer than I have."

Laura shook her head. "No. I've never even met him."

Belinda frowned. "I thought Isaiah said you were a friend of the family."

It was Laura's turn to laugh. "Sort of, I guess. My grandma lives next door to his mom."

"Ah. So you don't really know the family, per se."

"I know his mom pretty well. Sometimes when I go to Gram's she's over there for coffee."

"I see. Well, however it came about, I'm glad you got hired. Things will be hectic for you the next couple of weeks, but maybe after you settle in we can do lunch together and get better acquainted."

Laura's heart lifted with gladness. Lunch with a coworker. It was just the sort of thing she'd hoped might happen, but she'd never expected an invitation so soon. "I'd like that."

"Good. It's a date then." Belinda flattened her hand against the wire. "Catch you later, Laura. Welcome to the team."

Laura smiled to herself as Belinda walked away. *Welcome to the team.* For the first time in five years, she finally felt as if she were part of something again.

★ ★ ★

Belinda's prediction proved to be correct; the next couple of weeks were incredibly hectic for Laura. After training all morning at the clinic, she raced back into town to walk dogs, clean houses, and do people's ironing. As a result, she hit the floor running at five each morning and never slowed down until after five in the afternoon. She spent her evenings cooking dinner, doing dishes, cleaning her apartment, and doing her laundry. In short, she barely had time to take a relaxed breath.

But it was worth it. She absolutely *loved* her job at the clinic. She had expected kennel keeping to be a fairly lonely occupation, but it wasn't. Employees from both wings frequently entered the kennel area to check on dogs or administer medications, affording Laura an opportunity to get acquainted with some twenty-odd people. In addition to Belinda, Trish, Angela, Susan, Mike, and James, who worked in the south wing with Isaiah, there were a number of people from Tucker's team whom Laura really liked, namely Sally Millet, a short, stocky technician with curly brown hair and merry brown eyes who loved to tell jokes and had a raspy, contagious laugh; Jeri Gibson, a plump, out-of-a-bottle redhead in her late fifties who waged an ongoing war with gray roots; Tina Moresly, a tall, big-boned lady in her forties with a fun-loving personality; and Lena Foster, a white-haired grandmotherly type who had retired as a vet assistant five years ago and had now returned to the field part-time to supplement her Social Security income.

Laura enjoyed having so many new friends. It felt good to walk through the clinic and have people calling out hello. During coffee breaks she listened to gossip, laughed at jokes she didn't get, and enjoyed a sense of belonging that had been lacking in her life for far too long. Judi always had amusing anecdotes to share about her granddaughters. Lena was always trying to get pledges for walkathons, trying to raise money for MS and breast cancer research. Tina, married but childless, brought in snapshots of her nieces and nephews. It was fun, and Laura always felt a little sad when break times ended.

The sadness never lasted long. Working so closely with the animals gave her a deep sense of joy and satisfaction. There were sweet-faced felines who purred and nuzzled for more petting when she held them, and dogs with all types of personalities to keep her from growing bored. Every time Laura washed a blanket, cleaned a cage, or stole a moment to give an animal special affection, she knew she was making a difference. That felt indescribably wonderful.

One day she had just finished cleaning the last dog kennel and was about to leave for home, her thoughts on the upcoming weekend, when Isaiah appeared in the aisle behind her. "Hey," he said. "Long time, no see."

It had been days since they had spoken. She had caught fleeting glimpses of Isaiah occasionally as she scurried about, doing her job, but both of them had been too busy to do more than nod. Seeing him up close again kicked her pulse to a faster rate. How did he manage to look so good? His plaid shirt was in sore need of ironing, his boots were nicked and dusty, and his Wranglers were faded almost gray. He clearly put very little effort into his appearance.

In a classically masculine stance, he stood with his hands resting loosely at his hips, one knee slightly bent, his broad shoulders relaxed. A stethoscope was looped around his neck. His dark hair fell in attractive, tousled waves over his high forehead. When she looked into his blue eyes, every rational thought in her head leaked out.

"Hi," she managed to say. "It has been a while."

He rested an arm against the dividing wall between two kennel stalls. "Two weeks, to be exact." His gaze warmed on hers. "It's time for your first performance review."

Performance review? Laura's stomach dropped. *Oh, God.* If he fired her, she would just *die.* She loved this job, and she'd made so many new friends. Val Boswell, the office manager, a thin, sun-baked blonde in her late fifties, was always ready with a warm smile, and being a dog lover she often visited the kennels just to hang out for a few minutes. And that wasn't to mention all the techs and tech assistants from both wings. Laura's favorite person of all was Trish Stone, one of Isaiah's techs, a petite brunette with merry brown eyes who talked incessantly about her kids, and about her dogs, two rambunctious Airedales named Kip and Rip.

And the animals. Laura's heart squeezed at the thought of leaving them.

"Would you like me to come to your office?" she asked, and then wanted to kick herself because her voice quavered.

"Nah, nothing so formal as that." He flashed her a slow, crooked grin that made her feel as if she'd just swallowed a dozen live goldfish. "Everyone tells me you're doing great, the best kennel keeper we've ever had. You're well liked. Tucker's people think you're fabulous, and so do mine. You're always eager to work, no matter how nasty the chore. I'm even told that you hang around after your shift is over to spend extra time with the animals."

Laura released a breath she hadn't realized she'd been holding. "I get to stay, then?"

He threw back his dark head and laughed. As his mirth subsided, he said, "Try to leave, and everyone may stage a revolt. As far as I'm concerned, we can forget our original agreement to keep you on probation for thirty days. The position is yours, Laura. Everyone here, including me, feels that you're ready to become a bona fide member of the team. Stop by to see Val on Monday. She'll have a work schedule drawn up for you."

Laura was so delighted that she almost hugged him. "Oh! Well, then. I, um — thank you, thank you very much."

"Don't thank me. You've been working your tail off back here. I thought about waiting until tonight and calling you at home. During the day I'm always so busy that there's hardly any time to talk. But there's really nothing we need to discuss, no areas where you need improvement, no areas where you particularly shine. By all accounts you shine at everything."

A quick, informal performance review suited Laura just fine. In fact, she was anxious for him to go so she could hug herself and do a happy dance.

Instead of leaving, he frowned slightly. "Can I pick your brain about something?"

The question tickled her funny bone. "I don't have much of a brain to pick."

He narrowed an eye at her. "Don't say things like that."

Laura shrugged. "Sorry. It's just not often that someone asks me for advice."

"Mark the moment. I have this birthday party to attend tonight, and" — he glanced at his watch — "after I leave here, I'll have approximately thirty minutes to stop somewhere and buy a gift. It's for this older guy, Sly Glass, who works as a ranch foreman for my brother-in-law's family. He and his wife just remodeled their place, and she says he'd like something for their den. You're good with rooms. I thought maybe you'd have some ideas and possibly know a store where I can go."

Laura thought for a moment. "What's he like?"

"Sly?" Isaiah rubbed his jaw. "He's a wiry old cowboy in a droopy tan Stetson with a face like a crinkled brown paper sack."

"The Stubborn Mule," Laura said.

Isaiah gave her an odd look. "He is a little stubborn, I guess."

"No, no, not your friend. The Stubborn Mule is a Western store. They have some neat stuff, things an old cowboy might like."

The perplexity in his expression gave way to another lopsided grin that creased the corners of his eyes. "The Stubborn Mule, huh? I've seen it, I think. Out by the overpass, isn't it?"

"That's right."

"Any ideas about what kind of gift?" he asked. "What'd work for a den?"

"For an old cowboy, I'd look for horse stuff. An old saddle would be cool. Or a picture of a field with horses in it, maybe? They also have some pretty leather throw pillows, all hand-tooled."

"An old saddle, did you say?"

"Lots of people keep old saddles in a den. They set them on a . . ." Laura's brain went blank. "I can't recall the word." She gestured helplessly. "I hate when this happens."

"A sawhorse?"

She snapped her fingers and nodded. "Right, a sawhorse, only a pretty one."

"You know, he might really like that. He's a saddle kind of guy."

Laura smiled. "You'll find the right thing there. It's a fun store."

After Isaiah left, Laura hugged her waist and twirled down the aisle, so happy she wanted to shout. *A bona fide member of the team.* She tucked in her chin and tugged her name badge around to look at it. Right now it read, LAURA, TRAINEE. Next week, she'd get a new one that said, KENNEL KEEPER in big block letters.

It was official. She was here to stay.

Midshift on Monday, Laura went to Val's office to get her new work schedule. Val, slumped behind her desk and frowning intently at a blank notepad, finally glanced up. "Hi, Laura," she said, her voice lacking its usual enthusiasm.

"Hi. Isaiah said you'd have a new work schedule ready for me today."

"Oh, damn." Val made a fist in her short blond hair. "I totally forgot. Can you stop back by before you leave?"

"Sure." Laura studied the office manager's face, noting the way her mouth turned down in weary defeat. "Is something wrong?"

Val rocked back on her castered chair. "At the staff meeting last week, Isaiah and Tucker decided we should decorate for all the holidays from now on, starting with Halloween. They think it'll lift everyone's spirits and make the clinic seem friendlier."

"It is pretty bare," Laura observed. "But then, I like lots of color."

"I'm all for the place looking better." Val thumbed her bony chest. "But guess who got elected to do the decorating?"

"Uh-oh. And you're not happy about it?"

Val tossed down her pen. "I'm terrible at decorating. Out front, they want it to look tasteful."

Laura rocked back on her heels to glance around the door frame toward the front desk. "It won't be so bad. Almost any old thing will go with cedar trim and white walls."

Val gave Laura a speculative look. "Are you good at decorating?"

Laura lifted her shoulders. "Okay, I guess."

"They don't want cutouts of jack-o'-lanterns and witches plastered everywhere."

"What do they want?"

Val puffed at her bangs. "Tasteful stuff, not that Tucker or Isaiah would recognize tasteful if it ran up and bit them on the butt."

Laura snickered. "Ah, now. You'll do fine."

"No." Val wiggled her eyebrows like the villain in a children's cartoon. "You will."

Laura threw up her hands and fell back a step. "Oh, no."

"Oh, yes. You're bound to be better at it than me." Val propped her bony elbows on the desk blotter and leaned forward, her expression suddenly pleading. "Please, Laura, please, please, *please?* Just bring me the receipts, and I'll reimburse you for anything you buy. I *hate* to decorate."

Laura loved to decorate, and she liked Val so much that she really hated to say no. "I can't promise it'll look good," she tried.

"If I do it, I guarantee it won't."

"It's almost Hallo-ween," she reminded the office manager. "There's not much time."

"Tell me about it. *Men.* They have no clue what it takes to decorate a lobby. Save me, Laura. Please?"

On Friday Laura had called and quit all of her odd jobs. Over the coming week she would have plenty of time to take on an extra project. "Okay," she agreed. "I'll try my hand at it. Why not? If you don't like what I do, I'll pay you back for the stuff and use it at home."

"Deal!" Val beamed a grateful smile. "Just be sure to log in the additional hours so I can add them to your paycheck."

"I don't have to get paid," Laura protested. "I'll have fun doing it."

"Are you sure? If I stayed over to do it, I'd get paid. Why shouldn't you?"

Laura shook her head. "There's a cap on how much I can earn."

"Dinner out, then, my treat."

"That sounds great."

"It's settled then." Val shoved aside the notepad. "You came in here for a reason. Now I can't remember what it was."

"My hours," Laura reminded her.

"Oh!" Val rolled her eyes. "I think I'm coming down with something. My brain feels like mush, and I'm a little sick to my stomach."

"I hope you start feeling better."

"Oh, I will. Some crackers and tea may help." She rubbed her forehead. "Can you stop back in before you leave, Laura? I'll have a schedule ready for you."

After leaving Val's office, Laura paused near the reception desk to peruse the waiting room, which was milling with customers and their pets. In her mind's eye she pictured what kind of decorations might look good. Seasonal wreaths would be fabulous against the cedar. Baskets filled with gourds would lend touches of much-needed color, with the added convenience that the baskets could be redone for Thanksgiving and Christmas and filled with season-appropriate floral arrangements the rest of the year.

That thought propelled Laura into a U-turn. Val looked up questioningly when Laura appeared in front of her desk again. "About the walls," Laura began. "They're all bare."

"That's a news flash? Two bachelors own this joint."

"The whole clinic is bare. I know we can't have a lot of stuff on the walls. That would make it hard to dust. But with nothing at all, it feels so cold. I go to garage sales a lot. What if I start buying this and that? It wouldn't cost much to dress up the place."

"It is pretty boring out there." Val considered the suggestion. "If it doesn't cost an arm and a leg, I'm sure Isaiah and Tucker won't object."

"I see nice framed paintings at garage sales all the time. They never cost a lot."

Val nodded decisively. "Go for it, then."

After leaving Val's office, Laura trailed a finger along the wainscoting as she walked up the hallway. Decorating a clinic would be a challenging endeavor. Her experience ran more to houses. She wasn't sure what kind of wall hangings would work best. Maybe she could get some ideas by leafing through magazines.

Yes, that was a good idea, she decided. At the end of the hall, she turned to study the waiting area again, trying to envision how it might look. A clear picture wouldn't take shape in her mind. She only knew that the Crystal Falls Animal Clinic was about to get a makeover.

Chapter Four

Laura was cleaning kennels five and six the next morning when Isaiah appeared at the end of the aisle. He wore a blood-smeared blue lab coat, a surgical cap, and a mask. His eyes burned with urgency above the swatch of white cloth.

"I need you in the surgery, stat!" he yelled.

Laura dropped the soiled bedding she'd just gathered into her arms, latched the kennel gates, and hurried after him. When she entered the surgery, he tossed her a sterile smock, a cap, and a mask. "Hurry. Over half the staff called in sick. We've got a compound fracture of the femur. A main artery is severed."

Rooted to the spot, Laura stared in mounting horror at the dog on the operating table. An IV tube, fed by a see-through bag of clear liquid suspended from a tripod, was already taped to the animal's front leg. Its left hind leg rested at an awkward angle and had been tightly wrapped in a towel, which was now soaked with crimson. Beads of blood dripped from the stainless steel table onto the tile floor.

"Laura?" Isaiah gave her a sharp look. "I know this isn't part of your job description, but you're all I've got."

Laura just shook her head. Surely he didn't mean for her to assist him in surgery? *No, no, no!* She would make a horrible mistake. The dog would die because of her. She couldn't do this.

Isaiah drew the towel from the dog's leg and loosened the makeshift tourniquet that someone had applied to slow the bleeding. "You have to help me, Laura. There's no one else. Jennifer and Gloria are alone up front. They're doing their best to get some more people in here, but everyone they've called so far is knocked flat with some kind of flu. Belinda called in sick. Trish's husband phoned to say she's been puking her guts up all night. We haven't heard from Angela, but she's late. Chances are she's too sick to call in."

"But —"

"No buts. Tucker's got three emergencies in his wing and only Susan to assist him. Normally Val fills in when we get shorthanded, but she's not here either. That leaves only you to help me."

Still shaking her head, Laura managed to

push out, "I — can't. I'm sorry, but I just can't."

"You have to." His blue eyes locked with hers. "This dog's life is on the line. There's no time for his owners to take him somewhere else. He'll bleed to death."

Laura clutched the surgical scrubs to her chest, wishing she were sick, too. How come everyone else had gotten the bug, and she felt fine? "I don't know what to do."

"I'll talk you through it." He inclined his head at the sink as he grabbed a shaver to prep the unconscious canine. "That dispenser above the faucet is surgical soap. There are sterile gloves in that blue box at the end of the counter."

After jerking off her soiled smock, Laura quickly donned the clean one and rushed to the sink. Pushing at her hair with numb fingers as she pulled on the cap, she glanced in the mirror to make sure all of her head was covered. Her eyes, huge and dazed, stared back at her from a chalk-white face.

"Hurry," Isaiah urged from behind her. "I don't want to lose him."

Laura was trembling so violently she sent soap lather flying as she washed her hands and arms. Moments later she grew light-headed as she approached the table. Blood had pooled around the dog's hind-quarters.

"Don't pass out on me," Isaiah warned softly. "Pretend it's something on television. That's what I used to do."

He seemed so calm, so unaffected by the gore, that Laura found it difficult to believe he'd ever felt as queasy as she did.

As though he guessed her thoughts, he said, "The first time I observed an operation, I almost fainted. Happens to a lot of people. All you can do is find a way to separate yourself."

Laura nodded. Pretending it was something on television didn't quite work. The coppery smell of blood coated her mouth, shivered over her tongue. Her gaze kept shifting to the stand beside him. A dozen different instruments lay on a white towel, the pieces of stainless steel glinting in the bright light. She didn't know the names of the tools, which of them he might need. She'd watched enough medical shows to realize that a surgical assistant had to anticipate a doctor's needs and respond to his orders without hesitation.

Her legs felt as if they'd turned to water, but she forced herself to move closer. "I don't know what to do," she said again, her voice quavering and thin.

"No worries. All I need is an extra pair of hands." He nodded at the instruments. "Right now I need the scalpel." When Laura hesitated, he described the implement and then winked at her when she grabbed the right one. "See there, sweetheart? Already a pro."

When he made a long incision in the animal's leg, Laura gulped audibly. Little black spots danced in front of her eyes. She turned her gaze to the dog's head. Its eyes were only partially closed, and its mouth hung open. It looked to her as if Isaiah had pulled the animal's tongue out over its teeth. Her stomach tumbled and rolled. To hold down her gorge, she focused on the cotton blanket that now draped the canine's body.

"What kind of dog is it?" she asked, desperate for something, anything, to take her mind off what was happening.

"He's a mongrel just like me, part this and part that. Mostly shepherd of some kind, I think. 'Mongrel' isn't a very flattering term. I prefer the term 'mixed-breed' myself." He glanced at the monitor to check the dog's vitals and adjusted the IV drip. "Do you know what capillary refill is?"

Laura nodded. She knew the meaning of many terms that she could no longer say.

"Every few minutes, pinch his tongue and press on his gums to check his refill for me. Try to use only one hand for that. Keep the other one sterile to pass me instruments. If you forget, change gloves."

Laura stared stupidly at the dog's tongue. "His name is Humphrey," Isaiah said, as if he sensed her reluctance. "When he wakes up, he'll lick your hand to say hi. You do want him to wake up again, don't you?"

The question worked on her shocked system like a glass of ice water in the face. She gingerly pinched the dog's lolling tongue and pressed a fingertip to his upper gum. Because she couldn't say *capillary* to save her soul, she settled for, "His refill looks fine. The color comes back pretty fast."

"Good, good. His vitals are within normal range, but that can change in a blink when an animal has lost so much blood."

Laura's heart caught. This was *real,* she thought dizzily. This dog's life rested partly in her hands. Because it did, she reached deep for courage she hadn't realized she possessed. A strange calm settled over her.

She could do this. She *would* do this. She wanted Humphrey to wake up soon, wanted to feel the rasp of his tongue on her hand and see life in his now expressionless eyes.

"Tell me about him," she said shakily. "Is he a new patient?"

Isaiah's gaze flicked to hers and held for only an instant, but in that instant his eyes warmed on hers. "I've been seeing him for about a year, off and on." He asked her to sop up some of the blood with a piece of gauze so he could see what he was doing. While they worked, he went on to say, "Just office visits — shots, deworming, that kind of thing. We haven't had a lot of getting-acquainted time, but judging by the little I've seen, he's a great dog, smart and very friendly."

Beneath the mask, Laura smiled slightly. "He has a friendly look. What are his people like?"

He cast her another twinkling glance. "You have it turned around, don't you? The people own him."

Laura disagreed. "I don't think it's about who owns who. It's about love. Does he have nice people?"

Isaiah nodded. "A man, woman, and a cute little girl with big brown eyes and pigtails. I'll leave you to guess who Humphrey loves the most."

"The little girl," Laura quickly replied. She could almost see the dog playing with the child, barking and running happily after a ball. She was suddenly very glad that Isaiah had asked her to assist him. If Humphrey lived, she would be able to say that she'd helped in some small way to save his life. "He looks like a dog that loves kids."

"Right on target. And as of this morning, he became quite the hero." He winked at her, a habit she was coming to suspect he had cultivated because his hands were so often occupied and the lower part of his face was covered by a mask. "The little girl ran out in front of a car."

"Oh, *no.*" The last of Laura's squeamishness vanished. "Is that how he got hurt?"

Isaiah nodded. "The owner says Humphrey leaped into the street just in the nick of time and knocked the little girl out of the way. Unfortunately for Humphrey, the woman in the car says it happened so fast that there was no way she could stop. If it weren't for Humphrey, she would have hit the child."

"Oh, my God."

Though Laura couldn't see Isaiah's mouth, the creases that suddenly fanned out at the corners of his eyes told her he was smiling. "You ever saved a hero's life?"

"No."

"First time for everything. Humphrey deserves a medal." He parted the animal's flesh, revealing tendon, bone, and the damaged artery. Laura had one bad moment when she looked into the wound. Then she thought of Humphrey chasing a ball again, and the black spots in her vision went away. She grabbed fresh gauze to dab away the blood. Isaiah nodded in approval. "Do I remember your saying you couldn't do this? I think I'll keep you in here full-time."

Laura gave a weak laugh. "No way. I'm happy in the kennels." Her smile faded when she looked back down at the dog. "Will he make it, do you think?"

Isaiah reared back to avoid a spurt of blood. "Clamp!"

Laura grabbed frantically for what looked like a clamp, handed it to him, and nearly collapsed with relief when he used the apparatus to stop the bleeding. "Oh, *God*."

"He's right here," Isaiah said huskily, "looking over our shoulders and guiding our hands." He glanced up. "God, I mean. Some people would call me crazy for believing that."

Laura wasn't one of them. In that moment, as she looked into Isaiah Coulter's eyes, she understood what had led him to become a vet. Not a desire for money or a yearning for prestige. He was here, doing what he did, because he loved animals and felt a calling to help them.

"With God on duty, maybe Humphrey has a chance," she said tremulously.

"No maybe to it. God cares about all of us, man and animal alike. Humphrey will make it." He threw a look at a speaker in the ceiling above them. "Next time around, remind me to turn on some music. I work better to a beat."

Laura's stomach squeezed. "Next time around?"

"Got a pup with a chicken bone stuck in his intestines." He winked at her again. "Unless Gloria can work a miracle and get some more people in here, I'm going to need you most of the day. Unless, of course, you have other commitments you can't weasel out of."

Laura had intended to start decorating the waiting room when she got off at noon. A puppy with a bone in his bowel definitely took precedence. "No, nothing," she said.

"It's a date, then, darlin'."

An awful thought occurred to Laura. "I won't have to help with your horse patients, will I?"

He burst out laughing. "No, we have specially trained techs out in the equine center for that. You're safe."

Laura was relieved. Surgery on dogs and cats was one thing, but surgery on a horse would be something else entirely.

For Laura, the morning passed in a surreal blur. She soon stopped thinking about the blood. There were far too many other things to occupy her mind — the names of different implements and surgical techniques, disinfectants, and medications. When she wasn't standing at Isaiah's side, assisting in a procedure, she was racing about sterilizing tables or gathering the necessary items to do surgery on another patient.

Shortly after noon, right in the middle of an operation, this time on a Newfoundland with a stick caught in his throat, Laura noticed that Isaiah's hands were quivering. Concerned, she studied what she could see of his face above the surgical mask. There was a pale cast to his dark complexion, and his skin shimmered with sweat.

"Are you all right?"

He nodded, but Laura wasn't convinced. "Isaiah?"

"I need to eat. Got the weak shakes."

"What did you have for breakfast?"

"Nothing. I meant to go by McDonald's on the way in, but then I got the call about Humphrey and never went."

The moment they had the Newfoundland safely deposited in an observation cage and covered with warm blankets, Laura stripped off her surgical scrubs and hurried to the refrigerator. Inside she found mostly soft drinks. The only food items were containers of fat-free yogurt and low-fat string cheese, not the most desirable fare for a large, hardworking man. She filled the crook of one arm and both hands with food and then motioned to her boss, who was already putting on a fresh lab coat to do surgery on a cat with a plugged urethra.

"Food first," she said firmly as she arranged the makeshift meal on a paper towel on the counter.

"No time. That bladder is ready to pop."

Laura sent him a scolding look over her

shoulder. "You have to eat. You can't cut on a cat with shaky hands."

Isaiah was unaccustomed to being looked after by an employee. Normally on a busy day, it was every man or woman for himself. Nevertheless, he had to admit that it felt kind of nice. After joining her by the sink, he straddled a stool and grabbed a yogurt container.

"Thanks, Laura." He peeled the wrapper from a plastic spoon and practically inhaled the yogurt. Before he took the last bite, she had pulled the safety seal off another container and was pushing it toward him.

"Take a few sips of pop, too," she told him. "It'll get your blood sugar up faster."

Isaiah took several swigs of Coke. As he set the can back on the counter, he realized how badly his hands were shaking. "Thanks," he said again. "I'm feeling a little better already."

Her pretty hazel eyes were dark with concern. "You really should eat more often. No one can work this hard without food."

The simplicity of the statement wasn't lost on Isaiah. Most people would have used the words *nourishment* and *energy.* Her avoidance of those terms drove home to him just how extraordinary her performance this morning had been. While working with her, he had forgotten for long stretches that she was handicapped.

"Have I told you how much I appreciate your help this morning? I know it hasn't been easy for you."

Her mouth curved up at the corners when she smiled, lending her full lips a kissable sweetness that was difficult to ignore. "Easy is for sissies." Her eyes danced with devilment. "And, yes, you have thanked me." Her gaze shifted to the cages at the far end of the room where Humphrey now lay awake. The dog was weak but could lift his head, which Isaiah took as a positive sign. "The truth is," she went on, "I'm the one who should thank you. I got to help save lives today. That's not something I thought I could do."

Isaiah understood her sense of wonder. The first few times in surgery, he had felt it himself. Over time he'd lost that, something he hadn't realized until he worked with Laura and saw the awe in her eyes. "It's an incredible rush, isn't it?"

She nodded and looked down at her hands. "Even now, I can't believe I did it."

He couldn't help but smile. "You not only did it, you did a great job."

Isaiah almost added that she would make a great technician with the proper training, but he caught himself before the words were out. Laura had done well under his direction, amazingly well, but that was as far as it could ever go. The realization saddened him.

The blush of pleasure that stained her cheeks told him how much the compliment had meant to her, which saddened him even more. If not for the accident, she would have had such a brilliant future.

He tossed the empty yogurt containers into the trash. "You going to eat?" he asked as he peeled the plastic from a cheese stick.

She wrinkled her nose and shook her head. "Later. I don't feel very hungry."

It occurred to Isaiah that she probably felt too queasy to eat. He remembered those days, too. "Sorry. I forget that other people don't see this kind of stuff on a regular basis. After you've done it for a while, you get used to it."

"Hmm." She gave him a dubious look. "Maybe."

By five o'clock, Isaiah's back was killing him. They'd been standing for hours without a break. When the last surgery had been successfully completed, he sank wearily onto a stool, leaned his head back, and sighed.

"What a day."

Laura was at the sink, washing her hands. "If we're done, I need to go and make sure all the animals in the kennels have been taken care of."

Isaiah groaned. Jennifer had found a kennel person to fill in for Laura this morning, but the afternoon person had called in sick. That meant a good four hours of work still had to be done. "I'll help."

"I can handle it."

"And have you here until God knows when?"

"I may have to work the night shift if all the kennel people are sick, too."

"Jennifer got in touch with Dan Fosworth. He says he feels fine, so he's got tonight covered. Good thing. I may need you in here again tomorrow."

She paused in drying her hands. "You think?"

"It's possible. Depends on what kind of flu everyone has. Unless it's the twenty-four-hour kind, chances are we'll be short-handed again."

"Who'll work in the kennels tomorrow?"

"Lena needs the hours. Gloria says she agreed to work the whole day."

Thirty minutes later they were cleaning the kennels together. Laura gathered the soiled bedding while Isaiah hosed and disinfected the floors. As had happened in the surgery, they soon found a compatible rhythm and managed to get a lot accomplished in record time. Isaiah no sooner got a cage cleaned than Laura was putting down fresh bedding. Then she brought the animal back in while he washed the dishes and refilled them with food and water.

In a hurry to finish and go home, Isaiah almost snapped at Laura when he noticed that she was lingering in each cage to pet the dogs and talk softly to them. Hello? They'd already put in a twelve-hour day. At this rate they'd be here all night. But just as he opened his mouth to say something, he saw the look in one of the dog's eyes: pure adoration.

Isaiah smiled wearily and leaned a shoulder against the wire mesh of a kennel gate. *This,* he realized, was what made Laura so good at her job. She truly loved the animals, and they truly loved her. She spent only a minute with each dog before moving on to the next. All totaled she would waste no more than ten minutes, and it would be time well spent. Each and every dog in her care got its share of affection.

"You are amazing," he finally said.

She straightened and gave him a bewildered look.

Isaiah pointed at his watch. "You've been here since six this morning, and I know you have to be beat. Yet you still take the time to make all these dogs feel loved. I think that's pretty special."

"They're lonely."

That was all she said, but the response told Isaiah more about her than she could possibly know. His mother had called it right: Laura Townsend was every bit as sweet as she looked. It wasn't an act. She wasn't out to impress him. In her estimation, the affection that she doled out to every animal was just as important as fresh bedding and food.

"Pizza," he said.

Again she looked bewildered.

"Dinner, you and me, my treat. What d'ya say?"

"You don't have to feed me."

"We both have to eat, and I hate going anywhere by myself." He narrowed an eye at her. "Are you or are you not the same lady who was lecturing me about eating earlier?"

Her cheek dimpled in a smile. "You make it hard to say no."

"Then don't."

Wednesday was pretty much a repeat of Tuesday, with over half the staff out sick and only Laura to assist Isaiah in surgery, the only difference being that fewer emergencies came in. The slower pace gave Laura more opportunities than she liked to notice the man beside her — how the tendons in his bronzed forearms bunched and moved as he worked, how his eyes darkened when he concentrated, and how he smelled, an enticing blend of spicy cologne, traces of soap, and a sheer male essence that made her want to move closer for a better whiff. Bad situation. Laura's only hope was that a couple of the techs would be well enough by tomorrow to return to work so she could go back to the kennels where she belonged.

At ten she found a few minutes between patients to put on a fresh pot of coffee. When the machine had finished its cycle she grabbed Isaiah's sleeve and escorted him from the operating room. "Time for a snack," she informed him. "This time in your office, so I can eat a little, too."

"A snack?" A glimmer of interest came into his eyes. "What? More yogurt?"

"Nope. Something much better than that."

Isaiah stopped dead just inside the door. "Cinnamon rolls? I've died and gone to heaven!" He circled the desk, dropped onto his chair, and leaned forward to sniff. "They smell just like my mom's."

"Safeway has nice baked goods." It wasn't a lie; Safeway did have a fabulous bakery. Laura just preferred not to tell him the rolls were some that she'd made herself. She wasn't sure why — possibly because it seemed too personal. "They'll be good with fresh coffee."

He sighed as he took a bite. Laura took a roll for herself, setting it on a paper towel. Before having a taste, she tried the coffee. It was the first pot she'd ever made with the clinic's coffeemaker, and she hadn't been sure how many scoops to use. She was relieved to discover that it tasted all right.

"This is wonderful," he said, licking sugary glaze from the back of his thumb. "Cinnamon rolls are one of my favorites. I swear, these taste homemade."

Laura smiled as she sank her teeth into her roll. It was good, she decided, not one of her best batches, but acceptably light, with just the right amount of cinnamon and icing. It was Gram's recipe, a one-step dough that eliminated the kneading process, so she'd had time to make a batch last night before she collapsed into bed. "I'll bring some more one of these mornings," she promised.

He nodded. "Just be sure to reimburse yourself. I don't want the cost coming out of your wages."

The cost had been mostly in time and labor, but she couldn't bring herself to tell him that. Better that he believe the rolls had come from the store. That way she could make them again without feeling funny about it.

"For lunch I got sandwich makings, some chips, and a bunch of instant soups. Thank goodness Safeway is open twenty-four hours. Starving isn't my thing."

"Sandwiches will be great." He grabbed a second roll and rocked back in his chair, the expression on his dark face the very picture of contentment. "Better than great. Keep this up and I'll want you in the surgery full-time."

"I can keep the fridge stocked no matter where I'm working," she pointed out. "The market is on my way to work."

"That would be wonderful, Laura. When we have a full crew working, the techs give each other lunch breaks, and they usually go out somewhere to eat. I don't normally have time for that."

An overabundance of dedication was more Isaiah's problem than a lack of time, Laura had determined. He wasn't merely a good vet; he was totally devoted to his profession and the animals entrusted to his care. In her recollection, she'd never worked quite as hard as she had yesterday. She had a feeling that Isaiah gave one hundred percent each and every day.

Gazing across the desk at him, she once again found herself hoping that at least a few of the technicians would return to work tomorrow. She would be glad for things to return to normal. Familiarity didn't always breed contempt. Sometimes, deep in a foolish female heart, it planted the seed for feelings that ran much deeper.

Laura couldn't allow that seed to take root. She needed to return to the kennels, safely away from Isaiah, before she did something totally stupid, like fall in love with him.

Chapter Five

Laura got her wish. The following day most of the other employees returned to work and resumed their normal duties. Happy to have the worst of the flu epidemic behind her, Laura was able to go back to the kennels. Working with Isaiah had been challenging and exciting, but being with the animals was where she belonged. She had the routine down pat, she felt more relaxed, and though she loved all the animals that came briefly into her care, she was in no danger of permanently losing her heart to any of them.

When her shift ended at noon she went out to her car to collect the bulging plastic bags that had been crowding the backseat since her shopping spree on Monday night. Just as she opened the trunk, a truck pulling a horse trailer pulled into the parking lot. An older man in Levi's and a lined denim jacket exited the vehicle.

"It okay if I park over here?" he called. "All the spots are taken in front of the equine center."

Laura glanced over at the large metal building where Isaiah and Tucker treated horses, and sure enough a long four-horse trailer had been parked sideways and was taking up all the available parking space. "I think that'll be fine."

While Laura gathered bags of decorations from the trunk, the man unloaded a pretty reddish-brown horse from the trailer. The animal favored its right front leg and was limping badly. "Oh. How did he hurt his leg?" she asked.

"Just a sprained tendon, I hope," the man replied. "But he's limpin' pretty bad. I thought I'd better have Isaiah take a look."

"Ah." Normally Isaiah made farm and ranch calls three mornings a week so he could treat the minor injuries and common ailments of large animals on site. "You must live quite a distance away."

The man nodded. "Sixty miles north of here, a tad too far for a vet to come to me."

Laura knew that both Isaiah and Tucker had far too many patients to travel so far to treat only one. "I see. Well, I hope your horse's leg gets better soon."

She gazed after the man as he led the gelding toward the equine center. A tech in a blue lab coat emerged from the front office to raise a large slide-up door so the horse and its owner could enter the building.

A few moments later, when Laura stepped into the front waiting area with her arms laden with bags, Debbie, one of the secretaries, asked, "What have you got there? Do you need help?"

Laura couldn't tell Debbie what was in the sacks. *Halloween* and *decorations* were multisyllabic words. Trying to say both, back-to-back, would have set her to stammering.

She settled for grinning and wiggling her eyebrows. Debbie, who could best be described as nondescript, with short, light brown hair, blue eyes, regular features, and an average body type, was normally a reserved person with a businesslike air. But now curiosity was clearly getting the better of her. She pushed up from her chair and circled the counter.

"What do you have?" she asked, craning her neck to see into a sack.

Laura gently deposited her burdens on the floor. With a wave of her hand, she said, "Look and see."

A woman sitting on an end chair in the waiting area leaned sharply forward as Debbie opened one of the bags. Exclamations of delight followed, and before Laura knew quite how it happened, her Halloween purchases were under siege, with all of the receptionists fishing through the merchandise while patrons with dogs on leashes hovered behind them, trying to see. Even Gloria, a seemingly humorless woman, said, "Oh!" and "Ah!" as she examined the decorations.

The commotion brought Val from her office. "What on earth is going on out here?"

"Halloween decorations!" Jennifer Bacchi, a tall but nicely proportioned redhead, held up a miniature tree, a denuded deciduous branch painted black to make it look delightfully spooky. "Come look, Val." Compliments of tinted contact lenses, today Jennifer's blue eyes were emerald green, and they sparkled with excitement. "She got the cutest stuff to hang on the branches."

Pixie-cut blond hair in a wind-ruffled stir from her having recently stepped outside for a cigarette, Val came around front to bend over one sack and then another. The scent that surrounded her, an oddly pleasant blend of smoke and perfume, filled the air as she moved.

"Am I good or what?" Her sun-parched face went all crinkly in a pleased smile when she looked up at Laura. "I *knew* you'd be great at this."

"Get a load of these candied apples!" Debbie cried. "Don't they look real?"

Val grabbed a yellow basket from Debbie's bag. "Oh, Laura, these are wonderful. What are you going to put them in?"

Normally when Isaiah got back to the clinic after making farm and ranch calls, he entered the building by a rear door, but this morning a horse trailer blocked his regular parking place. Isaiah recognized the truck that pulled the conveyance as one belonging to a client of his who lived out of the area. Isaiah didn't recall the fellow's having an appointment with him today, but that didn't mean much. His schedule was so busy that his daily appointment roster was all that saved him.

The lack of parking space in the rear lot forced Isaiah to leave the Hummer out front. Peeling off his leather gloves, he circled the vehicle, leaped onto the front walkway, and measured off the stretch of paw-printed cement with long, hurried strides.

He heard the shrieks before he reached the building. Just inside the door, he drew to a stop and stared. His normally efficient, devoted employees had abandoned their posts to squat, kneel, and sit on the floor of the waiting area, all of them intent on a colorful array of Halloween stuff. As they plucked items from the cluster of plastic bags, they emitted sounds like a flock of startled chickens.

Her cheeks flushed with pleasure, Laura stood over the group, explaining in her slow, soft way where she hoped to put this or hang that, a telltale sign to Isaiah that his pretty blond kennel keeper was responsible for all the chaos. Given the fact that the female patrons seemed to be having as much fun as the employees, Isaiah could only grin. Nothing, it seemed, was going to stay the same at the clinic now that Laura had been hired. Her sunny disposition and warmth seemed to rub off on everyone.

A golden retriever caught his owner unaware and lunged against the leash to shove his head into one of the sacks. Laura gave a startled laugh and crouched to hug the dog's neck. "Aren't you a smart boy?" She tousled the animal's ears, then thrust a hand inside the bag and drew out a package. "Yes, I got doggy treats." She rewarded the sniffing canine with a liver-colored biscuit. "Tasty ones, not those icky healthy things that Isaiah and Tucker buy."

The dog made fast work of devouring the goody. Laura smiled, gave him one more, and then grabbed a plastic pumpkin with a removable lid as she pushed to her feet. She was in the process of emptying the dog treats into it when she saw Isaiah.

"Isaiah!"

The laughter instantly subsided, and all heads turned. Isaiah straightened away from the door frame. "Ladies," he said by way of greeting.

Debbie shot to her feet. Jennifer's face went nearly as red as her hair. Gloria, always the cool and collected one, returned the items she'd removed from a sack before she joined the sudden exodus back to the workstation. Only Val held her ground, a four-foot triangle of space on the tile littered with gourds of various colors.

"At the last staff meeting, you did ask for the clinic to be decorated," she informed him. "Remember?"

Isaiah recalled making the request. At the time he had imagined that it would be a one-woman task. Now he could see the error in his thinking. "It looks like a worthwhile project to me. Carry on."

At his words, the receptionists who had scurried back to their posts froze in midmotion. Isaiah winked at them. Shoulders began to relax, smiles peeked back out, feet retraced their steps, and soon feminine chatter was bouncing off the walls again. Only Laura didn't move. Eyes still round, she continued to stare at him.

"I guess I should have saved this for after hours," she said. "I didn't mean to mess up the normal routine."

"The normal routine needs to be interrupted every once in a while." Isaiah only wondered how Laura had gotten stuck with the decorating detail. He glanced at the paraphernalia strung across the tile. Jennifer was playing with what appeared to be a battery-powered miniature jack-o'-lantern. It glowed orange, then blinked out. "Where on earth did you find this stuff?"

"Season's Delights, a shop in Old Town down by the park. I went in there last Christmas, and now that's where I always go. Some of their stuff is spendy, but mostly not."

Isaiah was coming to suspect that Laura liked to shop. She seemed to know exactly where to go for any given item. "I'm impressed. Pumpkins that light up?"

"They're for the tree." Laura plucked a black thing affixed to a base from the jumble of stuff at her feet. It looked more like a glorified twig than a tree. "I found witches on brooms and little goblins to hang on it, too. And cobwebs. It'll be cute. I think it will look nice on the counter."

She hurried on, showing him a number of other items she'd bought — baskets, gourds, fake candy apples, autumn wreathes and swags, treat containers shaped like pumpkins, and a collection of Halloween standards that included paper witches, goblins, and skeletons.

Isaiah had eyes only for the woman. She wore a rust-colored knit top that went so well with all the autumn tones that she might have popped out of a sack herself. As he ran his gaze over her tidy figure, he found himself wishing that she had. He would have tucked her under his arm and taken her home to brighten his house for Halloween.

"So . . . what do you think?" she asked.

He snapped back to awareness. What did he think? That he was losing his mind was a strong possibility. "I, um . . . it's all great," he said.

"I tried to choose tasteful stuff."

Isaiah had no vision when it came to decorating, but he'd seen Laura's apartment. She had a knack for taking odds and ends, assembling them into groups, and making them look good. "I'm sure it will all look great when you've finished."

Laura's heart lurched oddly in her chest when Isaiah stepped closer. This morning he wore a tan Stetson that added to his already impressive height, the brim casting a shadow over his chiseled features. His brown canvas coat, cut long at the hem for riding horses on chill winter days, only enhanced his rugged good looks. The chatter of the women beside her grew dim until only the sound of her breathing hummed in her ears.

"You okay?" he asked.

Laura straightened her shoulders. "Fine, just fine." Only she wasn't. Just looking at him made her heart squeeze. Working with him for two whole days had not been a good thing. She wanted to ask if he'd eaten any breakfast. She had to bite her tongue to keep from reminding him to have lunch. "Just glad you like my choices."

He nodded and swept off the Stetson. His dark hair lay in rumpled waves over his forehead, making her fingertips itch to smooth it. He smiled slightly — one of those off-center grins that twitched up only one corner of his mouth.

"I guess I should go so you can get back to work." He toed a sack. "Just don't work too long. All right? That flu bug may still be making its rounds. Don't overdo and wear down your resistance. I don't want you getting sick."

The concern in his deep voice sounded sincere, giving Laura cause to wonder if he was as confused by his feelings for her as she was by hers for him. The thought no sooner slipped into her brain than her blood went cold. *Stupid, stupid, stupid.* A man like Isaiah would never be interested in someone like her. With his intelligence and drive, he could make his mark in the world of veterinary medicine. With that future success would come wealth and exciting opportunities. The last thing he needed was a brain-damaged woman to hold him back.

The squeezing sensation around her heart grew painful even as she forced a smile. "It won't take me very long." She gestured at the other women. "I have lots of help."

His beautiful blue eyes held hers, and for just an instant Laura felt as if they were the only two people in the room. Then he pivoted on his boot heel and walked away.

Once inside the surgery, Isaiah slapped his hat on a hook and shrugged out of his coat. *Damn.* Most times he had no trouble squelching feelings of attraction when they were inappropriate. Take Zeke's wife, Natalie, for instance. She was beautiful, talented, and charming. Any guy with eyes in his head drooled a little the first time he met her. Isaiah had been no exception, but the instant he'd felt a twinge of yearning, he had stamped it out and never allowed himself to feel it again.

Why in the hell couldn't he do the same with Laura? Yes, she was pretty, but so were thousands of other women. He never had a problem resisting any of *them.* In fact, busy as he was, it was the rare female who even made him look twice.

"Hi!" Trish turned from a cat cage. Her welcoming smile faded the instant she saw his face. "Uh-oh. Problems?"

"Nothing related to here." *Liar.* Laura was carving out a place for herself at the clinic, proving to be a valuable asset. He had to get his head screwed on straight where she was concerned. Men who lusted after female subordinates were slimeballs, and he wouldn't allow himself to go there. "Just feeling out of sorts."

"Laura brought in homemade cookies — the big, fat, chewy kind with gobs of milk-chocolate chips. They should cheer you up."

Isaiah almost groaned. *Laura, Laura, Laura.* In almost every conversation, her name seemed to crop up. Determined to focus on his work, Isaiah glanced over his roster for the day. Sure enough, Roger Petty had a one-thirty appointment with Isaiah for his quarter horse gelding, Rusty. Bad limp, right front leg. Isaiah hoped it was nothing serious. The old guy loved that horse as if it were a child.

Rolling up his shirtsleeves, Isaiah stepped to the sink to wash his hands. When he turned to grab a paper towel, Trish went up on her tiptoes in front of him and shoved a cookie in his face.

"Come on. Big bite. Chocolate brightens the mood."

Just the smell was enough to lift Isaiah's spirits. Breakfast, a half bag of cheese puffs that he'd eaten while driving, had been six hours ago. He took a huge bite of the cookie.

As he started to chew, Trish added, "Some studies say that chocolate gives people the same feeling they get when they're falling in love." Isaiah froze with his teeth imbedded in yummy chunks of chocolate. The last thing he needed was a hormone enhancer. Unfortunately, the chips were already melting over his tongue, and he was only human. What normal, rational person could resist swallowing?

The cookie was delicious. Isaiah practically inhaled the rest of it and grabbed two more from a deep orange party tray trimmed with little black witches. As he ate, he decided there was some truth to the old adage that the way to a man's heart was through his stomach.

After Laura finished decorating the waiting area, she moved on to Tucker's wing of the clinic in the hope that Isaiah might be busy in the examining rooms by the time she was ready to tackle his. No such luck. He was in the middle of an operation on a gray tabby when she entered the south-wing surgery.

At the sound of the door closing behind her, he glanced up and gave her a long, contemplative look. Accustomed to a friendlier reception, Laura wondered if she'd done something wrong.

Trish, looking like a masked elf beside her tall employer, flicked Laura a mischievous look. "There you are. If your ears have been burning, it's because we've been talking about you."

Belinda turned from cleaning an observation cage. "Yeah, lady," she said with a grin, "you're in big trouble."

Laura sent Isaiah a questioning glance. He caught the look and finally winked. "Not in a bad way," he assured her. "We're just grateful for the cookies, is all. They're delicious."

"I'll say. And the trays are totally cute. Puts me more in the mood for Halloween." Using her forearm, Trish scratched her nose through the surgical mask. "Hurry up and finish here, Isaiah. I'm hungry for another cookie."

"Yes, ma'am." Isaiah bent to resume his work. "By the way, Laura, I understand that you and your grandmother are invited to have Thanksgiving dinner at my parents' house."

"Thanksgiving?" Belinda wadded soiled newspaper in her hands. "Puh-lease. Can't we get Halloween out of the way first?"

Trish laughed. "Heck, no. We'll be on the holiday fast track for the next two months."

Belinda huffed and rolled her eyes.

With Laura's parents living in Florida and her sister in Portland, she had been counting on spending the holiday with her grandmother. "I haven't talked to Gram," she settled for saying. "And she's said nothing about going to your parents' for Thanks-giving."

He didn't look up. "Well, it's early on. My mother always plans everything for the holidays well in advance. I was just wondering if you might be there." He dabbed sweat from his forehead with the sleeve of his lab coat. "No big deal if you have other plans."

Pleasure radiated through Laura, suffusing her whole body with warmth. He wanted to know if she'd be having Thanksgiving dinner at his parents' house. She couldn't help but wonder if that meant he was hoping she might. The thought no sooner came than Laura pushed it from her mind. *Dangerous ground.* Where this man was concerned, she needed to keep her feet firmly rooted in reality. He thought of her as a friend, nothing more.

"Gram hasn't said any-thing. But that'd be fun," she heard herself say.

"If you guys decide to be there, you'd better brush up on your checkers game then," he said with a grin. "I'm the all-time champion."

Laura had always enjoyed checkers, and it was one of the few games that she could still play. "I'm not so bad myself."

His eyes crinkled at the corners, a sure sign that he was smiling. Then he gave her a thumbs-up and returned his attention to the cat. "Uh-oh. I don't like the looks of that."

Trish followed his gaze. "Does it look malignant?"

"Shit." Isaiah sighed wearily. "We'd better do a biopsy."

Trish stepped over to a cupboard. "Shania and Trevor love chocolate-chip cookies, Laura. Can I have your recipe?"

Laura was staring at the unconscious cat and thinking of its owners. If the feline had cancer, they might have to put it down. "What?" She refocused on Trish. "I'm sorry."

"Christ," Isaiah said softly. "This is cancer."

Returning to the table with a clear plastic slide, Trish replied to Laura's question. "I said I'd like your cookie recipe."

"Sure." Laura pushed the word up a tight throat. "I'll copy it for —"

"Son of a bitch. There's more than one tumor. Forehead." Isaiah angled his head toward Trish so she could wipe the sweat from his brow. Then he bent low again, intent on his work. "What rotten luck. She thinks the world of this cat."

Belinda abandoned her task to approach the table. "Oh, no. We can't lose him, Isaiah. Mrs. Palmer will be heartsick."

Trish's brows knitted in concern. "How bad, do you think?"

Beneath the mask that covered the lower half of his face, Laura could see Isaiah's jaw muscle ticking. "I don't know if I can get it all. But I'm sure as hell going to try. No wonder he's been off his food. Poor fellow's eaten up."

Trish looked at Laura. "Have you met Mrs. Palmer?"

Laura shook her head.

"She's a sweetheart," Belinda inserted. "A little old lady. Seymour is all she's got now. Her husband died about six months ago."

Isaiah swore again. Laura's heart hurt for him. In that moment there was such anguish in his eyes.

"Jesus." The whispered word was like a shout. He straightened and closed his eyes. "Hold the fort for me," he told Trish. "I have to go call her." He ripped off the mask as he stepped away from the table. "Be right back."

Laura's stomach rolled with nausea as he left the surgery. Trish stood over the cat, her eyes devoid of the mischief that was so characteristic of her. Belinda returned to cleaning cages, her expression glum.

"This is the downside of veterinary medicine," Trish said huskily. "That isn't going to be a fun phone call for him to make." She stroked the cat's head. "Poor kitty." She hauled in a deep breath. "Better this way than how some of them go. He'll just never wake up. Off he goes to Rainbow Ridge."

"Rainbow Ridge?" Laura echoed.

Belinda interrupted with, "Not that ridge bunk again. Animals don't have souls, Trish. Therefore they don't go to heaven."

"They do so," Trish argued, "and Rainbow Ridge is where they wait for their owners — a wonderful place halfway between here and heaven. They romp and play there in animal paradise, waiting for their owners to join them for the rest of the journey to heaven."

Laura hugged her waist. To her horror, she realized that she was about to cry. It didn't help any to see tears in Trish's eyes.

"I hate days like this," Trish said. "I wish we could save all of them."

"Yeah, well, we can't," Belinda said brusquely, kneeing the garbage can ahead of her as she advanced on another cage. "If you're going to last in this field, Trish, you can't be a bleeding heart. You'll burn out."

Laura thought of her grandpa Jim, who'd

left them a little over two years ago. The doctor who'd come out afterward had held her grandmother's hands and gotten tears in his eyes as he'd given her the news. There was life, and then there was death; it was a sad reality that no one could escape. The doctor who held himself apart was in grave danger of losing his compassion.

Isaiah reentered the surgery just then. He didn't speak, didn't make eye contact with anyone. He went directly to a cupboard, withdrew a vial, and filled a hypodermic needle with clear liquid. When he approached the table without washing his hands or putting on another mask, Laura knew what he was about to do. Moments later a hushed silence fell over the room as he bent to press a stethoscope to the cat's chest.

"Does she want him cremated?" Trish asked, her voice still oddly thick.

"No, she wants to take him home," Isaiah replied.

"Does she have kids in town?" Belinda asked. "She can't bury him by herself. She's a little old lady. The ground is starting to freeze."

"I'll run over and do it." Isaiah turned the edges of the surgical sheet over the cat and carried it from the chamber.

Trish shook her head and gave Laura a sad look. "Like he has time to do that. He's such a sweetie sometimes."

Laura found Isaiah in his office, tipped back in his chair, one arm angled over his eyes, his feet propped on the desk. At the sound of her entrance he bolted upright, his boots slapping the floor with a loud thump. She could tell by his expression that he was embarrassed to have been caught grieving. Why, she didn't know. His ability to care was one of the things she found most wonderful about him.

"Laura." He swiveled to face her and flashed a stiff grin. "What are you still doing here?"

Laura thought it was more appropriate to ask what he was doing there. He had patients waiting for routine exams and inoculations. All the examining rooms were full, and the waiting area was becoming crowded. It wasn't like Isaiah to keep people waiting. In fact, she'd never once known him to neglect his duties. The fact that he had chosen to now told her a great deal.

"I just wanted to tell you how sorry I am about Seymour."

He grimaced and forced another smile

that didn't reach his eyes. "Ah, well. You win some, you lose some — no big deal."

Only it *was* a big deal. He was feeling sad, and Laura ached for him. She'd seen the look in his eyes when he'd realized the extent of the cancer. She'd also seen the grim resignation on his face as he had administered the lethal injection. Until now she'd never stopped to think of all the sadness that came with this man's profession. She'd thought only of how talented he was and how that talent opened doors for him that were forever closed to her.

"They're all a big deal." Laura broke off to swallow. "A little old lady lost her only friend. If you didn't feel awful about that, what kind of vet would you be?"

"A happier one?" He ran a hand over his hair and propped his elbows on the desk. Passing a hand over his eyes, he softly confessed, "Okay, I feel like shit. I admit it. Feeling like shit goes with the territory."

Laura sank onto the chair where she had interviewed for her job. It seemed like a lifetime ago.

"She's all alone," he whispered. "Seymour was all she had left. I learned in college not to let things like this get to me. I guess it didn't stick. She's such a sweet old gal. She brought Seymour in because he'd been off his food. When I saw a mass in the X-rays, I hoped it was benign."

Laura knew that a lot of people, Belinda included, might remind him that Seymour was only a cat. But she'd been present the morning before last when it had been Humphrey on the table. To this man, all animals were important.

"You can't save them all. It's the same with people. When we get old and our bodies wear out, it's over."

He nodded. "I know." His mouth twisted. "It's just hard when I'm the one making the decisions and putting them down. It's particularly hard when I know a sweet old lady trusted me so implicitly and put her whole world in my hands."

Laura could almost feel his pain and couldn't think of anything comforting to say.

"She didn't expect that phone call," he said hoarsely. "She thought I'd perform a miracle, that Seymour would come home tomorrow feeling better." He grimaced and slumped his shoulders. "She can't afford the bill. She's on Social Security. I think Seymour ate better than she did."

"How sad."

"Yeah." He shrugged and rubbed his jaw. "I'll play around with the charges. She'll have to pay the fixed costs. Tucker and I jointly purchase the inventory. But I can shave off a lot by not charging for my services."

Laura wanted to hug him. "That's very kind of you, Isaiah."

"Kind? I killed her cat." He pinched the bridge of his nose. "*Damn.* I know she's sobbing her heart out right now. It just makes me sick."

When Laura left his office moments later, she did so with a heavy heart.

About six that evening, Isaiah was about to wrap up for the day when Laura appeared unexpectedly in his surgery. Bundled up against the cold in a pink parka with fake-fur trim on the hood, she looked adorable, her eyes shimmering with excitement, her cheeks flushed from the evening chill. Hands crossed over her chest, she appeared to be hiding something under her coat.

"What are you doing here?" he asked, even though he felt absurdly pleased to see her.

Cheek dimpling in a conspiratorial smile, she said, "I have an emer-gency."

His heart caught. "What happened?"

She stepped closer, parting the front of

the jacket. A fluffy gray tabby kitten was curled against her breast, sound asleep. "This poor baby came crying at my door. He's a stray, and I can't have pets."

"Uh-oh." Isaiah couldn't shake the feeling that this was a joke and he had somehow missed the punch line.

"I have to find a home for him," she went on in that slow, halting way of hers. "Do you know anyone who might take him, someone special who'll love him? Maybe a little old lady who just lost her kitty?"

Isaiah stepped closer. The kitten was the exact same color as Seymour. "Ho," he said, the utterance more an exclamation of amazement than a word. "My God, he's *perfect!* Where in hell did you find him?"

"On my porch." She fixed him with an innocent look. "That's my story, and I'm sticking to it."

Isaiah didn't buy it. Coincidences happened, of course, but Laura's self-satisfied expression told him that wasn't the case this time. "Seriously, Laura, where'd you find him? He's a miniature version of Seymour."

She cupped a gentle hand over the sleeping kitten. "The shelter was a dead end, so I looked in last night's paper. He was at the last house I checked. And he's a male. Lucky, huh?"

Isaiah felt as if a golf ball had gotten stuck behind his larynx. He stared stupidly at Laura's sweet face. In that moment she seemed to glow, looking more angel than human. He couldn't quite believe she'd spent her whole afternoon combing Crystal Falls for a gray tabby kitten that looked exactly like Seymour. It was such a kind thing for her to have done — and way beyond the call of duty. She had never even met Mrs. Palmer.

Belinda emerged from the cloakroom just then. "What's up?" she asked when she glimpsed Isaiah's stunned expression.

Prying his gaze from Laura's uplifted countenance, Isaiah replied, "A kitten for Mrs. Palmer. Laura spent her whole afternoon responding to classified ads, trying to find a gray tabby."

Belinda came over to see the kitten. "Oh, isn't he sweet?"

Laura was the sweet one, Isaiah thought, but he refrained from saying so. The two women cooed and awwed over the sleeping kitten for a moment. Then Laura shifted her gaze back to Isaiah, her expression expectant.

"Well, what do you think?" she asked. "If

we dump him in her lap and tell her he's homeless, do you think she'll sucker in?"

Isaiah burst out laughing, the sadness that had plagued him all afternoon vanishing. "Of *course* she'll sucker in. If she hesitates, I'll give her my famous spay-and-neuter speech about the glut of kittens in our area and how many are destroyed each week because they can't find homes."

Belinda grinned at Laura. "Trust me, he's got that spiel down pat. Mrs. Palmer won't be able to say no."

"You should have seen her when I was digging the grave this afternoon," Isaiah said. His heart panged at the memory. "She sat on the back porch, cradling Seymour in her arms and sobbing. There was nothing I could say or do to make her feel better. She looked so alone that I hated to leave her."

Laura lifted the kitten to her cheek. "She won't be alone now."

Mrs. Palmer lived in an old double-wide mobile home with a covered front patio chock-full of yard furniture and decorations, many of them plywood cutouts that had been artfully painted. A mobile of bluebirds dangled from an exposed rafter beam. From another hung a little boy and girl perched on swing seats. Near the front porch a bearded old farmer in blue overalls held a WELCOME sign in gnarled hands. There was so much to see that Laura could scarcely take it all in.

"Her husband was a woodworker," Isaiah explained. "When he retired, he stayed busy making yard stuff to sell."

Laura was admiring a collection of cutout animals crowded around the steps: raccoons, rabbits, squirrels, and countless others that were lost in the throng, all of them darling. "He was very good. Look at that robin. Doesn't it look real?"

Isaiah skirted a family of miniature black bears to mount the steps. As he knocked, he said, "I think he made decent money selling his stuff. Most people don't have the time or talent to make this kind of thing."

They fell quiet, waiting for an answer to his summons. When the old woman finally opened the door, Laura's heart twisted. As though her frail body lacked the strength to remain upright without support, Mrs. Palmer stood with one arthritic hand braced against the door frame. An oversize polyester blouse and baggy slacks nearly swallowed her bony frame. Her white hair encircled her head, fluffy wisps poking out here and there.

"Dr. Coulter?" she said weakly.

"Yes, it's me, Mrs. Palmer. I have a problem that I'm praying you can help me with."

"Oh, my." With trembling fingers, she pushed feebly at the sagging screen door. "Come in, come in."

Isaiah caught the door and drew it wide. "I brought a friend along. I hope you don't mind."

Mrs. Palmer peered past him at Laura. "I'm a little under the weather, you know. I'm not sure I'm up to having guests."

"We'll be only a minute, I promise," Isaiah assured her. "Like I said, I've got a problem."

"Oh, well . . . in that case." She tottered back a step to allow them entry. "I haven't any cookies on hand, but I can make us a nice cup of tea."

"That isn't necessary," Isaiah said as they invaded the old lady's tiny living room. "This is Laura Townsend, Mrs. Palmer. She works for me at the clinic."

Mrs. Palmer squinted to see. "It's good to meet you, dear. I'm sorry I look such a fright. It's been an awful day for me."

Keeping her left hand splayed over the front of her coat, Laura extended her right to shake the old woman's hand.

170

"I'm sorry about your kitty."

Tears slipped onto Mrs. Palmer's cheeks. With quivering fingers, she brushed them away. "I'm a crazy old woman, crying over a flea-bitten cat."

"No, it's not crazy at all," Laura protested. "You loved him."

The inside of Mrs. Palmer's house was as cluttered as her patio. Laura took in all the dusty doodads on the cheaply paneled walls and then shifted her gaze to a huge wicker basket filled with balls of yarn placed next to a worn brown recliner. She could almost see the old lady relaxing there with Seymour asleep on her lap while she crocheted and watched her television programs. How lonely the house must seem to her now that her beloved pet was gone.

Isaiah grasped the old lady's creped elbow and guided her to the recliner. Mrs. Palmer sank gratefully onto the cushion, which had become wallowed at the center from years of use. She fluttered a hand at a green, afghan-draped sofa that was in no better condition.

"Please have a seat."

The kitten tucked securely under her jacket, Laura sat at one end of the couch. Isaiah forwent the offer and crouched by the old lady's chair. In the brown riding jacket, he could just as easily have been hunkered by an open fire with a tin cup cradled in his big hands. Laura could almost see the firelight playing over his chiseled features.

"Here's the problem," he told Mrs. Palmer solemnly. "Tonight when Laura went home, she found a tiny stray kitten on her porch."

Mrs. Palmer's rheumy blue eyes widened. "Oh, *my.*"

"He's homeless and starving," Isaiah went on, "and there's no way Laura can keep him. If we can't find a home for him, she'll have to take him to a shelter."

"Oh, no," the old lady whispered.

"It's a sad situation," Isaiah went on. "There are so many cats and kittens without homes right now. The Humane Society has about thirty on any given day. They're wonderful about sheltering homeless animals until they're adopted, but with so many . . ." Isaiah's voice trailed away, the implications of what he left unsaid hanging in the air. "I'd hate to see this little guy be destroyed."

Mrs. Palmer shook her head. "If you're thinking I might take him, I simply can't. My precious Seymour isn't even cold in his grave yet."

Isaiah nodded his understanding. "I'd have been in total agreement with you an hour ago, Mrs. Palmer. But seeing this kitten changed my mind." He hesitated a moment. "Do you believe in fate?"

"Fate?" the old lady echoed.

"Yeah, you know, that some things in life happen for a reason? Like when you met Alfred, for instance. Do you think that happened by accident?"

"Meeting my Alfred?" Mrs. Palmer shook her head again. "Heavens, no. We were meant for each other. Both of us always believed that."

"Some things are just meant to be," Isaiah agreed. "And I'm sure this is one of them. When I clapped eyes on this stray kitten I got cold chills. He's a dead ringer for Seymour. It's as if God plopped him on Laura's doorstep just for you."

"He looks like my Seymour?"

Isaiah turned to Laura. Taking her cue, she drew the kitten from beneath her coat. As she held him up for Mrs. Palmer's perusal, she said, "Can you believe it? He even has the little white tufts in his ears."

Mrs. Palmer clamped knobby fingers over her mouth and stared with tear-filled eyes at the kitten.

"Now you know why I got cold chills

when I saw him," Isaiah said, taking the kitten from Laura as he spoke. "All my life my mom has told me that God will never allow us to be burdened with more than we can bear. Six months ago you lost your husband. Today you lost Seymour. I think God knows how sad you are and sent this little fellow to Laura's door so he could find his way to you."

Isaiah placed the sleepy kitten on Mrs. Palmer's lap. The old woman's hands hovered shakily over the tiny feline, her fingertips barely grazing the soft fur. "Oh," she whispered. A sob caught in her throat, shaking her frail shoulders. "Oh, my, he *does* look like Seymour. Almost *exactly*. Doesn't he?"

"I've never seen the like." Isaiah sent Laura a triumphant smile. "It's too much of a resemblance to be a coincidence. I'm convinced this kitten is heaven-sent."

"Oh, my." Mrs. Palmer finally lifted the kitten in her hands to look at his funny little face. "He's so terribly thin. I can feel his ribs!"

Having left his mother only that afternoon, the kitten was actually quite plump, but Isaiah nodded in agreement. "No telling how long it's been since he ate. It's a mean old world for a tiny kitten without a home."

Mrs. Palmer drew the kitten to her chest. "It's a wonder he survived!"

"I know it's a big imposition, but would you give him a home, Mrs. Palmer?" Isaiah shifted his weight to sit back on his heels. "I'm never at my place. I couldn't take proper care of a kitten this young, and Laura lives in an apartment where pets aren't allowed."

"It's awfully soon," Mrs. Palmer said, but her tone indicated that she was wavering.

"I know. But given the striking resemblance, I don't think Seymour would mind. In fact, he'd probably like the idea — another cat exactly like him. It's an honor to his memory, in a way. Don't you think so, Laura?"

"Oh, yes." Laura nodded emphatically. "I think Seymour would be glad. He loved you, Mrs. Palmer. He wouldn't want you to be all alone."

"He'll need his shots and have to be neutered when the time comes," the old lady observed.

"I'll take care of all that," Isaiah offered. "You'll be doing me a big favor if you take him. That's the least I can do."

Mrs. Palmer pushed up from the chair. Cuddling the kitten to her breast, she tottered off to the kitchen, saying, "We'll just pour you some milk while I'm thinking it over. Poor starving baby."

Isaiah grinned at Laura as he stood up. "Got her nailed," he whispered.

Mrs. Palmer was beaming when she returned. "My goodness, how he's going after that milk! I think his tummy is so empty, it's buttoned to his backbone."

"I brought some special food to put some meat back on his bones," Isaiah told her. "I'll go get it. If you'll take him, that is."

Mrs. Palmer glanced down and laughed delightedly. Seymour the Second had followed her from the kitchen and was attacking her yarn basket. Before anyone could react, a ball of red yarn was rolling across the floor, and the kitten was giving chase. The old lady sprang after her new charge, scooped him up, and wagged a scolding finger at his pink nose.

"You'll have to learn that my crochet basket is a no-no." She cuddled the kitten close and smiled. "He does look so very much like my Seymour. Perhaps he is heaven-sent." She rubbed her cheek on the kitten's fur. "Yes, I'll keep him. How can I say no? I can't let Seymour's look-alike be put to sleep!"

While Isaiah went out to get the cat food, Laura sat with Mrs. Palmer and watched the kitten play with the ball of yarn. The old lady was chuckling by the time Isaiah returned. He carried a large bag of kibble and a case of canned food, which he deposited in the kitchen.

"If you'll bring him in tomorrow," he said, "I'll give him his first round of shots, free of charge."

"Oh, you needn't do that," Mrs. Palmer protested.

"I insist. Like I said, you're doing me a big favor by taking him. It'd break my heart to take him to a shelter. You never know for sure that an animal will be adopted. I know he'll be loved and well cared for here."

"You can count on that," Mrs. Palmer agreed.

"In return, free vet care." Isaiah watched the kitten do a somersault and get tangled in the yarn. "He's going to be a handful."

Mrs. Palmer nodded happily. "I'll have to get him some toys first thing. He's full of mischief."

When Isaiah and Laura left a few minutes later, it was to the sound of Mrs. Palmer's laughter. Isaiah stopped at the edge of the patio and gazed back at the lighted windows, smiling.

"This feels good."

Laura agreed completely. It felt wonderful. "I don't think she'll cry anymore."

"No, and it's all thanks to you. As bad as I felt for her, I never would've thought to find her a look-alike kitten. Brilliant move."

As they continued toward his Hummer, Laura replied, "I'm just glad she took him. I really can't have a pet at my place, you know."

He laughed as he opened the passenger door. "What was your plan if she didn't take him?"

Laura grinned. "You don't have a clinic kitty. Most vets do."

"A clinic cat, huh?" He took her arm to assist her into the Hummer. The heat of his hand radiated through her jacket sleeve. "There's a thought."

He shut the door. As Laura fastened her seat belt, he circled the front of the vehicle and climbed in beside her. "I'm starving. Have you eaten?"

Laura almost wished she could say yes. Spending too much time with Isaiah Coulter wasn't a wise idea. With each passing day she found it more and more difficult to keep her feelings for him in check.

"No, I haven't eaten," she confessed.

"Good. How's Italian sound?"

Even though she wasn't overly fond of Italian food, Laura thought it sounded fabulous. And therein lay the whole problem: Anything and everything about Isaiah Coulter appealed to her.

Chapter Six

For Laura, the following weekend was filled with final preparations for Halloween, which marked the end of daylight saving time and the beginning of her favorite time of year, the holiday season. On Saturday morning she went to the grocery store to get the ingredients for sugar cookies, which she baked and decorated that afternoon. Then she spent part of the evening with her landlord, Mr. Evans, who came over to set all her clocks and appliances back an hour, a tedious, frustrating, and almost impossible task for Laura.

After attending church with her grandmother on Sunday morning, Laura returned home and listened to a novel on tape by Jeffery Deaver while she bundled handfuls of individual candies in squares of plastic wrap tied with orange and black ribbons. Each gaily beribboned package went into a large basket to sit by the door for the trick-or-treaters who would come calling later.

The novel, entitled *The Blue Nowhere*,

was about an evil hacker who invaded the computer systems of his victims and lured them to their deaths. Suitably spooky to set the mood for Halloween, it was a nice complement to the witches and goblins hanging in Laura's windows and the two lighted jack-o'-lanterns in her kitchen, one on the counter, the other serving as a centerpiece on the table. Her apartment smelled divine, a pot of steeped cinnamon cider simmering on the stove and filling the rooms with its spicy essence.

By four o'clock Laura was as ready as she'd ever be for all the children she felt certain would soon be knocking at her door. Taking a cup of hot cider with her to the bathroom, she grabbed a quick shower and then slipped into her Halloween costume, a pair of footed pink pajamas and a set of matching rabbit ears she'd crafted with velvet over lightweight, pliable wire. Voilà, she was almost a Halloween bunny. After attaching a pom-pom tail to the seat of the pajamas, she set to work on her face, using a black pencil to create exaggerated lashes and whiskers, rouge to dot her cheeks, and lipstick to stain her mouth a bright rose.

She'd just completed her transformation when the phone rang. Dashing into her bedroom, she grabbed the portable. "Hello."

"Hi, sis."

"Aileen!" Laura sank onto the edge of the bed. "I'm so glad you called."

"I can't talk for very long. I have to get the kids into their costumes. I've been thinking of you all day, remembering Halloweens gone by."

Aileen lived on the outskirts of Portland, a four-hour drive away. Laura would have liked to see her older sister more often, but city driving, with all the off-ramp signs and strange names, was too confusing for her. Aileen came home to Central Oregon for visits as frequently as she could, but a husband, three kids, and a full-time job kept her pretty busy. As a result, the two sisters hadn't seen each other since their parents had moved to Florida six months ago.

"I've been thinking of you, too," Laura said with a wistful smile.

"Did you make Grandpa Jim's cider today?" Aileen asked.

"Yep. It's on the stove. I'm having a cup right now."

"Me, too. Mine's spiked with wine. I'll need something to warm my innards when I hit the streets with the kids tonight. It's so cold out there! Jim's going to be our chauffeur, and I get to do sidewalk duty.

How's the weather down there?"

"Cold. I'm wishing for snow." Laura glanced out the ruffle-draped window. "Nothing yet, though. Ah, well. I'm going to light my little gas fireplace. That'll make it cozy and cheerful."

"You wearing your bunny costume?"

"Have to get in the spirit. You dressing as Cleo again?"

"I'm too fat for Cleopatra this year."

"You aren't fat."

"Tell it to my halter top."

"What are you going to be, then?"

"A wicked witch. Go ahead, laugh all you like. It'll be a lot more practical. I can wear a heavy coat under my witch cape to keep from freezing my tush off, and I can scream and act like a witch, a definite plus when you're trying to corral three kids on Halloween night. Trevor and Cody have one speed — high."

Laura could hear her sister's children in the background. It sounded as if the boys, age six and seven, were bedeviling their ten-year-old sister, Sarah. "What are they fighting about?"

"Whose jack-o'-lantern is whose. Sarah did the nicest one. Trevor laid claim to it, and she's fit to be tied."

Laura could remember a time when she

and Aileen had quarreled all the time, driving their mother to distraction. "We were such angels."

"Yeah, right. Remember the time we toilet-papered the police station?"

Laura chortled. "That was so much fun. All the cops were away on prank patrol. The perfect crime."

"You sound so good. I think you're talking better."

"I am?"

"Yeah, faster now, and . . . well, I don't know, smoother, I think."

"No long words," Laura pointed out. "I'm getting good at talking around them."

"I can barely tell anything's wrong. How long has it been since I saw you?"

"Six months."

"You still taking that brain-enhancement stuff?"

"Gag. Now that Mom's gone, I throw it out. I have a real job now. Did you hear about that?"

"Gram mentioned it. Mom's so busy going to water aerobics and community potlucks that she hardly ever calls me. How do you like it? The job, I mean."

"I love it." Laura listed her job duties and then went on to describe Isaiah and how handsome he was. "I've got a huge crush on him. I know it's dumb, but I can't seem to help myself."

"What's wrong with having a crush on him?"

"It'll never happen. He's got so much going for him, and I . . . well, I don't."

Aileen snorted. "You're a very pretty lady, Laura. Jim says you're a dead ringer for Charlize Theron."

Laura laughed so hard that she fell back on the bed.

"You *do* resemble her," Aileen insisted. "Any man who snags you will be one lucky fellow."

"I love you, too."

Aileen sighed. "Your aphasia is a problem. I won't say it isn't. But it's not that bad. Isaiah is obviously interested in you. A guy doesn't take a woman out to dinner twice unless something's up." She laughed theatrically. "And, yes, I meant that literally."

Laura rolled her eyes. "Don't be gross."

"I'm an old married woman. I can be gross if I want."

"The dinners weren't like that, not dates or anything. It was really late both times, and he only asked me to be nice."

"Yeah, right."

Laura stayed on the phone a few more

minutes, getting updated on all the family news. Shortly after she and Aileen hung up, the phone rang again, and it was her parents. Laura fielded questions from her mother. Was she taking all her pills? *Yes, Mom.* Had she noticed a difference since she'd started taking the seaweed tablets? *No, Mom.* Laura was relieved when her father finally came on the line. Mike Townsend was much more down-to-earth than his wife.

"How's my girl?" he asked.

"Good, Daddy. I miss you, though."

"Got a jack-o'-lantern?"

"Two."

"Got cider?"

"What would Hallo-ween be without it?" she countered.

When her father was finally satisfied that she was happy, healthy, and celebrating the holiday properly, he said good-bye, sending hugs and kisses to her grandmother before hanging up.

Laura rushed to the kitchen to heat up some leftover stew for dinner.

And then she waited for the kids to come. Dusk, normally the time when small children were out in droves on Halloween, came and went without any knocks on the door. Laura stood at her kitchen window and watched throngs of trick-or-treaters descend on her landlord's house, but none of them seemed to realize that someone lived over the garage. Laura considered opening the window to holler at them. But how silly would that be?

Disappointed, she called her grandmother.

"Oh, honey, I'm sorry. I know how you love to see all the little kids in their costumes. Next year you'll have to come over here. I've had oodles of kids, so many I'm almost out of candy."

Just then Etta's doorbell rang again, so Laura said a fast good-bye and let her go.

There was nothing interesting on television, so Laura spent the next hour listening to more of her novel on tape. She had just paused the tape player to go wash the makeup from her face and doff her rabbit ears when a knock finally came at the door. Her heart leaped with gladness. One group of trick-or-treaters was better than none at all.

When Laura opened the door, she found her miniature counterpart standing on the steps, a darling little girl dressed as a pink bunny. The child had huge brown eyes and dark ringlets that cascaded to her shoulders.

"Trick or treat!" she cried.

An older boy stepped up behind her and chimed the same words in a deeper voice. He was dressed as a vampire with blood dripping from the corners of his fanged mouth.

Delighted, Laura opened the door wider. "Step in where it's warm," she invited. "You're my first trick-or-treaters tonight, and I have scads of candy. I'll load you up."

"Can I come in, too?"

Laura peered past the children to see a tall, lean cowboy standing just beyond the circle of illumination cast by the porch light. Convinced that her eyes were deceiving her, she said, "Isaiah?"

He stepped closer so she could see him clearly. He wore the brown canvas riding jacket and tan Stetson again, and he looked achingly good to her hungry eyes — long, powerfully muscled legs sheathed in denim, shoulders hunched against the chill, face cast into shadow by the brim of his hat. Her heart lurched oddly in her chest.

"Meet Rosie and Chad, my niece and nephew. Their mother, Natalie, owns the Blue Parrot, and she's hostessing a Halloween karaoke party there tonight. Zeke, my brother, is handing out candy at his ranch supply store. I volunteered to take the kids trick-or-treating. Their aunt Valerie, Natalie's sister, couldn't do it. She's staying at Zeke and Natalie's place to hand out treats so their windows don't get soaped."

Forgetting that she wore rabbit ears, Laura reached up to smooth her hair. When her fingertips encountered velvet, she winced. Why was it that she never looked her best when he dropped by?

"Please come in!" She drew the children over the threshold. "Do you guys like cider?"

"I'm quite fond of it," Rosie replied. "Chad prefers soda pop. It's his mission in life to rot out all his teeth."

"Is not!"

"Is, too!"

"Is not!"

Isaiah entered behind the kids. "Rewind! No fighting. That was the deal. Remember?"

Flashing Chad daggers with her expressive eyes, Rosie pursed her lips and wrinkled her nose. Under his breath, Chad said, "You're such a little puke sometimes."

"Better to be a little puke than a big one," Rosie popped back.

Laura stifled a startled laugh. Isaiah appeared frazzled. Over the tops of the children's heads, he gave her a look rife with woe, which made her want to laugh again. She'd never seen a big, powerfully built man look more helpless or outflanked.

"I just happen to have some soda pop in my fridge," she assured Chad. Pushing the door closed on the chill night air, she added, "I also have heaps of cookies. If you'll take off your coats and sit at the table, I'll fix you right up."

"Cookies?" the children echoed. "Yum!"

As the children doffed their outerwear and raced to the kitchen, Laura sent Isaiah a wondering glance. "You live at the other end of town. What brings you over this way?"

He swept off the Stetson and smoothed a hand over his tousled dark hair. "Poisoned candy."

Laura frowned. "What?"

"Their mother is convinced that it's dangerous for kids to take candy from strangers. The school threw a big Halloween party on Friday night, but it's not quite the same as trick-or-treating. My assignment is to haul them all over God's creation to the homes of people we know. Mom suggested that I take them by your grandmother's house.

Your grandmother mentioned that no kids had visited your place and encouraged me to stop by."

"I'm glad you did. I was feeling a little blue. I like to see all the kids."

"They're cuter at a distance."

Just then Rosie shrieked. Laura turned to see Chad tugging on his sister's rabbit ears. "Hey!" Isaiah yelled. "Chad, stop that. Rosie, stop hitting."

"Chad's being obnoxious!" the little girl cried.

"Am not. You tried to jerk my fangs out."

"Only because you can't eat while you're wearing them."

Laura hurried into the kitchen to straighten Rosie's ears, reinsert Chad's fangs, and generally calm the waters. When she looked down into Rosie's tear-filled brown eyes, she melted. "It's okay, sweetie. You're all fixed."

Rosie reached up to check her headpiece. When the child had assured herself that her ears were undamaged, she gave Chad another glare and then turned a questioning look on Laura. "Do you have a speech impediment?"

"Rosie!" Isaiah sounded appalled as he advanced on the kitchen. "That isn't a nice thing to ask."

"It's all right." Laura turned the child toward a chair. "I do have trouble talking, Rosie. Five years ago, I dove off into the river and hit my head on a rock. When I woke up, I couldn't talk."

"Not at all?" Chad sat down across from his sister. "That sucks."

"Yes," Laura agreed as she went to put cookies on a plate and get each of the children something to drink. "Pepsi or orange, Chad?"

"Orange. How come you can talk now, then?"

"I went to rehab and learned how all over again."

Stetson in hand, Isaiah stood with his lean hips braced against the counter, long legs crossed at the ankle. He sent Laura an apologetic look.

"It's fine," she assured him. And it truly was. Despite her sister's recent avowals that her speech problem was barely noticeable anymore, Laura knew better, and she didn't mind answering the children's questions. As she carried their refreshments to the table, she said, "That's how come I talk so slow and stop between words. I know it bugs people, but for me it's better than not being able to talk at all."

Rosie nodded in agreement. "You do pretty good, actually."

"Thank you."

"Yum!" Chad cried when he saw the cookies. "They're frosted." He grabbed a handful and laid them on his napkin. After taking a big bite from a cookie decorated like a jack-o'-lantern, he moaned and said, "Soft, too! My mom's are always burned on the bottom and hard as rocks."

"Our mom's a singer and songwriter," Rosie revealed. "As a result, our dad does most of the cooking because Mommy gets distracted and burns everything."

"I see." Laura couldn't recall ever having met a little girl with such an impressive vocabulary. "How old are you, Rosie?"

"I'm six."

"Liar, liar, pants on fire," Chad cried in a singsong voice. "You won't be six until February!"

"So?" Rosie cried. "February is nearly here."

"You still aren't six yet. Don't tell fibs. Mom will scrub your mouth out with soap."

"She's *almost* six," Laura intervened.

Mollified but still disgruntled, Rosie took a dainty bite of cookie. "Uncle Isaiah, you really must try one of these. They're delicious."

Laura returned to the kitchen, all but shaking her head in amazement at Rosie's command of English. "Does it run in the fami-ly?" she asked Isaiah.

He grinned. In a voice pitched low so only Laura might hear, he said, "We aren't actually related. My brother Zeke is their adoptive father. Their real dad was killed."

"Oh, I'm sorry to hear that."

"Robert wasn't much of a father." He shrugged out of his jacket. Underneath he wore a cardinal red, long-sleeved, Western-cut shirt that lent his already dark skin a deeper burnish. "The kids are a lot better off with my brother. Zeke loves them like his own, and he's shaping up to be a great dad."

Laura followed him with her gaze as he went into the living room to hang his jacket and hat on the coat tree. "You aren't wearing a costume," she noted.

"Rosie tried to make me into a ghost, but the sheet only went to my knees."

"It's probably just as well. The cowboy look is more you." Laura went to ladle them each some cider and arrange more cookies on a plate. Cupping a hot mug in her hands, she leaned against the work island across from him. With a glance at the children, whose mouths were now too

194

stuffed with cookies for either of them to fling insults, she asked, "Is your night of torture almost over?"

"Don't I wish. There's a big subdivision on this side of town that Nattie says is safe. Mostly young people with families live there. I'll let them run amok for a while. Hopefully they'll wear themselves out and be able to fall asleep at the regular time. School tomorrow."

"You'll keep a close eye on them, I hope."

"I'll walk with them. Chad's old enough to look after Rosie, but you never know what kind of kooks may be out on the streets tonight." He cocked a dark eyebrow. "You want to come?"

Laura hadn't been out on Halloween in years. It sounded like fun, and she wanted very badly to say yes, but her deepening affection for him was starting to alarm her. "Thanks for asking me. But I should stick around here just in case any kids come."

"No one's knocked on your door all night."

Laura felt herself wavering. He was so nice, and she enjoyed his company so much. As long as she kept her head out of the clouds, what harm could come from their being friends? "Only if I can go as I am and trick-or-treat with the kids."

She fully expected him to hoot with laughter. Instead he grinned, shrugged, and said, "Whatever turns your crank. I'd appreciate some adult company." He tipped his head, arched a dark brow, and gave her a pleading look. "Please? If you don't come along, I may strangle them before the evening's over."

Laura wasn't at all worried that Isaiah might do his niece and nephew physical harm. She'd seen him with animals and knew how limitless his stores of patience could be in trying situations. And wasn't that the whole problem? She didn't just like this man. She admired him as well.

For the second time in as many minutes, little warning bells jangled in her mind. Unfortunately Isaiah Coulter had an irresistible way about him, even when he wasn't trying. When he shifted into persuasive mode, Laura found it difficult, if not impossible, to tell him no.

For Isaiah, what had begun as a begrudging duty — playing chauffeur to two quarreling children — turned out to be a delightful evening. Just as Laura had threatened, she wore her bunny costume to the upscale subdivision, her only concession to practicality the pink parka she sometimes wore to work, donned for warmth. Isaiah had always thought Laura was beautiful, but watching her traipse up countless steps with Rosie to knock on doors and holler, "Trick or treat!" in that slow, halting way of hers drove home to him that real loveliness ran much deeper than the skin.

Over the years he had dated countless women, most of them physically gorgeous, but never had he known anyone as natural, spontaneous, or sweet as Laura Townsend. Oh, sure, he'd known gals who made a good show of it, pretending to love animals, kids, and spur-of-the-moment activities. But then an acrylic nail got broken, hosiery got snagged, or a child's gooey hands met with perfectly styled hair, and the pretense ended.

There was no pretentiousness in Laura. When a barking, growling Great Dane managed to slip past its owner onto a porch, she didn't tumble backward down the steps in terror as many women might have. Instead she removed her bunny ears to look more normal and crouched down to make friends with the snarling beast. When Rosie got Snickers chocolate all over her hands and touched Laura's cheek,

Laura laughed, licked a fingertip to clean away the stickiness, and then popped the digit back in her mouth, saying, "Yum, can I have some more?"

In short, the kids absolutely loved her, and Isaiah found her pretty hard to resist himself. Even with rabbit whiskers and floppy ears, she managed to appeal to him in a way no other woman ever had.

Over the course of the evening, Isaiah kept recalling how she'd looked earlier when she opened the door to Rosie — all dressed up with nowhere to go. The decorations inside her apartment indicated that she really got into celebrating the holidays. Seeing her surrounded by Halloween cheer, yet so terribly alone, had saddened him. It seemed a shame that someone with so much to offer had no one to share it with.

"I got more than you guys!" Chad cried as he raced ahead of Laura and Rosie back to the sidewalk, where Isaiah waited.

"No, you didn't!" Rosie cried.

"Did, too!"

"Did not!"

Isaiah was about to break a molar from clenching his teeth when Laura held up her sack and cried, "I got the most!"

Chad and Rosie both yelled, "Did not!"

Laura cried, "Did, too!"

And the word fight began again. Only this time, there was a twist at the end that set Isaiah to laughing. Laura engaged in the volley for a time, saying, "Did, too," until the kids fell into the rhythm, and then she suddenly switched sides on them, crying, "Did not!" Chad and Rosie automatically countered with, "Did, too!"

Laura laughed. "Gotcha!"

Soundly trounced, the children giggled and hurried away to the next house. Before they'd covered three sections of sidewalk, however, they were elbowing each other off the cement, trying to trip each other, and spilling much of their candy in the process. Isaiah was about to collar both kids and give them a scolding when Laura cried, "Finders keepers!"

The next instant she was dashing about, collecting the lost candy and putting it in her sack, her powder-puff tail flashing beneath the hem of her coat every time she bent over. Laughing, Isaiah followed her lead, grabbing all the candy he could before the kids were able to retrieve it.

"That's *mine!*" Rosie protested.

"Not now." Laura scooped up more of Chad's loot before he pounced on it. "I don't need to ring doorbells walking behind you guys. I can get more candy this way."

Chad and Rosie hurriedly retrieved the spillage that hadn't yet been confiscated.

"You're adults," Rosie complained. "You're not supposed to take candy from children."

Unabashed, Laura flashed a triumphant grin at Isaiah before replying, "Kids aren't supposed to fight, either. If you break the rules, I guess we can."

Clearly at a loss, Rosie pursed her lips and frowned. Chad huffed in disgust. "Come on," he said to his sister. "We can get more candy at the next house."

As the kids walked ahead, Isaiah heard Chad mutter to his sister, "No more fighting. Okay? If Uncle Isaiah tells on us, we're gonna get in big trouble."

"You pushed me first!"

"Only because you elbowed me."

"Only by accident!"

"Ha."

"Yes, sir! I was trying to see inside my sack and just bent my arm. I didn't mean to elbow you."

"Why didn't you say so, then?"

"Because you pushed me!"

Chad sighed, straightened his sister's ears, and compromised with, "I'll say I'm sorry if you will."

Rosie sighed theatrically. "I'm sorry."

"Me, too."

Having reached a tentative peace agreement, they broke into a run. Isaiah shook his head, wondering if Laura's slow speech made the children listen more closely to her than they did to him. "That's amazing. Do you know how many times I've asked them to stop fighting tonight?"

Laura only smiled.

"You're great with kids," he told her. "It's a shame you don't have any of your own."

She fell into step beside him, her breath forming little puffs of steam in the crisp night air. In the illumination of the streetlights, her eyes shimmered like polished topaz. "I planned to, but then I got hurt, and things changed." She wrinkled her nose and shrugged. "It was very hard for my friends. I couldn't talk to them, so after a few visits they stopped coming to see me. My boyfriend felt bad for me, but there was nothing in it for him anymore, and it wasn't long before he broke it off."

Essentially the same thing had happened to Isaiah's sister, Bethany, after her riding accident. Isaiah had no use for men who bailed out when a woman needed them the most. That was the way it often went, though. Some guys loved a woman only as long as loving her was easy.

"It's still not too late for you to have a family," he told her. "You're young yet."

"I'm thirty-one, Isaiah."

"*That* old?" he teased.

"It's not the same for me."

Isaiah cocked his head to see her face. "I'm not following."

She avoided his gaze by fussing with her coat. "Someday maybe I'll meet a man who won't care about my aphasia. But chances are good that I won't meet him soon. I can't have a baby all by myself."

Isaiah's heart caught, and he wanted to give himself a swift kick for being such an idiot. A beautiful woman like Laura normally had men standing in line to take her out on dates, and he had just assumed . . . *God,* he was such an airhead sometimes. The general rules of thumb couldn't be applied to her. As lovely as she was, her speech alone would put a lot of guys off. She also had a host of other problems.

"You don't necessarily need a man to have a child nowadays," he reminded her.

"Getting pregnant isn't the worry. It's afterward. I couldn't raise a child by myself."

Isaiah cautiously circled that. He'd been

in her apartment, and it was not only spotlessly clean, but charming. She was also a wonderful cook. "I think you'd be a fabulous mom."

"Thank you. I only wish you were right. But there are too many things I can't do."

As far as Isaiah could see, she had all the basics covered. "Like what?"

She laughed. "Do you want a list?" Then, with a self-deprecating snort, she added, "Forget I said that. Making out lists is one of the things I can't do very well. Writing is hard for me." She gestured helplessly with her hands. "A lot of things you do without thinking are hard for me. I can't write checks, either."

"How the hell do you pay your bills?"

"I take them to the bank and have a clerk make out money orders for the right amounts. Then I drive around to pay in person."

Isaiah couldn't imagine it. He paid his bills over the Internet with a credit card, which he paid off once a month.

As though she guessed his thoughts, she flashed a smile and said, "It's not so bad. I just work around things. When I go food shopping, I walk slow, cover the whole store, and really look at things. Most times

I get home with all the stuff I need."

"How do you pay?"

"Mostly with a card, sometimes with cash. I just hand my money to the clerk and hope she doesn't cheat me."

Isaiah had known from the first that Laura had trouble counting, but he'd never stopped to consider the ramifications of that when it came to everyday living. She had to give people her money and trust in them not to shortchange her?

Pulling himself back to the original subject, he said, "All that aside, you get along all right. If you can manage for yourself, why not for a child?"

Shadows had darkened her eyes when she looked up at him. "Kids need help with homework. I couldn't give it. They get sick and need medi-cine. I can't read labels very well. They want bedtime stories, too, and I'd take until midnight getting just one read."

Never more than in that moment had Isaiah realized just how drastically that swimming accident had altered Laura's life. All the things most women took for granted might never happen for her — no challenging career, no husband, no kids, no grandchildren. She loved animals and couldn't even have a pet because she lived in a little apartment over someone's garage.

"Don't," she said with a prideful lift of her chin.

"Don't what?"

"Don't feel sorry for me. I hate it."

"I don't feel sorry for you. It just seems so unfair."

"I'm glad for what I've got. I'm happy. I have a good life. Maybe it isn't what I wanted before, but it's enough."

Enough. Someone like Laura shouldn't have had to settle. Granted, she was handicapped, and any man who married her would have to compensate for her shortcomings. But there would be trade-offs. Laura would probably enjoy being a stay-at-home mom. Her husband might have to read the bedtime stories, help the kids with their homework, and handle all the finances, but on the plus side, he'd never come in after a hard day and be responsible for fifty percent of the domestic duties, either. There were a lot of men, himself included, who would feel damned lucky to come home every night to a hot meal on the stove, with a beautiful woman like Laura to serve it.

The thought brought Isaiah up short. *Red alert.* What the hell was he thinking?

He cast her a sidelong glance, taking in her cameo-perfect profile. A guy could do worse, no question there. But he wasn't ready to settle down. Just the thought made him want to run.

He had too many other fish to fry first.

The following evening Laura was scheduled to work her first night shift. When she arrived at the clinic shortly before nine, she sat in her car for a few minutes with the dome light on, going over and over the number code that would, if keyed in properly, disarm the security system. After any door of the building was opened, a four-number code had to be entered on the console pad within one minute to prevent the alarm from going off.

For anyone else, it would have been a simple enough thing. For Laura, it wasn't. The code, 6925, was an evil combination of numbers for her. She sometimes saw letters and numbers upside down and backward, making sixes, nines, twos, and fives very tricky. An upside-down and inverted six, for instance, looked like a nine, and vice versa. In a slightly different way, twos and fives were equally treacherous.

Laura had come into the clinic that afternoon to practice entering the code under

Val's supervision, and everything had gone well. But that didn't mean nothing would go wrong when she tried to do it by herself.

After taking a deep breath for courage, she exited the car and strode resolutely toward the rear of the building. Her heart kicked hard against her ribs as she inserted the key in the door lock. *Please, God, don't let me screw up.* In order to keep this job, she had to be able to set and disarm the security system. Otherwise she'd be able to work only during the day, when other people were present. That wouldn't be fair to the rest of the kennel keepers. One week a month, everyone was required to work the night shift.

Laura's pulse was racing as she pushed open the door and entered the dimly lighted back room. *Hurry, hurry.* A minute was only sixty seconds long. How many of those seconds had already passed? She closed and locked the door, just as Val had instructed. Then, clutching a paper with the code written on it, she hurried over to the alarm console, a small rectangular panel affixed to the wall. *Stay calm. Just look very carefully at each number before you punch it.*

With a trembling finger Laura entered the code and then pressed 1 to disarm the system. Then she stood frozen in place, half expecting the sirens outside to start wailing. Instead the little red light blinked and turned green, which meant the system had been successfully disarmed. She closed her eyes and went limp with relief. *Thank you, God.* She'd done it right. Now all she had to do was reset the alarm so no unauthorized person could enter the building while she was in here alone.

With painstaking care Laura reentered the code and then pressed three, per Val's instructions. The little green light blinked and turned red again, just as it was supposed to do. Laura grinned and almost danced with happiness. She could do this. Heck, yeah, not a problem.

Tucking her thermos and lunch sack under one arm, Laura shook free of a coatsleeve as she proceeded through the storage area to the door that opened into the kennels. She'd taken perhaps ten steps when the alarm went off. The shrieking wail was so loud it seemed to bounce off the walls and arrow straight to her eardrums. The noise startled her so badly that she almost wet her pants. *Oh, God.* Horrified, she dropped her things on the floor, scrambled to open the door, and spilled into the kennels. As she ran up the center aisle, the frightened dogs added to the din, barking and howling and pawing at their cage gates.

Until now Laura had never appreciated how large the clinic was. She was out of breath by the time she entered the front hall that divided the examining rooms from the offices. In the event that the alarm went off, the security company was supposed to telephone the clinic before alerting the police. Laura had never used any of the phones in the back rooms and wasn't sure where they were. She needed to be at the front desk to take the call.

She had just reached the lobby when the siren abruptly turned off. Almost instantaneously the telephones started to ring. Laura circled the counter to grab a receiver. "Hello?"

A woman replied, "Hello, this is Harris Security. As I'm sure you know, the alarm at the clinic just went off."

"It was an acci-dent," Laura huffed. "I must have punched a wrong number when I came inside."

"Ah, I see." The woman laughed. "No harm done. It happens now and again. All I need is the password."

Laura's brain went blank. *The password. Oh, God.* She clamped a hand to the side of her head and almost mewled with dismay. She'd been so worried about re-membering the code that she hadn't thought to refresh her memory on the password. It had something to do with dogs. The name of a particular breed, maybe? Only she couldn't remember *which* breed. Poodle, cocker, Aussie? None of those sounded right. What on earth was she going to do?

"It's some kind of dog," Laura said shakily.

"Yes, but I need more than that," the woman informed her. "If you can't tell me the exact word, I'll have to call the po-lice."

Laura made a fist in her hair. *Stupid, stupid, stupid.* The password, she needed the password. *Please, God.* Her mind re-mained stubbornly blank. "I have brain damage," she explained. Just then she heard a crashing noise come from one of the offices. She jumped and looked over her shoulder, wondering if someone else was in the building. "The office mana-ger told me the password," she explained. "But when I'm upset, I get confused."

"I'm sorry," the woman said. "But that's the policy. I need the password."

Laura took a deep breath, trying to calm

down. "Can you just call one of the vets? They'll tell you it's okay."

"No, I'm sorry."

Isaiah had just finished eating and was tossing the plastic dinner tray into the recycle bin under the kitchen sink when the phone rang. He groaned and grabbed the portable from the counter before the answering machine could pick up. As was his habit, he bypassed saying hello. "This is Isaiah."

"Dr. Coulter?" a man asked.

"Speaking." Thinking it was a client with a question about a pet, Isaiah grabbed the bottle of beer he'd just uncapped and circled the bar to sit down while he talked. After he'd been on his feet all day, his back was killing him. "How can I help you?"

"This is Officer Radcliff, Oregon State Police."

Isaiah shifted his hips to sit on a bar stool. The rattan creaked as he settled his weight. It wasn't always bad news when law enforcement called. Only last week, the Oregon State Sheriff's Association had hit him up for a donation. Nevertheless, Isaiah's heart beat just a little faster. "Is there a problem?"

"That's what I'm hoping to find out.

The security alarm at your clinic went off a few minutes ago. The woman inside the building was unable to give the security company the correct password, so we were notified."

The tension eased from Isaiah's shoulders. He glanced at his watch and saw that it was shortly after nine. A picture of Laura's face flashed in his mind, and he smiled slightly. "I see."

"She says she works for you, a lady named Laura Townsend."

"Ms. Townsend does work for me. This is just her first time on night shift. She's never had to deal with the security system before."

"So she said. Well, that's good. She isn't a burglar, at least."

"Nope, she's authorized to be there."

"According to her, the problem with the alarm could happen again. She says she has a condition of some kind that can make her see letters and numbers backward. That being the case, it might be best if you keep her on days so she doesn't have to mess with the alarm."

The officer had a point. "I'll come in and take care of it," Isaiah said. "Tell Ms. Townsend I'll be there in about thirty minutes."

★ ★ ★

After the police left, Laura decided to work in the kennels until Isaiah arrived. The time would pass more quickly if she kept busy, she assured herself, and that way, when another employee was called in to take over her shift, she wouldn't be leaving a mountain of work for someone else to do.

As Laura collected soiled bedding from one of the cages, she fought back tears. From the start she and Isaiah had agreed that he would let her go if she couldn't do the work. Part of her job description was to work nights one week a month, just as the other kennel keepers did. Now that she'd proven herself incapable of fulfilling that requirement, Isaiah would have no choice but to fire her.

For a number of reasons, the thought made Laura sad. This was more than just a job to her. She was going to miss all the friends that she'd made here at the clinic. And, oh, how she would miss working with the animals. Her niche. The other kennel keepers did just what was required of them and nothing more. Only Laura took the time to give each cat and dog some extra attention every day. And why not? She had no one waiting at home for her — no kids, no husband, not even a significant other. If she wanted to dawdle in the kennels after her shift was over, she could and often did. As a result, in a very short while, this job had become the center of her life.

She suspected that Isaiah knew how much she loved working for him. He would probably feel terrible about having to let her go. At the thought, Laura wiped the tears from her cheeks and straightened her shoulders. Time to put a cheerful face on it. She didn't want to be all puffy-eyed and blotchy when he came in. That would only make him feel worse. They had made a bargain, and she meant to hold up her end of it.

She was hosing out cages when he finally arrived. The instant she saw him striding up the center aisle, she shut off the nozzle, hooked it through the wire, and went out to meet him. He wore a dark blue sweatshirt that looked as if it had been washed almost as many times as his faded Wranglers, yet he still managed to look wonderful.

"Hi," was all she could think to say.

His blue eyes twinkled with laughter. "Sounds like your first night-shift started off with a bang. Or should I say with a bell?"

Forcing a smile, Laura pushed up the sleeves of her pink knit top. "I'm sorry you had to come in so late. I practiced setting the alarm with Val today, and I thought I could do it."

He tucked the tips of his fingers into the front pockets of his jeans. "What's the problem, exactly? Maybe we can work around it."

"I wish. But I don't think we can." Her throat felt tight. "Numbers and letters are hard for me. Sixes can look like nines. Twos can look like fives." She shrugged and attempted to laugh. "Now you know why I don't write checks."

His eyes clouded with concern. "It's no big deal, you know. Practically everyone sets off the alarm at some point. We'll figure out a way to —"

"I'm quitting," Laura inserted, cutting him off in midsentence.

A taut silence fell between them. Even the dogs seemed to sense the tension and stopped whining. Isaiah slowly lifted a hand. "Whoa."

"It's what we agreed," she reminded him. "I never wanted the job if I couldn't do the work." She shrugged as if it were no big deal. "I can't, and that's the end of it."

"Isn't that a little hasty?"

"You can't trust me to touch the alarm, Isaiah. That means I can't work nights. All the kennel keepers have to work nights. It's part of the deal. I don't want special treatment."

"I'm not offering you special treatment. I just think we can work around the problem."

She lifted her hands in defeat. "I went over the code again and again. It's not a matter of needing more time. I see the numbers wrong at times, and no amount of practice will fix that."

"How are you with eights?"

"Eights?" she echoed bewilderedly.

"Yeah, eights." He traced one in the air. "Upside down, inside out, or sideways, they always look the same."

That was true, but Laura couldn't see how it pertained. "What do eights have to do with it?"

He grinned and winked. "One nice feature of our security system is different authority levels. Just by pressing a few buttons, I can assign you your own user code. How does four eights sound?"

Laura could scarcely credit her ears. "All eights? You can do that?"

"If eights are easy for you, I not only can, but I will."

Laura had been so certain she would have to quit the job that the suggestion threw her completely off balance. Tears stung her eyes again, and it was all she could do to keep her chin from quivering.

"That'd be great," she said. "Only what about the password? I couldn't think of it, either. Right after the police left and I calmed down a little, it came to me. But I couldn't for the life of me remember when the alarm person called."

"Is there any one word you think you could remember?" he asked. "One that always comes to mind when you get rattled and can't think clearly?"

Laura didn't need to think very long to answer that question. "Stupid."

"Ah, honey." Before Laura could guess what he meant to do, he hooked a hand over her shoulder and drew her against him. "You're not stupid. Don't even think that way."

His breath stirred the tendrils of hair at her temple. For just an instant Laura allowed herself to relax in the circle of his arm. *Ah.* She let her eyes drift closed. He felt so big and strong and solid. He settled a hand on her hair, his touch so light and insubstantial that it might have been a whisper.

"Don't put yourself down," he scolded softly, his lips feathering her hair. "You were an environmental scientist, for God's sake."

"Was. Past tense."

"It still means you had the brains to get a degree. Aphasia doesn't affect intelligence." He ran a big, soothing hand over her back. "You're just as smart now as you were then."

His sweatshirt rasped against her cheek. The scent of him — a wonderful blend of male muskiness, aftershave, and faint traces of soap — filled her senses. All the starch went out of Laura's spine. *Isaiah.* Oh, how she yearned to simply lean into him. But those warning bells were jangling again. This man could have any woman he wanted. She was mad to wish for things that would never happen.

Bracing the heels of her hands against his broad chest, Laura tried to lever herself away from him, only to come up short against the circle of his arm. Heat rose to her cheeks when she met his gaze. His gaze searched hers questioningly — and perhaps wonderingly. His firm mouth, shimmering like polished silk in the fluorescent light, tipped into a slow, off-center grin. For just an instant she thought he might kiss her, and she felt sure her heart would stop beating if he did. Instead he curled his hands over her shoulders and gently set her away from him.

Retreating a step, he said, "As much as it gripes me, I guess 'stupid' will work as a password. I'll call the security company and ask them to put it in our file as an alternate."

"They'll do that?"

"Sure. As long as we don't get carried away, they don't care how many passwords we have. A lot of businesses have more than one. Some people can't remember a password unless it has a personal meaning for them."

Laura followed him from the kennel into the storage room and watched as he programmed the system to accept her user code. After going over the steps with her several times, he went up front to call the security company. With a longing so intense it was almost an ache, Laura gazed after him.

Stupid. In that moment, she was more certain than ever that the word suited her perfectly. She was falling in love with Isaiah Coulter. If that wasn't stupid, she didn't know what was.

After working nights only twice, Laura was counting the hours until she could go back to days. Little wonder all the kennel keepers hated working the late shift. Being alone in such a huge building would have been spooky in broad daylight, but it was downright eerie at night. The rooms, which never appeared that large during the day, seemed cavernous without people in them. The dark hallways and shadowy alcoves made Laura's skin prickle. Just the sound of a door swinging closed behind her seemed deafening.

She had never been afraid of the dark or uncomfortable with solitude, but working the third shift alone was enough to make even her imagination run wild. Several times a night, she found herself looking over her shoulder, unable to shake the feeling that someone was watching her. At certain times she could have sworn she heard movement in another part of the building as well — the stealthy whisper of footsteps or the muted click of a door swinging closed.

She might not have felt quite so uneasy if only the dogs had stayed awake to keep her company, but even their inner clocks seemed to be set for the daylight hours. They barely stirred when she entered their cages to collect the soiled bedding and wash their dishes. She missed their insistent nudging for pats and scratches, the excited barking when she walked up the center aisle, and the sense of purpose that interacting with them always gave her.

She also sorely missed the camaraderie with her coworkers. At night she couldn't look forward to coffee breaks with Lena, Jeri, and Tina. Sally wasn't there to tell her funny jokes. James never sneaked into the kennels to slip the dogs a treat. In short, night shift was downright boring.

Boredom in the wee hours of the morning made each minute seem like a small eternity. Laura was bleary-eyed, exhausted, and ready to go home by midnight. The last two hours of the shift seemed to last forever.

By Wednesday Laura missed everyone at the clinic so much that she decided to drop in for a visit. After sleeping in late that morning, she grabbed a quick shower, threw on some old grubbies, bagged a bunch of frozen cookies left over from Halloween, and drove to her workplace. Before exiting the car, she allowed herself only one brief glance in the visor mirror to check her appearance. No makeup, she realized, and almost dug in her purse for a lipstick. *But no.* Isaiah was probably finished making his ranch calls by now, and she'd undoubtedly see him, but that didn't mean she should primp. They were friends, nothing more. She had to keep that foremost in her mind.

The women at the front desk were delighted when they saw that Laura had brought them treats.

"Oh, yum!" Jennifer exclaimed. Hair caught at the crown of her head with a green clasp to match her tinted contacts, the redhead bounced up from her chair. "I think they should put you on days full-time. No one else brings goodies in to work."

As much as Laura would have loved working only the day shift, she knew that would be unfair to the other kennel keepers.

"Sugar cookies?" Debbie, normally the reserved and quiet one, smiled impishly and grabbed a cookie before Jennifer could beat her to the draw. "Mm, and they're frosted! Thanks, Laura."

Tucker and his crew were equally pleased to receive cookies. Tucker had just finished a surgery and was rummaging through the north-wing refrigerator for something to eat when Laura appeared. His blue eyes, so very like Isaiah's, twinkled with interest when he saw the bags in her hands.

"Food?"

Laura laughed. Unlike Isaiah, Tucker never forgot to eat.

"Just some cookies left over from Halloween." She extended a bag to him. "Enjoy."

He'd taken a bite of cookie and was already chewing when he said, "What are you doing here? You're working nights this week."

"Just stopping in for a visit."

"Any more trouble with the alarm?"

"No, thank goodness."

"That's good." He looked at the partially eaten cookie in his hand. "Wow, these are good. You missed your calling, Laura. You should open a bakery."

"There's a thought."

"Speaking of callings." He held up a finger to keep her from leaving. "There's something I need to talk with you about. On Monday night you got your wires a little crossed when you fed the dogs. It wouldn't have been any big deal, but the golden retriever in kennel four was on a special diet. Eating the wrong food made him a little sick."

Laura knew the dog. A raid of a neighbor's garbage can had thrown him into acute gastric and intestinal distress, necessitating intravenous feedings the first twenty four hours and temporary hospital-ization. The animal had a hypothyroid dis-order of long standing that required medication and a bland, low-fat diet to keep it under control. He'd be going back home soon.

"I gave him the wrong food?" she echoed incredulously.

Tucker shrugged. "It was your first time working nights alone, and with the alarm going off and everything, I know it was a tough shift. Fortunately Susan caught the mistake when she got here at six, so the mixup was corrected before too much damage was done. It's just . . ." He smiled kindly. "Last night you did everything per-fectly. I'm sure you will from now on. Just don't become too relaxed again. All right? Other mistakes might not be so easily fixed."

Laura's stomach felt as if it had dropped to her knees. She couldn't believe she'd gotten the cages confused. She was always so careful. A person like her had to be. That being the case, how on earth had she managed to get the food mixed up?

"I'm sorry," she said thinly. "It won't happen again."

Tucker nodded. "Good." His smile faded. "Because we can't let it happen again. You understand?"

Laura swallowed and bobbed her head. Oh, yes, she understood. As nicely as possible, he was telling her that she'd be fired the next time.

Laura was frowning as she made her way along the short connecting hall to Isaiah's surgery. A second later, when she entered the large chamber and saw all the familiar faces, it was like coming home after a long absence.

Trish, standing at the sink and washing her hands, began wailing like a siren the moment she spotted Laura. Shaking off the sense of impending doom brought on by Tucker's reprimand, Laura laughed and rolled her eyes. "So you heard about that."

Trish grinned broadly. "When I first came here, I tripped the alarm, too. It's a tradition around here, a rite of passage, if you will." Drying her hands, she turned from the counter. "What brings you in so early?"

"I miss my babies," Laura confessed. "The stinkers sleep all night. I'd like to spend a little time with them while their eyes are open."

"Ah."

"Hi, Laura." Belinda closed a cupboard door and smiled over her shoulder. "We've missed you around here. The yogurt's all gone, we're down to one kind of pop, the sandwich stuff's all gone, and the soup's running low."

Laura grinned and held up the remaining bag of cookies. "Emer-gency rations."

"Ooh!" Belinda grabbed the package, opened the seal, and sank her teeth into a sugar cookie frosted with orange. "Chewy ones. I love them this way."

"Don't eat them all." Trish tossed the paper towel into the trash. "I want my share."

Isaiah and Angela stood at an operating table at the far end of the surgery. A sheet concealed the patient, making it impossible for Laura to tell what kind of animal was under the knife. She waved and started for the door that opened into the kennels.

"Laura!" Isaiah called.

She turned to look questioningly at him. "Yes?"

His blue eyes were uncharacteristically solemn above the surgical mask that covered the lower half of his dark face. "Have you seen Tucker?"

Laura nodded. "Yes, just now." That awful sinking sensation attacked her stomach again. "We talked."

Isaiah nodded, looking relieved. The familiar twinkle slowly returned to his eyes. "Good cop, bad cop. We take turns. I hope he didn't come down too hard on you."

Silence had fallen over the room. Belinda and Trish had become unaccountably busy. Laura's cheeks went fiery hot with embarrassment. For an instant she deeply resented Isaiah's lack of tact. Maybe she had screwed up, but he could at least discuss it with her privately.

Before the anger could get a good foothold, Laura's sense of fairness came into play. There were no secrets at the clinic. Everyone in the room undoubtedly knew about the food mishap already.

"No," she said. "Tucker was very nice. And I'm really sorry I made a mistake."

"Two mistakes," Belinda inserted even as she smiled to soften the comment. "You got kennels three and four mixed up somehow, so two dogs got the wrong food, not just one. That's why we're all so careful around here. It could happen to anyone."

No, not to just anyone, Laura thought bitterly, *only to a retard like me.* It was still difficult for Laura to believe she'd gotten the cages confused, but if two dogs had received the wrong food, there was no other explanation. She had been misreading numbers that night. The alarm fiasco bore testimony to that. Normally she never confused threes with fours, though. They looked nothing alike, no matter how you turned them.

"I'll be more careful from now on," Laura promised. She glanced uneasily at Isaiah, whose eyes had gone solemn again. "Really," she assured him. "It won't happen again."

Laura let herself out into the kennels. Almost instantly the dogs began to bark joyously. She hauled in a deep breath, slowly released it, and gave herself over to the pleasure of eager nudges, wet noses, and dog breath. As she moved from one cage to the next and finally came to kennel three, she stared hard at the number, painted in bold black, high on the rear wall of the cement-block enclosure. Some numbers were extremely difficult for her to read correctly each and every time, but a three wasn't one of them.

An hour later, when it came time for Laura to go, she reentered the surgery to get her coat and purse. Belinda had just lifted a huge Angora cat from a cage by the scruff of its neck. Evidently the feline didn't appreciate the manner in which Belinda had picked him up, for he immediately began hissing and swatting at the air.

"Got a live one!" Belinda cried.

"Bring him over," Isaiah ordered.

Belinda hurried to deposit the cat on the stainless-steel table. The instant the feline's paws touched down on the metal surface, he began frantically fighting to escape, twisting, scratching, yowling, and trying his best to bite. Startled by the animal's ferocity, Belinda released the feline and leaped clear. Only Isaiah's quick reaction kept the cat from jumping from the table. He snaked out a hand, caught the Angora by its scruff again, and lifted him high in the air.

"Hey, buddy," he said soothingly. "Let's be friends. Okay?"

In Laura's opinion, Belinda was responsible for the cat's misbehavior. The poor thing was in a strange place. He'd been locked in a cage as well, which was probably something he wasn't used to. Then, to make matters worse, the tech had made no attempt whatsoever to befriend the animal before she picked him up.

Hissing and spitting, the feline took a swipe at Isaiah's face. Isaiah jerked his head back in the nick of time. "Has he been declawed?" he asked Belinda.

"He's a first-timer, and we don't have his

records yet." Belinda grabbed the cat's front leg, pressed a thumb to the back of his toes, and said, "Yeah, I think he's clawless."

"I need a muzzle!" Isaiah called over his shoulder to Trish. To the cat he said, "Look, Cuddles, we can do this the easy way or the hard way. Your choice."

Rhhaa! was Cuddles's reply, quickly followed by vicious but futile swipes at Isaiah's face and chest.

"What's his owner smoking?" James asked from across the room. "Cuddles isn't a good name for him. How about Terminator?"

Laura smiled and approached the table. Belinda's blue smock was covered with so much white fur that Laura was surprised Cuddles had any left on his fat body. Before Isaiah could guess what Laura meant to do, she curled her hands around the feline's belly, tugged gently to loosen Isaiah's hold, and drew the terrified kitty to her chest.

"Poor baby," she crooned.

Cuddles snarled and hissed, attempted to claw his way up and over Laura's shoulder without success, and then gave up the fight.

"Shh-hh," Laura soothed, lightly stroking

the cat's fur. "Such a pretty kitty. Yes, you are. It's okay." Responding to her gentle tone, Cuddles ceased his struggles. "There, you see?" she whispered. "No one's going to hurt you."

Brushing fur from his green shirt, Isaiah shook his head. "That's amazing. I can't believe he isn't biting you."

The cat pressed close to Laura's chest and nuzzled his nose under her collar. "He's scared," she explained. "You can't just take him from the cage and start doing mean things to him. Someone should hold him for a little while first."

Belinda huffed under her breath. "Unlike some people, we have a schedule to keep."

Isaiah held up a hand. "No, Belinda, she's right." He reached out and touched a fingertip to the cat's head. "I'm not much of a cat person, I'm afraid." He, too, began stroking the cat's fur. "But I treat a lot of them. I need to develop a better rapport with them."

"He's a sweetie." Laura rubbed her cheek against the cat's soft fur. "I can see why they named him Cuddles. He's very loving when he's not scared."

Isaiah chuckled. "He is with you, at any rate."

Laura shifted the huge cat to hold him more easily. Cuddles began to purr, which made Isaiah grin. "What's the matter with him?" Laura asked.

"Something with his ear," Isaiah said. "So far I haven't gotten close enough to tell what the problem is."

Laura kept stroking the cat and turned so Isaiah could see one side of the animal's head. "You can have a look now."

"Come on," Belinda said impatiently. "He's liable to go ballistic. Obviously you've never dealt with cats or experienced a feline bite. I prefer to keep all my fingers, if it's all the same to you."

Trish arrived just then with the cat muzzle, an awful-looking contraption that fit over a feline's entire face and was anchored with crisscrossed straps behind the head. Laura couldn't see how a kitty could even breathe wearing one. She gave Isaiah a pleading look.

"I'll hold him while you look," she offered. "If we're careful not to scare him, I don't think he'll bite."

Isaiah narrowed his eyes at her even as he plucked a penlight from his pocket. Leaning in close, he peered in the cat's ear. Laura gently turned Cuddles's head so Isaiah could get a better look.

"Foxtail," he murmured.

"Uh-oh." Belinda stepped around to look. "How deep is it?"

Laura knew firsthand how treacherous foxtails could be. The arrow-shaped stickers grew on tall grassy stalks that dried to a yellow-brown over the summer. The foxtails came away from the parent plant with the slightest touch or breath of wind and stuck to clothing and animal fur. Once attached, their sharpness and shape enabled them to burrow. Animals often got them in their feet, ears, mouths, and eyes. Many horses in the area wore eye guards while out in the pasture to protect them from foxtails.

"It's not bad, actually," Isaiah replied.

"She brought him in as soon as he started shaking his head," Trish inserted.

"Good thing," Isaiah replied. "The little bugger would just keep going deeper."

"Must be a field near her house," Belinda observed.

Isaiah went for some long-nosed tweezers. When he returned a moment later, he slanted a look at Laura. "If you can keep him still, I think I can pluck it out easily enough."

Laura nodded, and soon Cuddles's ordeal was over. Laura held the cat awhile longer before she returned him to the cage. Behind her, she heard Isaiah giving orders for follow-up care. When Laura turned, she saw that Trish was taking notes while Isaiah cleaned his hands. Laura went to get her purse. Just as she drew the strap over her shoulder, Isaiah glanced around.

"Are you *sure* you want to be a kennel keeper? Your talents are wasted back there."

"Yeah!" Trish seconded. "You'd be a fabulous tech assistant."

"Oh, no." Laura shook her head vehemently. "I'm not cut out for it. Remem-ber me, the lady who got the dog food mixed up?"

At the reminder, Isaiah's encouraging grin faded and his eyes went dark. He said nothing, but words weren't necessary. He had clearly forgotten for a moment that Laura had been put on notice. One more mistake and she'd be gone.

Chapter Seven

"What picture should I use?" Etta Parks asked.

Peering over her grandmother's shoulder, Laura squinted to see the small cell phone screen. She'd come knocking on Etta's door at ten that morning to get the number to the clinic programmed into her phone. "A dog or a cat would be nice."

Etta took a drag from her Winston and exhaled smoke, which drifted up into Laura's face. "You used the dog for Mrs. Kessler and the cat for the Segals. You've got a party balloon, a wineglass" — Etta scrolled down through more choices — "a book, a cake, a printer, a car, and a coffee cup. There are no animals left."

Because Laura had such difficulty in reading numbers and letters, she had purchased a cell phone with symbols that could be assigned to people she called often. That way she could scroll quickly through the electronic phone book, recognize people's names by the pictures that accompanied them, and make calls without always having to dial numbers. "Use the cake. That'll work."

"The cake? For a veterinary clinic?"

Laura nodded. "I'm always taking in food."

"A cake it will be, then." Shoulder-length silver hair held back by a glittery purple headband that matched her brightly decorated sweatshirt, Etta set herself to the task of programming the phone. "What kind of food do you take in?"

"Lots of stuff. At home I'm always making too much, and my freezer's getting full. Isaiah forgets to eat unless there's something handy, so I can get rid of all my extra and feed him while I'm at it."

"Taking care of him, are you?" Etta grinned. "Sounds pretty cozy."

"We're just friends," Laura replied, thinking as she spoke that those words had become her mantra.

While her grandmother pressed phone buttons and grumbled under her breath about newfangled inventions, Laura went to get a drink. Leaning her hips against the cupboards, she surveyed the familiar kitchen while she took slow sips of water. It was a room dear to her heart. As a child she'd often sat at the oblong table with Grandpa Jim, sharing a predawn breakfast before they went fishing at the lake. She'd also spent many a summer evening in this room with her grandmother, putting up produce from the vegetable garden. It had involved a lot of hard work, but Gram had always managed to make it seem fun. Remembering those days, Laura almost wished she were a child again.

Over the years, the kitchen had undergone many transformations — new appliances, different color schemes — but it had remained essentially the same. The breakfast-nook window now sported lime-green Priscilla curtains that matched the darker green flecks in the new Formica counters and the swirling pattern in the indoor/outdoor carpet that her grandmother had recently had installed so she would no longer need to mop. A dark brown Mr. Coffee machine sat to the left of the stainless-steel sink, its carafe half-full and emitting the rich aroma of freshly brewed coffee. The front of the refrigerator was so crowded with doodads that the white door barely showed. Many of the magnets sported slogans that Laura now struggled to read, but they'd been hanging there for so long that she'd memorized most of them.

Say the word diet, *and you die. God bless this house. I'm not just a good cook;*

I'm a damn good cook. Laura smiled when her gaze came to rest on her favorite magnet of all, which she'd gotten as a gift for her grandmother years ago. It read, *Me and you, and you and me, that's the way it'll always be.* Oh, how true that was. All these years later, here she was, standing in Gram's kitchen, one of her favorite places to be.

"Almost done," her grandmother said.

As Laura's gaze came to rest on her grandmother, she smiled to herself. Even at seventy-six Etta was beautiful, a slender, fine-boned woman with delicate features. A lot of people claimed that Laura looked like her, but Laura had never seen the resemblance. Their coloring was similar, she supposed, but that was as far as it went.

The cell phone in Etta's arthritic hands suddenly rang. "Dear God!" she cried, giving such a start that she nearly dropped the apparatus. "I detest these things."

Laura laughed as she crossed the room. Taking the device, she pressed the little green telephone symbol to answer the call. "Hello?"

"Hi, Laura," a deep, masculine voice replied. "This is Isaiah."

Her heart thumped just a little faster. "Hi."

Long silence. Then he said, "There was

a spot of trouble here this morning. I only just now got back from making ranch calls and found out about it. I think we need to talk. Is there any way you can come in to see me today?"

Laura's glad smile faded. Isaiah's voice was taut, almost grim. "Sure. What kind of trouble? Did I get the food mixed up again?" Laura frowned even as she asked the question, for she'd been extra careful last night, checking and double-checking her work at every turn. "I can't believe I made a mistake."

"We'll talk when you get here."

Laura was starting to get a very bad feeling. Isaiah also sounded distant. "All right. What time is good for you?"

Another silence. "Just come in when you can. I'll be here the rest of the day."

After ending the call, Isaiah rocked back in his desk chair and rubbed his eyes. Tucker, sitting on a corner of the desk, heaved an audible sigh, fiddled with the stapler for a moment, and then said, "We have to let her go, Isaiah. It's nothing short of a miracle that that dog didn't die."

A brutal fist of emotion squeezed Isaiah's throat. "She's so careful, Tucker. I can't believe she left that kennel gate unlatched."

Tucker hissed a vile curse through clenched teeth. "Damn it, Isaiah, don't go there. She was the only one here last night. Who else could have done it?"

Isaiah had no reasonable explanation. He knew only that Laura was meticulous in all that she did. "Okay," he tried. "Just for the sake of discussion, let's say she did leave the gate open. It could happen to almost anyone. Why can't I just chew her out and let it go at that? It seems pretty harsh to fire her over a mistake she may never make again."

Tucker threw up his hands. His blue eyes sparked with anger. "You didn't see the condition that dog was in. There was so much blood, the kennel looked like a war zone. He could have died, Isaiah. He's an expensive animal. The owners might have sued. Leaving a kennel gate unlatched is no small mistake."

Isaiah nodded. "I realize the gravity, Tucker. You're missing my point. Laura is fabulous with the animals. I think we should work with her and give her another chance."

"How many chances?" Tucker pushed up from the desk. "We're financially liable for her screw-ups." With each word, his voice grew louder. "We can't just slap her on the wrist and take the risk that she may

240

do it again. That makes no sense."

Isaiah rose from his chair. Fists braced on the desk, he leaned forward to look his brother in the eye. "I'm the one who decided to hire her. I think it should be me who decides when to fire her. I've worked with the lady. I know her a hell of a lot better than you do."

"That's what worries me. Do you have a thing for her or something?"

"No, of course not."

"Then why this reluctance to cover our asses? Use your head, brother, and I'm not referring to the one behind your fly."

"What the hell is that supposed to mean?"

"She's an attractive woman."

"We have a number of attractive women working here," Isaiah pointed out. "I'd argue against firing any one of them if I felt she didn't deserve it."

Tucker took a calming breath, raked a hand through his hair, and stared at the floor. Watching him, Isaiah had to wonder if he looked as intimidating when he grew angry. The muscles that roped Tucker's shoulders were bunched, his cheek was ticking, and his large hands curled into fists each time he lowered his arms to his sides.

"All right," he finally ground out, his

tone conveying intense displeasure. "You've worked with her and I haven't. You're right in saying that you know her better. I'll let you make the call. But if anything happens again, no matter how insignificant, she's gone, no discussion. Agreed?"

Isaiah nodded. "Agreed."

Tucker opened the door and started out. Then he swung back around. In a voice pitched low so it wouldn't carry to the front desk, he said, "Keep your head about you, Isaiah. Laura's a sweetheart, and there's no denying she's pretty, but she's packing a lot of baggage. Don't go falling in love with her."

Isaiah shook his head. "The warning is completely unnecessary."

Muscles locked, Laura gripped the arms of the chair as she waited for Isaiah to stop fiddling with things on his desk and tell her what she'd done wrong. He obviously dreaded this conversation. He seemed unable to look her directly in the eye, and it was totally unlike him to fidget.

All her life Laura had wondered why people sometimes described silence as being so loud it was deafening. Now she knew. It was so quiet in the office that she could have sworn she heard the sweat oozing from her pores.

Finally Isaiah settled back and looked at her. Once he made eye contact, his blue gaze was direct and unrelenting. "Last night you left a kennel gate unlatched."

Laura's heart caught. "But that can't be —"

"The dog got out," he went on, cutting her off in midprotest, "a black Lab that underwent abdominal surgery yesterday. He was on an IV drip. When he left the cage the fluid bag was jerked loose from the hook, fell to the floor, and the dog dragged it around behind him. At some point he jumped up on some packing crates under one of the windows, probably in an attempt to get outside, and the fluid bag was at a lower level than the IV, resulting in reverse flow."

Laura had no idea what that meant. Evidently he saw the confusion in her expression, for he went on to explain: "That means that instead of infusing fluid into the patient's vein, the blood is siphoned out. In this case, thank God, the dog must have jumped up on the crates just before Susan arrived. He'd lost a lot of blood, both from the IV insert and the incision, which, at some point, was ripped open, but he wasn't dead. She called Tucker, he transfused the animal, performed emergency surgery, and, by the grace of God, it looks as if he'll make it."

Laura was so stunned she could only shake her head. "No," she finally managed to whisper. "No, that can't be."

As if she hadn't spoken, he went on to say, "I'm sticking my neck out by not firing you on the spot. I have only one reason for taking a chance on you — because you're so wonderful with the animals. I honestly believe you're the best kennel person we've ever had."

"Thank you," she squeezed out.

"But we can't have things like this happening. The dog could have died. Do you understand the ramifications of that? The owners might have sued our pants off."

"Yes, I under-under-stand." Laura's mind felt all fuzzy, and her stomach lurched as if she might vomit. "It's just that I checked all the gates to make sure they were latched," she said faintly. "That's the last thing I do right before I leave."

He rocked back in his chair. His jaw muscle rippled from his clenching his teeth. "Last night you must have forgotten." He spread his hands. "How it happened isn't important. What we have to deal with is that it occurred on your shift and a dog almost died. Tucker and I met to discuss what should be done. On my recommendation he's agreed to give you another chance, with the understanding that you'll be terminated if anything at all happens again. Our reputations as vets are on the line."

Tears burned at the backs of Laura's eyes. Pain radiated through her chest. "Maybe I should save every-one a lot of trouble and quit right now."

Isaiah put his elbows on the desk, folded his hands, and rested his chin on his knuckles. Once again his eyes offered her no quarter. "Is that what you want?" he asked softly. "To just quit?"

"No, of course not. I love this job. But I don't like being blamed for something I didn't do. I *checked* those gates. I always do. I know I didn't leave a cage open."

"Someone did, and you were the only someone here."

Laura pushed up from her chair. "Are you sure?"

His face a mask of stunned incredulity, he stared up at her. Laura curled her hands into throbbing fists. Words crowded at the back of her throat. She wanted so badly to defend herself, but he would undoubtedly think she'd lost what was left of her mind.

"Look," he said reasonably, "let's reverse that question. Can you swear to the fact — are you absolutely positive — that you couldn't have accidentally left that one gate unlatched?"

Laura almost said yes, but right then she was so upset that the previous night was a blur in her mind. She needed to go back over everything she'd done last night before she could be absolutely sure. "I'm almost posi-tive," she settled for saying.

"Almost? That's not good enough."

Laura distinctly remembered walking up and down the center aisle, checking the gates on both sides before she left the clinic. Had something distracted her? Could she have accidentally passed by one gate without trying the latch? She'd worked out a routine while on the day shift, and now she always stuck to it. Routines were vital to someone like her, who tended to be more forgetful than other people.

"I hope you'll stay on, Laura," Isaiah said softly. "I fought hard to give you another chance. It'll be a shame if you quit."

She was too upset right then to discuss it further, so she just nodded her head.

"Maybe," he went on, "you can develop a few new habits to prevent something like this from happening again."

246

He went on to offer her several ideas, all safety precautions that she'd already instituted. By the time he stopped talking, she felt numb.

When she turned to let herself out of his office, all she could think to say was, "I'm sorry about the dog, Isaiah."

"We all are."

It was almost seven when Isaiah left the clinic that night. A vague ache had taken up residence behind his eyes, and his mind swam with bits and pieces of several phone conversations he'd had with respected colleagues. One of Isaiah's patients, a neutered Chesapeake, was dying of autoimmune disease, and the usual treatments, heavy doses of antibiotics and prednisone, weren't working. It was time to go for broke and try something new: hormone replacement therapy.

It was difficult for Isaiah to believe that injections of testosterone might save the Chesapeake when the more traditional approaches had failed. But, hey, compared to Rodney Porter, head man at Eastern Oregon Veterinary Research Center, Isaiah was still a rookie. If Porter felt that the deprivation of natural hormones could weaken the immune system, Isaiah would try giving the Chesapeake injections of testosterone.

Why the hell not? Bone-deep weariness and a leaden feeling of defeat tempted Isaiah to try a testosterone cocktail himself.

As he walked through the crisp night air toward his Hummer, he pressed the switch on the remote to unlock the rear doors so he might stow some research tomes on the backseat. It was going to be another late night, he thought dismally. He wouldn't be able to sleep until he'd read everything he could get his hands on about autoimmune disease.

When the Hummer's door locks disengaged, the clearance and interior dome lights blinked on. The sudden illumination brightened the dark parking area. Isaiah was surprised to see another car on the opposite side of the hulking SUV. Someone from the cleaning company who was working overtime, maybe? As he drew closer, he was even more surprised to see that it was Laura's red Mazda.

After tossing the books inside the Hummer, he glanced at his watch, thinking it might be later than he thought. But no, it was only seven. Laura's shift didn't begin until nine. What on earth was she doing here so early?

Retracing his steps, Isaiah reentered the building and made his way to the kennels. Instinct led him directly to the black Lab's cage. He found Laura sitting inside the enclosure on the cold cement, the dog's massive head cradled on her lap. Expression sad, shoulders slumped, she put him in mind of the little lost angel in one of his nephew Garrett's storybooks. Golden wisps of hair trailed forward over her cheeks. There was a stricken look in her large, hazel eyes.

At the sound of his footsteps she didn't even glance up. "You haven't been here ever since we talked, have you?"

"Yes," she said hollowly.

"*Why?* You work the late shift tonight, Laura. You'll be dead on your feet by two in the morning." *And more likely to make another mistake,* he thought.

She trailed a hand lightly over the dog's shoulder. "Dusty almost died. He's still feeling pretty bad. Sitting with him is the least I can do."

His heart caught at her flat tone of voice, which accentuated the halting way she spoke. When he'd stood there for several seconds and she still hadn't looked up, he opened the gate and entered the cage. Bracing his back against the cement, Isaiah slid down the wall into a crouch. "Well," he said softly, "I can see you're still upset with me." When she continued to avoid making eye contact, he tried a chuckle to lessen the tension. "Hey, it's not *that* bad. You're still on the payroll. Dusty will recover. Before you know it this whole mess will be nothing but a memory."

She finally lifted her gaze to his. Her hazel eyes burned with resentment. "If I had left the gate open, I wouldn't mind being blamed for it. I wouldn't even mind being fired. Only it wasn't me who did it."

It wasn't like Laura to so stubbornly deny responsibility for something that was so obviously her fault. From the very start she'd been uncommonly humble and uncertain of her ability to do this job.

"This cage was left open," he said evenly. "You were the only person in the building. Who else could have done it, Laura?"

"I don't know. I only know that I *always* check the gates to be sure they're closed." Her hand stilled on the dog's shoulder. "I'm not like other people, Isaiah." Her voice quavered as she said his name. "I can't even keep track of the scoops when I make coffee without my counting beans."

He cautiously circled that, not entirely sure how her coffee-making ability pertained to the situation. He was about to ask when she added, "Knowing that about myself, do you really think I'd come in here, where *all* that I do is so impor-tant, and leave *any-thing* to mem-ory? I'm more careful than other people. I have to be."

A sinking sensation attacked Isaiah's middle. He'd said almost exactly the same thing this morning to Tucker.

She waved her hand to encompass all the cages. "I *love* these dogs. I'd never take a chance with their safety. I have a strict rou-tine, and I always, *always* follow it. Other-wise I might forget something." Her larynx bobbed as she swallowed. "I was worried about Dusty last night and checked on him right before I left."

"Isn't it possible that you accidentally forgot to drop the latch when you exited the cage?" he suggested kindly.

"No." She looked him dead in the eye. "This morning when we talked, I was upset and couldn't recall the details clearly, but now I can." She jutted her small chin at him. "I checked *twice* to make sure the latch was down after I left his cage."

Isaiah drew up his knees to create a rest for his arms. Gazing into her bruised, hurt-filled eyes, he had no choice but to believe

251

her. She was almost ritualistic about her little routines. Over time he'd noticed that she did exactly the same things in the same order, day after day. When she left the clinic at the end of her shift, for instance, she always followed a pattern — going first to check on the snack supplies when she entered the surgery, and then going to get her coat and purse before saying good-bye. Other people might deviate, saying good-bye first and stopping by the refrigerator last, but Laura never altered the pattern, undoubtedly because she might overlook something important if she did things out of sequence.

"I want to believe you," he confessed, his voice gravelly with regret. "And if it had happened on day shift when other people were in the kennels, I would believe you. But I'm having a problem getting past the fact that you were the only person here last night."

Tears shimmered in her eyes. She gazed at him for an interminably long moment, and then she looked away.

"What?" He leaned sideways to see her face. "You almost said something. What?"

"You'll think I'm crazy."

"No, I won't. Spit it out."

The tendons in her throat went taut. She

drew in a deep breath. On the exhale, she blurted, "I think someone is sneaking in here at night."

She was right; he thought she was crazy. *"Why?"*

"To get me fired."

That was even crazier. So far as he knew, everyone at the clinic liked Laura.

"Why would someone want you to be fired? I'm sorry. It's not that I don't believe you, Laura, but who would want you to lose your job?"

Her lips quivered at the corners. "I don't know. I only know someone does. Maybe some-body who doesn't like me because I have brain damage, and it's easy to set me up. If the dog food gets mixed up, I must have done it. If a kennel gate is left open, I must have done it. Well, news flash: It's true that I misread numbers sometimes, but I never get my threes confused with fours."

Again, Isaiah didn't get the connection.

"The dog in kennel f-four got the food for the d-dog in kennel three," she explained, agitation slowing her speech even more. "A th-three is the same no matter how you turn it, and a f-four looks nothing like a three, upside down, inside out, or s-s-sideways." She stopped petting Dusty to gesture at the seven painted in bold black high on the back wall of the enclosure. "It's not like the numbers are small or hard to read. I'm brain-d-damaged, Isaiah, not blind."

Isaiah stared thoughtfully at the seven, and then drew his gaze back to her pale face.

"Earli-er this week when T-Tucker chewed me out about mixing up the f-food, I wondered how I could have made such a d-dumb mistake. I'm always so careful. Now I'm almost sure that s-someone came in here and switched the bowls."

Normally Isaiah was analytical to a fault, a man who dealt only in facts and carefully gathered data. But even though Laura's allegations made no sense to him intellectually, he found himself believing her. She wasn't a person to dream up something this wild, and for the life of him he couldn't think of anything she stood to gain. She hadn't lost her job, so this wasn't a ploy to get it back. She was also smart enough to realize that making such allegations could easily backfire, casting even more doubt on her credibility.

"I knew you'd think I'm c-crazy," she whispered accusingly. "Well, if you th-think that's bad, you're really going to think I'm n-nuts when I tell you the rest. I don't think I s-set off the alarm Monday night."

Isaiah slid the soles of his boots forward and plopped his rump on the cement. *In for a penny, in for a pound.* If he could believe that someone had sneaked in here to switch the feeding dishes and leave a gate open, it wasn't difficult to go a step farther and believe someone else had tripped the alarm.

"I practiced s-setting the alarm with Val that day," she hurried on. "She told me to watch the little light on the c-console. When it's red, the alarm is set. When it's green, the alarm is off."

"That's right."

"Monday night it was all still new to me," she went on. "I thought maybe I'd done something wrong, even though the light had turned the right colors. Now I know better. I did nothing wrong. The light never turns green unless the alarm is off, and it never turns red unless the alarm has been set."

"You're sure that the light turned green when you disarmed the system?"

She nodded emphatically. "And it was red when I left the console to go into the kennels. I was about halfway across the storage room when the siren went off."

If the light had been red when she left the console, the alarm had indeed been set. "Have you ever seen or heard anyone in the building at night?" he asked.

She looked imploringly at him. "If I answer that qu-question, are you going to think I'm n-nuts?"

"No," he replied, and sincerely meant it.

"After the alarm went off M-Monday night and I was talking to that lady on the ph-phone, I could have sworn I heard a crash in the one of the of-fices."

"Which one?"

"I'm not sure. I just know I heard a loud c-crash. I never checked to see what it was. I was so upset about every-thing else that I forgot about it until later."

Isaiah could understand that. "Anything else strange?"

"At night when I've been working, I've heard sounds. Sometimes soft footsteps like you might hear if someone was in ano-ther part of the building. Sometimes it was the faint sound of things being moved — scraping noises or thumps. Until today, I kept telling myself it was all in my head. Now I'm sure it wasn't."

"If you properly rearmed the system Monday night, opening a door or window is the only thing that would have tripped the alarm. Because of the animals, we don't have motion detectors."

She shook her head. "I was taking off my coat. I never touched a door or window. It just went off."

Isaiah stared thoughtfully at the wall. "There are two alarm consoles in the building, one at the front and one at the rear. If someone had been standing near the front doors, watching that console, he would have known by the indicator light when you got the system rearmed. Then he could have hurried into one of the offices to open a window. Once the alarm went off, he could have closed the window and remained in the office until after the police came and left."

Laura's eyes went wide and filled with tears. "You believe me?"

"I don't know who's crazier, me or you, but yes, Laura, I believe you. Why would you lie about something like this, and for what purpose?"

She squeezed her eyes closed. Tears spilled from under her dark lashes, making sparkling rivulets on her pale cheeks.

"Hey!" he said.

She opened her eyes and gave him a tremulous smile. "I'm sorry. I just didn't think —" She broke off, caught her lower lip between her teeth, and shook her head again. "I didn't think you'd believe me, is all."

"Yeah, well, you thought wrong." Isaiah reached out to brush the tears from her cheeks. Then he drew his feet back under him and pushed erect. "All that remains is for me to substantiate your story."

"How can you do that?"

"By calling Harris Security." At her questioning look, he smiled. "Nobody can enter or leave this clinic after the alarm has been set without leaving an electronic trail. The console sends a signal to Harris Security via a secure phone line every time the security code is used to activate or deactivate the system."

"It does?" Her eyes went even wider. "So it'll show that someone else was in here on Monday night?"

He nodded. "Absolutely."

In that moment Isaiah knew he'd been right to believe Laura. She didn't look frightened or uneasy, as a person might if she'd been lying and suddenly realized the game was over. She clearly believed that the security records would vindicate her.

"Want to come?" he invited. "You can listen while I make the call."

Chapter Eight

Tucker's Victorian farmhouse sat on forty acres at the east side of town. Some sections of the land were treed and others were in pasture, creating a perfect balance for a busy veterinarian who wanted to keep a few horses but didn't have time to operate a full-scale ranch. The yard itself was defined by a white, ivy-draped picket fence. An old, dented mailbox on a post stood next to the front gate.

When Tucker had purchased the property, he'd taken a lot of razzing from his father and brothers. They'd asked him if his feminine side was coming out, teased him about getting a white cottage with a picket fence, and wondered aloud if Tucker would start serving tea in fancy cups when they came to visit. Finally, when their mother had been out of earshot, Tucker had held up all five fingers of one hand and cheerfully informed them it was a bouquet of F-yous, one for each of them. That had pretty much put a stop to the teasing.

Secretly, Isaiah admired his twin's attitude. There was nobody tougher or more masculine than Tucker, but he wasn't hung up on cultivating that image. He was who he was and didn't worry about what other people thought. He'd liked this house and its location. Turrets, elaborate porches, gingerbread trim, and English gardens appealed to him. Isaiah was more into gleaming wood and simple architectural lines, but to each his own. If Tucker was happy, that was all that mattered.

As Isaiah strode up the stepping-stone path to the veranda steps, he scrunched his shoulders to push the collar of his jacket higher on the nape of his neck. In November, the nighttime temperatures in Central Oregon dived to freezing, crystallizing the air with particles of ice and frosting the pine branches. A full moon bathed the landscape in silvery light, making the trees look more gray than green.

Too cold for snow, Isaiah thought as he scaled the steps to knock on his brother's front door. Faint light shone through the windows, telling Isaiah that Tucker was home and still up.

Moments later Tucker appeared in the large entrance hall, which encompassed a central curving staircase with runners of forest green. Through the oval of etched door glass, his silhouette was distorted, creating a copper-and-blue blur where his bare upper torso met with the waistline of his jeans.

He cracked open the door. "Isaiah? What's brought you here?" He drew the portal wide, rubbing his furry chest as the chill air curled around him. "I was crashed in the recliner. It's after nine."

"I need to talk to you."

Isaiah had known several sets of identical twins over the years, and a fair half of them hadn't felt that they resembled each other all that much. Such had never been the case with him and his brother. Their coloring, features, and builds were so markedly similar that sometimes they both felt as if they were looking in a mirror. This was one of those moments for Isaiah. Maybe it was the soft glow of a lamp coming from behind Tucker, casting his face partly in shadow. Whatever the reason, Isaiah got the uncanny feeling, if only for an instant, that he was having an out-of-body experience.

Tucker retreated a step to allow Isaiah entry. "Everyone missed you at the party."

"What party?"

"Earth to Isaiah." Tucker pushed the

door shut. "Natalie's grandfather's birthday party, tonight, six sharp. Does that ring a bell? Everybody showed but you."

"Shit." Isaiah remembered now. He'd gotten a gift and attended Sly's party, but had forgotten to attend Natalie's grandfather's party. "I even have a present for him — a whole case of cheap burgundy to keep under his bed."

Tucker grinned. "Drop it off and apologize. With a case of wine as a peace offering, he'll forgive you almost anything." With a shiver, Tucker asked, "What do you need to talk to me about?"

Isaiah swept off his Stetson. "There's a situation at the clinic."

"Shit. What's happened now?"

"Nothing more has happened, exactly. I've just become privy to some information that we need to discuss."

"Tonight?"

"It can't wait until morning."

Cursing under his breath, Tucker padded barefoot up the hall to the library, situated to the left of the stairs. He reached around the door frame to flip on the overhead chandelier before they entered the room. The sudden spill of light made the hardwood floor gleam like polished glass.

"I can tell by the look on your face that

it's not good news," he told Isaiah. "As far as I'm concerned, bad news at this hour calls for a drink."

It called for immediate action, but Isaiah knew his brother well and refrained from dropping that bomb until the moment felt right. He tossed his hat on a fancy settee that was new since his last visit. "Wow. Aren't we getting classy? Actual furniture?"

"Wallpaper, too." Tucker stepped over to an ornate liquor cabinet of hand-carved mahogany. "I liked the tea roses. What do you think?"

It looked as if a woman had taken up squatting rights, but Isaiah only nodded as he perused the little roses that trailed over a swirled hunter-green backdrop. "Pretty," he settled for saying. Prissy stuff usually was.

Tucker drew two crystal tumblers from a shelf and sloshed a measure of Irish whiskey into each. He looked too big, dark, and rugged to be messing around with a crystal decanter. "I got tired of making do and hired an interior decorator."

Isaiah swept a wondering glance over the mahogany office furniture that took up one corner of the room. There was even a secretary with curlicues across the top. The last time he'd been here, a cheap drafting table had filled in as a desk, and the only furniture had been two metal chairs and an apple crate serving as an end table. He crossed to stand before the hearth and chafe his hands.

"Why do people do that?" Tucker asked.

"Do what?"

"Warm their hands at a hearth when the fire's dead out."

Isaiah glanced down, and sure enough he was holding out his hands to nonexistent heat. He laughed and folded his arms. "Good question. Habit, I guess. It's colder'n hell outside."

Grinning, Tucker shook his head.

Isaiah studied a nature painting in an oval frame that hung above the mantel. "This is really great, Tucker." And Isaiah realized he actually meant it. The house had a warm, lived-in feeling now. "Maybe I should hire a decorator. I've been in my place for over six months, and I'm still sitting on beanbags in the living room to watch TV."

"That's no way to impress the babes." After handing Isaiah a whiskey, Tucker sank onto a sage-green wingback chair set at an angle in front of the hearth. "Females go for well-established men with refined tastes." A devilish twinkle entered his blue eyes. "Not to mention that it's harder than hell to seduce a woman on a folding chair."

The picture that formed in Isaiah's mind brought a smile to his mouth. "I imagine so."

"The gal's name is Lisa Banning, if you're interested."

"Who, the woman you seduced on a folding chair?"

"No, lamebrain, the decorator."

Isaiah took a seat opposite his brother. As fancy as the wingback seat looked, he was pleased to find that comfort hadn't been sacrificed for appearance. The cushions were luxuriously soft, and deep enough to accommodate his large frame. "Maybe I'll give her a call."

Tucker took a sip of whiskey. After swallowing and giving an appreciative whistle, he asked, "So what can't wait until morning?"

Isaiah leaned back, his drink balanced on one knee. "Laura didn't leave that kennel gate open last night. We were wrong to jump to conclusions."

Tucker didn't immediately respond. He swirled the whiskey in his glass, his expression thoughtful. When he finally met Isaiah's gaze again, all the laughter had left his eyes. "Do you realize how crazy that sounds, Isaiah? One person works the late shift. Last night that person was Laura. If she didn't leave the gate open, who did, a mischievous gremlin?"

Isaiah refused to get angry. "She was set up, Tucker. I think someone's trying to get her fired."

Tucker sat forward on his chair. "Come on, Isaiah, get real. Who'd want to do that? As far as I know, everybody at the clinic likes Laura. I know for a fact that none of my techs have a beef with her. Lena sings her praises. That kennel keeper Danielle Prince, with the hair that changes colors once a month, thinks she's the greatest thing since the invention of popcorn because Laura never leaves shit details unfinished for the next shift. Tina thinks she's a saint. I repeat, who'd want to get her fired?"

"I don't have all the answers yet," Isaiah replied. "I only know she was set up."

Tucker arched a dark eyebrow. "We're not talking about a corporate position here. She's a kennel keeper, for God's sake. Who'd want her job?"

Taking care not to spill his drink, Isaiah shifted on the chair to fish in his coat pocket. He drew out a folded piece of paper. "Your guess is as good as mine." He handed the paper to his brother. "But facts don't lie. Have a look."

"And this is?" Tucker began to scan the printout. "Dates, times? I'm not following."

"That was faxed to me a while ago by the night person at our security company. Whenever anyone turns the alarm at the clinic on or off, Harris Security receives a signal via the phone line, and it's recorded in a computer log."

"I remember something about that." Tucker's voice rang with weary impatience. "And this is important because . . . ?"

"That's a record of all our alarm activity this week. If you'll notice, someone disarmed and rearmed the system on Monday night at eight, almost an hour before Laura got there. Also notice that, according to that record, Laura successfully disarmed and rearmed the system just before nine. Less than thirty seconds later the alarm went off. Pay attention to the cause that's listed, please. It says 'perimeter breach.' That means the alarm was properly reset and someone opened a door or possibly a window to make it go off."

Tucker studied the first few lines of the printout. "If she disarmed and rearmed the system correctly, why the hell did she open an outside door and set off the alarm?"

"She didn't. The alarm went off as she was heading into the kennels."

"So she says."

An image of Laura's sweet face moved through Isaiah's mind. "Don't accuse her of lying, Tucker. Making a mistake I can handle, but not out-and-out lying."

"A little sensitive, aren't you?"

"Right now I'm just royally pissed off. Look at the damned readout. It speaks for itself. Someone else was already in the building that night when Laura got there." Moving his drink to the arm of the chair, Isaiah rested a boot on his knee. "*Think,* Tucker. At night, when you visit the clinic and plan to stay for a while, what procedure do you follow with the alarm?"

"I unlock the door," Tucker said, his tone laced with sarcasm. "Then I immediately relock it. After that's done, I hurry over to the console, enter our user code, and turn off the system. When the light turns green, I reenter our user code and rearm the system by hitting three."

"And when you leave?"

"I go through the whole process again to exit the building."

Isaiah inclined his head at the printout. "Exactly. Just before eight o'clock, a full hour before Laura entered the building, someone disarmed and rearmed the system. There is no record of that being done again before Laura arrived."

"That doesn't necessarily mean that the person remained in the building. Maybe someone forgot something, Isaiah. I've disarmed the system and raced into my office for a file or research book before I rearmed the system and left."

"Did you make it to your office and back to the alarm console in less than ten seconds?" Isaiah countered.

Tucker considered the printout again. Then he whistled softly. "Damn, you're right. Whoever went in at eight reset the alarm three seconds later."

A cold sensation moved over Isaiah's skin. "That's right. Nobody could run inside for something and reset the alarm in less than three seconds. The pattern you see there is congruent with the pattern that occurs when someone enters the building at night, planning to stay for a while."

"Why would anyone hang around in the middle of the night if they weren't working a shift?"

"To trip the alarm after Laura entered

the building and make her look like an incompetent imbecile."

Tucker's eyes darkened to a turbulent gray. "Did she see anyone in the building?"

The question told Isaiah that Tucker was beginning to believe him. "No, but she did hear a crash in one of the offices while she was talking on the phone. Unfortunately, in all the confusion, she didn't think much about it and never went to investigate."

"My paperweight," Tucker whispered.

"Your what?"

"My paperweight," he said more loudly. "That big ceramic bull Mom got me for Christmas last year. On Tuesday morning I found it on the floor in a hundred pieces. I thought one of the cleaning crew had knocked it off my desk and left it there, not wanting to get in trouble."

"It's possible, I guess. But it's more likely that the crash Laura heard was the paperweight being knocked from your desk."

Tucker scanned the sheet of paper again. "The clinic was as busy as Grand Central that night. Look at all the entries around a quarter of ten."

"That was me, reprogramming the console to give Laura her own user code." Isaiah set his drink on the hearth and vacated the chair to crouch beside his brother. He tapped the paper to point out other pertinent entries. "The police left here. This is where I arrived. All this garble was a little later, when I assigned Laura her own user number."

"I'm with you," Tucker said softly. He pointed to some entries farther down. "Is this when you left?"

Isaiah studied the record. "Ten thirty. Yeah, that was me." He trailed his fingertip down to another line. "Look at this. Someone disarmed and rearmed the system in quick succession at eleven forty. I think that's when our mysterious alarm tripper finally left the building. Laura was working in the kennels and laundry room, nowhere near either console, so she wouldn't have seen the indicator light change colors. She never even realized someone else was there. The dog food bowls in cages three and four were probably switched while she was in the laundry room."

Tucker lowered the paper and closed his eyes. "Give me a second to process this."

"What's to process?" Isaiah asked. "It's as plain as the nose on my face, and that's pretty damned plain. Someone else was in the clinic that night, and last night as well.

It's not just Laura's word, which I happen to believe is golden. The entries corroborate her story."

Tucker perused the readout again. "Sweet Christ. Someone entered the clinic after Laura left this morning. That dog almost died. Who'd do something like this?"

For the moment Isaiah was content with the knowledge that Laura had been exonerated, even in Tucker's estimation. "That's a damned good question," he said. "And one we'd better find an answer for pretty damn fast."

Tucker sat back, the printout held loosely on his lap. "So Laura didn't forget to latch that gate after all."

"No," Isaiah agreed huskily. "She left the building at two this morning, right when her shift ended. At shortly after five, someone else went in."

Tucker smoothed the printout over his thigh to review the entries again. "Son of a bitch. That poor dog. This makes me want to do murder." He sent Isaiah a burning look. "Someone deliberately left that cage open and unhooked the fluid bag from the wire, knowing a reverse IV flow would probably occur."

"That's how I see it."

Tucker's jaw muscle started to tic. "I

don't know about you, but I think this was painstakingly orchestrated so Susan would arrive less than an hour later to save the dog."

"The aim wasn't to kill the Lab, Tucker. It was to get Laura canned."

"Who could possibly hate her that much?"

Isaiah could only shake his head. "You've got me."

Normally a dark, burnished brown, Tucker's face had gone ashen. "Whoever did this could face legal charges."

"We have to catch the person first. I think our chances of doing that are pretty slim."

"You think it's a man — or a woman?"

Isaiah shrugged. "We have more women working for us than men, but when I try to imagine which one of them it might be, my brain shorts out. As gruff and militant as Susan can be, she's a kind person, and she seems to really like Laura. Trish is an absolute sweetheart, too. And Belinda has worked way too hard to get her certification as a vet assistant to put it at risk."

"It could be someone on my team, I guess," Tucker mused aloud. "Only I can't imagine who. Everyone in my wing seems to like Laura and think she does a great job." Tucker frowned slightly. "We can't rule out the possibility that it could be one of the men in your wing, James and . . . what's the other guy's name?"

"Mike. But neither of them sees Laura all that much."

Tucker swirled his drink again. "Never underestimate a scorned man. Laura's very pretty and likable. Could be one of them has a thing for her. Unrequited love can make people who already have a few screws loose do some pretty off-the-wall things."

Isaiah nodded pensively. "I suppose that's true."

Tucker sat farther forward on his chair. "What the hell are we going to do, Isaiah? We could chase our tails for a month trying to figure out who did this. Meanwhile, what's to stop it from happening again?"

Isaiah, his thoughts on Laura and how easily a man might fall in love with her, pulled himself back to the conversation. "I've already taken steps."

"What kind of steps?"

"I took the liberty of changing our user code before I left the clinic. The old one is now defunct. If anyone enters the building tonight and tries to disarm the system using the old numbers, the alarm will go off."

"Good thinking. What's our new number?"

"We used the last four digits of my Social Security number last time. I decided it would be too easy for someone to guess if we used yours this time. Instead I combined the last two digits of the years Dad and Mom were born."

"Four-two-four-six?" Tucker nodded. "That'll work. No one at the clinic knows when they were born. Someone could find out, I suppose, but it'd take some digging."

"That was my thought, too."

"And what about our employees? If the old code is defunct, how will they disarm the system to enter the building?"

"I've assigned each of them an individual user code." Isaiah glanced at his watch. "We need to call Susan with hers so she can open in the morning. The others will get theirs tomorrow." Isaiah drew another sheet of paper from his pocket. "I made you a copy."

Tucker accepted the printout. "You never cease to amaze me."

"How's that?"

"All those brains in a head exactly the same size as mine." Tucker flashed a quick grin. "You're always one step ahead of me. Been that way all our lives."

In Isaiah's opinion, Tucker was every bit as smart. He just looked at everything through a broader lens, whereas Isaiah had a tendency to hyperfocus. When confronted with a problem, he couldn't relax until it was solved.

"At least no one besides you, me, and Laura will be able to enter or leave the building tonight without setting off the alarm. And as of tomorrow, when we assign the new user codes, everyone will have to finger himself to operate the alarm."

"We may never find out who did it," Isaiah said.

Tucker nodded in agreement. "The most important thing is that the animals are safe."

And so was Laura's job, Isaiah thought with an even greater sense of relief.

Before driving home, Isaiah dropped by the clinic to fill Laura in on his meeting with Tucker. When he entered the kennels she was nowhere to be seen. He moved up the center aisle, glancing into each cage to be sure she wasn't inside with a canine that needed a cuddle. All he saw was dogs, some happily eating from freshly filled bowls, others asleep on clean bedding. Not even Laura could clean a kennel well enough for someone to eat off the floors, but she came damn close. The cement gleamed in the fluorescent light. The whole place smelled primarily of lemon cleaning solution. The lady was a wonder.

When Tucker reached the Chesapeake's cage, he reeled to a stop and stared. The big red dog was on his feet. That morning and again this evening, when Isaiah had administered the injections of testosterone, the Chesapeake had been almost comatose.

"I'll be damned."

Visibly shaky and weak, Rocky tried to wag his plumed tail and wobbled forward to poke his nose through the wire mesh.

"Hey, buddy." Delight swept through Isaiah. He opened the cage and went inside. As he settled his hands on the animal's silky fur, Rocky sank exhausted to the floor and whined. "You're still a mighty sick boy." Isaiah checked the canine's gums. "You're getting some color back, though. I can't believe it. I thought you were a goner."

"Isaiah?"

Laura's voice startled him. He glanced over his shoulder and smiled. "Hey." He looked back at the dog. "It worked, Laura. He was dying. Now look at him."

She entered the cage and crouched down to join him in petting the weak animal. "I noticed how sick he seemed. What's wrong with him?"

"Autoimmune. None of the usual treatments worked. A colleague of mine suggested that I try testosterone injections. He says spayed and neutered animals are deprived of their natural hormones, and that it can affect their health and immune systems." Isaiah remembered he was talking to a woman with brain damage and broke off. "Sorry. I don't mean to bore you."

Her eyes shone with interest. "I'm not bored. I've thought for a long time that fixing dogs and cats might be bad for them. They get so fat and lazy. That can't be very fun."

"It's not a popular theory in veterinary medicine," Isaiah replied. "I sure as hell wasn't taught that at vet school, and no vet I interned with ever mentioned it, either. Just the opposite."

Laura sat beside the Chesapeake. In the spill of light she looked beautiful and cute, both at once. Over a pink knit top she wore an old flannel shirt that was so oversize it nearly swallowed her. Her hair lay in tousled disarray, the shiny wisps tempting his fingertips to touch them. Her mouth, a delicate rose pink, curved sweetly in a Madonna smile.

"That doesn't mean all those vets were right." She sent him an impish grin that dimpled her cheeks. "When they spayed my mom, she had an awful time."

Isaiah had never heard anyone refer to a hysterectomy as a spay, and he almost laughed. Then he remembered that Laura couldn't say *hysterectomy,* and sobered. It wasn't the words she said that mattered, he decided. What did matter was that she could comprehend his line of reasoning, be a sounding board, and give him intelligent feedback.

"Go on," he urged. "What happened with your mom?"

She shrugged and wrinkled her nose. "They couldn't get her hormones right. She gained weight and got cranky. She cried a lot. Hair came on her upper lip and chin. Even on her toes!" She lifted her finely arched brows. "It was pretty bad. When they finally got the dose right, she got better and lost the whiskers. If messed-up hormones could do all that to her, why wouldn't it be just as bad for a dog or cat?"

Isaiah nodded. "It's a foreign concept to me, but you're absolutely right. Hormones are important." His were raging at the moment. He wanted to kiss her so badly, he caught himself leaning closer, until her faint perfume teased his senses. Not a good plan. Being friends with her was fine. Taking it beyond that would be exhilarating, but Laura might take it seriously, and he wasn't ready for anything serious.

He lowered his gaze to the dog. "It calls for more research. Thank God there are fabulous vets who devote their careers to that. Rocky just might make it, thanks to them. Maybe it's a fluke. Maybe it's not. I only know he's turned around since I gave him the testosterone injections."

Laura ran a slender hand over the dog's glistening coat. "Give yourself some credit. You were willing to take a chance and try the shots."

"I couldn't see how it would hurt."

"And it didn't. He's getting well." She leaned forward to look into the dog's sad eyes. "Aren't you, Rocky? And it's all because Isaiah tried something new."

It felt good to talk with Laura like this, he realized. To share his concerns and get some thoughtful feedback. She had some interesting insights. Maybe she couldn't wrap her tongue around long words anymore, but her mind was as sharp as ever.

"I dropped by to tell you about my talk with Tucker."

Her eyes darkened. "What did he say?"

"He feels rotten for jumping to conclusions this morning. He's also mad as hell. He wants to find out who left that gate open and rack his ass."

The tension eased from her narrow shoulders. "He believes it wasn't me?"

"Absolutely. Those records prove it wasn't."

Before Isaiah left, he did a quick walk-through of the clinic to be absolutely sure no one was hiding somewhere in the building. *Silly.* Nothing had been done directly to Laura. She would be perfectly safe, and he shouldn't have felt worried. Only he was. Leaving a kennel gate open wasn't overtly hostile, but the result definitely had been. No matter how Isaiah cut it, the perpetrator of that act had meant to harm Laura. When Isaiah factored in the pain and suffering of Dusty, a poor, defenseless dog, it made his blood run icy.

The person who'd left the cage open was an employee at the clinic. It followed that the individual had known in advance that the consequences of his actions would inflict pain and possibly even death on the animal. That was not indicative of someone with a conscience, and Isaiah couldn't shake his concern that the next prank might be aimed more directly at Laura.

If it hadn't been for the fact that assisting him was so taxing for her, Isaiah would have removed Laura from the kennel position immediately and started training her to be his assistant. She'd done a fabulous job when everyone had been off sick.

Plain and simple, Isaiah didn't like the thought of her being in the clinic alone at night. Not to mention that he enjoyed being around her and wished he could work with her all the time. He liked the other techs. Trish was a doll, he enjoyed Belinda's dry sense of humor, and Angela was a whiz with anesthesia. All in all, they comprised a fabulous team.

It was just that none of them were as fun to be with as Laura.

Chapter Nine

On the following Monday Laura returned to day shift. Even though the new alarm procedures had been instituted the prior Friday, she still heard some grumbling about the changes. Over the weekend Trish had lost the piece of paper her user code had been written on, which earned her a chewing-out from Isaiah. As a result, he called a staff meeting and insisted everyone in the building show up, even the office personnel. It was the first time Laura had attended a meeting at the clinic. It felt strange to see both vets and all the employees gathered together in one room. Tucker's team huddled together in a group, and Isaiah's people collected in another. Only the kennel people worked essentially for both vets. Because Laura was the only kennel keeper working that shift, she was the only one present.

Isaiah opened the dialogue by stressing to everyone, not once but twice, that each person's security code was unique and highly confidential. "I strongly advise that all of you memorize your number," he said, "and then destroy the paper it's written on. Treat it like a PIN number for your cash card. Guard it with your life."

Laura expected that to be the end of it, but Isaiah surprised her. With a thoughtful glance in her direction, he went on to say, "Last Thursday morning, a dog was found almost dead when Susan opened the clinic. The animal nearly bled to death because a kennel gate had been left unlatched."

Everyone looked at Laura. Her cheeks burned with humiliation. The room went so quiet that she could hear the people around her breathing.

"Because Laura worked the Wednesday night shift, everyone, including Tucker and me, assumed she was responsible. We all owe her an apology."

Tucker flashed Laura a grin and touched a fingertip to his brow in a mock salute. "You've definitely got one coming from me, Laura. I'm sorry for jumping to the wrong conclusions."

Isaiah smiled slightly and then went on. "Because Laura so vehemently denied all responsibility, I decided to check the security company's alarm records to see if anyone else had entered the building on Wednesday night, and sure enough, someone had. We also discovered that it wasn't the only time last week that someone slipped into the building while Laura was working. It wasn't Laura who tripped the alarm on Monday night. We've proven that beyond a shadow of a doubt. That leads us to wonder if it was Laura who got the dog food mixed up in kennel three and four that same night. There's every possibility that our prankster switched the bowls while Laura was working in another part of the building."

James, who stood nearly a head taller than all the female techs, sent Laura a horrified look. Belinda put a hand on Laura's shoulder and said, "That's terrible. Laura could have been fired."

Tucker acknowledged the point with a nod. "Instead of focusing on that, though, we'd like to concentrate on prevention. Nothing like this can happen again." Tucker spoke for several more minutes, concluding with, "If Dusty had died, the clinic could be facing a lawsuit, which would have affected everyone's job." He winced. "Including mine. Isaiah and I are just getting our feet solidly under us. We can't afford to pay off a large settlement and keep the doors open."

"Surely you have liability insurance," Belinda said.

"We do," Isaiah inserted. "But there's a ceiling on each claim." He glanced at his brother. "Being fairly new vets, we went for the economy package with a rather large deductible. As we've all come to realize from working here, people love their pets. They're upset enough when they lose a dog or cat to unavoidable complications or an incurable illness. Just imagine the reaction if they learned that a pet was deliberately harmed by someone in our employ."

"Lawsuit time," one of Tucker's techs chimed in. "I'd sue if it was me. Wouldn't you?"

"I think most pet owners would at least consider suing," Tucker agreed. "And in the event that they did, Isaiah and I would be looking at a whole lot more than the cost of the animal. We'd probably get stuck for pain and suffering as well, not to mention wrongful death. And the cost of our liability insurance would go clear through the roof.

"And," Tucker added, "there's also our reputations to think about. Things like that make the local news. People might hesitate to bring their pets here for medical care.

As a result, our practice would suffer. No question about it: If that dog had died, it would have had a negative effect on everyone in this room. For that reason we want to take every possible precaution to protect you and ourselves until this individual is caught."

"Which is why protecting your security code is so important." Isaiah paused to look each person in the eye. "If you lose your number and it falls into the wrong person's hands, you could find yourself in a very unpleasant situation. If your code is used to enter the building and do harm to an animal, you'll look guilty, and Tucker and I won't hesitate to file charges against you."

"You're making me feel like a criminal," Trish said with a humorless laugh.

"I'm feeling that way, too," James seconded. "Most of us have worked here for a while now. Seems to me that we've earned a measure of trust."

Isaiah smiled. "You're each, in your own special way, an important member of a team, whether you work primarily with Tucker or with me, so please don't take this personally. We aren't pointing the finger at anyone. We're just giving you a stern warning so you don't lose your codes and inadvertently get blamed for something you didn't do."

Val spoke up. "It bothers me to think that someone deliberately left the gate open." She looked Laura's way. "As upsetting as it was to think that Laura might get fired, at least I knew she hadn't done it maliciously. What kind of person does? And why in God's name did such a person go to work in a veterinary clinic, where we're all supposed to love animals?"

"We don't have any answers," Tucker replied kindly. Then he added, "Yet." His voice rang with grim promise. "Eventually we hope to learn the person's identity. Perhaps then we can tell you more."

As uncomfortable as the meeting was for Laura, she could hold her head a little higher once it adjourned. She had received a public apology from both Tucker and Isaiah, and she'd been cleared of any wrongdoing. Nevertheless, there was a downside. She found herself looking into the eyes of her coworkers at unexpected times, wondering if he or she was the person who'd so cleverly framed her.

With Thanksgiving fast approaching, Laura once again found herself in charge of decorating the clinic for the holiday, which made the following two weeks seem to pass in a blur. To her great relief, nothing more happened at the clinic that was notable during that time. It was almost as if the tightened security and the revelations made by Tucker and Isaiah at the staff meeting had frightened the prankster and made him or her back off.

On the Monday prior to Thanksgiving, when Val posted the holiday work schedule in both surgeries, Laura anxiously studied it. Over the upcoming four-day weekend, only the office personnel would be exempt from having to work a few hours. Even though the clinic itself would be closed, the hospitalized animals would require care. Laura was glad to see that her holiday shift was on Friday morning, which gave her the remainder of the long weekend off. She would be able to spend Thanksgiving Day at the Coulters', as planned.

When Laura wasn't working during Thanksgiving week, she spent her time dressing up her apartment with season-appropriate colors and baking all kinds of goodies. She made cookies and tarts to take to the clinic. She baked pumpkin and apple pies, storing them in the freezer until she could cart them over to the Coulters' for Thanksgiving dinner.

Before she knew it, Thanksgiving eve

arrived. She'd just put in the oven a casserole of baked beans, which she'd prepared as a side dish for the holiday meal the next day, and was rummaging through her closet, searching frantically for something to wear, when her phone rang. Groaning, she threw herself across the bed to grab the portable.

"Hello?"

"Hi, Laura. This is James."

Laura smiled and rolled onto her back. She liked James Masterson. Though he was a tech and worked primarily with Isaiah, he often visited the kennels to care for the dogs. He always came bearing treats and spent a few minutes with each canine. There was a gentle air about him that Laura considered to be rare in a young man.

"James! Hello. To what do I owe this honor?"

"I, um, I . . . I just —" He broke off and gulped audibly.

Normally it was Laura who did the stammering. Her smile faded, giving way to concern. "Are you all right?"

"Fine, I'm fine." He swallowed again, the sound a hollow *plunk* over the line. "Look, I know I'm calling at the last minute and you p-probably have plans, but I was, um, just wondering what you're doing tomorrow. My folks are in Reno. I thought we might get together and, well, you know, just hang out."

Laura's heart caught. It had been a very long time since she'd heard a young man stammer with nervousness as he asked her out. *James?* She guessed him to be in his very early twenties, which was way too young for her. Still, it was flattering to know that he had a crush on her.

Not wishing to hurt his feelings, she searched her mind for the right thing to say. "Oh, James, I would have loved to hang out with you, but I've already made plans."

"Ah."

She sat up and pushed her hair from her eyes. "I'm sorry. I'm going with my grand-mother to a friend's house for dinner." Laura thought it best not to mention that the friend was their boss's mother. "This is the first big holi-day since my parents moved away. I'm the only fam-ily Gram has left in town, and I really should spend the day with her."

"Oh." He sounded deflated. "Well, sure, you'll be spending the day with her then. I totally understand. It was just a thought. You know — me facing the day alone. I thought maybe you were in a similar fix and might want company."

Laura wished with all her heart that she could invite James to the Coulters' for dinner, but that wasn't her place. "I'm sorry. No one should be alone on Thanks-giving."

"Ah, well. I'll rent some flicks and have a few beers. Well . . ." His voice trailed away.

Laura quickly said, "Thank you so much for thinking of me, James. It was sweet of you. If I didn't have plans, I'd love to say yes."

"Oh, well, sure. Of course I thought of you. We work together and all."

Laura frowned as she hung up the phone. It bothered her to think that James would be alone on Thanksgiving. She went to the kitchen to fish her cell phone from her purse. Punching the keys to bring the symbols up in the window, she scrolled down until she saw the balloon, which her grandmother had programmed for Isaiah the same morning that she'd assigned the cake to the clinic. Laura had never bothered her boss at home before, but she felt this was important.

"Hello?" His voice came over the line, deep and silky.

"Hi, Isaiah, this is Laura."

"Laura! I was just going to call you."

"You were?"

"Yeah, to confirm for tomorrow. You still planning to go?"

Laura leaned her hips against the cupboards. "I am. That's sort of why I phoned. James just called to see if I'd like to hang out with him tomorrow."

Silence. Then, his voice suddenly taut, Isaiah said, "Is that so?"

His change of tone took Laura by surprise. "Yes. His parents went to Reno, and he'll be alone. I feel bad about it."

"I didn't know you and James were that thick."

"We're just friends. Of all the techs I see him the most. When he visits the kennels he always stays for a bit."

"He does, does he?"

Laura raised her eyebrows. "You sound upset. Am I missing something?"

He hesitated, then said, "Thursday night when I met with Tucker, we discussed the possibility that the person who set you up might be a man who fancies himself in love with you — someone you've inadvertently ignored or offended."

Knees suddenly weak, Laura walked to the table and sank onto a chair. *James?*

"He is a man, and he obviously has a thing for you."

"I think of him more as a kid."

"My point exactly. Being treated like a kid can piss a guy off. Hurts his ego. You understand?"

Laura understood perfectly. It was just that she'd never picked up on any anger in James.

"Normally a man doesn't ask a woman to spend Thanksgiving Day with him unless he has the hots for her," he added.

Laura recalled how James had stammered when he phoned, giving her the impression that he had a crush on her. "I've always been nice to James. If he has a thing for me, as you say, I've given him no reason to be mad at me."

"Maybe you just haven't been nice enough to suit him," Isaiah countered. "Whoever did this has some screw loose, honey. And that's not always something you can tell just by talking to a guy. What you may perceive as being nothing more than a friendly-coworker kind of thing could be the romance of the century to him. At some point maybe he was talking to you, and you got distracted. Or walked away because you had work to do. You just can't know what might set a fruitcake off."

James, a fruitcake? Laura felt sick. Someone was out to get her. That was an undeniable fact. But, oh, God, she didn't want it to be James. When she thought about it, though, she couldn't think of anyone at the clinic she did want it to be.

"Oh, Isaiah," she whispered shakily. "And here I was, calling to ask if he could be in-vited to the dinner."

He sighed, and then she heard the sound of his footsteps, Western boots walking on tile. "We can invite him, I guess. His having a thing for you doesn't necessarily mean he's guilty of anything. It only means he bears watching."

"I just hate for him to eat dinner alone."

"I'll give him a ring and invite him to join us." The sound of running water came over the line. "The more the merrier."

"Will your mother mind?"

He chuckled dryly. "The house will be so packed she probably won't notice. Coulter holiday dinners all begin with the chaotic placement of chairs."

Laura forgot her worries about James and smiled into the phone. "Chairs?" she repeated.

"Oh, yes. Eating until we're stuffed is only one of the many highlights. Chairs are the first order of business. I'm one of six kids, remember, and Tucker and I are the only ones who haven't gotten married and started multiplying. Bethany and her husband, Ryan, have two kids. Jake and his wife, Molly, have one and another on the way. Then there's Hank, Carly, and their baby. Zeke, Natalie, and their two kids make four more, and Mom absolutely has to invite the entire Westfield clan."

"Who are they?"

"Zeke's wife's family. Then, at Mom's insistence, Tucker will bring a date. Your grandmother and some guy named Frank will be there. You and I make another couple. And, knowing my mom, she invited the Kendricks, all their shirttail relatives, and half the hands from Zeke and Hank's ranch, the Lazy J." He paused, muttering numbers under his breath as he tried to take a head count. "How many does that make?"

"You're asking *me?*"

He laughed again. "Get out your beans, lady."

"I think that's more than twenty," she pointed out. "You're on your own."

"Damn. I forgot to count my folks. Picture sardines squirming in a can. My parents' house isn't that large. I always wonder how my mom pulls it off, but somehow she always does. They rent folding tables and chairs, and she gets those white plastic tablecloths that look like linen. We don't put the tables up until it's time to eat. Until then we just line the living room with two rows of chairs. First thing when we arrive, we all go to work. That way everyone can find a place to sit. It's always mass confusion, with everybody talking at once, and kids darting through the maze, narrowly avoiding injury from a chair leg to the head."

It sounded like fun to Laura, who had always enjoyed her own family gatherings. Only the thought of facing such a large number of strangers made her palms go sweaty. "What should I wear?"

"Clothes."

She snorted and then blushed at the noise she'd made. "You know what I mean. Do they dress up?"

"You'll see a little of everything, jeans, slacks, dresses. Don't worry about it."

"I want to fit in."

"You'll look great no matter what. Honestly, it's not a worry."

Laura had just been looking through her closet for something suitable to wear. Now she wished she'd gone shopping for a new outfit — or possibly whipped one up on her sewing machine.

A silence fell over the line — the kind of silence that occurs when two people find themselves on the phone with nothing more to say.

"Well." He cleared his throat. "I'll phone James and give him an invite."

Laura nodded, then realized he couldn't see her. "If you're sure it'll be all right with your mother, that will be nice. At least he'll have somewhere to go."

"I'll be there about noon. If you can make it that early, great. If not, the actual meal will begin around three thirty."

Laura didn't want to arrive right before dinner was served. It seemed rude not to socialize or offer to help in the kitchen. "Noon works."

"Great. I'll see you there, then." Another silence. Then, "Sleep tight. Don't let the bedbugs bite."

When the conversation ended, Laura returned to her bedroom to resume the search of her closet. She'd just unearthed three winter dresses and was trying to choose among them when her phone rang again.

She grabbed the portable from where she'd tossed it onto the bed. "Hello?"

"Hi, Laura. Isaiah again. I just called James. He refused the invitation."

"He did?"

"Flat." He cleared his throat. "I got the

impression he was none too happy to know that you'll be spending the day with me."

"It's not like that, though."

"You know that, and I know that, but James doesn't. The guy definitely bears watching. I'll give Tucker a heads-up. James could be our man."

Laura didn't want to believe that. James didn't strike her as the type to harm an animal. He seemed to truly love the dogs and was always so kind to them. Granted, he usually chatted with her when he visited the kennels. It was possible that he'd been carrying a torch for her since she'd first started at the clinic. But if she had ever made him angry, he'd never given her any indication of it.

"Watch yourself with him. Okay? Just to be on the safe side," Isaiah said. "If James ever shows up at the clinic when you're there alone, you call me immediately. All right?"

Laura assured Isaiah that she would. After they hung up, she sat on the edge of her bed, staring blankly at the floor. Maybe she was just a phenomenally poor judge of character, but all her instincts told her that James was innocent.

Bent at the waist, one leg extended behind him, Isaiah stood at the kitchen sink, his arms braced on the edge of the basin. He stared thoughtfully out the window into the night, illuminated only by stars and a first quarter moon. *It's not like that,* Laura had insisted when he'd told her that James had sounded miffed about their spending the day together. Intellectually, Isaiah was in complete agreement. It wasn't like that between them — couldn't be like that. He needed a couple more years to build his practice before he got locked down with one woman. A serious relationship? No way. And with a lady like Laura, a serious relationship was the only option.

Then why was he anticipating tomorrow like a green kid looking forward to his first date? And why in the hell had he encouraged her to come so early? *Duh.* A couple of checkers games would take about an hour. What the hell would they do the rest of the time?

He needed to get his head screwed on straight about her. On the one hand, as pretty and sweet as she was, he was totally not interested. But somehow, when the uninterested part of him wasn't on guard, another part of him seemed to be working at cross purposes, asking her to show up early at a family dinner. Not a good thing. If he wasn't careful, he might give her the wrong idea.

Laura was a dear heart. He didn't want to unintentionally give her hope where there was none and end up hurting her.

At ten minutes after twelve the next day, Isaiah, who'd been setting up chairs with one ear cocked toward the front door, heard the bell chime. He had to elbow his way through a throng of chair-bearing relatives to reach the entryway. Then, when he got the door open, all he could do was stare. A gray wool coat folded over one arm, Laura stood on the porch. She wore a dark burgundy dress with a V-neck and long sleeves. Made of soft wool knit, the dress was fitted at the waist, then flared into graceful folds that hung to midshin, revealing a pair of shiny black dress boots that emphasized her slender ankles and shapely calves. *Wow.*

"Hi." She flashed one of those dazzling smiles that showed her dimples. "I hope I'm not too early. You did say noon."

All Isaiah could do was shake his head. *Beautiful.* She was so damned beautiful. It was enough to make a man's tongue stick to the roof of his mouth. He stepped back to let her enter. When she crossed the threshold into the dimmer light, he still couldn't take his eyes off her. She put him in mind of a glass of wine shot through with candlelight, a locket at her throat glinting gold against her pearly skin. Three of his brothers had married gorgeous women, but in Isaiah's opinion Laura had them all beat hands down.

Watch your step, bucko, a little voice whispered in his mind. Otherwise he was going to fall in love with this lady — completely, head-over-heels, irrevocably in love. "You're right on time," he finally managed to say.

She was staring, wide-eyed, at all the people in the living room. Isaiah followed her gaze and almost winced. His family was okay in small doses, but when everyone got together, it was pretty overwhelming. Hank's kid, now eight months old, was squalling, and Hank was doing the baby-on-the-shoulder two-step while his wife, Carly, a cute little blonde, hovered anxiously at his elbow. Zeke was moving through the room with four folded chairs held high over his dark head to avoid smacking anyone. His wife, Natalie, was belting out "Forever and for Always," their favorite song, as she arranged the chairs in a tidy row. Jake, the oldest brother, had an arm around his pregnant wife, Molly, and was trying, not very successfully, to execute a waltz step without stepping on anyone's toes. Their son, Garrett, who would turn three in February, and Bethany's son, Sly, who would turn four in April, were taking turns beaning each other with a foam hammer, which they seemed to think was grand fun, judging by their giggles and shrieks. To add to the confusion, Gramps, Natalie's crotchety eighty-five-year-old grandfather, who was deaf as a post, was hunched over her two kids, Chad and Rosie, who sat on the floor in front of the television. He kept yelling, "PlayStation, did you say? Well, I'll be!" Or, "Would you just look at that!" Or, "What'll they come up with next?"

"Sorry," Isaiah said. "My family's a little much." Lifting his voice to a yell, he said, "Hey, everybody! This is Laura. Mind your manners and introduce yourselves!"

Jake whirled his wife to a stop and drew her snugly against him, his big hand resting possessively and with teasing familiarity on her well-rounded hip. Molly, her amber hair a halo of short curls around her face, giggled, moved his hand back up to her waist, and playfully slugged his shoulder.

"Hi, Laura, and welcome!" she called. "I'm Molly. This big galoot is Jake, Isaiah's oldest brother."

Hank shifted little Hank on his shoulder and peered at Laura over his son's diapered behind. "I'm Hank, second youngest."

Carly squinted her big blue eyes to see. "Hi, Laura. Carly, here. I'm Hank's wife. I can't see very well at a distance yet. I had eye surgery a while back, and my focus is —"

"Terrible," Hank inserted, cutting Carly short. "What's she's trying to say is, don't take offense if she sees you later and introduces herself all over again."

Carly laughed and made kissing sounds at the wailing baby. "This is little Hank. He's presently trying to break Nana's crystal with a high note."

Ryan Kendrick, also carrying in chairs, deposited a load against one wall, smoothed a big hand over his black hair where it had kicked up in the wind while he was outdoors, and smiled in their direction. "Hi, Laura. I'm Ryan, Bethany's husband." He glanced around, obviously in search of his wife. "She's buzzing around here somewhere."

"Right here!" Bethany spun through the archway from the kitchen in her wheelchair. "Hi, Laura. You're just in time. Mom is trying to stir four pots at once, and I can't reach the stove to help."

Laura glanced down at her coat, then back up at Isaiah. "I've got food to bring in. On the backseat of my car." She thrust the coat at him. "Would you mind getting it for me?"

And just like that, Isaiah lost her.

When he entered the kitchen a few minutes later, carrying a cookie sheet laden with two pies, he found Laura at the stove, her pretty wine-colored dress already covered by one of his mother's embroidered white bib aprons. She was stirring stuff, adjusting burner temps, and laughing at something his mother had just said.

"Oh, Laura, you shouldn't have," Mary cried when she saw the pies. "My goodness, how lovely." With a sly smile at Isaiah, she said, "Imagine it, a modern-day young woman who can actually bake. Will marvels never cease?" She directed her attention to the desserts again. "My pumpkin got just a little too brown this year. Yours is perfect, Laura."

The smell of the roasting turkey and ham made Isaiah's stomach growl. He set down the tray and reached for one of the canapés arranged on a platter, earning himself a slap on the wrist from his mother.

"Stay out of those!" Mary scolded.

"But I'm hungry."

Mary rolled her eyes, poked one little canapé in his mouth, and then moved the others around to fill in the vacant spot. "Fix a sandwich. These are for company."

"What am I, chopped liver?"

It was an exchange that Mary had had with all her sons at every holiday gathering since their childhood. "Out of here," she grumped. "Or else I'll put you to work."

Normally Isaiah ran when that challenge was issued, but today he was tempted to stay. He glanced at Laura's slender backside. "What can I do?"

Mary raised her eyebrows. She, too, looked at Laura. Then she gave him another sly smile. "You can grate orange peel for the cranberry sauce if you like."

Isaiah liked. Afterward he helped Laura chop up fruit for something called ambrosia. Then he trimmed the smoked turkey, which his folks had picked up at the meat market completely prepared and would serve warm from the microwave. After that he poured oil into the kettle outside on the deck and lighted the propane flame beneath it for the deep-fried turkey, a dish that had been added to the Coulter Thanksgiving menu a couple of years before.

"Three turkeys?" Laura said in amazement.

Isaiah laughed. "We have a lot of people to feed. You ever tried fried turkey?"

"No."

"Delicious," he'd said, kissing his fingertips. "So moist and flavorful you can't believe your taste buds. It's also a fairly quick process, compared to baking a turkey the old-fashioned way."

Cooking wasn't usually his thing, but as always when he was with Laura, he enjoyed himself. There was also the added benefit that he could sneak bites of food without getting caught. Every once in a while Laura would rearrange the appetizers on the trays to hide the fact that he'd been grazing.

That worked until Bethany joined them in the kitchen to nurse her seven-month-old daughter, Chastity Ann. When she saw Isaiah snitch a deviled egg from the refrigerator while their mother's back was turned, she cried in a singsong voice loud enough to wake snakes in five counties, "Mom, Isaiah's sneaking food!" The accusation was reminiscent of childhood, and she spoiled the effect by laughing. "You said we couldn't have any yet, and he's not minding!"

Mary sent Isaiah a scolding look. "If I don't have enough appetizers for my guests, I'll have your head."

"Tattletale," Isaiah said to his sister. Then to his mother, he raised his voice to a squeaky alto and complained, "Mom, make Bethie stop telling on me!"

Mary laughed and rolled her eyes. "Thank God those days are over."

Laura straightened away from the oven, her cheeks flushed from the heat, her eyes sparkling. "Did they fight a lot when they were small?" she asked.

"A lot? With six kids underfoot, the quarreling never stopped."

"Brat." Isaiah stepped across the room to tweak his sister's dark hair and then bent to kiss Chastity's sable ringlets. Crouching beside the wheelchair, he admired his niece for a moment and then whispered, "She's so beautiful, Bethany Ann." He lifted his gaze to his sister's face. "The very picture of her mama."

Bethany, modestly holding a hand towel over her breast while the baby nursed, beamed a proud grin at him. "She doesn't look that much like me. I think she has her daddy's nose."

"Bite your tongue!" Ryan entered the room. Leaning over his wife's shoulder, he studied his baby girl and then said in a dictatorial tone, "No daughter of mine will have the Kendrick schnozzle."

"I love your nose," Bethany protested.

"Yeah, well," Ryan replied, "I'm not a girl."

"A fact for which I'm very grateful," Bethany quipped.

The doorbell rang just then, and the rest of the Kendrick family entered. Ryan left to greet his parents, Keefe and Ann Kendrick, and then his older brother, Rafe, a tall, lean man with jet-black hair and dark skin who might have been his double. Rafe's wife, Maggie, a petite and very attractive brunette, stood at her husband's side. Flanking the couple were their children, Jaimie, who'd turned seven in September, and Amelia, who'd turned five only a couple of weeks ago.

As Isaiah pointed people out to Laura, she interrupted to say, "You know how old each person is?"

He thought about it and laughed. "You know all those birthday presents I'm always shopping for? Now you know why. Seldom a week goes by that there isn't a party."

The living room was now filled to bursting. Etta Parks, Laura's grandmother, arrived on the arm of a dapper, elderly gentleman she introduced as Frank. Isaiah decided that his mother was certifiably insane to have invited so many people. He led Laura through the throng to a chair.

"You're one of the guests," he insisted. "You've done enough in the kitchen. Stay out here and get to know everybody."

Laura's eyes widened as she scanned the crowd. "Oh, I don't think —"

Before Laura could complete the protest, Jake's wife, Molly, sat down beside her. "So you're the fabulous kennel keeper I keep hearing about."

"Oh, well." Laura blushed. "You've heard about me?"

Molly laughed and motioned for Maggie and Natalie to join them. By the time Isaiah walked away to offer his mother more help in the kitchen, Laura was deeply engaged in conversation.

The dinner was fabulous. The living room had been emptied the prior day of all regular furniture, and when all the meat was done to a turn, the men set up ten six-foot tables, end to end, to accommodate the diners. The moment the tables were out the women went to work, spreading tablecloths and arranging place settings. Nothing matched. Every set of dishes Mary Coulter owned was called into service, including Grandma McBride's wedding china, plus two forty-piece sets of dishes belonging to Ann Kendrick. Some people got clear plastic wine goblets instead of genuine crystal. There wasn't quite enough flatware, so everyone got only one fork.

But the food was plentiful and wonderfully prepared, and everyone had fun. Jokes were told, and everyone laughed whether they were funny or not. Gossip was shared. Children spilled their milk. More than once during the meal, Isaiah glanced sideways at Laura and apologized for all the confusion.

She smiled back and said, "I love it."

Isaiah glanced around at all the faces, some as familiar to him as his own, others not. Hank and Carly's son sat in a high chair between them, forcing the couple to lean forward or back to hear whispered exchanges. Zeke and his wife, Natalie, were glued together at the hip, still so much in love that they had eyes for no one else but their kids, who occasionally demanded their attention. Jake and Molly, who'd been married the second longest, were content to lock gazes only occasionally, the looks passing between them filled with a deep and abiding love. Because of her wheelchair, Bethany sat at the end of one table, her husband, Ryan, to her right, her son to her left. Ryan held their daughter on his knee, feeding her mashed potatoes and gravy in between bites for himself.

At each end of the center table, which accommodated all the older folks, Isaiah's parents sat in places of honor, talking in louder-than-normal voices so as not to exclude their guests. Mary Coulter looked sweet and matronly in her pretty blue dress as she chatted gaily with Laura's grandmother, who sat to her right, and Ann Kendrick, to her left. At the opposite end, Harv was an older version of his sons, a lean but well-muscled man with dark skin, his graying sable hair now gone completely silver at the temples. He carried on a lively debate with Natalie's father, Pete, and Keefe Kendrick while he ate, only occasionally pausing to repeat himself when Gramps, Natalie's grandfather, cupped a hand behind his ear and bellowed, "What's that you say?"

Family. This was what it was all about, Isaiah thought, feeling suddenly nostalgic.

312

The kids grew up, fell in love, got married, and had kids of their own, until pretty soon one good-sized living room could barely hold them all. Before long, when he and Tucker got married, they'd have to rent a hall to celebrate the holidays. But that would be fine. It wasn't about the surroundings, be they fine or makeshift. It was about being together. It was about spilled milk, deaf grandparents, sibling rivalry, and the trials of everyday life, which were overcome or overlooked because, beneath it all, love made the little irritations seem like blessings.

More than once Isaiah caught Laura gazing at the babies and young children with a wistful smile curving her lips. When Isaiah followed her gaze, he wanted to feel smug and self-satisfied. There were no soiled diapers for him to change. He'd let his brothers have that pleasure. But instead he felt oddly sad, too.

It was just the occasion, he assured himself. Over a holiday, all the festivities and family gatherings could make anyone feel a little sentimental. Only Isaiah knew it wasn't just that. Watching his married brothers, seeing the love and pride in their expressions when they looked at their wives and kids forced him to admit, if only to himself, that he was growing weary of being single. As soon as his practice was rock solid, he needed to start thinking seriously about settling down.

Tonight, when the party ended, Jake, Zeke, and Hank wouldn't leave alone, and when they got home they wouldn't wander by themselves through oversize, unfurnished rooms that echoed like tombs. Instead they would each leave with a sleeping child in their arms, taking a measure of the noise and laughter and confusion home with them.

Isaiah glanced thoughtfully at Laura, and the feeling that had grabbed him by the throat when she'd first arrived came over him again. He tried to push it away, and failing that, tried his damnedest to ignore it. But he couldn't drag his gaze from her lovely profile. *Sweet.* The word circled in his mind whenever he looked at her. He loved the way she laughed, the sound light, musical, and unaffected. Over time he'd even come to appreciate the way she talked — always so slowly, every word carefully chosen. The cadence of her speech soothed him, perhaps because it forced him to slow down himself.

Keefe Kendrick pushed to his feet and rapped his crystal wineglass with the edge of his dinner knife. "Before this wonderful meal is over, I'd like to express my thanks to Mary and Harv for so kindly opening their home to all of us." He glanced around the room. "Quite a crowd. Putting a meal on the table for so many isn't an easy feat." He smiled and inclined his head toward Mary. "A fabulous meal, Mary. Not even my Annie could do better, and she's one of the best cooks this side of the Divide."

Ann Kendrick blushed and pooh-poohed the compliment with a moue of her lips and a flap of her wrist. "You're buttering me up for something."

Keefe grinned and winked at her. Then he turned toward his host. "Unfortunately, a woman can't show off her culinary skills to so many without making a serious dent in her husband's pocketbook, so some of the thanks must go to the ornery old cuss that Mary's hooked up with. Thank you, Harv. And now, I gotta know. Where in hell did you get the idea to deep-fry a turkey?"

"Infomercials," Gramps informed him. "Don't you ever watch televison?"

Everyone laughed and echoed Keefe's sentiments about the meal. When the talk died down a bit, Harv said, "Enough of this

315

sappy stuff. Mary, it's time for dessert!"

Groans erupted from every table, but they were followed by laughter and loudly stated preferences. "Pumpkin pie for me!" "You can have the pumpkin. I want a piece of that pecan." "Ice cream on mine, please!"

After the meal, Laura and Isaiah's mother were banned from the kitchen because they'd both worked so hard to prepare the meal. Tucker's date, a long, tall drink of water named Grace who'd come to dinner in skintight Wrangler jeans and a fringed Western shirt, insisted on helping with the cleanup. While Ryan watched the baby, Bethany cleared the tables, zipping her wheelchair tirelessly back and forth from the table to the kitchen with soiled plates and flatware piled on her towel-draped lap. Isaiah's father and two of his brothers, Tucker and Jake, rolled up their shirtsleeves to do their part.

"Get out of here," Isaiah was told by his father when he tried to enter the kitchen. "You helped cook."

Isaiah hadn't done that much, but he accepted the edict gratefully and invited Laura to go for a walk. After helping her on with her coat and donning his jacket, he led her out into the deepening twilight.

"Ah, the quiet," he said appreciatively when they gained the front porch. He didn't actually mind the noise, but to someone who wasn't used to it, it seemed a polite thing to say.

She shivered and turned up her coat collar. Along both sides of the street, houses with lighted windows created a golden, cheery backdrop for the gnarly, denuded oaks that grew along the grass median.

"I like all the noise," she retorted with a laugh. "With so many people, you never get bored."

"True, but so many talking at once makes my ears tired after a while."

As they traversed the cement walkway that ran from the front porch to the sidewalk, she tipped her face up to the leaden sky, the gray of which was quickly darkening to charcoal. "I think winter is here."

"Afraid so." Isaiah zipped his jacket. In the crisp twilight, their footsteps sounded sharply on the frozen cement, her boots tapping out a feminine, slightly faster rhythm than his. Man and woman. He could smell her perfume, a light, sunshiny scent that suited her. Whenever he ventured a look at her, he couldn't keep his gaze from straying to the graceful curve of her jaw and the ivory smoothness of her throat above her coat collar. "Won't be long before the snow starts to fly."

Thinking of the trials of driving in the wintertime, Isaiah was surprised when she smiled dreamily. "I just *love* the snow. Don't you?"

As they turned left onto the sidewalk, he shortened his stride and fell into step beside her. "Oh, yeah," he said with an edge of sarcasm. "Snow is great. There's nothing to beat scraping the windshield at five in the morning — or discovering, always when I'm running late, of course, that the car doors are frozen shut. Slipping on the steps is a real blast, too. I just *love* it."

She wrinkled her nose. "Don't be an old fuddy-duddy. What about all the good stuff?"

The irritated look she sent his way brought a smile to his mouth. "Such as?"

"Such as sitting by a window with a cup of hot soup and watching the snowflakes drift down."

"There is that," he conceded.

"And making a pile of snowballs for a snowball fight."

He grinned. "You like snowball fights?"

"Doesn't every-one?"

No, not everyone, he thought. In fact, he

couldn't remember the last time he'd been with a woman who would countenance any part of that activity. Wet hair, snow down the neck, taking one in the face. Most females over eighteen shuddered at the thought.

"And making snow angels!" she tacked on. "We can't forget that."

Isaiah could imagine her lying in the snow on her back, blissfully enjoying herself as she flapped her arms and moved her legs back and forth to create an angel impression.

"Sliding down hills on plastic garbage bags is fun, too," she said.

Isaiah couldn't remember the last time that he'd careened down a snowy slope. "Don't leave out making snow ice cream," he inserted. "When I was a kid we could barely wait for the first snowfall. My folks always made us wait for a bit and collect only the top layer of snow to make sure it wasn't impure."

"Mine did that, too." She rolled her eyes. "Like snow is ever really clean. If I had kids, I wouldn't make them wait."

"Ah, come on. The anticipation was half the fun." Isaiah remembered standing with his brothers and sister at the living room window, their noses pressed to the glass. "I wonder if snow ice cream would taste good now."

"Of *course.*" She sent him a scandalized look. "Snow ice cream is *wonder-ful.* Don't you ever make it now?"

Isaiah chuckled. "Can I take that to mean that you do?"

Delicate knuckles pink from the cold, she clutched the front of her coat at the collar. "If it was fun when I was a kid, it's still fun now. Why do people think they have to stop doing all the good stuff when they grow up?"

That was a very good question and, without a doubt, one of the reasons he so enjoyed Laura's company. She reminded him not to take life quite so seriously all the time. "It's hard for me to find the time for that kind of thing anymore."

"Make time." Her eyes sparkled like chips of clear amber when she glanced up at him. "Once a day, ever-y single day, we should take the time to be kids again. If we don't, why bother? What's life all about if it isn't any fun?"

"You're right," he said softly. "I know you're right. It's just hard to remember that there's more to life than work."

She lifted her shoulders and sighed, her breath coming from her rosy lips in a steamy puff. "Make yourself a sign," she suggested. "Hang it on your rearview mirror." She grinned up at him. "Something simple like, 'Have Fun Once a Day.'"

Isaiah was more inclined to enjoy this moment while it lasted. It was only a simple walk on a winter evening, but somehow being with Laura made it seem special. "When it snows, I bet I can build a better snowman than you," he challenged.

"Nuh-uh. I make the best snowmen ever."

"You've never seen mine."

"You're on," she agreed with a laugh. "What are we betting?"

Still gazing at her face, Isaiah almost proposed that the winner should get a kiss from the loser. Then he'd be a winner either way. Instead he said, "The loser has to cook the other person a full-course dinner."

She nodded. "All right." Then she frowned slightly. "I didn't know you could cook."

"Can't." He flashed a satisfied grin. "So if you're smart, you'd better let me win."

She rewarded him with a startled laugh. "No fair."

"You already agreed," he retorted. "No reneging now."

When they returned to the house, old and young alike had gathered in groups at the tables to play games. Ann and Keefe Kendrick were partners against Isaiah's parents in a game of pinochle. Tucker and Grace, Hank and Carly, and Zeke and Natalie were playing a boisterous card game called Spoons. At another table, canasta was in full swing, with Bethany and Ryan playing against Natalie's parents, Pete and Naomi. Natalie's grandfather sat cross-legged on the floor before the big-screen television, totally absorbed in a PlayStation baseball game.

Isaiah picked his way around babies asleep on the floor in blanket-lined carriers to find two free chairs where he and Laura might play checkers. They ended up sharing a table with Jake and Molly, who were playing Go Fish with all the kids at the opposite end. Confident in his ability, Isaiah wasn't concerned about the distractions that chortling, arguing children might present.

Thirty minutes later Laura had a king, and Isaiah was in serious danger of getting his ass kicked. Lower lip caught between her teeth, she gave him an innocent look. "Sorry. I told you I was good."

"You did not. You said you liked

checkers. There's a difference."

To make Isaiah's defeat worse, his family gathered around to watch Laura trounce him. "Go, Laura," Zeke cheered. "He's been kicking butt at checkers for years. It's about time he got whipped."

Isaiah slanted his brother a murderous look. "Do you mind? You're interfering with my concentration."

Tucker leaned over Laura's shoulder to peruse the board. "Concentration won't save you, bro. She's got you cornered nine ways to hell."

Isaiah fought to the end. When Laura gingerly removed his last piece from the board, he gave her a long, searching look and said, "Best of three."

She glanced at her watch.

"Don't *even* think of pleading that it's getting late," Isaiah warned. "My championship is on the line."

"I'm putting ten on Laura," Hank said loudly.

"Ho!" Harv Coulter fished in his hip pocket for his wallet. "I'll take that bet. She just got lucky. Nobody beats Isaiah at checkers."

Ann Kendrick nudged her big, broad-shouldered husband in the ribs. Keefe bent his dark head to hear what she said. Moments later he was opening his wallet. Ann held up a twenty-dollar bill. "My money is on the lady. We gals have to stick together."

Bethany grinned. "I'm with you, Mamatoo." She held out a hand to her husband, Ryan. "Money, honey. I want to place a bet on Laura."

"Me, too!" Etta Parks cried. "Ten dollars on my granddaughter."

"I can't believe this," Isaiah complained. "So far there's only one bet on me." He looked at Tucker. "You gonna be a turncoat, too?"

The next checkers game was the center of attention. Some people stood to have a better view of the board. Others made themselves comfortable on chairs. Isaiah and Laura, who'd begun the first game laughing, faced off during the second play-off, solemn and grimly intent on every move.

By the time the game ended, Isaiah was vowing to brush up on his snowman-building skills. Otherwise he might find himself cooking a seven-course meal for his opponent.

He gave her a calculating look. Never more than in that moment had he appreciated the gleam of intelligence that he saw in her hazel eyes.

"Do you play chess?" he asked.

She dimpled a cheek at him, jumped his last piece, and said, "Not often. I'm not very good."

Isaiah had an image to preserve. "Want to make the third game a little more challenging?" he asked. "The winner is the undisputed champion."

She shrugged and nodded her assent. Isaiah ran to get the chess set.

That proved to be a mistake. An hour and a half later, when Laura said, "Checkmate," he stared incredulously at the board, muttering, "No *way*. I thought you said you weren't very good."

She grinned mischievously and leaned across the board to whisper, "I lied."

Chapter Ten

The morning after Thanksgiving, Laura arrived at the clinic ten minutes before six. After entering the building, she locked back up and disabled the alarm. Then, just as she started to reset the system, a knock came at the door. She jumped with a start, began to answer the summons, and then thought better of it. Hands shaking, she entered her personal code and quickly rearmed the system. Only then did she approach the back door.

"Who is it?" she called.

"It's me, James. Can you let me in for a second?"

Laura's heart caught. Isaiah had asked her to call him if James ever came around when she was working a shift alone. She groped in her purse for her cell phone.

"I just need to talk to you for a minute," he urged.

Caught in indecision, Laura stared at her phone. *James.* Despite Isaiah's warnings, she found it difficult to believe that the young tech had had anything to do with the trouble at the clinic. James might have a crush on her. Laura wouldn't argue the point. But that didn't necessarily mean he was guilty of anything else. In fact, all her instincts told her just the opposite.

With a sigh, she dropped the cell phone back into her purse. "Just a second, James. I need to disarm the system."

She stepped over to the console, turned off the alarm, then returned to the door and disengaged the locks. When the portal swung open, James hurried inside. He wore a bulky blue parka. His curly brown hair was mussed by the brisk morning wind.

"Hi," he said, flashing a sheepish grin as he pushed the door closed. "You must be wondering what the heck I'm doing here."

Laura had been wondering exactly that. The sun wasn't even up yet, and it was his day off. Most people wanted to take advantage of that and sleep in. She was probably out of her mind to let him inside the building, but when she searched his eyes, she saw nothing sinister.

"It is pretty early," she settled for saying.

He turned and locked the door. "Yeah, well." He folded his arms as he turned back toward her. "Early's good, actually. I'd just as soon nobody else knows about me stopping by."

For just an instant Laura felt uneasy. But before the feeling could take a firm hold, James said, "About the other night and my asking you to spend Thanksgiving with me. When Isaiah called me right afterward, I about had a heart attack."

"You did? Why?"

He sighed and raked a hand through his hair, his motions agitated. "There's a rule here that employees aren't supposed to date. I thought he was going to fire me."

"Oh, *no,*" Laura whispered with genuine dismay.

"Oh, yeah." James nodded and scratched his chin. "You're a very pretty lady, Laura, and there's no denying the chemistry between us. I've felt it, anyway. But no way can I put my job on the line. I hope you understand."

Laura had no idea what to say.

"I really love this job," he hurried to add. "Isaiah's been totally cool about letting me study on the side to get my tech credentials. Last year he even gave me time off and paid for me to get my X-ray certification. At my last review we talked about my going to college next year, maybe to become a full-fledged assistant like Belinda. He's willing to keep my position open while I'm away at school and kick in on my tuition. That'd be a really sweet deal for me."

"Yes, it would," Laura agreed, not at all surprised to hear of Isaiah's generosity.

"So you can totally understand why this thing between us has to stop before we get in too deep."

"Oh, *yes.*"

He looked deeply into her eyes. "I think it could be really special between us, Laura, I honestly do. But who can say for certain? My future here at the clinic is a pretty sure thing. All I have to do is keep my nose clean."

It was all Laura could do not to smile. "Then that is what you must do, James."

He gave her another soulful look. "I wish it could be different. A few people here have dated on the side, and nobody ever found out."

"They were lucky," Laura was quick to say. "No, James. The risk is too great for you. Your whole future is on the line." She swallowed hard. "Some things aren't meant to be."

"Totally. It's just —" He broke off and gave her another melancholy look. "If only. You know?"

Laura put a hand on his jacket sleeve. "We can be friends. There's no rule against that, is there?"

The tension eased from his shoulders and he grinned. "Nope. Friendship is okay."

Returning his smile, Laura said, "Friendship it will be, then."

He sighed and rubbed a hand over his face. Then his gaze sharpened on hers. "Isaiah doesn't suspect, does he? He sounded sort of weird when he called me."

"No," she assured him. "Isaiah has no idea. It's our secret."

"Thank God. When he called I broke out in a cold sweat. I just knew he'd found us out. He was nice and everything. But I could have sworn I heard a hint of suspicion in his voice."

Laura shook her head. "I don't think so. Isaiah has a lot on his mind at times. Maybe that was it."

"I hope so." He puffed out his cheeks with an expelled breath. "We're agreed, then. From here on out we'll be friends and nothing more."

"Friends and nothing more." With a glance at her watch, Laura reached to unlock the door. "Out of here. It's almost six. The alarm sends a signal each time a code is entered. I don't want the record to show that I started work late. There would be questions. This way I can say I forgot something in my car to explain why I disarmed the system."

"Oh!" He swung around to leave. Once the door was open, he glanced back. "Thanks for understanding, Laura."

"No problem. I'm just glad you came by to talk with me."

"It only seemed fair. My decision affects you as much as it does me."

Laura was still smiling a moment later when she activated the alarm. Isaiah had been correct on one count: She'd been involved in the romance of a lifetime. She simply hadn't known it.

At a little before ten, Laura nearly jumped out of her skin at the sound of footsteps on the concrete behind her. She fumbled not to drop a bowl of dog food and, whirling around, flattened her free hand at her throat, limp with relief when she saw Isaiah standing just outside the enclosure.

"Sorry," he said. "I didn't mean to startle you."

"Well, you did. What are you doing here?"

He planted his hands at his hips. This morning he wore a lined denim jacket, open at the front to reveal a red plaid shirt neatly tucked into a belted pair of faded Wranglers. His dark hair lay in silky waves over his high forehead, some of the strands so long they touched his brows. "You haven't been here alone for a while. I just wanted to stop by and check on you."

Laura couldn't help but feel touched. "I'm fine."

"No problems?"

For an instant she considered not telling him about James's early-morning visit, but honesty was always the best policy. "Not a problem, really."

Isaiah's expression became more intent. "What?"

"James dropped by to talk with me."

Isaiah's jaw muscle started to ripple. "I thought we agreed that you'd call me if he came around."

"I'm sorry." Laura could think of little to say in her own defense. Letting James into the building hadn't been the smartest decision she'd ever made. "I got out my cell phone and almost did. But I just couldn't believe he posed a threat."

"What if you'd been wrong? Damn it, Laura. If the guy is a fruitcake, he could go from pussycat to tiger in a blink. You could have been hurt, lying here for hours waiting for help to come."

"But he isn't a fruitcake. My instinct was right."

She went on to recount the conversation with James. Toward the end of her tale, Isaiah's eyes were twinkling with laughter. "He thought I called that night to fire him?"

Laura nodded. "That's what he said. I think that's why he wouldn't go to dinner at your parents' house. He felt sure you were on to us."

His firm mouth slid into a slow grin. "Well, I was right on one count. He fancies himself in love with you."

Laura bent to give the dog a farewell pat before exiting the cage. "Not anymore. To protect his future, we've agreed that we have to ignore our feelings and just be friends."

Isaiah chuckled. "A great sacrifice for both of you, I take it?"

Laura gave him an innocent look. "Of course. I think James feels bad about choosing his job over me. But, as he pointed out, we're not a sure thing, and the job is. I had to applaud his good sense. His future is at stake."

Isaiah shook his head. "You're a sweetheart. You know it? A lot of women would have told him he presumed too much and where to get off."

Laura dropped the gate latch and tugged to make sure it had caught. "Why do that? He already wanted out."

"No matter that you never even realized he was in?"

Laura shrugged and smiled. "He's a nice young man. I wouldn't want to hurt his feelings."

"Like I said, a sweetheart." He fell into step with her as she moved up the center aisle. Glancing at his watch, he said, "You're about finished here, aren't you?"

"Almost."

"How about an early lunch?"

The invitation took her by surprise. She gave him a questioning look. "Lunch?"

He flashed a crooked grin that gave her a glimmer of how devastatingly cute he must have been as a boy. "Yeah, you know." He pretended to shovel food into his mouth. "The meal most people eat midway between breakfast and dinner. You hungry?"

The bagel that Laura had eaten at five that morning had long since evaporated. "Starving."

"Well, then? There's a great little diner in Old Towne. Fabulous food, a view of the river. We can eat hot soup and watch the snowflakes drift down."

Laura's eyes widened. "It's snowing?"

"That's one of the drawbacks of working in a huge building without many windows. A blizzard could happen, and you'd never even know."

As Isaiah navigated stop-and-start traffic to reach the diner, he had to ask himself what the hell he was doing. *Lunch?* What was it about Laura that made him go brain-dead? So it was snowing. Big deal. Just because she loved the white stuff and seeing it had made him think of her was no sign that he had to sit with her by a window and eat soup for lunch.

He absolutely *had* to get a handle on the impulsive behavior that seemed to besiege him whenever he was around her. He wasn't in the market for a wife, and a wife was what he might get if he didn't damned well watch his step. A quick lunch, he promised himself. Afterward he'd drop her off at the clinic to get her car, and from that moment forward he'd stop this craziness before it got him in trouble.

"Stop!" she suddenly shrieked.

Isaiah's foot hit the brake almost before he registered the word. The Hummer's antilock brakes caught and then released as the vehicle went into a slide. *Ice.* It went hand in hand with snow. Even as he struggled to bring the heavy SUV to a safe stop, Laura was unbuckling her seat belt and fumbling to open the passenger door.

"Oh, *God!*" she cried. "He'll get run over!"

Who would get run over? Before Isaiah could verbalize the question, Laura had spilled from the vehicle. They were still in a traffic lane, and cars were coming from both directions. "Laura?" *Sweet Christ.* Isaiah's heart shot clear into his throat when she careened, slipping and sliding on the ice and slush, around the front bumper of the Hummer, the only visible part of her the top of her blond head. "Laura!"

He threw open the driver-side door, tried to leap out, and found himself anchored by the seat belt he'd forgotten to unlatch. A car skidded to a stop behind them, its front bumper getting too up close and personal with the rear end of the Hummer for Isaiah's peace of mind.

"Laura!" he yelled again when his boots finally connected with the slush-covered pavement. Through the downfall of snow-flakes, he glimpsed the shimmer of her golden hair. *Damn.* She was jogging right up the center of the street, heedless of the automobiles that braked and fishtailed to avoid hitting her. "Have you lost your mind? Get back here!"

Isaiah's shouts never even slowed her down. Leaving the driver door open, he took off after her, shouting her name every few steps. Ahead of him she'd finally stopped, her slender, denim-sheathed legs spread wide, her arms held out at her sides to stop traffic. Isaiah wore slick-soled Western boots and almost fell several times as he raced up the street. By the time he arrived at his destination, the cars going in both directions had come to a dead halt, and Laura was scooping an oversize puppy into her arms.

"What the hell are you trying to do, kill yourself?" he cried.

"Oh, Isaiah, isn't he *sweet?*"

Laura was nose-to-nose with the puppy. Before Isaiah could reply that the dog was the homeliest critter he'd ever clapped eyes on, she was making kiss-kiss noises.

"Are you *out* of your mind?" he cried again.

She gave him a wide-eyed, incredulous look. "He was about to get run over. I had to save him."

The drivers of the cars backed up in both directions, bumper to bumper, were starting to blow their horns. Isaiah grasped

Laura's arm. "We've got to get back in the Hummer. We're blocking traffic."

Laura tightened her arms around the puppy. A second look at the mutt confirmed Isaiah's first impression: It was the ugliest puppy he'd ever seen. *Oversize* didn't say it by half. The thing had paws the size of flapjacks, and its block-shaped head promised to be massive in adulthood. Worse than the puppy's incredible size, though, was its coloring. It looked as if it were part dalmatian, with rottweiler ears tossed in for good measure, and the loose skin of a shar-pei to make *homely* downright ugly. The poor thing was white with black splotches and spots, only the splotches and spots had run together, creating an overall blue effect.

"Come on." Isaiah led Laura toward the Hummer. Once there, he said, "The cars have stopped now. You can turn him loose."

Her eyes went as round as quarters. "I can't do *that!*"

Isaiah was starting to get a very bad feeling. He met her imploring gaze over the hood of the vehicle. "Why?" he asked cautiously.

"Well, *because!*"

He hated it when women said that. *Because.* What the hell did that mean? In

338

Isaiah's experience, it usually led to trouble. His mother used this tactic. So did his sister, Bethany, and all of his sisters-in-law. When they had no rational explanation for a decision, they always said, "Well, *because*," the overall implication being that no male of the species could possibly understand the intricacies of their reasoning because all men were somewhat mentally impaired.

"Laura," he said in a reasoning tone, "he probably belongs to someone."

"No, sir. He has no collar."

Oh, boy. Through the drifting snowflakes he gave the dog a long look, ignoring the fact that people were now beginning to lay on their horns. Both the animal's eyes looked as if they'd been blacked. And its ears were oddly asymmetrical, one partially black and cocked forward over its right shiner, the other gray and hanging straight.

"The absence of a collar means nothing with a puppy," he tried. "Some people don't put a collar on a dog until they're older."

"His ribs are poking out. I'm not leaving him. He was nearly killed!" She looked at Isaiah as if he'd suddenly been transformed into a monster — a heartless puppy murderer. "How can you ask me to do that?"

Oh, boy. Isaiah glanced at the cars. Those in the opposite lane were now starting to move, and the street was narrow. He would have to shut the Hummer door for them to get by. He sighed, accepting that this discussion would have to be resumed later.

"Get in the car then," he commanded. "We're blocking traffic."

"With the puppy?"

"Yes," he replied resignedly, "with the puppy."

Once all three of them were safely inside the Hummer, Isaiah drove slowly up the street. Laura crooned to the puppy, saying, "Poor hapless baby." The windshield wipers went *swish-whack, swish-whack,* pushing snow into mounds at either side of the glass.

"You can't keep him, honey."

"Of course I can't. But I can find a home for him." She made more kiss-kiss noises and brushed her cheek over the top of the puppy's head. "Isn't he darling?"

Isaiah had just been thinking that no one in his right mind would adopt the poor thing. He was the last person on earth to hold a dog's bloodlines against it, but this

340

pup had a really bad case of the uglies. Laura held him as she might a baby, on his back in the crook of her arm, putting his nether regions in full view. Definitely a male. And he was going to be a *huge* animal. Normally Isaiah could look at a mongrel and make an educated guess as to its origins, but this pup was a boiling pot with blotched fur. Part mastiff, possibly? Those ears were definitely rottweiler, though, and the loose, wrinkly skin around the head and shoulders still screamed shar-pei. Some fool hadn't kept the gate locked. Maybe several damned fools. A generous dose of dalmatian blood had surely been tossed into the mix.

"Well," he said cheerfully, "we'll just drop him off at the Humane Society before we go for lunch. How's that for an idea?"

"No!" she cried. "What if no one adopts him?"

So, Isaiah thought sagely, he wasn't the only one who thought the pup's looks were lacking. "A cutie like that? He'll get sprung from jail in a couple of days."

Laura thrust out her chin. "He isn't going to the pound."

"Pound? Sweetheart, the term is archaic." Isaiah fleetingly wondered when he had gone from calling her Laura to calling her sweetheart. Even worse, it felt really *right.* "Nowadays strays are in high cotton until they're adopted. They have bedding, just like at the clinic, and all the volunteers who absolutely *love* animals take care of them. The Humane Society even has a Web site. They have pictures and write-ups about each animal. They also advertise on the radio. He has the best chance of finding a good home there. They screen applicants very carefully."

"I think we should call him Hapless," she said. "Isn't that a cute name? It was almost the first thing I said, that he was a poor hapless baby."

Inwardly, Isaiah groaned. He'd known that drawn-out *because* would lead to trouble. "Sweet—" He caught himself and backtracked. "Laura," he said with exaggerated patience, "let's really *think,* okay?" When he glanced over at her, the sharp gleam of intelligence in her eyes had been replaced by bewildered confusion. She clearly wasn't in the mood to be rational. "Where will you keep him until you can find him a home?"

She just kept looking at him. At *him.* Isaiah returned his gaze to the road, saw that the light had turned red, and slammed on the brakes so hard that the puppy almost catapulted from Laura's arms into the dash. "Jesus Christ."

"*That* is uncalled for," she said heatedly. "Just because you're miffed is no excuse to take the Lord's name in vain."

"I'm sorry." When had she turned into his mother? "It's just . . ." It was just what? That he'd almost killed all of them, including the self-satisfied-looking Hapless, by running a red light? "I can't keep a dog, if that's what you're thinking."

"He's not a dog."

True. He was a spotted version of Attila the Hun. "If not a dog, what is he?"

"A tiny puppy."

Tiny was not a word to describe that dog. Isaiah glanced askance at one of the paws dangling over Laura's arm. "Well, puppy, dog, whatever, I can't keep him. Get it straight out of your head."

Forty minutes later Isaiah was making a bed for Hapless in the metal shop behind his house. As he plumped up an old pillow on a pile of towels and blankets, he found himself understanding his father for the first time in his life. More than once he'd watched his dad wage verbal war with his mother and always come out the loser. Given the fact that his mom wasn't much bigger than a minute and Harv Coulter was a rugged, well-muscled man who stood over six feet tall, Isaiah had never understood the dynamics that took place between his parents during an argument. How could a big man who'd never taken shit off anybody always end up the loser in a disagreement with his wife?

Now Isaiah had an inkling. He couldn't recall volunteering to keep Hapless at his place, but somehow Laura had maneuvered him into it anyway. It was something about her eyes. She'd looked at him in a certain way, which in retrospect Isaiah could describe only as pathetic, and the first thing he knew, he'd been saying, *Well, okay, but only for a couple of days.* Now here he was, creating a dog bed for a puppy who had missed his calling to the stage.

"Oh, sweetie, you'll like it here," Laura was saying in that slow, soft way of hers. "You'll see. Isaiah is a vet. He'll take very good care of you."

Hapless made a mournful sound, half whimper and half growl. When Isaiah glanced over his shoulder, he saw that Laura had crouched down to pet the puppy, which was now draped over her bent knee.

"Don't carry on so." Laura looked up. "I'm afraid he'll get cold out here."

There was absolutely no way that Isaiah meant to put a pooping, peeing puppy in his house. "Nah. He'll be fine. Dogs are amazingly resilient."

"He isn't a dog. He's just a baby."

He was also a con artist, Isaiah thought, but that was beside the point. Laura had taken the bait, hook, line, and sinker, and Isaiah couldn't quite bring himself to tell her no. What was that all about? He'd never had a problem telling a woman no. It was a simple word, no, and it could be expressed in several creative ways, by simply saying, "No," or by saying, "No way, babe." In pressing situations, he'd even been known to tell a woman, "No damned way." But somehow, with Laura, not even the short, straight-to-the-point version had found its way to his lips.

"Do you have a heating pad?"

Christ. Next thing Isaiah knew, the damned mutt would be sharing his bed. "No. A heating pad's not necessary. He was wandering the streets, Laura. This shop is warm enough. It'll seem like a palace to him."

"Oh, sweetie," she whispered, her tone

aching with sympathy. "I wish I could take you home with me."

"He'll be fine, Laura. He's got plenty of food." Isaiah pointed to the sack of Science Diet puppy kibble that they'd picked up at the clinic. "That stuff isn't cheap, you know. It's the canine version of T-bone steak. And he's got water and chew bones. Not to mention a nice bed. He'll be absolutely fine out here for a couple of days." Just as a precaution, Isaiah tacked on, "He'll only be here long enough for you to find someone to adopt him. Right?"

Laura nodded and kissed the top of the puppy's head. "You'll be fine, Hapless. Yes, you will."

Hapless groaned and whimpered, stretching his neck as far as possible to lick Laura's face. Isaiah straightened and put his hands on his hips — a typical stance for a Coulter male when he felt outflanked. He'd seen his father and all his married brothers assume the same posture when they tried to reason with their wives.

"I don't know about you, but I'm famished. Let's leave Hapless to eat his lunch while we go have ours."

Groan, whimper, groan. Isaiah could have sworn the mottled, overgrown puppy had a Mensa IQ, and he was quickly becoming convinced that this particular canine had played the part of Romeo Montague in a former life.

"Come on, honey. I've agreed to put him up for a few days. He's got great accommodations here. What else do you want?"

She gave him a look that made him wish he hadn't asked. "I'd just feel better if he were in the house, where it's warmer. He's so little and helpless. What kind of person dumps a tiny puppy on a busy downtown street?"

Isaiah raked a hand through his hair. "I don't know why people dump animals, period, let alone a young puppy," he finally replied.

The admission forced Isaiah to take a mental step back and try to analyze his unreasoning reaction to this puppy. He was a vet. He spent every hour of every day devoting himself to the welfare of all kinds of animals. Why, then, did this young dog, who'd never done anything to deserve this kind of abuse, make him feel so resentful?

Normally Isaiah loved all animals on sight, but he'd taken an instant dislike to Hapless, undoubtedly because Laura had so foolishly put herself in danger to rescue him. Every time Isaiah remembered how she'd dashed out into traffic, causing countless drivers to slam on their brakes to avoid hitting her, he did a slow burn. Even worse, each time he recalled how the automobiles had fishtailed on the ice, his balls shriveled to the size of peanuts.

Okay, he thought, *this isn't about the dog.* Only, if it wasn't about the dog, what the hell was it about? Laura, he guessed. And admitting that, even to himself, was going to take him places he was reluctant to go. It seemed a lot safer, all around, to blame the entire incident on the dog. It was a lot less complicated, at least.

"He'll be fine out here for a little while," he offered. "I have the day off. After we have lunch I'll come home and check on him."

Laura sighed. Then, after she'd gazed deeply into the puppy's eyes, her expression went all soft and luminous. "He is *so* darling. Don't you think?"

Isaiah stepped around to give the puppy an assessing look. He was sort of cute, he guessed. Sometimes babies and puppies could be so ugly they were oddly appealing.

After returning Laura to the clinic parking lot after lunch, Isaiah headed toward home to check on Hapless, as promised. He had just turned onto Old Mill

Road where his house was located when his pager beeped. When he phoned in to get the message, he pulled a U-turn and rushed back to the clinic. A dog had raided its owners' garbage can and dined on the remains of a turkey carcass wrapped in tinfoil. Unfortunately for the dog, the owners suspected that more foil than turkey had found its way into the animal's stomach.

Belinda came in to assist Isaiah in surgery. Preliminary X-rays showed a blockage in the large intestine, so the operation was more complicated than Isaiah had first hoped. When he had finally closed up, Belinda gave him an inviting smile.

"How about a hamburger? It's about time to eat, and I'm starved."

The atmosphere in a hamburger joint was pretty safe, and given the fact that Belinda had just sacrificed a whole afternoon to help him out, Isaiah would have liked to buy her supper to show his appreciation.

"I'm sorry, Belinda. I have a young boarder at home, and I need to go check on him."

"A boarder?" Her eyes gleamed with curiosity. "Do tell."

Isaiah recounted the harrowing rescue of Hapless. It was one of the few tales he'd ever told that required no embellishment to make it interesting.

"Oh, he sounds so precious!" Belinda cried. "Hapless. What a cute name."

"It's the only cute thing about him." Isaiah went on to describe the puppy. "He looks like he fought with an ugly stick and lost. Poor little guy. Laura is convinced she can find a home for him, no problem, but I'm not so sure."

Belinda smiled. "Ah, now. He can't be *that* bad. If nothing else, maybe Laura can keep him."

"No way. Even if her landlord would relent and allow her to have a pet, her place isn't really suitable."

"You've been there?"

"Yeah, a couple of times." Isaiah pictured the small rooms chock-full of breakable knickknacks, and a grown Hapless slapping them from the tables with his tail. "No fenced area, and hardly room to turn around in the house itself. It'd never work."

Belinda's smile faded. "That's too bad. Hopefully some kind soul will take him. Poor little fellow."

An hour later Isaiah discovered that the "poor little fellow" had gone on a chewing rampage in the shop building. An entire new pack of shop towels, made from particularly strong and absorbent paper to absorb grease, had not been able to withstand his puppy teeth. The interior of the building looked as if it had been heavily sprinkled with confetti. Isaiah might have just shrugged and hauled out the Shop-Vac to clean up the mess, but when he went to get the barrel-shaped vacuum, he found that the hose now had holes in it. Even worse, his nylon ski bag had been torn open, and every Velcro strap had been cleanly removed from his three-hundred-dollar ski boots.

"No!" he yelled. "Not my *boots!*"

Hapless was lying on his pillow, looking altogether too innocent and unconcerned. Isaiah stalked toward him.

"You miserable, vicious little cur. What else did you destroy while I was gone? I left you chew bones. Why didn't you teethe on those?"

The puppy's response was a deep, happy-sounding growl. He bounded from his bed to attack Isaiah's pant leg. Once the denim was secure between his sharp teeth, he braced on all fours and backed away, dragging Isaiah's foot with him.

"Let go. I'm mad at you. Let go, I said."

In the end, Isaiah had to pick the puppy

up to rescue his jeans. Growling again, Hapless immediately began licking Isaiah's face.

"She should have named you Growler. Better yet, how about Velcro Breath? That suits you better." Isaiah turned to survey the remaining valuables inside the shop and was glad to see that his wall tent had escaped the puppy's notice. "Well, this cinches it. You'll have to sleep in the utility room until Laura finds you a home."

Chapter Eleven

Isaiah awakened to mournful howls, followed by a quick succession of shrill yips. He groaned, rolled over to peer through the darkness at the red digital readout of his alarm clock, and pulled the pillow over his head. Two o'clock in the morning? It was a holiday weekend, one of his few opportunities to get a full night's sleep, and that ungrateful little wretch wanted to get up at two in the morning? No way.

As though sensing that Isaiah had covered his ears, Hapless raised his volume a notch. *Yip, yip, yip, howl.* Over and over the sounds reverberated through the house, growing louder and louder. Isaiah tried to ignore them. He tried using two pillows to block out the noise, but succeeded only in almost smothering himself. He even tried counting the yips as if they were sheep in an attempt to go back to sleep.

Finally he slapped back the covers, swung out of bed, and stormed through the house. "All right, damn it, you win."

He opened the utility room door. "But it's only for a couple of nights. Understand? The minute Laura finds a home for you, you're out of here."

Just as Isaiah said that, he stepped in something cold and squishy with his bare foot. "Son of a-a-a *bitch!*" He was too far from the door to flip on the light. Judging by the smell, he stood in the middle of a puppy-poop minefield. The dog food, he thought dismally. Puppies often got loose bowels if their diets were abruptly changed. "Damn it," he said as the stuff oozed up between his toes.

An hour later, after the utility room was cleaned and both Isaiah and Hapless were freshly showered, the pair snuggled down for a long winter's nap in Isaiah's bed. In Isaiah's estimation, it was the only way he would get any sleep. Hopefully Hapless wouldn't cry if he could curl up against a warm body, and this way Isaiah would wake up if the puppy needed to go outside. As Isaiah's eyes drifted closed, he gruffly whispered, "Don't get used to this, mutt."

Hapless emitted a happy little growl and thrust his wet nose in Isaiah's armpit.

Over the next week Isaiah frequently repeated that refrain, or facsimiles thereof.

"It's only temporary. The last thing I need or want is a dog. Got it?" These proclamations generally came on the heels of a notable event, such as the purchase of Hapless's first bed, a huge, contoured thing made of foam cushions and lined with sheepskin, or after a visit to the pet shop, where Isaiah and Hapless could shop together for puppy toys, a pastime they frequently engaged in after they left the clinic in the evening. Oh, yes, Hapless accompanied Isaiah to work. It was the only practical solution, Isaiah told himself. Otherwise the puppy chewed on everything *except* his toys while Isaiah was gone. At the clinic Hapless could be around people, and there wasn't much that he could damage. It was also an ideal place to housebreak a puppy, with indestructible floors and lots of watchful adults to escort Hapless outside before he had accidents.

"I am not keeping that dog," Isaiah was often heard to say to anyone who would listen, and in the beginning he meant it. But after a week a bond between man and dog began to be forged. At the clinic Hapless followed at Isaiah's heels everywhere he went, parting company with his unwilling master only when a door was closed in his face. At home Isaiah discovered that having a dog around made the big, empty rooms feel less lonely. Hapless particularly enjoyed their homecomings. En route to the house, he bounded wildly around the yard, still so short of leg that he sometimes disappeared entirely in the drifts of snow. Then, the moment Isaiah opened the door, the puppy ran excitedly through the house, growling and barking as he sniffed out his toys.

The second week Isaiah sought Laura out once a day to ask, "Has anyone responded to the ad yet?"

The ad Isaiah referred to was a three-line description of Hapless in the lost-and-found section of the *Central Oregon Bargain Shopper*, a small weekly newspaper with cheap ad space that practically everyone read.

"No," Laura always replied. "I check with Val every day to see if anyone's called, and so far nothing. I don't think any-one is going to claim him."

At the end of the week, Isaiah came to a decision that surprised no one but him. "Just cancel the ad," he told Laura. "No one's going to claim him, and it doesn't look like you're going to find him a home. I'll keep him."

"Really?" Laura struggled not to smile,

for it was apparent to everyone at the clinic that Isaiah had fallen in love with the big, clumsy puppy. "Are you sure, Isaiah? My friends the Kesslers are still talking about taking him."

Isaiah frowned and then shook his head. "There are plenty of other strays out there that need homes. Hapless has settled in with me. It'd be mean to uproot him again."

Laura knew it was ornery, but she couldn't resist saying, "You think he's ugly, though. Wouldn't you rather get a dog you like?"

Isaiah narrowed an eye at her. "You're enjoying this, aren't you? I didn't like him at first, and now you're rubbing it in. A guy can change his mind, can't he?"

"Of course." Just then Hapless entered the kennels. When he saw Isaiah he bounded up the center aisle, growling happily and wagging his tail so hard that his whole body whipped back and forth. Laura crouched down to greet the puppy. "Well, I guess you're here to stay," she said as she stroked the puppy's head. To Isaiah she added, "A clinic dog instead of a cat. I'm glad it's worked out between you. He needed a home, and you needed a dog to love. It must have been fate."

"Maybe so." Isaiah hunkered down, too. They fell silent for a moment, petting the puppy that squirmed with delight between them. "I didn't know I needed a dog, but I guess maybe I did. I really like having him around. It's weird, actually, how the best things in my life are always the things that happen along when I least expect them."

Laura got a wet puppy kiss on the mouth. She laughed and sputtered. "Yuck!"

Her amusement faded as she met Isaiah's gaze. He was looking at her oddly — almost speculatively. "What?" she asked.

"Nothing. I was just thinking."

"About what?"

A mischievous gleam slipped into his eyes. "That's for me to know and you to find out, I reckon."

What Isaiah couldn't tell Laura, what he could scarcely admit to himself, was that she was one of the wonderful things in his life that had just happened along when he least expected it. If not for Laura, the clinic wouldn't have been aglitter with Christmas lights and garlands. If not for Laura, there wouldn't be a staff Christmas party planned. If not for Laura, the fridge and cupboards would still be empty every time he went foraging for food. If not for

Laura, he might never have gotten a dog because he'd always considered himself to be far too busy to care for a pet.

If not for Laura. Ever since he'd hired her that October evening, she'd been systematically altering his world. Everyone at the clinic seemed to laugh more now that she was around. Coffee breaks were no longer brief, dreary affairs where people sipped bitter brew, wishing for cream or sugar. Thanks to Laura, the condiments were well stocked, and along with the coffee there were always cookies, doughnuts, and cinnamon rolls, all of them tasting homemade. Isaiah no longer felt as exhausted when he left the clinic at night because he now ate snacks throughout his workday and didn't drain his energy stores to such critically low levels.

Laura. When Isaiah tried to recall what it had been like at the clinic before her arrival, he had difficulty remembering. It was the oddest thing, but he felt as if she'd been a part of his life forever. For that reason he was vastly relieved that nothing more untoward occurred at the clinic while she was working. If someone had been plotting to get Laura fired — and Isaiah would always believe that had been the case — then the enhanced security procedures and the candid comments that both he and Tucker had made at the staff meeting had discouraged the perpetrator.

Late in the afternoon in mid December, Isaiah was about to call it a day when a pregnant rottweiler was rushed into the clinic. The dog had been left at home alone while her owners were at work, and she'd gone into labor. As sometimes happened with first litters, the rottweiler experienced complications and started to hemorrhage. By the time her owners returned home, the dog was near death. The instant Isaiah saw her, he knew it would take a miracle to save her — pale gums, cold lips, dull eyes.

"C-section!" he yelled. "Belinda, Angela, I need you, stat."

Everyone rushed to get a table ready, and with efficient speed Susan prepped the dog. In the end, though, all the hurry was for naught. The animal had lost too much blood, and she died during surgery.

Isaiah felt sick about it. She was a beautiful dog, a purebred with fabulous markings and conformation. He left his techs to care for the pups and went to the waiting area to speak with the dog's owners, a husband and wife who sat huddled in a corner. Isaiah guessed they were in their mid-thirties, professionals judging by their dress, the man in a blood-smeared street coat over a tailored gray suit, the woman in a dark skirt and blazer. She was sobbing on her husband's shoulder, saying, "Oh, God, I hope she'll be okay. My poor, poor Phoebe."

"Hello," Isaiah said, extending his right hand to the man. "I'm Dr. Coulter."

The fellow patted his wife's shoulder and gently pushed her away as he stood up to shake Isaiah's hand. "How is she, Doc?"

Before Isaiah could reply, the woman cried, "She went into labor while we were at work!"

"Ah." Isaiah might have pointed out that leaving the dog alone near her due date had been irresponsible, but that would only have made the situation worse. The people had learned their lesson the hard way and would do better the next time. "That happens sometimes."

The woman nodded and sniffed. "When we got home there was blood everywhere. We had made her a birthing bed in our closet." Her voice went high and thin. "She was just lying there like she was dead."

Experience had taught Isaiah that bad news was best delivered quickly and simply. That made it no easier for him to say what had to be said. "I'm so sorry, but Phoebe didn't make it."

The woman covered her face with her hands. The man made a strangled sound and bent his head.

"We did our best to save her." Isaiah always felt helpless at times like this. "But we were too late. We lost her on the table."

"I shouldn't have left her alone!" the woman cried brokenly. "Oh, God, my poor Phoebe."

"Complications like these aren't something anyone can predict," Isaiah said gently. "It's always easy to second-guess ourselves after the fact, but all that accomplishes is to make us feel worse. What you need to focus on right now is that you loved her and did your best to give her a good home. Not all dogs are so fortunate."

The woman's husband inserted, "That's right, honey. Don't start blaming yourself. We had no way of knowing that she'd have problems." He glanced at Isaiah. "We did everything to make her comfortable. We just had no idea."

Isaiah nodded. "Next time around you'll know from experience that complications can arise. But you didn't know that this morning." He waited for the woman's sobs to abate somewhat. Then he said, "I don't know if this will be any comfort, but we were able to save Phoebe's puppies."

"You saved them?" The woman's eyes lit with hope.

Isaiah smiled. "She left you thirteen beautiful babies. I got only a glimpse of them before I came out to talk with you, but they all looked healthy."

The woman sent her husband a wet, tremulous smile. "Oh, Stanley. Did you hear that? Her babies made it."

Stanley shook his head. "Their mother's gone, Nan. We can't take on thirteen puppies when we're both working like we are."

Isaiah held up a hand. "There are puppy formulas available. Orphaned newborns can do very nicely. You just have to bottle-feed them every two hours."

"Every two hours?" Nan echoed. "All day and all night?"

Isaiah nodded. "In cases like this most people wean the pups at four weeks. It'll be a rough month. I won't kid you about that. But Phoebe was a beautiful dog. It's my guess that her puppies will sell for a lot of money. Perhaps, considering the financial reward of such an endeavor, one of you can afford to take a month off from work."

Stanley shook his head again. "I can get time off for emergencies, but the death of a dog doesn't qualify." He looked at his wife. "And you have the art show in two weeks. You can't drop the ball right now."

Nan wiped her cheeks. "I own an art gallery."

"Ah," Isaiah said again. It was his favorite word at times like this, noncommittal, meaningless. People could take it to mean whatever they liked.

"You know how it is," Stanley went on, rubbing his brow as though his head hurt. "Nan's running herself ragged twenty-four/ seven right now, and I'm a project manager, trying to meet a deadline." He looked sadly at his wife. "We have to be practical, honey. There's just no way we can do it."

"What are you saying, that we should have them put down?"

Stanley looked at Isaiah. "Would anyone here be interested in bottle-feeding a litter of pups? You're right about Phoebe's being a nice dog. She had champion German bloodlines, and the stud had equally impressive ancestry. Depending on their quality, the pups will sell for anywhere from eighteen hundred to twenty-five hundred dollars apiece."

Isaiah could promise nothing. "I can ask my techs. Maybe one of them will be interested."

"In return for pick of the litter, we'd be willing to sign off on all the other pups." He glanced at his wife. "Right, Nan? Somebody could make a lot of money, and we'd get one of Phoebe's puppies."

Nan's mouth trembled as she attempted to smile. "Oh, yes. That would be wonderful."

Isaiah nodded. "I'll pass the word. Maybe one of my techs will take them on. If not, what would you like me to do?"

Stan's expression grew grim. "If nobody's interested in bottle-feeding them, we'll have no choice but to put them down."

None of the techs could bottle-feed thirteen puppies for the next month. Isaiah had no idea what the stories were in Tucker's wing, but in his own everyone had a reason that made such an endeavor impossible. Trish wept as she refused the offer, but between her job, a husband, two kids, and a pair of rambunctious Airedales, she was already stretched too thin. Susan lived with her mother and didn't have room for thirteen puppies in so small a house. Belinda lived in an apartment that didn't allow pets, as did Angela, James, and Mike.

Isaiah considered trying to raise the puppies himself, but when he got down to the practicalities, he knew it was an insane idea. The first couple of weeks the puppies would have to be fed every two to three hours, making it impossible to leave them at the clinic overnight. There was a four-hour lapse after nightshift ended until six in the morning, when the clinic opened, and it would be at least another hour if not more before someone could devote time to the puppies. Such young dogs needed to be fed frequently and regularly. Isaiah would have to take the puppies home every night so they wouldn't miss a feeding. What would happen if he got called back in on an emergency? He couldn't cart around thirteen puppies everywhere he went.

With a heavy heart, Isaiah prepared to euthanize the litter. He'd just filled a syringe with anesthetic, which would be injected into each puppy's heart, when Laura entered the surgery. Isaiah was surprised to see her. It was almost six o'clock. Her afternoon shift had ended two hours earlier.

"Hi!" she called as she crossed the room to take an inventory of the snack supplies before she left.

"What are you still doing here?" Isaiah

asked, his tone just a little sharper than he intended.

"I was sitting with Rambo. His leg still hurts."

Rambo, a pit bull mix, had jumped off a deck onto cement and fractured a front leg. It wasn't unusual for Laura to hang around when one of her charges needed a little extra TLC, but today Isaiah really wished she hadn't. She would not be happy if she learned that thirteen puppies were about to be put down. He already felt bad enough. If she started to cry — and it was a sure bet that she would — he wasn't sure he'd be able to do what had to be done.

He gazed after her as she stepped into the adjoining cloakroom. When she emerged a moment later, juggling her purse as she pulled on a jacket, she spotted the puppies.

"Oh, how *sweet.*"

Isaiah hadn't bothered to ask Laura if she would be interested in bottle-feeding the babies. Her landlord had a strict no-pet policy.

"Don't look at them," Trish told Laura with a loud sniff. "It'll only break your heart. Isaiah has to put all of them to sleep."

"Why?" Laura's eyes widened with dismay. As she moved across the room toward Isaiah, her gaze remained fixed on the squirming black puppies lying on the towel. "What's wrong with them?"

"Nothing," he replied. "Their mother died. The owners can't bottle-feed them because they both work. For the next several days they'll need to be fed every two hours, or they won't make it. After that, it'll be every three hours, at least, until they're weaned."

Laura curled a slender hand over one of the puppies. Isaiah knew by her expression that she was frantically trying to think of a way to take on the job.

"Forget it, honey. Your landlord would blow a gasket." He thumbed the syringe plunger to spurt a little anesthetic. "It's just one of those things. We all hate it, but that's the downside of veterinary medicine. Sometimes I dance on clouds when I leave here. Tonight I'll feel like hell."

"No," Laura whispered. Her gaze flashed to his, and she said the word again, louder this time: "No." Her larynx bobbed as she swallowed. "You can't kill them, Isaiah. In three or four weeks they'll be big enough to eat normal food."

Isaiah saw her heart shining in those big,

hazel eyes. "Sweetheart, what else can I do?" *Sweetheart?* Where had that come from? "You can't keep them at your place. No one else can do it, either. Thirteen puppies? Think about it."

"Let me call Gram," she said in a quavering voice. "Maybe she'll let me keep them there."

Isaiah sighed and capped the syringe. "Okay. Go for it. It's not like I want to do this."

Laura returned to the cloakroom to make the call. Moments later, when she reappeared, Isaiah knew without asking that her grandmother had said no. Her eyes were swimming with tears. Her chin was trembling. She came over to the table and picked up one of the tiny, wrinkle-faced puppies. After brushing her cheek the length of its small black body, she laid it back on the towel.

"New carpet," she said softly. "Indoor/outdoor in the kitchen and baths. If they got out of the box they'd ruin her rugs."

She gave him a final, agonized look and then fled from the surgery. The door swung closed behind her with such force that it jiggled on the hinges. Isaiah stared thoughtfully after her and then lowered his gaze to the puppies. *Damn it.*

He despised this part of his job.

"Maybe someone at the Humane Society would take them," Trish suggested with forced cheer.

"We could call and see," Belinda agreed.

Angela piped in with, "If that's a dead end, why not call around to some other vets? There's got to be someone out there who'd like to make some extra money doing a good deed."

Isaiah stepped over to the hazardous-waste receptacle and pushed the capped syringe through the flap. "I have a better idea. Would you get a blanket from the warmer and cover the puppies, Trish? I don't want them getting chilled while I'm away."

"Where you going?" she asked.

Isaiah grinned mysteriously. "I'll be back shortly."

Laura was about to climb into her car when a shout stopped her short. Recognizing Isaiah's voice, she turned to look back. Shrugging into a jacket, he moved toward her through the dusky gloom, his breath forming puffs of steam. She waited while he picked his way across the icy parking lot. When he reached her, he drew to a stop and gazed at the darkening sky for a long moment.

"I've got a proposition for you," he finally said.

Laura tossed her purse in the car. She felt helplessly angry and was battling tears. "What's that?"

A lazy grin moved slowly across his mouth, deepening the creases in his lean cheeks. "You ready for a really wild idea?" His eyes shimmered like molten silver in the fading light, in startling contrast to his dark hair and skin. "How about you staying out at my place to take care of the puppies until they're weaned?"

Laura took in the words, but for a moment their meaning danced inside her brain like droplets of water on a red-hot griddle. "What?"

His grin broadened. "I told you it was a wild idea. But it's not really when you think about it. I've got all wood floors or tile. A litter of puppies can't really hurt anything."

"You want me to stay at your house?" she asked incredulously.

"Yeah. When I built the place, I went for broke and put in five bedrooms. Someday — not anytime soon, of course — I hope to get married and have a family, so it's not like I don't have room. My brother Jake has a plastic wading pool out in the barn.

They work great for a litter of newborn puppies. You just toss in some towels for bedding, and the slick sides keep them from climbing out. When they get older, we can get one of those portable wire kennels and cover the floor with newspaper."

Laura couldn't think what to say.

"You'll have to bring them with you when you come to work," he tacked on. "That'll be a major pain in the ass. But once you get here you can put them in one of the kennels until you're ready to leave. Could be that you'll even be able to recruit volunteers to help feed them while you're working."

Almost from the start Laura had been battling her feelings for this man. Now she lost the war. He had such a good heart. How could she help but love him? He was, without question, the handsomest man she'd ever known, and now, by making this offer, he had convinced her that he was also the kindest. She wanted to throw her arms around his strong neck and give him a great big kiss.

Not a good situation. Staying at his place would be a recipe for heartbreak. As it was, she struggled to keep her feelings for him in check. How could she possibly hope to do that if she saw him constantly, not only at work, but at home as well? They'd probably share meals. There might even be times when they'd spend an evening watching television together. She'd be like a chocolate lover living in a chocolate factory, endlessly subjected to temptation but unable to indulge her cravings.

If it weren't for the puppies, Laura would have declined the offer. But how could she possibly do that when thirteen lives hung in the balance? Yes, she needed to protect her heart, but at what cost? If watching out for herself meant that those puppies had to die, the price was way too high.

"Come on," he urged with a low laugh. "It's not like I'm a stranger. No funny business, I promise."

"I'm not worried about that." Laura took a bracing breath. *If only.* Butterflies of dread attacked her stomach. "It's a lovely offer, Isaiah. How can I say no?"

"Now you're talking." He struck the heel of his boot against a patch of ice, sending shards flying. "We've got puppy formula here at the clinic. One of us can stop at a department store tonight and pick up some doll bottles. Until then we can feed them with a syringe."

Laura's thoughts were going in circles.

"I'll need to pack some clothes. And my fridge! I can't just leave stuff in there to spoil."

"No problem. Go home. Do whatever you have to do. I'll swing by Jake's to get the wading pool and take the puppies on out to my place. We'll manage fine until you arrive. I'll get them settled in and feed them. After you do everything at your apartment, can you swing by a department store to get some doll bottles?" He went on to describe the kind they would need. "To make feeding times simpler, I'd get thirteen if you can. I'll pay for them. Just bring me the receipt."

"I'm not sure I can find your house. The day we took Hapless out, I didn't watch the way."

He gestured toward the clinic with a swing of his head. "I'll draw you a map."

That evening was one of the busiest in Laura's memory. After stopping by her apartment to remove perishables from the fridge and pack personal items for her stay at Isaiah's house, she went to town for doll bottles. Small bottles with pliable nipples, suitable for a puppy's mouth, weren't easy to find. She finally ran across some in a dollar store, the plus side being that they were inexpensive, the downside being that she had had to make five stops before she found them.

By the time she reached Isaiah's, it was almost eight o'clock. As she parked in the circular drive, she stared in awe at the huge log house, which looked entirely different at night than it had during the day. Butter-yellow light poured through the massive front windows, which stretched clear from the floor to the lofty peak of the center gable. Smaller gables flanked it on each side, sporting French doors that opened onto second-story balconies. Directional flood lamps had been tucked among the shrubs that bordered the home's foundation. Light fanned upward from the snow-laden greenery to bathe the logs in an amber glow.

Laura had just exited her car and pushed the driver's seat forward to retrieve stuff from the backseat when Isaiah and Hapless emerged from the house. The puppy gave a happy bark and came tumbling down the steps to greet her. Isaiah's grin was just as welcoming.

"I was worried that you'd gotten lost!" he called as he descended the steps with considerably more grace than the puppy.

"No, the map was great." Laura set a

cardboard box on the roof of her car and bent back inside to grab an oversize satchel stuffed with clothing. "It just took me longer than I hoped. I had trouble finding the bottles. Most stores don't carry them any-more."

"Little girls don't play with baby dolls like they used to. You found some, I hope."

Laura held up a sack. "Thirteen. The clerk made sure I counted right. I think they'll work."

He took the bag and opened it toward the light. "Right on. These will do great."

Arms laden with belongings, Laura bumped the car door closed with her hip. "I went to five stores before I found them."

"Five? Jeesh." He stepped over to take the box and overnight case from the top of the Mazda. "You must be beat."

"A little."

Working in tandem, they began carrying her things to the house and depositing them just inside the front door. As they went back and forth, they spoke in starts and stops. He told her that he'd fed the puppies with a syringe and put them in the wading pool for a snooze. "I called the people who owned their mother. When the puppies are weaned, they'd like to have their pick of the litter. You can sell the others and keep the money."

When Laura heard how much each puppy might bring, she couldn't believe her ears. "How much did you say?"

"You heard me," he said with a grin. "If they all live, and I see no reason why they shouldn't, this endeavor will be very profitable."

Laura hadn't given a thought to the financial rewards. "I didn't know a dog could cost that much."

"Oh, yeah. Certain breeds, anyway. Evidently the mother and father were both show quality. German bloodlines, they said. Some of the puppies will command a very high price."

When they had carried everything inside, Isaiah closed the front door and swung a hand to encompass the house. "Welcome to my humble abode."

Laura took in the spacious living room, which seemed all the larger because it was almost empty. A wrought-iron chandelier hung from the center beam of the knotty-pine ceiling. Its mellow light combined with that of a fire crackling cheerfully in a large rock fireplace at the opposite end of the room to wash the unadorned log walls with amber. Two burgundy beanbag chairs sat before the raised hearth. A big-screen television was the only other piece of furniture.

"It's a great house." Empty, but pretty.

She wondered why he had no sofa or regular chairs, but before she could think of a polite way to ask, he said, "I keep meaning to do something with the rooms, but I never seem to find the time."

"Oh." Laura bit back a smile. That was so like Isaiah, always racing from one task to the next, with never enough hours in his day. "Finding the right pieces takes a lot of time, and it's not something you should rush. Once you get a couch and chairs, you'll be stuck with them for a while."

"Exactly." He gave her a speculative look. "You'd be good at it, I bet."

"Good at what?"

"Picking out furniture. I thought about hiring a decorator, but every time I start to call, I chicken out and hang up."

"Why?"

He sighed and rubbed the back of his neck. "I don't know. Tucker's decorator did a great job with his place. It's just . . ." He gestured with his hand. "I'm afraid she'd do it up fancy like his, and I'd hate that. I want my home to reflect my personality, not someone else's. You know what I'm saying?"

Laura understood exactly what he meant. It wouldn't do for some decorator to come in there and create a spectacular showplace with delicate knickknacks cluttering every surface. Isaiah was a hard-working man with an outdoorsy lifestyle. He needed furniture and wall decorations that suited his personality. Laura envisioned a durable leather sofa and oversize easy chairs, flanked by distressed-wood tables — chunky, comfortable furniture in keeping with the style of the house and the man who lived there.

As she stepped farther into the room, she ran her gaze over the loft above her. She loved the railing, made of yet more logs, none of them planed, so each post had natural twists and knots to lend it character. A staircase to her left angled up the wall, providing ingress to the top floor.

"There are three bedrooms up there and two more down here," he explained. "I'd offer you your choice of sleeping accommodations, but only the first-floor guest room has a bed."

Laura couldn't help but laugh. She was just pleased to know that she wouldn't be expected to sleep on the floor. "Down here is fine."

"It's probably just as well." He gestured

at the railing above them. "If a puppy escaped from the wading pool up there, it'd be a mighty long drop."

Laura shuddered at the thought. "Did you design the house?" she asked as she turned to see everything.

"Why do you ask?"

"Because it's like you somehow."

Laura had no better words to explain it, only that the house reminded her of him: big, attractive, solid, and straightforward, yet imaginative as well. She liked the window seats to the right of the front door. They were wider than most and ran quite deep, providing enough room for a person to recline. With some bright, overstuffed cushions, they would provide cozy reading areas with all the natural light that would pour through the windows during the day.

"Let me take your coat," he offered. "Then I'll show you through."

As Laura drew off her jacket to hand it over, Hapless reared up on her leg for petting. "Hello, Hapless. Oh, yes, I love you, too." Laura gave the puppy a scratch behind the ears. "You're a sweetie. Yes, you are."

"He's a pest," Isaiah corrected as he closed the coat closet. "If you get tired of him, just push him down."

"I never get tired of dogs."

With a final pat on the dog's head, Laura trailed after her employer for her first look at the inside of the house. Behind the double-sided stone fireplace was a spacious dining room devoid of furniture. Beyond that was an equally large kitchen, divided from the living area by a long bar lined with wicker-back stools.

"What a nice kitchen," she exclaimed. "And there are bar stools. How nice. You can sit down while you eat."

He narrowed an eye at her. "Keep it up and I'll have you shopping for furniture and decorating the place."

Laura almost wished he would carry through on the threat. She'd never decorated a brand-new house. It would be fun — and challenging.

"I wanted a gourmet kitchen," he explained as he showed her the Viking range top, the double ovens, a gigantic Sub-Zero side by side, and a custom work island with tons of under-the-counter storage. "State-of-the-art," he said proudly, even as he cast her a sheepish grin. "Too bad I can't cook."

Laura laughed again. Around Isaiah she seemed to do a lot of that. "Maybe you can take cooking classes."

He shrugged. "Yeah, right. In my spare time, maybe?"

"Perhaps your wife will enjoy cooking," she offered.

He smiled slightly. "Maybe so."

He led her into a nice-sized laundry room. "Washer, dryer." He grinned and winked. "Here we have laundry soap." He opened a door to show her the attached three-car garage. "While you're getting settled in your room, I'll park your Mazda out there," he informed her. "Forecast calls for snow tonight and tomorrow."

"It does?" Laura's expression brightened.

"Yep," he confirmed, sounding far less enthusiastic than she felt. "Tomorrow I'll be shoveling the drive, sure as the world. No point in having to scrape snow off the windshields, too."

Laura followed him through the kitchen again, her gaze trailing over him while his back was turned. It wasn't often that she saw him without a lab coat. She studied his Western belt, where his first name had been tooled into the leather. Then she admired the purely masculine shift of his lean hips as he walked. He had the gait of a man who'd spent much of his life in the saddle.

"Do you have any horses?" she asked.

"Not yet. Come spring I'm hoping to get a couple." He glanced back over his shoulder. "Do you ride?"

Laura shook her head. "Not for years, and then only a little."

"Well, now, we can't have that. I'll have to give you riding lessons. There are some great trails out here. The property backs up to BLM land."

Prior to her accident, Laura had occasionally done eco studies for the Bureau of Land Management and other governmental agencies.

"Thousands of acres, no houses. You'll love it."

Laura suspected he was right; she would love it. That was the whole problem: She loved everything about Isaiah Coulter, loved being with him. Once the puppies were weaned, she needed to avoid him. No more accepting impromptu invitations to go out to dinner with him. No more delivering kittens to sad old ladies. No more hanging out in the surgery for coffee breaks where she would be sure to run into him.

As they passed the stove, she saw a pot of something on one of the gas burners. The smell of tomato soup wafted from under the stainless-steel lid, reminding her that she'd yet to eat dinner. Isaiah led her back to the front of the house to a door positioned under the stairs. He pushed open the portal and flipped on the overhead light to reveal a large bedroom. As Laura moved to stand beside him in the doorway, she was acutely aware of him physically — of his height and breadth, of the heat that radiated from his body and the masculine scent of him. It took all her concentration to focus on the bedroom furnishings, a lovely sleigh bed, a matching dresser with mirror, and a tall chest of drawers where she could store her clothing.

"Sorry," he said. "I know you're used to lots of stuff on the walls."

"It's fine," she assured him. And it was. The bed had been made up. There was no bedspread, but the colorful patchwork quilts had a charm all their own that went nicely with the rustic log walls. She stepped over to test the mattress. When she sat on the edge and gave a bounce, the springs squeaked. "Comfy. I'll sleep like a baby."

Just then their gazes met. To Laura the air between them suddenly seemed charged with electricity. Man, woman, squeaking bed. She pushed to her feet so quickly she got light-headed.

He cleared his throat, looked away. "That leads to the bathroom," he said, gesturing to a doorway. "There's a jetted tub and shower. I think it'll meet your needs." He cleared his throat again. "We won't be fighting for a turn in the shower, anyway."

Feeling like an idiot, Laura stepped over to look in the bathroom. "Oh!" she said with delighted surprise that helped to dispel the tension. "How pretty." The tub was surrounded by what looked like an acre of forest-green tile. Above it the ceiling sported a glass dome, some of the panes stained ruby and green, others clear. "Oh, Isaiah." She imagined hanging plants around the deep tub, how they would thrive in the tricolored light that would pour through the dome all day. With a few decorative touches, it could have been a bathroom fit for royalty. "Did you design this?"

"More or less. I sketched what I wanted and hired a guy to draw up the blueprints."

"It's lovely." Laura wished she could say *fabulous* without getting tongue-tied.

"Thank you. The main suite is even nicer. No tour of that until I pick up in there, though. I'm a complete slob."

"The house looks clean to me."

"Cleaning woman."

"Ah."

As Laura turned from the bathroom, she spied a turquoise wading pool on the floor between the bed and the wall. "Oh, the babies!" she said softly.

He came to stand beside her. "What I wouldn't give to be able to sleep like that," he said with a low laugh.

Laura crouched down to admire her snoozing charges, all thirteen of them. She loved their stout little bodies, blockish heads, and squashed noses. "They have hearts on their butts."

He laughed again and hunkered down beside her. "They do at that. Tomorrow we need to take them to the clinic and dock their tails."

Laura hadn't thought of that. "Oh, ouch. Do we have to do it so soon? They're so tiny yet."

"Better to do it now. If you wait until they're older, it hurts a lot more."

Laura couldn't bear to think about it. "It seems so mean. Why can't we just leave them with tails?"

"We could, I guess." Hapless bounded into the room just then. Isaiah caught the rambunctious puppy back from jumping into the wading pool. "Off-limits, buddy. They're too little to play with you yet." He gave Hapless a knuckle rub on the head.

"The problem with not docking their tails is that rotts are such big dogs, and their tails are stout. As adults, they'll knock stuff off tables and slap people's legs every time they wag."

Laura didn't think that would be so terrible.

"We also have to remember that they're expensive purebreds. Rottweilers normally have docked tails. They'll look weird if we don't do it."

Laura supposed he had a point. Weird-looking dogs might be hard to place in loving homes. "Will it hurt?"

He considered the question. "I've never had it straight from a puppy, mind you, but I don't think it's that bad. A quick sting, maybe. We apply an analgesic ointment almost immediately, and most times they go right back to sleep."

Laura sighed. "I don't want to watch." She leaned forward over her knees to pick up a puppy. The sight of its disgruntled frown made her laugh. "Isn't he sweet?"

"He is a she." Isaiah considered the wrinkled little face that Laura turned toward him. "And, yes, she's pretty darned cute. It's hard to look at a face like that without smiling."

Laura gently returned the puppy to her

siblings. "Thank you for letting me keep them here, Isaiah. It's very kind of you."

He shrugged. "I'm as happy about saving them as you are, and you're the one who's kind. It's no easy project you've taken on. For the next four weeks you'll be losing a lot of sleep."

"I don't mind."

"No, I know you don't." He ran his gaze over her face as if to commit each line and angle to memory. "And that's what makes you so special."

After Laura had unpacked her things and arranged them in the bureau, she returned to the main part of the house. Isaiah was clattering around in the kitchen, doing something that filled the rooms with mouthwatering smells. When he saw her emerge from the bedroom, he called, "You hungry?"

Laura rubbed her hands on her jeans. This entire situation made her nervous. It was one thing to see Isaiah at the clinic and quite another to be staying at his house.

"Starving," she confessed.

"It's nothing gourmet, just grilled cheese sandwiches and soup from a can."

Laura hiked up a hip to perch on a bar stool. "It sounds good. I haven't eaten."

"Figured as much. On the way home I stopped at a store. We have the basics — eggs, bacon, bread, some fruit, and lunch meat. Tomorrow I'll do some more shopping. You'll want to cook while you're staying here, right?"

Laura couldn't imagine eating out for a month. "Yes. If that's all right."

"All right?" He laughed. "I'll love it. You mind cooking for two?"

"I always do, and sometimes for four. What I need is a cookbook for one person." Laura propped an elbow on the bar and rested her chin on the heel of her hand. "I can do the shopping if you like."

"I don't want you paying for the food."

"Why not? I want to pay half, at least."

He shook his head. "No way. Supplying you with room and board will be my contribution to saving the puppies. I'd just give you cash to cover the groceries, but paying that way is complicated for you. If you're worried that I'll get the wrong stuff, you can come along when I go to the store. That way you can get what you'll need for cooking, and I'll be there to cover the tab."

"Okay." Laura hoped he didn't talk a lot as they moved through the aisles. She had trouble enough remembering all that she needed without added distractions. "Sure."

He ladled the soup into bowls and then turned the sandwiches on the built-in griddle. As he worked, Laura indulged herself in another surreptitious study of him. His Wranglers were loose from wear and baggy at the seat, but the denim hugged his long legs just enough to showcase the powerful contours of his thighs. He wore a wrinkled green plaid shirt neatly tucked in at his trim waist. The bright, geometric design drew the eye to his chest, shoulders, and arms, which were also well padded with muscle and rippled under the cloth whenever he moved.

He glanced up and caught her staring. For an uncomfortably long moment he paused in his task to meet her regard. Then his firm mouth quirked at the corners and he returned his attention to the food.

Moments later Laura was dunking pieces of her cheese sandwich into the soup. She made appreciative noises as she ate. "Sorry. I know dunking isn't polite."

"Go for it. I like to dunk mine, too." Cheek bulging, he cast her a teasing look. "Don't tell my mother, all right? She's a stickler on table manners."

Laura laughed. "Aha. Now I've got something on you."

They fell into a comfortable silence as

they enjoyed the meal. He slurped when he spooned soup into his mouth, which helped Laura to relax and do a little slurping herself. When she accidentally dribbled on her chin, he grinned and winked at her.

They tidied the kitchen together, an endeavor that had Laura's heart leaping into her throat when she turned and ran face-first into his chest. "Whoa. Are you okay?" He caught her by the shoulders and bent slightly at the knees to check her face. "That had to smart."

Laura didn't know which was worse, the sting of her nose or the unsettling tingle of her skin where his big hands rested. "I'm fine."

"Do you want some ice?"

"No, no." She shook her head and gave in to the urge to rub her nose. "We didn't hit that hard."

When the dishes were in the machine and the counters were wiped clean, they washed the doll bottles and filled them with warm formula. The puppy-feeding operation took place in the living room in front of the fire, Isaiah on one beanbag, Laura on the other. They sat cross-legged, each with a puppy cradled in the bend of one arm.

"I've never done this," she informed him.

He chuckled. "With thirteen hungry

mouths to feed, you're going to be an expert in no time."

When the first two puppies had been fed, they went back to the bedroom for replacements. The moment they had returned the first puppies to the wading pool, Laura realized they had a potential problem.

"Uh-oh. How will we tell which ones we've fed and which ones we haven't? They all look alike."

Isaiah looked momentarily perplexed, but then his frown eased away. "You're talking to an identical twin. Tucker and I look alike, but anyone who knows us has no trouble telling us apart because we behave so differently."

"How does that help us with the puppies?"

He grinned. "Behavior differences, Sherlock. The puppies we just fed are sleepy. See?" He pointed to the pair of contented babies. "If it wiggles, feed it."

Laura laughed and grabbed a wiggler. When they returned to the fire, Isaiah said, "The novelty of this is going to wear off for me at about three o'clock in the morning."

"No worries. I brought my windup alarm. I can handle the night feedings without help."

"It's the weekend. I don't mind getting up."

Laura couldn't quite envision herself sitting beside him on a beanbag when she was wearing only a nightgown. "No, no. I wanted to do this. It won't be that hard."

As it turned out, the first middle-of-the-night feeding occurred at two o'clock, not three. Isaiah awakened with a start to the faint sound of a feminine voice. He'd already shot from the bed before he remembered the puppies and his pretty houseguest. He grabbed his jeans from the foot of the bed and dragged them on. Hapless lifted his head from the spare pillow and blinked sleepily.

"Go back to sleep, buddy. No point in your getting up."

The pup snuggled back down and closed his eyes. Isaiah pulled on a shirt as he entered the living room. Not bothering with the buttons, he followed the sweet sound of Laura's voice to the guest room. The door was ajar, and the light from within spread across the hardwood floor in a golden wedge. Craning his neck, Isaiah peeked around the door frame. Backside to the door, Laura was bent over the wading pool, cooing and talking to the puppies. She wore a flannel nightshirt that would have reached modestly to just above her knees had she been standing erect.

Only she wasn't.

Isaiah jerked back so fast that he cracked the side of his head on the door. Unfortunately that quick glimpse of bare, shapely legs and the shadowy triangle at their apex had been branded upon his brain. A certain recalcitrant part of his anatomy went rock-hard.

Laura whirled around, holding a puppy in one hand. With her eyes unfocused from sleep and her hair mussed from the pillow, she might have passed for a twelve-year-old if not for the womanly curves of her body, which, much to his dismay, were displayed in revealing detail by the soft, worn flannel. Without a fire the ambient temperature of the house had turned chilly, and her nipples had reacted to the cold, going hard and pointed.

"Isaiah," she said breathlessly. "You startled me. What was that thumping noise?"

It had been his head, knocking on wood. That worked. "I rapped on the door to let you know I was here."

"Oh."

"I heard your voice. I thought I'd come help."

"I'm not dressed," she pointed out.

Isaiah had noticed that, yes. Since the first moment that he'd clapped eyes on Laura, he'd been struggling not to feel physically attracted to her. Now he was having trouble remembering why. She was beautiful, sweet, and easy to get along with. He enjoyed her company and liked her as a person. What more could a guy want?

Nothing, he realized. She was everything he'd ever wanted and more. *Sweet Christ.* Two in the morning was a hell of a time to have this kind of epiphany. He needed a cup of coffee. Or maybe he needed his head examined. He was a confirmed bachelor. He had his life all planned out, and none of his plans for the near future included a wife, no matter how sweet and wonderful she was.

"Are you all right?" she asked.

Hell, no, he wasn't all right. He'd just been blindsided by the realization that he was in love with her. He wanted to wring his mother's neck. This was all her fault. If not for her he never would have met Laura Townsend.

"Isaiah?"

He blinked and refocused. The picture hadn't changed. Flannel had never looked so good.

"I'm fine," he said.

"Are you sure? Maybe you should go back to bed."

Alone? He rubbed a hand over his face. *Time-out.* He needed to think this through. A cup of coffee might help clear his head. Yeah, that was it. He was sleep-befuddled. Once he came awake, he'd laugh at himself. Isaiah Coulter in love? Not for another five years, at least.

"I'm fine," he said again. Gesturing vaguely behind him, he added, "I'll build the fire back up while you mix the formula. Sound okay?"

He went to the kitchen first to put on a much-needed pot of coffee. Then he laid a fire. As he huffed and blew, trying to make the kindling catch, Laura padded barefoot to the kitchen. He was relieved to note that she'd slipped on a pair of sweatpants, pink ones that went nicely with the itty-bitty roses on her nightshirt.

At least *her* good sense hadn't gone on hiatus. A tantalizing picture of her backside flashed behind his eyes again, and every thought in his brain crisscrossed. He *wanted* her. The masculine side of him wasn't exactly pleased that she'd decided to hide those gorgeous legs.

Coffee. He'd think more clearly — not to mention more rationally — once he got some wake-me-up pumping through his veins. He hurried to the kitchen. Laura stood at the sink, frowning intently as she mixed the formula. He poured a cup of java and took a huge sip, then another. The liquid was so hot that it seared his tongue.

Laura turned toward him with a bottle held aloft. He knew he was a goner when he found himself studying the delicate angles and planes of her face instead of sneaking a peak at her unfettered breasts.

"Is this the right amount of water?" she asked.

Isaiah forced himself to check the water level. "Perfect," he assured her, only he wasn't thinking about formula ratios. *She* was perfect. Almost from the start he'd been hooked. All those times when he'd wondered at himself for finding ways to be with her. His panic when she'd almost been fired. His anger with Tucker for implying that she was a liar. He'd loved her all along and just hadn't had the good sense to realize it.

Okay. Fine. Being in love wasn't a death sentence. As recently as Thanksgiving he'd toyed with the thought of settling down in two or three years. It was just happening sooner than he'd expected. No big deal. Granted, he was busy, and carving out blocks of time to spend with Laura wouldn't be easy. But that wasn't an insurmountable problem. He and Tucker had been talking for months about bringing in a couple of partners so they could each take more time off. If they followed through on that, they'd each have a lot more time for a personal life. Aside from the fact that his mother would gloat, he could think of no good reason why he shouldn't act on his feelings. It wasn't as if he fell in love every day of the week.

Problem. This was Laura's first night in his home. If he made a move on her — hell, if he even looked at her wrong — she'd probably think he was a lecherous creep who had maneuvered her into this situation, hoping to get her in the sack.

"Are you sure you're all right?" she asked.

He jerked back to the moment. "I'm great. The coffee helped."

And it had. He could think more clearly now, and being in love with her no longer seemed quite so alarming. His main concern, now that his brain was firing on all cylinders, was how he should proceed. Slowly, he decided. If he suddenly blurted out that he was in love with her, he might scare her off.

He couldn't have that.

Chapter Twelve

Two more feedings occurred during the night, and by six o'clock the next morning, when Isaiah faced the wading pool, romantic musings were the farthest thing from his mind. Thirteen puppies, tiny though they were, had a way of making a lot of messes when they were being fed every two hours. After contemplating the soiled towels through sleepy, narrowed eyes, he decided a cup of coffee should precede the unpleasant reality of cleanup.

Isaiah helped Laura feed the puppies while the coffeemaker went through its brewing cycle. Hapless squirmed and wiggled his way in between the beanbags, sniffed at the puppy in the crook of Isaiah's arm, and then let loose with a mournful growl.

"I think he's jealous," Laura said.

Isaiah chuckled and held the bottle with his chin while he petted Hapless. "I love you, blockhead. No other dog will ever take your place in my affection."

Hapless moaned again, which made

Laura laugh. "He's heard that pickup line before."

Isaiah smiled thoughtfully as he resumed feeding the puppy. *Pickup line?* He had no idea how much actual experience Laura had had with men before her accident, but she was clearly well versed in their treacherous wiles. He'd made a wise decision last night. This situation definitely needed some time.

When the last pup had been returned to its bed, Isaiah made a beeline for the kitchen, thinking that Laura would follow him. He was well into his first mug of wake-me-up when he realized she didn't mean to join him and went to find her. She was in the laundry room, humming the tune to "Frosty the Snowman" while she rinsed puppy poop from bedding towels before putting them in the washer. Unlike him, she hadn't yet indulged in a cup of coffee. Nor had she gotten dressed. Like a little soldier on a mission, she was taking care of her duties before she tended to her personal needs.

"What are you doing?"

Eyes still blurred from sleep, her hair going every which way with a rooster tail on top, she looked too beautiful to be legal when she turned to meet his gaze. "Taking care of the puppies," she said, her voice still husky with drowsiness. "What are you doing?"

Isaiah wanted to hide his mug behind his back. Instead he set it on the counter and said, "Taking over. Go have a cup of coffee and grab a shower."

"But this is my job."

"*Our* job," he corrected. "I never meant for you to do all of it, Laura."

"But —"

"No buts." He held up a staying hand. "I wanted to save the puppies as much as you did. There was just no way I could manage alone. Working together, neither of us will be overloaded."

She gave a towel a final swish under the faucet. "If you're going to help, then I insist that we split the profits when the puppies are sold."

Isaiah couldn't have cared less about the damned profits. But then, he knew that Laura didn't either. "Deal," he agreed. "You've done half the towels. I'll do the other half."

She nodded, scrubbed her hands, and reached for the towel on a hook above the sink. "I relined the wading pool with clean towels. The puppies are all sound asleep."

"Good. That'll give us time to have

showers and fix some breakfast."

Thirty minutes later Isaiah was stepping from the shower when a delicious smell wafted to him. He quickly got dressed and shaved. Then he followed his nose through the house and found Laura standing before his new Viking range top. She wore a dishtowel apron over a fresh pair of jeans and a Christmas-green sweater. Isaiah didn't know if it was the enticing aromas that filled the kitchen or the woman herself, but she looked good enough to eat. Hapless lay at her feet, gazing adoringly up at her.

"You're not feeding him, are you?"

She gave him an innocent look. "Heavens, no!" Even as she denied the charge, she tossed the mottled, loose-skinned pup a morsel of sausage. "He might become a beggar."

And Isaiah wouldn't blame him. Food had never smelled so good. "Yum." He lifted the lids from two of the skillets and saw hash browns in one, link sausage in the other. "What's in the oven?"

"Biscuits."

"Homemade?" Dumb question. He had no tube biscuits in the fridge. "I've died and gone to heaven."

"They're just drop biscuits." She

grabbed a whisk to whip some eggs with milk. "Nothing fancy."

This was the first real breakfast — the first actual meal, for that matter — that had ever been cooked in his state-of-the-art kitchen. "Any kind of biscuit is fancy in my book. What can I do to help?"

Seconds later Isaiah was putting paper-towel place mats on the bar and gathering condiments from the cupboard and fridge. His mouth was watering by the time Laura served the meal, homemade biscuits drizzled with butter and honey, hash browns, sausage done to a turn, and fluffy scrambled eggs with orange juice on the side.

Isaiah ate like a horse. Afterward he and Hapless helped clean the kitchen. Hapless's job was to stand on his hind legs, front feet planted on the open dishwasher door, to lick up dribbles of egg yolk and sausage grease the moment they hit the stainless steel.

"That is so gross," Isaiah complained.

"He's not hurting anything," Laura retorted. "The washer will kill any germs."

Hapless gave Isaiah a smug look and started licking the tines of a fork. When the dishwasher was humming industriously, it was time to feed the puppies again. Laura giggled as she collected a tiny rottweiler and poked a bottle nipple into its mouth. "He is *so* sweet!"

Isaiah was pleased to note that she had the gender right this time. "They are pretty sweet," he agreed.

In actuality, though, Isaiah thought Laura was the sweet one. She'd been up every two hours all night long, a schedule that would make anyone cranky. Instead she sat cross-legged on a beanbag, looking fresh, well scrubbed, and ready for anything. No one would ever guess that she'd slept in stops and starts for a total of six hours.

"We need to go grocery shopping," he said as they returned the last of the puppies to their clean bed.

"You don't have to go to the clinic at all today?"

"It's Tucker's weekend to work Saturday. I'm off unless there's an emergency after hours. We share anything that comes in on Sundays."

"Safeway?" she asked brightly.

Isaiah wasn't married to any particular store. "Sure, Safeway will be fine."

"Good. I know all the aisles. That's import-ant for someone like me."

Forty minutes later Isaiah was tapping his foot. Laura shopped like a snail, removing things from the shelves to stare at them, but only rarely putting an item in the cart. He finally determined that she had trouble reading the labels, and expedited matters by helping her find what she needed. They were soon moving through the store at a faster pace, and the cart was brimming with groceries.

As they checked out, Isaiah caught her ogling the cover of a new mystery novel. When he asked if she wanted to buy it, she shook her head. "I have to wait until they come out on tape," she said wistfully.

Isaiah waited until her head was turned and then tossed several novels into the cart. While Laura was staying at his place, there was no reason he couldn't read to her in the evenings.

As they exited the supermarket, Laura gazed longingly at the Christmas trees that were lined up along the front of the building. Normally Isaiah didn't decorate for the holiday. When he wanted to see Christmas lights, he went to visit his parents or one of his married brothers. No fuss, no bother. When the holiday was over, he didn't have to mess with taking down a tree or storing heaps of decorations.

Problem. He had someone else in his life

now — a very sweet someone who yearned for a Christmas tree. After stowing their groceries in the back of the Hummer, Isaiah led Laura back to the store. Her eyes went wide with delight when she realized that he meant to get a tree.

"Take your pick," he told her.

Five minutes later they were at a tree lot on the opposite side of town. Choosing a Christmas tree was a serious business to Laura. She circled. She eyed every branch critically. That tree had a thin spot. Another had a spindly top. Isaiah had begun to fear that they'd never find a tree to suit her when she finally came upon a spruce that pleased her.

"What do you think?" she asked him.

"It's a beautiful tree," he agreed, so glad she'd found something that he was tempted to kiss the boughs. "Let's get it."

She frowned in indecision. "Maybe we should look some more."

Isaiah glanced at his watch. "We have to feed puppies, remember."

Pressed for time, Laura settled on the spruce. While Isaiah was strapping the evergreen to the roof rack of the Hummer, he realized that he had nothing to hang on it. After racing home to put away their groceries and feed the puppies, they returned to town for lights and decorations. Isaiah had always hated to shop and planned to simply grab some things — a few strings of lights, several boxes of balls, and maybe some garland. But again, Laura took the business of buying Christmas decorations to a whole new level. Because Isaiah had a log home, nothing less than a country theme would do.

She took him to a shop that specialized in Christmas décor. Instead of ordinary lights, Isaiah got old-fashioned bubble lights. Instead of the usual shiny glass balls, he got handcrafted ornaments — Santa Clauses, cute little mice in people clothes, dogs, cats, horses, cows, angels in all shapes and sizes, and only God knew what else, with garland that looked like the popcorn he and his siblings had strung for the tree many years ago.

To Isaiah's surprise he enjoyed himself. There were about twenty decorated Christmas trees in the place, and all the ornaments were for sale. He spent almost twenty minutes at the dog tree, looking for a miniature Hapless. Unfortunately the mixed-breed pup was one of a kind. He settled for a dalmatian, a shar-pei, and a rottweiler to represent Hapless's boiling-pot ancestry.

The final tab was over three hundred dollars.

"Oh, that's too much," Laura cried when the clerk gave them the tally. "We'll put some things back."

"No, we won't." Isaiah handed over his credit card. "I like all the stuff. And it'll last for years. Right?"

"Yes, but —"

"We'll take it," Isaiah told the clerk.

When they got back home, they fed the puppies again and then carried in their purchases. Isaiah set up the tree in front of the living room windows while Laura went to the kitchen.

"We can't trim a tree without some of my grandpa Jim's mulled wine," she called over her shoulder.

When Isaiah joined her minutes later, she had already commandeered a seventy-dollar bottle of merlot from his wine rack and had the contents simmering in a pot. He didn't have the heart to tell her that she'd just uncorked a prize-winning wine from Oregon's famous Willamette Valley that he'd been saving for a special occasion. Just watching her in his kitchen made the occasion special enough for him. She had added some orange juice, cinnamon sticks, and other spices to the merlot. The concoction smelled divine.

"When can I have a taste?" he asked.

"It needs to simmer awhile longer," she informed him.

While the wine mulled, they strung the lights on the tree. Then they returned to the kitchen for cups of warm, spiced wine. "Mm," Isaiah said when he took a taste. "This is fabulous, Laura."

She dimpled a cheek and nodded. "Now we're ready to trim the tree."

Isaiah was a quick study. No haphazard placement of ornaments was allowed. Every decoration had to be hung in just the right spot.

Late that night, when they stood back to admire the finished project, both of them were just a little tipsy. Isaiah felt contented and happy as he hadn't in a very long time. The Christmas lights joined with the fire-light to fill the living room with cheerful warmth, making it seem more like a home than it had since he'd moved there.

"It's the pretti-est tree I've ever seen," Laura murmured.

"Beautiful," he agreed, only he was no longer admiring the tree. In the flickering light Laura looked so lovely, her hair shimmering like molten gold, her eyes luminous, her skin flawless and glowing. He'd never wanted to kiss anyone so much in all his life. Unfortunately he didn't think it would be wise to act on the urge just yet. With a woman — in this case, *the* woman — timing was everything. Instead he said, "Now all I need is some furniture."

She glanced around at the empty room. "You'll get some in time."

"I want some now." He forced his thoughts to safer channels by turning to regard the room. "Will you help me pick it out, Laura?"

"Me?"

He couldn't help but be amused by the incredulity in her tone. "Yes, you. I really like your apartment. It reminds me of my parents' house. You took a small rectangle of living area and turned it into a home."

"Thank you."

He met her gaze. "Help me turn this place into a home."

Her expression still incredulous, she shook her head.

"Please?"

"I wouldn't know where to start. This is your house. It should reflect who you are."

"You know me pretty well." He gestured at the emptiness around them. "Now that the tree is up, it looks so bare in here." He grinned slowly. "It'd be fun. Say yes."

She chafed her arms and turned in a slow half circle. "How much do you want to spend?"

"Whatever it costs. I make damned good money, and as you can see, I don't spend much of it. Help me blow a few grand."

She laughed and executed another turn to survey the room. "Leather," she said softly. "You want a rustic ranch feeling in this house. You like the outdoors. An-imals are a big part of your life. You won't feel at home if the rooms are fussy."

Isaiah totally agreed. He just hoped that she pleased her own taste as well as his, be-cause someday, if he had his way, the home she created would be for both of them.

The following week Laura was scheduled to work nights again, starting Monday. Isaiah volunteered to watch the puppies so she wouldn't have to take them with her to the clinic, but she refused the offer. He worked much longer hours than she did and needed eight hours of uninterrupted rest, whereas she could sleep in if need be. She bought a large wicker basket in which to carry the puppies back and forth, and once at work she divided her time between her regular duties and puppy feedings. That made her shift not only more

411

stressful but also longer. With the puppies to care for, she found it impossible to complete all her usual duties in the same amount of time.

When she got back to the house, usually at about four in the morning, Isaiah was asleep. Sometimes Hapless bounded from the bedroom to greet her, but otherwise Laura spent thirty minutes alone while she tried to wind down enough to sleep. When she got up around noon, Isaiah had long since left for work, and she didn't see him until he came home in the afternoon, some days earlier than others so they could shop together for furniture.

With the shopping trips to complicate the evening hours, Laura made good use of Isaiah's slow cooker, preparing their dinners ahead and leaving them to simmer until they got home. Isaiah didn't seem to mind. He praised her beef roast and vegetables and had three helpings of the chicken and dumplings she made.

The hectic pace should have made it easy for Laura to keep her head out of the clouds, but just the reverse occurred. When furniture began to arrive, she found herself feeling proprietary toward the rooms as they began to take shape. *Foolish Laura, spinning impossible dreams.* This wasn't her home, and it never would be, just as Isaiah wasn't her man and never would be. But she couldn't help but wish.

As she tried to choose the perfect wall to hang a mountain scene by a local artist, she wished. As she prepared meals to go in the slow cooker, she wished. When she greeted Isaiah as he came in at night, she wished.

It was partly his fault, she decided. He had a certain way of smiling at her that made her feel like the most special person in his world, and sometimes she could have sworn she saw yearning in his eyes when he looked at her. And just how, exactly, was she to keep her feelings in check when he went out of his way to be so thoughtful? After dinner of an evening, he took to reading aloud to her until it was time for her to leave for work. Even after a beautiful leather sofa and easy chairs arrived for the living room, they sat by the fire on the beanbags.

It was cozy and a little too intimate for Laura's peace of mind, with the fire crackling behind them and the Christmas-tree lights pulsing warm color over the room. Isaiah's deep, silky voice curled around her, working on her senses like an intoxicant. Sometimes she forgot to listen to his words and lost herself in imagining how it might be if he suddenly turned and kissed her.

She was falling in love with him. Correction: She'd been in love with him for weeks. Laura lectured herself constantly never to let him know. He was a wonderful boss and an even better friend. If not for him, the puppies, each of which she had come to love, would have been put to sleep. She absolutely couldn't abuse his kindness by making him feel guilty for not returning her affection.

No, she told herself firmly. Friendship was a lovely thing, and she had to be happy with that. Christmas was coming. She had always loved the season and tried to stay focused on that and enjoy every moment. During the afternoons, when she wasn't greeting deliverymen and trying to decide where to place furniture, she often baked. She went to her apartment for Christmas tins and filled them with goodies to go under the tree, cookies and candies, fruitcakes and bars. Isaiah was still too thin. She enjoyed seeing him devour the treats. She discovered that he loved chocolate and made him a batch of creamy fudge. Other afternoons she ran into town between puppy feedings to shop for the house, buying vases, throw pillows, and colorful rugs to brighten the hardwood floors.

By Thursday, the sixteenth of December, Isaiah's house had begun to look like a home. Laura was giving a silk flower arrangement some finishing touches when the phone rang. She gave the flowers a last pat and grabbed the portable from the kitchen counter.

"Hello?"

"Hello, dear heart. This is Mary, Isaiah's mom."

Laura had been in touch with her grandmother since coming to stay at Isaiah's, but she hadn't spoken with Mary. "Mary," she said with genuine gladness. "How nice to hear your voice."

"How are the puppies?"

"Growing," Laura said with a laugh. "I only have to feed them every three hours now. That makes it easier."

"Ah, good." Mary sighed. "I'm just wondering, dear. Has Isaiah mentioned his birthday to you?"

Laura perched on a bar stool to admire the flower arrangement on the kitchen table from across the room. *Just the right touch,* she decided. "No," she replied distractedly, "he hasn't said a word. When is his birthday?"

"Today."

Laura jerked erect on the stool. "What?"

Mary laughed. "You heard me. I called Tucker this morning and surprised him with best wishes, but Isaiah was out in the field, so I haven't talked to him yet. I'm afraid they both forgot."

Laura couldn't imagine forgetting her own birthday. "You're kidding."

"Don't I wish. Isaiah has always been my absentminded one, thinking deep thoughts and scarcely aware of what's happening around him. I might expect him to forget. But Tucker?" She sighed again. "Ah, well, I'm sure it's because they're both so busy."

Laura had brought only one cookbook from her apartment. Her grandmother had gone through the entire thing, drawing little sketches off to the side of all the recipes. A half-filled cup represented a half cup, etc. Laura used that cookbook a lot because she wasn't as likely to misread an ingredient amount with the sketches to clarify the measurements. Only she couldn't remember if the collection included a cake recipe. As a general rule, cakes weren't her favorite things to bake because they went stale quickly and didn't freeze as nicely as other goodies. But she absolutely had to make one for Isaiah's birthday.

"Anyway," Mary was saying, "how about

a surprise party over here tonight? Dinner, followed by cake and ice cream. Just family — and you, too, of course. Do you think you can maneuver my son into coming over without spilling the beans?"

Laura grinned. "Yeah, I think I can do that. Do you mind if I bring the puppies?"

When Laura informed Isaiah that they were going to his parents' house for dinner that night, he almost groaned. She had been staying at his place for almost a week, and he hadn't made a single move on her. Tonight he'd meant to rectify that. Surely she'd been there long enough now to know that he wasn't merely trying to take advantage of a convenient situation. He wanted to tell her how he felt about her, possibly even ask her to marry him, and let Mother Nature take it from there.

"I'm beat," he said when she told him about having dinner at his parents' house. "Can we make it for another night?"

"No. Sorry. Your mom and I are going to make Christmas cookies."

Isaiah thought of all the goodies under the tree and in his freezer. As it was, he'd weigh three hundred pounds if he ate them all. But when he looked into Laura's pleading hazel eyes, he found it difficult to deny her anything. He sighed. Maybe, he decided, tonight wasn't the best time to tell her he loved her, anyway. She had to work the late shift. If he waited until Saturday night they'd have the entire evening and night together.

"Okay," he agreed reluctantly. "Just let me grab a shower."

"Hurry. I don't want to be late."

Unbeknownst to Isaiah, he carried his birthday gift from Laura into his parents' house. When he collected the cardboard box from the backseat of the Hummer, he mistakenly thought it contained cookie-decorating paraphernalia. He about had a heart attack when he stepped into his folks' darkened living room. All the lights suddenly came on, and his entire family burst from the kitchen, yelling, "Surprise!"

Isaiah could only gape at them. Surprise? Then it dawned on him. It was the sixteenth of December, his and Tucker's birthday. He couldn't believe they had forgotten. His twin brother, who'd arrived ahead of him, grinned sheepishly and shrugged. "I had a lot on my mind. What can I say?"

Jake clapped Isaiah on the shoulder. "Happy birthday, little brother. You've been a pain in my ass for thirty-four years now."

Molly, Jake's wife, went up on her tiptoes to give Isaiah a hug. "Idiot," she whispered. "I've never heard of senility setting in at so young an age."

That was only the beginning. Except for Tucker, everyone in Isaiah's family felt obligated to razz him about forgetting his birthday. Isaiah took it good-naturedly. Like Tucker, he'd had his mind on other matters, namely a pretty little blonde with big hazel eyes who made him go brain-dead every time he looked at her.

Dinner was wonderful. His mom had prepared two main courses, seafood fettuccini for Tucker, and prime rib for Isaiah.

"I had to fix each of you your favorites!" she explained.

"You're a marvel, Mom," Isaiah said. Tucker bested him with, "You're the most wonderful mother in the world." When Mary turned away, Tucker gave Isaiah a smug grin and said in a low voice, "Now who's the number one twin?"

"Yeah, well," Isaiah popped back, "you got the charm and I got the brains."

After cake and ice cream were served, the puppies had to be fed, and everyone in the family participated. Sly and Garrett got into a fight over who got to feed the thirteenth pup. Laura settled the dispute by letting them each take turns until the bottle ran dry. Watching her with the children, Isaiah knew beyond a doubt that she would be a fabulous mother. All that remained was for him to convince her to have his babies.

When the puppies had all been returned to the wicker basket, Isaiah and Tucker sat on the living room floor, surrounded by loved ones as they opened their gifts. Isaiah got an appointment book from his mother, a new Stetson from his dad, a collection of shirts and ties from his brothers, and two twelve-count packages of gray wool boot socks from his sister.

"So your socks will always match," Bethany said with an impish grin.

Nowadays Laura was doing Isaiah's laundry, and his socks were all folded neatly into pairs. He glanced over at the lady in question before opening the gift that she'd gotten for him. It was in a heavy, gaily wrapped box about eight inches square. The attached card was from Hallmark, a beautiful outdoor scene on the front with a horse and rider in the distance. Inside she had painstakingly written,

*Thakn you for beign you. Love awlays,
Laura.*

Tears stung Isaiah's eyes as he returned
the card to its envelope. Instead of passing
it around, he tucked it under his leg. Eight
simple words, but they meant the world to
him. He could almost see her, hunched
over the card at the kitchen table, struggling to form each letter.

When he unwrapped the gift, the room
grew quiet. Isaiah slowly lifted the chunky
figurine from the box so everyone might
see it. Handcrafted from Mount Saint
Helens volcanic ash, it was a female rottweiler, surrounded by a litter of pups.

"A paperweight," Isaiah said huskily.
Only it was so much more, something to
remind him in years to come of this time
that they'd had together.

When Isaiah looked up, he saw Laura's
love for him shining in her eyes, along with
a shimmer of tears. He felt as if a mule had
kicked him squarely in the chest. She was in
love with him? His lungs deflated. His gut
clenched. His heart pounded like a sledge-
hammer against his eardrums. She loved
him. All this last week he'd been planning
and plotting ways to coax her into his arms,
and she'd been his for the taking all along.
How the hell had he missed that?

The answer was there in Isaiah's mind almost before he finished asking himself the question. Laura believed with all her heart that her aphasia made her undesirable. His throat went tight as he gathered the torn wrapping paper from all the gifts into a pile. *Laura.* She'd carefully kept her feelings for him hidden, undoubtedly convinced that he would never return them. She considered herself damaged merchandise. Her ability to be a wife and mother was impaired. What man in his right mind would want a woman who couldn't write checks, misspelled simple words, and had difficulty talking?

Isaiah knotted his fist over a clump of paper. He should have felt elated. The woman he adored with all his heart loved him just as much as he loved her. But instead he felt heartsick. It wasn't only that he'd been holding back sexually, never kissing her or touching her to let her know that he desired her. He'd also failed to let her know how wonderful he thought she was.

When the mess had been cleared away, Isaiah stepped outside for a moment to make a phone call. When he reentered the house he wasted no time in collecting his birthday presents, his pretty houseguest, and the puppies.

"I'm beat, Mom." He hugged his mother from behind where she stood at the sink rinsing dessert plates. "Would you mind if we bail out early? I want to go home and crash."

Mary turned in his arms to go up on her tiptoes and kiss his cheek. "Not at all, dear heart." She cupped a hand to the side of his face. "Maybe soon you can bring in some partners and stop working so hard all the time."

Isaiah meant to do that far sooner than his mother imagined. He didn't intend to get married and leave his bride alone twelve to fourteen hours a day. "Tucker and I are working on it." He placed a soft kiss on Mary's forehead. "Thank you for the surprise party. It was wonderful. And the prime rib was out of this world."

As Isaiah drew away, Mary patted his arm. "I'm so glad Laura managed to get you here without letting the cat out of the bag."

His birthday party wasn't the only cat that Laura hadn't let out of the bag. She loved him. The thought circled endlessly in his mind, as unbelievable to him after an hour as it had been when the realization first struck.

He definitely had some fences to mend

when they got home. If nothing else, she would go to bed tonight knowing that he thought she was the most wonderful woman in the world.

After making the rounds to tell everyone good-bye, Isaiah carried his gifts out to the Hummer, then returned for Laura and the puppies. When they were all settled in the vehicle, he peered at her through the gloom, trying to make out her expression in the light from the streetlamp that angled through the windshield. She was smiling, as always, only now he noticed how she avoided looking him directly in the eye. According to Isaiah's dad, the eyes were windows to the soul. Now Isaiah realized they were also windows to the heart.

Isaiah was quiet on the way home, making Laura wonder if he was angry with her about something. When they entered the house, Hapless leaped up on Isaiah's leg, then on Laura's. Then he ran in figure eights around them, growling deep in his throat and wagging his tail.

"Hello, Hapless." Laura set the puppy basket down so she might give the older dog some individual attention. Hapless shivered with delight when she crouched down to pet him. "I think he missed us," she told Isaiah.

Isaiah put his gifts on the sofa and peeled off his jacket. After a quick trip to the coat closet, he returned to the living room to add wood to the dwindling fire. With Hapless following at her heels, Laura carried the puppies to the bedroom. Because she had to leave for work in less than an hour, she decided to leave her charges in their basket. She had washed all the bottles at Isaiah's mother's house. She set the sack of formula and feeding paraphernalia on the floor by the wicker carrier.

She jumped with a start when she straightened and saw Isaiah standing in the doorway. He looked pensive, brooding, and so handsome that her breath hitched in her chest.

"You can put them in the pool," he said. "You aren't going in tonight."

Laura gave him a bewildered look. "But I —"

"I called Ellie Kingston. She's covering your shift tonight and tomorrow night."

"But —"

"It's my birthday," he reminded her. "Having you here the next two nights is my gift to myself. I'll pay you your usual wage if you're worried about the money."

"Don't be silly. I don't need the money."

"Good. Ellie needs the hours. Christmas and all that. You're doing her a good turn and making me happy, both at once."

Laura wished she could spend the rest of her life making him happy. But she would have to settle for only three more weeks. The puppies would be seven days old tomorrow. Her time here was flying by. Before she knew it she'd be going home to her apartment.

"Let's read for a while," he suggested. "I'll turn on the tree lights. It'll be a nice ending to a wonderful evening."

Something in his eyes — an intensity in the blue depths that she'd never seen before — made her nervous. She wondered once again if she'd said or done something at the party to upset him. Before she could ask, he turned away from the doorway. She put the puppies in their wading pool and returned to the living room.

Isaiah was already reclining on a beanbag, his back supported by the hearth, his long legs extended and slightly bent. On his lap he held the mystery novel that he'd been reading to her. The blue plaid shirt he wore brought out the color of his eyes.

Laura gingerly sat on the beanbag beside

him. Hapless immediately launched himself onto her lap. She cuddled the overgrown puppy to her chest, ruffling his ears as she glanced over at Isaiah.

"Ready?" he asked huskily.

Laura nodded and settled back, trying to recall the scene he'd read to her last night. A burglar had been rifling the home of the main protagonist, looking for a handgun. The implication was that the burglar meant to do murder. It was a strange novel, in Laura's estimation. No crime had yet been committed. She didn't know who was going to be killed. She only knew that the burglar meant to do the deed and pin the crime on the hero.

Isaiah began to read, his voice deep and silky, his pronunciation of every word perfect. Lulled by the story, Laura soon felt totally relaxed. Hapless fell asleep with his head nestled between her breasts, his snores adding yet another layer of coziness to the winter night.

Isaiah suddenly stopped reading and reached for another book lying on the hearth. As he opened to the first page, Laura gave him a questioning look.

"I'm in the mood for something lighter tonight," he explained. "Do you mind?"

Laura shook her head. In truth, she was

growing impatient with the mystery, waiting for something to happen. So far it was all buildup with no delivery.

Isaiah cleared his throat and began to read. "Looking back on that evening, I can only wonder why I didn't know the moment that I clapped eyes on her that she was the love of my life." He coughed again and settled deeper into the beanbag. "When I opened the office door and saw her for the first time, I was instantly attracted to her. But I blamed it on mere physical attraction. She was just another pretty woman, I told myself. But then, slowly, as I came to know her as a person, I realized she was far more. She literally changed my life, at first only in little ways, but over time all the little things added up and became huge. Now I love her so much that I feel panicky at the thought of losing her. Even worse, I'm not sure how to tell her."

He paused to look over at her. Laura wiggled more deeply into the cushiony beanbag. "A romance?" She flashed him a pleased grin. "How nice."

He gave her a long, penetrating look. Then he cleared his throat again and resumed reading. "I thought I could content myself with simply being friends. Best friends, I guess you'd say. Only now I want and need more than that. I'm praying that she wants more, too."

He stopped reading to turn the page. Laura shifted Hapless in her arms. "It's not in third person," she observed.

He gave her another odd look, then returned his attention to the page. "I don't know when it happened. When I fell in love with her, I mean. I wonder now if it was the first time that I saw her lovely face. Or maybe it was later, when I started to realize what a wonderful person she is. She has the most incredible hazel eyes. When I look into them, I feel as if I've been lost all my life and have finally found my way home."

Laura's heart caught. Hazel eyes? She searched his dark profile. Then she thought, *Get real, Laura. You're really reaching.*

"When it started doesn't really matter," he read on. "I only know it *did* happen. She fills my life with laughter, she makes me happy in a way no one else ever has, and sometimes I think she understands me better than I do myself. She knew how torn up I was when an old lady's cat died. She listens when I need to discuss my patients. She makes me fudge because I love chocolate."

Tears sprang to Laura's eyes. She wasn't imagining it. He was talking about her. "Oh, Isaiah."

He slowly closed the book and met her gaze. "Corny, huh? I never thought I'd have a problem telling a woman I was in love with her. But every time I try to tell you, I freeze up and the words won't come."

She could barely see him now for the tears. "You love me?" she squeaked.

He gently thumbed a tear from her cheek. "I adore you, Laura. You're the most wonderful person I've ever known. I want to spend the rest of my life with you." He gestured at the room around them. "I love the house. Now I want you to live here with me, not just for a few weeks, but always."

She shook her head. "But —"

"Please don't say that word. Whenever you say that word you're about to add something really dumb. I love you. My mother finally found me the perfect woman, God love her. You're beautiful, you're smart, you're funny, and you're my best friend. Even better, as a cook you're second to none."

Laura nearly choked on a giggle. "You love me because I can cook?"

He smoothed another tear from her cheek. "When you're in the kitchen, you aren't just cooking. You're preparing gifts."

It was true, she realized. When she cooked, she thought of the people who would enjoy the dishes. She especially enjoyed cooking for Isaiah, not only because he needed the nourishment but also because he was so appreciative.

He lightly grazed his fingertips along her cheekbone and then furrowed them through her hair. "Well?" he asked huskily. "I've had a great birthday so far. Are you going to make it the most memorable one of my life by telling me you love me back?"

It took all Laura's self-control not to throw her arms around his neck. "I have brain damage, Isaiah. There are a hundred little things I can't do now, things that may become huge irri-irri—"

"Irresistible glitches?" he supplied.

She laughed again. He had a way of making her laugh. "You know the word I'm trying to say."

"Irritations," he said. "But you're wrong about that. We balance each other out, Laura. It's true that there are a number of things you can no longer do, but there are also a number of things I'm miserable at. Together we're dynamite."

"You need someone who can help with your career."

"A surgical assistant in emergencies, maybe?"

Her cheeks went warm.

"Or possibly someone who's great with animals?" He leaned closer — so close that she could feel the steamy warmth of his breath on her lips. "Do you love me, Laura?"

Her heart squeezed with yearning so intense it made her bones ache. "I don't want to be a chain around your neck."

He cupped her chin in his hand. "Do you love me? It's a very simple question."

"Yes," she finally whispered.

Before the word had completely passed her lips, he angled his dark head and settled his mouth over hers. Wet silk. The kiss was as soft as a whisper at first, and then he deepened it, making questioning forays with the tip of his tongue. Laura's head spun. She couldn't breathe. Making fists on his shirt, she clung to him as she surrendered her mouth to him, parting her lips in invitation.

Hapless, squished between them, suddenly awakened and stuck his cold, wet nose between their chins. Isaiah cursed and pulled away. Laura fell back on the beanbag, her head reeling.

"It's time for you to go outside for a while," Isaiah told the pup.

He pushed to his feet and went to the front door. Once Hapless was dispatched, he strode slowly back to the fire. Laura stared dazedly up at him, aware of his raw masculinity as she'd never been — the decisive tap of his boots with each lazy step he took, the way his broad shoulders worked in harmony with each shift of his lean hips, and the play of muscle in his thighs under the faded denim of his Wranglers. His eyes burned with desire, turning them the dark blue of cobalt. A tendon along his jaw bunched with each clench of his teeth.

He stopped a foot shy of the beanbags and started unbuttoning his shirt. "I want you," he said in a voice gone gravelly with need. "I want you as I've never wanted anyone."

That was good. That was *great.* Only she needed just a little more lead time. "Isaiah," she said shakily. "There's just this one little thing."

He dispensed with another shirt button. "What's that? Just name it, sweetheart."

Laura cringed inwardly. At thirty-one years of age, she felt it was an embarrassing thing to admit, especially in view of the fact that he'd clearly been with countless women. "I've never — done this."

His hand stilled on a button. His gaze jerked to hers. "You've never done what?"

Laura sat erect and waved her hand. *"This."*

She heard him release a breath, the sound similar to air escaping from a partially deflated balloon. "You've never made love, you mean?" His tone was incredulous. When she nodded, he flopped down on the beanbag beside her. Legs bent, arms resting limply on his upraised knees, he gave her an unbelieving study. "Not even once?"

Laura's cheeks went fiery hot. "I, um, guess you might say I never got around to it. I was busy — first with school, then with my work." That sounded so lame, even to her ears. "There was just never time."

He arched a dark brow. "I see," he said.

Only he didn't see at all, because she was lying through her teeth. Laura took a deep breath for courage and blurted, "That's not true. I wasn't busy. I mean . . . well, I was busy. But that wasn't the reason." The fiery heat of embarrassment spread to cover her face and seep over her scalp. "I was waiting for that one special man. You, Isaiah. I know that now. Only you never came along. And then I got hurt, and no one asked me on dates, and I just —"

He touched a fingertip to her mouth. "Stop," he ordered softly. His gaze locked with hers. "Are you trying to tell me that you were saving yourself for your husband?"

She nodded and twisted her face away to say, "I know it sounds old-fash-ioned. But it never felt right with any-one else." She broke off and shrugged. "In my defense, I have to say it's not all that weird. Last year's Miss Amer-ica is waiting, too. No one thinks she's crazy."

Isaiah sighed and rubbed a hand over his face. "Sweetheart, I don't think it's old-fashioned. In fact, I think it's wonderful." He waited a beat. "I just wish I could say that I'd waited, too."

Laura considered that possibility for an instant. On the one hand it might have been nice if it were the very first time for both of them, but on the other hand there were the mechanics to consider. "I'm sort of glad one of us knows what to do."

He gave a startled laugh. And then, as naturally as though he did it all the time, he looped his arms around her and lifted her onto his lap. "No worries. Just in case I forget any of the steps, I keep a how-to manual in my nightstand."

Laura had a feeling he knew all the steps by heart, and the thought made her hurt inside. When they made love, would he think of women he'd been with before and find her lacking? It wasn't as if she were practiced in pleasing a man. The sum total of her experience had come from books, movies, and what little her sister had told her.

She searched his twinkling blue eyes. "Have you been with lots of women?" she couldn't resist asking.

"Not a good question." His mouth twitched at the corners. "My past is just that — past." He dipped his head to nibble seductively at her mouth. "The minute I saw you, I instantly forgot every other woman I've ever known. I can't remember their names, can't remember what they looked like. You're everything to me, Laura, my past, my present, and, I pray to God, my future. Will you marry me?"

Deep in her heart of hearts, Laura knew he was only saying what she needed to hear. But it meant a great deal to her that he bothered. It meant even more that he was asking her to marry him. Maybe she didn't eclipse every other woman in his memory, but he'd somehow come to value her above all others. That was good enough for her.

She felt as if she might burst with happiness. "Oh, yes, I *will* marry you, Isaiah. I will. I *will*."

He kissed her then, hesitantly at first, then more deeply, his lips like warm, moist silk on hers. Laura's head spun. She grabbed frantically for breath. Her arms quivered as she hugged his strong neck. "I don't know what to do," she whispered between kisses.

He trailed his lips down the side of her neck, setting her skin afire. "You don't need to do anything," he assured her. "Nothing, sweetheart. Just be with me."

Laura expected it to entail a little more than that and was taut with nerves. To her surprise he turned sideways to the fire and moved her off his lap to sit between his spread thighs. Hands overlapping on her belly, he hunched his shoulders around her, rested his chin atop her head, and merely gazed into the flames. *Just be with me.* She'd thought the request to be an oversimplification, a deceptive prelude to naked flesh and demands on her body that she might feel self-conscious about granting. But now he was reminding her that he never oversimplified. Isaiah was as straightforward as he was wonderful.

The hard press of his arms held her firmly against his chest. The heat of him soothed her worries away and soon drained the starch from her spine. She relaxed against his sturdy strength, her gaze fixed on the dancing firelight. She was acutely aware of him in those moments, attuned to every breath he took, every thump of his heart against her shoulder blades, every slight shift of his fingertips at her waist.

The mood that fell over them was inconceivably tender, a joining of bodies and hearts, but not in the way she had expected. *Isaiah.* It was so like him to sense her feelings and somehow ease her tension. Another man might have rushed her to the bedroom and availed himself of her body, giving little or no thought to making it easier for her.

Minutes slipped by. Laura had no idea how many, only that enough time elapsed for her initial panic about making love to evaporate. When Isaiah shifted to put his back to the room and turned her sideways on his lap again, she knew he intended to kiss her. And this time she was ready.

Just be with me. The words drifted softly through her mind as he bent his dark head toward hers. His lips grazed hers as softly as a butterfly wing. Her breath came in shallow bursts. Anticipation brought her hands to his shoulders. And finally he deepened the kiss, taking her mouth like a man who'd just found nourishment after months of starvation.

Firelight and Isaiah Coulter. In Laura's mind they became synonymous, both of them generating heat, both of them brilliant, even when she closed her eyes. He went to his bedroom and returned with a sheepskin rug that he spread out over the floor in front of the hearth. Then he made love to her just as he did all else, totally focused on the details and thoroughly attending to each before he moved on. He began with the palm of her hand, tracing each line and crevice with his lips and the tip of his tongue. Laura had never considered her palm to be an erogenous zone, but with Isaiah kissing it so lightly, sensation shot clear up her arm, pulled a U-turn, and streamed like jags of lightning to the core of her.

When she was trembling with the aftershocks, he seized the hem of her sweater and plucked it off over her head as easily as he might have peeled a banana. For just an instant Laura felt embarrassed. She'd gone out in public in a two-piece swimsuit, but somehow a bra seemed less modest. But Isaiah had her hand again, and now he was trailing kisses over the inside of her wrist. It was hard to remember that she had breasts when he was doing such marvelous things to another part of her body. Soon he reached the sensitive flesh at the bend of her arm. Then he was at her shoulder — her collarbone — and next her throat. And somehow, in between kisses and nips, he unfastened her bra. It seemed to melt away from her body like the chocolate coating on a candy bar in mid-August heat.

"Oh, God, you are so beautiful," he whispered.

Laura moaned and jerked when he flicked his tongue over her nipple. The next instant he tipped her over onto the soft rug, and before she could blink she was anchored there by six-feet-plus of muscular male. He drew her nipple into his mouth. Sensation exploded through her, so intense she couldn't breathe, only she didn't want him to stop. Just when she thought she could bear it no longer, he switched to her other breast and took her under again.

At the back of Laura's mind she knew she was supposed to do something. The women in the movies didn't just lie there, moaning and quivering. Only — *oh, God* — it was so wonderful. She couldn't think clearly. She made hard fists in his hair so he couldn't get away. *Oh, yes.*

Spiraling in a feverish delirium, Laura felt a tug that moved her body on the soft surface of the rug. Then she felt the graze of denim moving down her legs. With two hard jerks Isaiah divested her of the jeans bunched around her ankles, as well as her underwear, sneakers, and socks. *Naked.* She'd never been naked with a man. Only somehow she didn't feel bare, possibly because Isaiah was everywhere — his mouth, his big, hard hands, the steely press of his body.

His hand curled over the mound at the apex of her thighs. He slipped his middle finger between the folds. Laura's spine arched. Her hips came up. She gave a startled gasp.

"Easy," he whispered. "I just want . . . It's okay, sweetheart. Trust me."

It occurred to Laura, in between mind-boggling bursts of sensation, that he'd never finished the sentence. But it didn't matter. Sometimes actions spoke more clearly than words. With graduating pressure, he stroked her until she felt like a volcano about to erupt.

"Isaiah," she cried.

"Shh. It's okay. Just let it happen," he whispered.

As if she had a choice? With one fingertip he'd taken control of her body. She couldn't withdraw. Her hips lifted up to him as if of their own accord. Her back arched. She felt like a bowstring drawn taut to release its arrow. Only nothing happened. She made tight fists over the sheepskin beneath her. Her body quivered, right on the edge, but she couldn't seem to make it over that last little crest.

Isaiah swore softly. The next instant his mouth was at her breast again, and he put more force into the strokes below. The combination of sensations rocked Laura's world. And finally she sailed over the top and felt like a piece of glass, shattering into a million brilliant pieces to float in sparkling abandon through black space. Distantly she was aware that she gasped for breath. She was also vaguely aware of Isaiah moving beside her. But her senses were so scattered that she couldn't focus on him clearly enough to see what he was doing.

"You okay?" he whispered.

Laura pried her eyes open. He was a bronzed blur above her. She blinked to clear her vision. Blue eyes, dark, chiseled features. She managed a lopsided smile and a slurred, "Fine, I'm fine."

"Ah, honey. This is the bad part. I almost wish you'd let somebody else take care of it. I can't bear to hurt you."

Laura pried her eyes open again. She felt a nudge at her opening. *Hold it.* Definitely a big nudge. Not a finger. Before she could slap a hand on the middle of his chest and say, *Let's think about this for a minute. I don't think you'll fit,* he pushed his way in.

Laura felt as if she'd been cleaved in two by a baseball bat. Pain. *Oh, God.* This surely wasn't right. Small opening, large interloper. Where had she gotten the idea that penises were no bigger around than tampons?

"You okay?"

Laura was still quivering from the hurt and holding her breath. How could she say, *I'm dying,* when her teeth wouldn't unclench?

"Laura?"

The pain abated somewhat. She was finally able to drag in a breath. She stared up at him. He supported himself on straightened arms that bulged with tightened muscle. He held perfectly still. He looked so beautiful with the firelight limning his body in amber. Laura remembered floating deliriously through space and wished she were back there.

"It *hurts*," she managed to push out.

"Only for a minute."

How did he know? Laura felt betrayed. He'd known it was going to hurt before he did it. And how long was a minute? She was still hurting, just not quite as much now. It had gone from unbearable to almost tolerable, at any rate.

"I don't like it." Her prerogative. This was *not* fun. "I want to stop."

His body was quivering. The muscles in his shoulders and arms knotted. And suddenly his dark face contorted. "Oh, shit," he said.

And the next instant he moved inside of her — only a little, and the pain this time was minimal. Even better, when he bumped bottom, Laura got an inkling of the delightful possibilities. Her insides lit up as brightly as the Christmas tree. She dug her fingers into his shoulders, wanting him to bump bottom again. Only he was poised above her like a statue, his body knotted and vibrating.

So she lifted her hips to do the bumping herself.

"Oh, *Christ!*" he ground out.

Laura moaned in delight and nudged upward with her hips again. "Oh, Isaiah. Yes."

He gave an agonized groan and collapsed on top of her. Laura blinked and wiggled her chin out from under his shoulder in order to breathe. That was it?

"I'm sorry," he muttered near her ear.

He was sorry? It had just started to be fun.

"Are we done?" she asked.

"Oh, *Christ,*" he said again.

Chapter Thirteen

Isaiah turned his face up to the stream of hot water, whimsically wondering if anyone had ever drowned himself in the shower. It seemed a fitting end for a complete shit. *God.* Had he blown it, or what? Now he knew why his father had warned him never to mess with virgins. They were fragile and complicated, and no matter how you tried, you couldn't avoid hurting them.

He closed his eyes and clenched his teeth. He'd felt her flesh tear. He loved her so damned much, and he'd felt her flesh tear. Every time he thought about it, he felt like he might puke. Ever since his teenage years he'd heard guys brag about popping some girl's cherry, as if it were the greatest sex there was. Maybe he was abnormal, but hurting anyone, most especially the woman he loved, was not a pleasurable experience for him.

He stood for a while under the spray, letting the hot water loosen his knotted muscles and hopefully clear his head. When he finally slapped off the faucet, he felt marginally better. Every woman on earth went through it once. He'd pretty much managed not to move while he was inside her. In a couple of days, any injury that he might have inflicted would be healed. Maybe then they could try it again, hopefully with more success. Next time, no matter what it took, he would make it good for her.

A few minutes later, when Isaiah entered the living room, he found Laura sitting on a beanbag feeding puppies as if nothing had ever happened. She sent him an apologetic smile.

"I'm sorry," she said. "I didn't mean to ruin it."

Isaiah finished buttoning his fresh shirt, a solid blue one to suit his mood. As he sat beside her, he asked, "How are you feeling?"

"Fine." She shifted the puppy in her arms and went back to feeding it. "It only hurt awful for a minute. Then it got better. I'm bleeding a little. Nothing bad."

Isaiah winced. He knew some bleeding was completely normal. He also realized that at some point in a woman's life, her hymen had to be torn. He'd just never wanted to be the guy to do the honors.

"Maybe we can take another stab at it in a couple of days."

The instant Isaiah spoke, he wanted to bite off his tongue. Another stab? If she didn't run screaming from the room, it'd be a miracle.

Instead she smiled, shrugged, and said, "I was hoping sooner than that."

Not on her life. "You need some time to heal."

"I really don't think I'm injured."

"You're bleeding, aren't you?"

In Isaiah's mind, that settled that.

The following day Laura was left to ramble around in the huge log house while Isaiah was away at work. A dozen different times she stood over the beanbags, remembering their time together, and the picture didn't become prettier in her mind with repetition. She'd been a big sissy, asking Isaiah to stop. Thousands of babies were born each year, and unless a woman went to a sperm bank, she didn't become pregnant without engaging in sex.

Losing their virginity hadn't made those other women swear off, and neither would she. Isaiah wanted to wait for a few days? *Ha.* They would see about that.

Isaiah canceled all nonemergency appointments late that afternoon and rescheduled them for Monday so he could leave the clinic right at five o'clock. It was Tucker's turn to work Saturday again. Unless an emergency call came in after hours, Isaiah could look forward to an entire weekend off.

When he got home thirty minutes later, it was already full dark, and Laura was nowhere to be seen. The Christmas-tree lights were on, and a fire crackled in the hearth to welcome him. Smiling, he hung up his jacket and followed his nose to the kitchen. The slow cooker sat on the counter, the lid lifting with steam occasionally to emit a wonderful smell. He peeked inside and saw huge, man-sized meatballs simmering in a red sauce. *Spaghetti?* Oh, man, he absolutely loved the stuff.

Unable to resist, he got a spoon from the drawer and ladled out a piping-hot meatball. Cupping a hand under the spoon so no sauce would drip, he started puffing on the meat to cool it. When he judged it to be at an edible temperature, he blissfully sank in his teeth.

"Hi, there, big guy," a sultry voice purred from somewhere behind him.

Mouth full of meatball, he whirled around. Laura stood at the entrance to the kitchen, one slender arm angled up the end of the wall that divided the formal dining room from the cooking area. She wore — God, help him, he had never seen anything like it — a peach-colored drape of transparent stuff with long fringe at the bottom that jerked his gaze to her bare, shapely thighs. Underneath, her breasts were covered by a tidbit of peach-colored cloth, scarcely wider than dental floss. At the apex of her legs, a T of lacy black stuff served as panties. She was the most gorgeous thing he'd ever seen in his life. Her eyes issued a sultry invitation, and she stood with her body displayed to make a man's eyes pop from his head.

Caught completely by surprise, Isaiah grabbed for breath. Bad mistake. Particles of meatball went down his windpipe. He choked — and then he couldn't breathe. At first he didn't think it was a big deal. But after coughing and then gagging, he found that he still couldn't breathe. He ran to the sink and gagged some more.

"Oh, my *God!*" Laura cried.

The next thing he knew she was whopping him on the back. For several awful seconds, each of which seemed aeons long, Isaiah thought he might die. He'd never choked before. *Panic.* He couldn't breathe, couldn't talk — and toward the last, he couldn't even gag. He just stood there, his body convulsing with spasms, his head pounding with an awful airless feeling, and black spots dancing before his eyes.

Laura locked her arms around his midsection, her small fist planted just over his diaphragm. "Bend your knees!" she cried. "You're too tall."

Say what?

"Your knees, Isaiah! Bend your knees!"

Through the fog of panic, her words finally penetrated his reeling brain. He bent his legs, affording her more leverage, and with a strength he couldn't believe she possessed, she clenched her arms around him, shoving her fist upward with such force he wondered that it didn't connect with his backbone. Air propelled upward from his lungs, and one small piece of meatball shot from his mouth.

Air whistled down his windpipe. Isaiah collapsed over the sink, grabbing for breath. *Sweet Christ.* Laura hovered at his elbow.

"Are you okay? Isaiah, answer me, please. Are you all right?"

All he could manage was a nod. After dragging in several more breaths, he finally pushed out a weak, gravelly, "Okay, I'm okay."

"Thank God. I thought you were going to die."

Trembling from the experience, Isaiah straightened away from the sink. "Me, too." He gave the piece of meat a last look, deciding then and there that he'd never eat a meatball again. "Man. That's never happened to me before."

She patted his arm. He grabbed a towel and dampened it to wipe his face. When his vision cleared, Laura had vanished. He tossed the towel on the counter. Remembering that peach film of nothing that she'd been wearing, he smiled slightly and went to find her.

She was in the bedroom, jerking a sweatshirt on over her head. He got a quick glimpse of beautiful bare breasts before blue fleece became the only landscape. She'd already lost the black G-string and replaced it with modest white panties.

He could have wept.

She wrinkled her nose and reached for a pair of jeans draped over the foot of her bed. "I'm sorry. Bad idea. I didn't mean to make you choke."

Isaiah wanted the peach fringe back. "I choked because you took me by surprise. I didn't expect . . ." There were no words. "You looked so beautiful."

"And I took your breath away. Right?" She laughed and shoved a dainty foot into the jeans. "The lady at the shop said it would make you wild for me. She was old. I should have found someone younger who'd know more what guys like."

Isaiah waited until she got her other foot stuck into the jeans. Then he lunged across the room and caught her around the waist in a flying tackle, his target the bed. She shrieked and tried to catch her balance, but with her ankles shackled and his weight working against her, she went over like a ninepin. Isaiah followed her down to the mattress, catching his weight with his arms so he wouldn't crush her.

She blinked bewilderedly and peered up at him through tousled wisps of blond hair. "Are you sure you're okay?"

He'd never felt better. And she didn't need fringe to be hot. "Clarification. Were you or were you not trying to seduce me?"

She wrinkled her nose again. "I ruined it for us last night. I wanted to make up for it."

She already had. God, how he loved her. He bent to nibble at her delectable mouth. "Next time, two things. Don't appear in an outfit like that when my mouth's full. And you might also consider calling out some sort of warning. 'Isaiah, brace yourself' would work. Anything to let me know you're about to blow my socks off."

"You liked it?"

"You were a vision. If I go outside and come back in, will you put it back on for me?"

"The mood is sort of ruined."

His mood was perfect. "Please?"

Laura in see-through peach stuff, standing by the Christmas tree . . . In all his life Isaiah had never seen anything so beautiful, had never even dreamed such beauty could exist. The Christmas lights bathed her in a cheerful glow that accentuated the delightful curves of her body. All she lacked was a ribbon to be every man's Christmas fantasy.

"I love you," was all he could think to say.

"I love you, too." She dimpled a cheek at him. "Stop staring at me. You're making me feel funny."

He didn't want that. Isaiah felt as if he walked a mile to reach her. His hand trembled slightly when he touched her hair. "Ah, Laura, you're lovely. I'm almost afraid to touch you."

She giggled. "That's not the idea. This is

supposed to make you crazy for me."

Mission accomplished. Isaiah drew her into his arms. This time, he vowed, he would make it perfect for her.

Afterward Laura felt like a puddle of melted wax. She lay sprawled on the beanbags, one arm flung outward, the other locked around Isaiah's neck. He lay with his face buried between her breasts. She had no idea where her sexy outfit had gone. Overall, she decided that it had been a complete waste of money. He'd left it on her for only about three seconds.

But, oh, it had been lovely. She lifted her hand to his hair. The strands sifted through her fingers like cool threads of silk. His heart was still pounding. She could feel each violent thrum vibrating into her belly button.

"I'm really, *really* glad you didn't choke to death."

He gave a weak laugh and nibbled at the curve of her breast. "Me, too. Ah, Laura, you're fabulous. I love you so much."

She tucked in her chin. In the firelight it was oddly arousing to see his dark face pressed against her white skin. She trailed her hand down his back.

"It didn't hurt this time. Not at all."

"Hmm," was his only response.

That wasn't exactly what she'd been hoping for. She stared thoughtfully at the open-beamed ceiling. "Isaiah?"

"Hmm?"

She danced her fingertips over his bare hip. "If I put my outfit back on, can we do it again?"

He groaned. "Dear God, I've created a monster."

Laura lifted her head, trying to see his face more clearly. "You don't want me?"

He laughed and pushed up on his elbow. "Convince me."

Laura wasn't exactly sure how to do that. But she was willing to give it her best. In the end, she discovered that Isaiah didn't require a lot of encouragement. Hardly any, in fact.

In between puppy feedings that night, they didn't sleep. They were like two children who'd been turned loose in a candy shop, insatiable in their greed for each other. When dawn broke and the first faint light of day shone through the crack of the bedroom drapes, Isaiah was so exhausted that he could barely move. Laura lay over the top of him like a cover that was too short, her dainty toes poking him at the ankles, her silky hair teasing his chin.

Even drained of energy as he was, Isaiah wanted her again. She felt so damned wonderful, all soft and naked and warm, pressed full-length against him. But he was finished. He could move his toes, but only just barely.

Sighing, he groped for a blanket to cover them. Laura stirred and squirmed to get off of him, then curled her body into the lee of his for warmth. He splayed a hand on her belly, drew her even closer, and fell into an exhausted sleep.

When next Isaiah opened his eyes, Laura was gone, and the sheet beside him was cold. He tossed back the blankets, pushed to his feet, and grabbed his jeans. As he hopped to drag them on, he made his way to the door.

"Laura?"

She wasn't in front of the fire, feeding puppies. He took some wood from the box and tossed it on the dying flames. Then he went in search of her. He found her in the laundry room, rinsing out towels. She wore one of his shirts instead of a nightgown. The tails reached almost to the bend of her knees.

"Morning," he said.

She grinned at him over her shoulder and stretched her neck for a kiss, which he was happy to deliver.

"How can you look so perky?" he asked. "We hardly got any sleep."

"I'm high on love."

"I'm high on love, too. But even the sexiest man alive needs some sustenance. Let me finish that while you start some breakfast."

She rinsed her hands, gave him another kiss, and scurried off to the kitchen. Over the rush of the water, Isaiah could have sworn he heard her singing. He shook his head and chuckled.

"Thank God it's Tucker's turn to work Saturday again," he said when he entered the kitchen a few minutes later. "I feel like I've been run over by a tank."

She yawned as she turned the bacon. "The puppies are fed. After we eat we could go back to bed."

"Sounds like a plan to me."

Thirty minutes later they snuggled down in Laura's bed, as contented and sleepy as the puppies in the wading pool. Isaiah considered making love to her before he went back to sleep, but between thought and action, his eyes drifted closed. The next instant he was under.

They awakened to the sound of thirteen hungry puppies, yipping and mewling. Laura warmed formula while Isaiah washed bottles. "Are you sure you want kids?" he asked.

She smiled. "Yes, but maybe not thirteen."

They stayed in that day, content with only each other. In between making love, they watched a couple of movies, played a game of checkers, and fixed snacks to keep up their energy. Isaiah had never hoped to be this happy. Laura could scarcely believe that all her dreams, which she'd believed could never come true for a woman with aphasia, were now becoming reality.

Every once in a while they would look at each other and smile stupidly. "I can't believe you love me," she'd say. "I think I'm the luckiest man alive," he'd say. And pretty soon they were in bed again, as eager for each other as they'd been the first time.

Just after midnight, Isaiah's phone rang. It was his answering service. There'd been a car accident just north of Crystal Falls. A German shepherd, riding in the bed of a pickup truck, had been thrown from the vehicle.

"Do you want me to go?" Laura offered.

Isaiah would have loved to have her assist him, but he knew the dog's injuries might be severe, requiring a lengthy surgery. "You need to be here with the puppies. This could take hours. I'll call Belinda."

Minutes later, as Isaiah pulled away from the house, he saw Laura and Hapless still silhouetted in the open doorway. As if she sensed that he was looking back, Laura blew him a kiss.

"Oh, Jesus," Isaiah whispered when he saw the first X-rays. "Is there a bone in his body that isn't broken?"

Belinda stood at the table. The shepherd was already under the effects of anesthesia, a tube down its trachea, its tongue lolling. "He's in pretty bad shape," she said sadly. "Do you think we can save him?"

Isaiah rolled up his sleeves and jerked on a lab coat. He wished now that he'd gotten more sleep over the last twenty-four hours. Normally his and Tucker's weekend schedules worked out fairly well, with each of them covering two Saturdays a month so the other one could have two weekends off. The downside was that the guy who didn't work days on Saturday had to cover any emergencies that night.

"I don't know if I can save him," Isaiah finally replied. "But I mean to give it a try." As he approached the table, he asked, "What the hell was a Seeing Eye dog doing in the back of someone's pickup truck?"

Belinda shrugged. "I didn't get many details. I thought maybe you did when you talked to the police."

"Only that some blind lady flew in from Chicago to see her family. There must not have been room inside the cab for a dog."

"Idiots," Belinda said heatedly. "With all the seat-belt laws in Oregon, and all the public-awareness messages on television, you'd think people would understand that even dogs need some kind of safety restraints."

That was the end of all unnecessary conversation for a while. Isaiah focused intently on his work. If the shepherd died, there was no telling how long it might be before the blind woman could get another guide dog.

By four in the morning, Isaiah was so tired that his vision kept blurring. Belinda had made him coffee that was strong enough to paint walls, but it hadn't helped.

"Talk to me," he said. "Help me stay awake."

Belinda obliged, chattering nonstop

461

about her days at college as they worked on their patient. When Isaiah blinked and yawned again, she tipped her head questioningly. "I don't think I've ever seen you so beat," she observed. "Is everything okay at home?"

Isaiah stifled another huge yawn. "Laura and I didn't get much sleep last night."

"Uh-oh. Trouble with the puppies?"

He tried to bite back a smile, but failed. "No, other stuff."

Belinda busied herself straightening the instruments. After a long moment she said, "You're in love with her, aren't you?"

Isaiah started to deny it, but then decided it was pointless. He did have a life apart from the clinic, and from now on Laura was going to be a big part of it. He wouldn't be able to hide that fact, and he wasn't inclined to try.

"Yes," he admitted. "I'm very much in love with her."

Belinda smiled. "I'm so glad for you, Isaiah. If any guy on earth deserves to be happy, it has to be you."

"Thank you."

"And I adore Laura," she added. "But then, don't we all? She's such a sweetie." She grinned and gave him a look rife with curiosity. "Am I wrong to suspect that wedding bells may be ringing soon?"

"We've talked about it. Nothing set in cement yet."

Two hours later, Isaiah finally closed the last incision. The shepherd's vitals were still strong. That was a good sign.

"Get on the horn," he told Belinda. "This fellow has to be kept under close observation for the next several hours, and we're both too wiped out to stay. See if you can get a tech to come in and sit with him."

It was daylight by the time Isaiah got home. When he stepped inside the house, he saw Laura asleep on an easy chair. An afghan that his mother had made was draped over her shoulder. She'd drawn her legs beneath her, and her head was lolling on her shoulder.

He tiptoed across the room to kiss her awake. "Mornin', sunshine."

As Isaiah spoke, it occurred to him that she actually was his sunshine. She had brightened his whole world.

"Isaiah." She rubbed her eyes and sat up. "What time is it?"

"Going on seven."

"I waited up for you."

She looked as tired as he felt. "When did you last feed the puppies?"

"About an hour ago."

"Let's crash in your room. That way we'll hear them when they get hungry."

En route to the guest room, Laura slipped an arm around his waist. "You must be worn out."

"Pretty much wasted, yeah."

"Is the dog all right?"

Isaiah shook his head. "I've done all I can. God has to do the rest."

At nine o'clock, the puppies served as an alarm clock to bring Laura awake and rouse Isaiah momentarily from an exhausted sleep.

"Don't get up," Laura whispered. "I'll take care of them."

Isaiah wanted to argue, but he couldn't keep his eyes open long enough to form the words. *Laura.* It seemed that only minutes had passed when she shook him partially awake again and leaned down to beam a smile at him.

"I called in to check on the dog. Lena says he's holding strong."

"Good, good." Isaiah struggled to smile, but even curving his lips took too much effort.

★ ★ ★

When Isaiah finally resurfaced, it was almost three in the afternoon. Laura heard him stumbling about in the bedroom. She'd pulled the wading pool out into the living room so as not to disturb him during feeding times. Now she was keeping busy, putting puppies back in the pool.

"Coffee's fresh," she said when he emerged.

He had fastened his jeans, but his shirt hung open to reveal a swath of bronzed, muscular chest furred with dark hair. He blinked and peered blearily at a puppy as it gained the top edge of the pool wall and tumbled out headfirst onto the floor. "What the hell? They aren't supposed to be doing that yet."

Laura could only lift her hands. "Tell them that. All of a sudden they've got springs on their feet."

Isaiah yawned and headed for the kitchen. When he returned a moment later, he held a steaming mug of coffee in one big hand and looked a little more alert. He watched her put a puppy back in the pool, smiled, and shook his head. "Time for a portable kennel. You can't spend your whole day juggling dogs."

Laura knew he was right. But that wasn't to say she hadn't been enjoying herself.

465

"Hapless thinks it's great. They're almost big enough to play with him."

Isaiah sat in an easy chair. While he took a slow sip of coffee, Laura nibbled her bottom lip.

"Isaiah?"

"Hmm?"

"Can I keep one?"

"Keep one what?"

Laura rolled her eyes at him. "A puppy."

He frowned. "Hapless will be a big dog, Laura."

"I know." Laura patted Hapless, who lay sleeping beside her. "But he's yours. I want a dog of my own." Laura scooped up the little male who'd captured her heart. She couldn't look at his wrinkled nose without smiling. "I want to name him Frown Face."

"Frown Face? What kind of a name is that?" Isaiah studied the puppy. Then he finally smiled. "He is sort of frowny at that." His eyes darkened. "Laura, honey, the people who owned the mother get pick of the litter. There's every chance they'll pick him. He's a good-looking pup."

Laura's heart caught. "Can't I just hide him?"

"You don't think they can count? They already know there are thirteen puppies."

Laura held the puppy close to her heart. She thought for a moment. Then she brightened and said, "One of them just died."

Isaiah threw back his dark head and barked with laughter.

When Monday morning rolled around and the shepherd was still holding strong, Isaiah finally breathed a sigh of relief. He called the police to give them an update on the dog's condition, happy to report that the guide dog would probably make it.

"That's wonderful news," a female dispatcher said. "His owner has been inconsolable. He isn't just a dog to her, but her best friend in the entire world."

"If he's her best friend, why did she let him ride in the back of a pickup on icy roads? It's one thing in the summer for short trips, but it's pure lunacy in the winter when the asphalt is slick."

"I know," the woman agreed. "Trust me when I say she'll never allow it again. Next time she says she'll hire a cab. It was just one of those things, I guess, a single-seat pickup, and two people at the airport to pick her up. With three people up front, there was no room for the dog. She didn't think it would hurt to let him ride in the back. They were only going a short distance."

"Icy roads are hazardous no matter how short the distance." Isaiah realized that he was complaining to the wrong person. "I'm sorry. It's just hard sometimes. I see more idiots walk through our door than I care to count. It doesn't take a rocket scientist to properly care for a pet. All you need is a little common sense."

The woman made a commiserating sound. "Tell me about it. You see the dogs that have been thrown from vehicles. We see the kids."

Isaiah's stomach turned just at the thought. He stayed on the line only long enough to verify the billing information with the police.

On Tuesday Isaiah realized that there were only three shopping days left before Christmas. He was writing out a prescription in one of the examining rooms. As he wrote the date, it suddenly dawned on him that it wasn't the twenty-first of just any old month, but the twenty-first of December.

Laura had already pulled her morning shift and left for the day. After returning to the surgery, Isaiah plucked his cell phone from his belt, dialed his home number, and paced until she answered.

"Can you bring the puppies to the clinic at about four?" he asked after she'd said hello.

"Why?"

"Because I'm going to hire someone to stay here and watch them while we go Christmas shopping."

"You aren't finished yet?"

Isaiah rubbed the spot between his eyebrows that always throbbed when his nerves were on edge. "Finished? Sweetheart, I haven't started."

Long silence. "But, Isaiah, it's almost Christmas."

"I know. I don't know where my head was. I thought I had plenty of time left. Would you mind helping me out?"

"How many people do you have to buy for?"

"At a quick count, about thirty, not counting all the older hands at the Lazy J. I grew up with most of them, and they're like family. And you, of course. I suppose I should get something for your parents and grandmother as well. And your sister and her family, too, I guess. Probably, when it's all said and done, about forty, maybe forty-five."

"That's a lot."

"I know," he agreed miserably. "I have a big family, and it's getting bigger every year." He sighed. "I was thinking that we could take the Hummer and leave your car here until tomorrow."

"Won't we have to go back for the puppies?"

"Yeah. But we'll be coming to work about the same time in the morning. Why drive your car clear back to the house and waste gas? It'll be fine parked behind the clinic."

"Okay. I'll see you at four, then."

"I appreciate this, sweetheart. We'll do dinner out. Sound good?"

When Isaiah ended the call, Belinda was laughing and shaking her head. "You forgot to go shopping again." It wasn't a question.

"I didn't forget, exactly. I was thinking I could go sometime next week."

"Next week?" Belinda raised her dark eyebrows. "What planet are you living on?"

Laura was late arriving at the clinic. Isaiah had funneled all the appointments he couldn't cancel into Tucker's wing, and he'd been watching for her out a kennel window for almost fifteen minutes. When he finally saw her car pull into the parking

470

lot, he let himself out through the storage room door and hurried to meet her.

"Sorry," she said as she spilled from the car. "I had puppy problems."

"What kind of problems?"

She looked like a cheerful little Eskimo in the hooded pink parka. Fake fur framed her face, with tendrils of blond hair poking out. "They wouldn't stay in the basket. I got on the road and the first thing I knew, I had a puppy under the brake pedal."

Isaiah's heart caught. "You could have had a wreck."

"Tell me about it. I couldn't use the brake. I had to turn the key off and roll to a stop."

"Dear God." Isaiah bent to peer through a rear window. "Where are they?"

"In the trunk." She popped the lid just then. Isaiah stepped around the rear bumper. Puppies were popping up like jack-in-the-boxes. "Help!" Laura started grabbing puppies before they tumbled out and fell to the ground. "I don't have enough hands!"

Isaiah couldn't help himself; he started to laugh. His amusement quickly faded when he grabbed for a tumbling puppy and almost missed his mark. Before he could put that dog in the basket, another one toppled out. "Sweet Lord. They're too little to be doing this. What are you lacing that formula with?"

Puppies were coming out of the basket quicker than they could put them in. Isaiah slipped off his jacket and threw it over the wicker to create a lid. Then he helped slip puppies inside and held the jacket taut while Laura rounded up more. When all thirteen babies had been stuffed in the basket, they worked in tandem to carry it into the clinic, Laura dancing around Isaiah as he walked to catch furry little escapees.

"I have never in all my life." Isaiah was out of breath when he set the basket down inside a kennel cage. "And you want one of these little monsters?" A black ball with legs tumbled from the basket and waddled blindly over the toe of his boot. Isaiah was afraid to move for fear of stepping on a tiny paw. He reached down to collect the puppy and was rewarded with a snarl for his trouble. "The little shit. He just growled at me."

"Don't call him a little shit. That's Frown Face."

Isaiah turned the puppy around to stare into its milky eyes. "As soon as you can see me clearly, you little pill, we're going to get a clear understanding."

★ ★ ★

Isaiah hated to go shopping for Christmas presents. His usual mode of operation was to hit a department store and scoop things off shelves as he passed through a section: housewares for women, the tool section for men. On his last sweep he hit the toy section for the kids.

The first crack out of the bag, he realized that he and Laura didn't see eye-to-eye on the appropriate way to select gifts. She stared at him in appalled dismay when he grabbed a toaster for his mother.

"Isaiah, your mom has a toaster."

"This one has four holes, though."

"That isn't the point. You're sup-posed to get people things that they want. She doesn't *need* a toaster, and it isn't a fun present, either."

"She loves toasters."

Laura gave him an incredulous look and started to tap her foot. "Please don't tell me you've gotten her toasters before."

Isaiah couldn't see what was so bad about buying someone a toaster. People ate toast, didn't they? If his mother already had a toaster, it was bound to break sooner or later. Then she'd be really glad that he'd thought to buy her a new one.

"Here's the deal," he said. "I have forty-five people to buy for. If I stand around thinking it to death every time I pick a gift, it'll take me a week."

Laura put the toaster back on the shelf. "If we can't find something better, we'll come back for it later."

Isaiah almost groaned, but he dutifully followed her through the store. When she picked something up and examined it from all sides, including from the bottom, he just smiled. Why not? Hell, they had three more days to shop. *Piece of cake.*

To his surprise, shopping Laura's way turned out to be fun. Maybe it was because his head had stopped hurting, but putting a little thought into a gift was rewarding. They found a kitchen stool for his mother — a handy fold-up thing with a projecting seat so she could sit down while she prepared meals. More than once at family dinners Isaiah had seen Mary with swollen ankles and rubbing her lower back. The stool was something she'd really use.

After that Laura led Isaiah through the mall, stopping at specialty shops to browse and find thoughtful presents for everyone they loved. In between stores they made mad dashes through the winter night to stash their purchases in the Hummer. It was snowing, which made it all perfect.

At the mall commons, she insisted that they circle the gigantic Christmas display filled with animated figures. This year it was Santa's workshop at the North Pole. Reindeer lowered their heads to eat. Through frosted windowpanes they could see Santa's elves working industriously in a golden glow of light to complete their projects before Christmas Eve.

"Oh, Isaiah, look at Mrs. Claus!" Laura cried. "Isn't she sweet?"

Isaiah bent to peer through frosted glass and study a cute little Mrs. Claus, complete with granny glasses, rosy cheeks, a blue dress, an apron, and chunky shoes. Beaming a smile, she was extending a tray to a very happy and satisfied Santa, who kept grabbing cookies and saying, "Ho, ho, ho! Thank you, Mrs. Claus."

"Wouldn't it be neat if there really were a Santa, and we could all make a wish and have it come true?" Laura asked.

She looked up at Isaiah with shimmering eyes, and in that moment he decided that he'd already received a lifetime's supply of Christmas wishes. She was everything he'd ever wanted, everything he'd ever needed, and more than he'd ever dreamed of, his every desire all rolled into one. Christmas carols were playing over the mall's sound system — at that instant "Silver Bells" — making him realize that he didn't have a stereo, let alone a Christmas CD. Even worse, he'd been so focused on work that he hadn't gotten Laura a gift yet or even thought about what she might like.

He didn't like the picture of himself that was taking shape in his mind. He'd become a modern-day Scrooge, almost mechanical in the way he lived his life. Granted, his work was important, and it was fine to be dedicated, but not to the exclusion of all else. There was Christmas magic in the air. Soon they'd be celebrating the birth of Christ. It was a glorious occasion, a time of year that he never wanted to ignore again.

"There is a Santa," he assured Laura. "If you believe in him, he's as real as we are. Just keep telling yourself there is a Santa."

She laughed, squeezed her eyes closed, and said, "I'm making my Christmas wish."

"What did you wish for?" he asked when she lifted her lashes.

"I can't tell. Then it won't come true."

At the opposite side of the North Pole scene they came upon a Christmas tree for the poor, decorated with envelopes. At the top of the tree a paper star bore the message, PICK A FAMILY. Normally Isaiah went straight past such displays. He already had enough family to buy for at Christmas. But tonight he couldn't keep walking. He had so very much, and there were others who had little or nothing.

"Let's give a poor family a nice Christmas," he suggested.

Laura looked hesitant. "I don't know if I've got the money. When I pay off my credit card, the lady at the bank tells me how much I've got left. But it's almost the end of the month, so she hasn't told me for a while."

Isaiah couldn't imagine how it would be, never to know for sure how much money he'd spent or how much he had left. "I'll pay for everything," he assured her. "I'm blessed with the resources to be able to do it and never notice the expenditure." He turned her toward the tree. "Close your eyes and pick an envelope."

Laura's groping hand landed on a red envelope that contained the physical descriptions of five individuals, a mother and four children of varying ages. There were three girls, ages six, nine, and eleven, along with boy of fourteen. Each child had written a Christmas wish list, all fairly modest requests and some sadly practical, such as snow boots or insulated gloves. Although the mother's clothing sizes were supplied, she'd asked only for five frozen turkey dinners, a can of cranberry sauce, a package of dinner rolls, and a frozen pumpkin pie.

"Oh, Isaiah," Laura whispered shakily as he read the lists aloud. "They aren't going to have a Christmas dinner."

"Oh, yes, they are." Isaiah bent to kiss her, right there in front of God and everybody. Her mouth met his tremulously. She tasted as warm and sweet as the mulled wine she'd made for their tree-trimming party, making him yearn for home and privacy so he might do a more thorough job of tasting. Not possible. He drew reluctantly away, smiling as he watched the dazed, dreamy look slowly leave her eyes. "And these kids will get everything on their lists, and then some. We're going to play Santa."

Isaiah caught her hand. "Come on, lady. Make like an elf. It's almost Christmas!"

The dreaded Christmas shopping expedition turned out to be one of the most wonderful evenings of Isaiah's life. He and Laura erred on the side of absurd generosity as they shopped for their tree family, buying the mother a robe, nightgown, and slippers, and getting everything on the children's lists, including extra things — toys, books, art supplies, sports equipment, and clothing. To cover dinner, they decided to include a hundred-dollar gift certificate from a local supermarket so the mother could prepare a real Christmas dinner with all the trimmings, and a little left over for goodies.

For his paraplegic sister, Bethany, they found a pair of battery-powered slippers that heated up, something to keep her feet warm on cold winter evenings. They got Hank's wife, Carly, a magnifying glass with an attached light suspended from an adjustable metal arm that would clamp onto almost any surface. Isaiah knew that his sister-in-law spent every spare moment trying to train her visual cortex. Reading and looking through magazines would be much easier on her eyes with a magnifying glass.

Midway through the shopping expedition, Isaiah and Laura both got hungry. They stopped at a wine-and-cheese place. When they were seated at a table, Isaiah gazed over the candlelight at Laura's oval face, thinking that she was the best Christmas gift of all. He still had no idea of what to get her, though. He only knew that he wanted to give her the world.

"Do you have any idea how wonderful you are?" he asked.

She popped a green olive into her mouth and smiled at him around the lump. "No, but feel free to tell me."

"You're the most fabulous thing that's ever happened in my life."

Her eyes sparkled with happy tears. "And you're the greatest thing that's ever happened in mine."

"I love you so much. I've always detested Christmas shopping, but you make it fun."

She helped herself to another olive from the relish plate between them. "I'm glad. Shopping is like most other things. You can think of it as a chore — or you can turn it into an art."

Isaiah had never thought of it like that, but now that she'd mentioned it, he realized that she approached most things that way, putting her whole heart into everything she did.

"You're incredible. You know it? No list of names, but so far you haven't forgotten anyone. How the hell do you do that?"

"I may have trouble reading and writing, Isaiah, but my memory is fine."

"I have a great memory, too, but I'm not organized like you are. No matter how many balls you have to juggle, you never seem to drop any. You're working, taking care of puppies, decorating the house, keeping it clean, doing laundry, and you still manage to have a great supper ready every night. I don't know how you do it. Do you realize that I once had a customer pluck a fabric-softener sheet from the back of my shirt?"

She laughed so hard that she hugged her sides, making him wonder how she might react if he told her about the sock that he had found dangling out the bottom of his pant leg when he had been in the bank one afternoon. When her mirth subsided, she reached across the table to touch his hand. "You're saving lives, Isaiah, not juggling balls. You forget all the little things because you're always worried about big things."

He sighed. "I guess. But sometimes it's frustrating. All I do is work, but I never seem to get anything done. The shopping, for instance." He turned his hand to squeeze her fingers. "Thanks for helping me get it done. I honestly don't know what I'd do without you."

"No worries. I don't intend to let you find out."

Chapter Fourteen

It was still snowing when Isaiah and Laura finished the Christmas shopping and left the mall.

"You saved my life," Isaiah said as they stepped out into the night air. "Gift certificates from specialty shops. I've done certificates before, but never for specific sections of stores or from places just ladies or guys would like."

"With so many people and so little time, it's a case of what-ever works," Laura replied with a laugh. "It would have been nicer if we could have picked a nice gift for each person, but failing that, it's okay to let them do their own choosing, I think."

"I'm just thrilled to be *done*."

After stowing the last of their purchases in the back of the Hummer, Laura flung her arms wide and raised her face to the sky to catch snowflakes on her tongue.

"Try it," she said with a laugh. "Didn't you ever do this when you were little?"

Isaiah felt silly, but he decided dignity was highly overrated and opened his mouth.

"No two snowflakes are alike. Did you know that?" She blinked as floating white missiles drifted into her eyes.

Isaiah dropped his chin to look at her. In the soft light from a nearby lamppost she looked like an angel. She was definitely unique, he decided. If he were to search for a hundred years, he'd never find anyone else quite like her.

Back at the clinic Isaiah dug through one of the storage rooms for a portable wire kennel. That took nearly an hour, because it was behind a bunch of boxes. Then they had to collect puppies and introduce them to their new jail cell.

"They won't be climbing out of that," Isaiah said with a laugh when a puppy bumped its nose against the wire mesh. "Your Houdini days have come to an end, Frown Face."

"When they get bigger, will there be enough room in there?" Laura asked.

"No, but it'll do for now." Isaiah hooked an arm around her neck and planted a deep kiss on her soft mouth. "I'm glad you're riding home with me. I've been wanting to get my hands under that parka all evening."

Her eyes drifted almost closed. "Promise?"

When they arrived home, Hapless burst past them to get outside, almost making Isaiah drop the packages in his arms. Laura deposited the wire kennel full of puppies on the floor and hurried back to the Hummer ahead of Isaiah to get another load of gifts.

When everything had been carried in, she surprised Isaiah by dashing back outside to romp with Hapless in the snow. Isaiah stared at the mountains of packages that had yet to be wrapped and seriously considered starting on that immediately. But the sound of Laura's laughter drew him like a magnet out onto the porch.

"Laura, it's after nine o'clock. Don't you think it's a little late to be fooling around out here?"

Whop. A snowball hit him squarely in the face. Isaiah brushed white stuff from his cheek and narrowed his eyes. "Have I mentioned that I pitched for the Crystal Falls Comets four years running?" he said.

She danced away into the darkness, and a moment later another snowball nailed him on the chest. Isaiah realized that he was at a serious disadvantage, standing in the light. He leaped off the porch, grabbed a handful of snow, and bounded after her. "You want war, lady, you'll get war."

She laughed and stuck her tongue out at him. Isaiah let fly with a perfect pitch, nailing her in the face with a loosely packed snowball. She sputtered and dove for a snowdrift to gather more ammunition.

Thirty minutes later they were both drenched with melted snow, and Hapless was exhausted from running back and forth, trying to fetch balls that melted in his mouth. Isaiah sank onto the porch. Laura came to sit beside him. Together they stared out into the darkness at the snowflakes drifting down.

"This is beautiful," he whispered.

"Yes." She stared off for a moment. And then she sprang to her feet. "We haven't made snow ice cream yet!"

"You're kidding. It's almost ten."

"Do you turn into a pumpkin at midnight?"

He pushed to his feet and followed her into the house. She was already taking a bowl from a shelf. "You want to get the snow while I get the other stuff ready?"

What he wanted was to make passionate love to her on the kitchen table. But one look into her dancing hazel eyes told him that snow ice cream would have to come first. He went back to the living room for the portable stereo and CDs that he'd bought. If they were going to make ice cream, they'd listen to Christmas carols while they were at it.

Isaiah and Laura arrived at the clinic at just a little before six the next morning. As Isaiah executed the turn into the parking lot, his heart shot into his throat. Police lights seemed to be flashing everywhere, creating a spiral effect of red and blue on the fresh snow. In the predawn darkness it was a frightening sight.

"Oh, God. Something's happened!" Laura cried.

Isaiah jockeyed the Hummer into a parking slot, slammed the gearshift into park, and cut the engine. He and Laura spilled from the vehicle almost simultaneously. When they reached the rear door, they found a police officer standing outside.

"Sorry, sir. You can't go in."

Isaiah grasped Laura's arm. Even through the parka sleeve, he could feel her shaking. "Are the dogs and cats all right?" she asked thinly.

"The animals are fine," the officer assured her. "They were after drugs."

"Drugs?" Isaiah repeated incredulously. It was true that the clinic had a large store of narcotics. Practically any medical facility did. He also knew that it wasn't uncommon for veterinary clinics to be burglarized by addicts. But this was Crystal Falls, Oregon, not a big city. "Someone broke into our clinic for drugs?"

"Yes, sir. Are you one of the owners?"

"Isaiah Coulter. My brother Tucker and I own the place. If there was a break-in, why weren't we notified by the security company?"

"Alarm didn't go off." The cop pulled a tablet from his pocket. "Coulter, did you say? What's your first name again?"

Isaiah provided the information. "How the hell did someone get inside without setting off the alarm?" he asked the policeman.

"It looks like an inside job. The perpetrator used a security code to disarm the system. One of your employees" — he glanced at his notes — "a lady named Susan Strong, called us when she got here to open up a few minutes ago."

The police were inside dusting for fingerprints, and it was over thirty minutes before Isaiah and Laura could enter the building. When Isaiah saw the drug cabinet, he couldn't believe his eyes. The locks had been jimmied open, and the shelves were almost bare.

"Damn," he muttered to Laura, "someone's going to be high for six months."

Laura was shivering, even in her coat. Isaiah hooked an arm around her shoulders and pulled her close. "It's no big deal, sweetheart. The cabinet can be fixed, and the medications can be replaced."

"The first thing I thought of was the dogs," she whispered. "That they might be hurt."

"I know, but they're fine."

Over the top of Laura's head Isaiah saw a police officer step into the doorway of the drug room. The man glanced at Laura, removed his hat, and tucked it under his arm. "Excuse me, Dr. Coulter?"

Isaiah set Laura away from him. "Yes?"

The officer glanced down at a tablet in his hand. "Do you have a woman named Laura Townsend working for you?"

For the second time in less than an hour, Isaiah's heart leaped. "Why do you ask?"

"We just found her automobile out in the parking lot. The stolen drugs are in the trunk."

Isaiah glanced at Laura. Her face had gone as pale as milk. "I'm Laura Townsend," she said in a quavering voice.

The officer gave her a startled look. Then his eyes narrowed. "Can you explain how the controlled substances found their way into the trunk of your car, Ms. Townsend?"

"No."

Isaiah stepped forward to put Laura slightly behind him. "Wait just a damned minute. Laura wasn't involved in this. I know she wasn't. She was with me all night." Isaiah quickly related the events of the previous afternoon. "We left her car here. She didn't even have transportation to come back."

The cop glanced at Laura. Then he gave Isaiah a sharp look. "Would it be possible for us to talk alone, Doctor?"

Outrage roiled within Isaiah. "No, damn it, that isn't possible. I have no secrets from her."

"It's all right, Isaiah." Laura touched his hand. "I'll be in the kennels."

Laura was frightened. On the one hand she knew it was silly. People didn't get arrested for things they hadn't done. But another part of her wasn't so sure. The drugs had been found in the trunk of her car. She had no idea how they'd gotten there. But that was beside the point. The police dealt in facts, and right now all the evidence pointed directly to her.

She busied herself with work — changing bedding, refilling dishes. Even so, it seemed as if an eternity passed before Isaiah appeared in the center aisle. Laura took one look at him and knew she was in big trouble. His blue eyes were filled with anguish. His firm mouth was drawn into a grim line.

"Well?" She stepped from a kennel to meet him. "Don't make me wait. I'm dying."

He curled his big hands over her shoulders. "Before I say anything, Laura, I want you to know I already called a lawyer."

"A what?"

"A lawyer." He bent his dark head to rest his brow against hers. "Narcotic theft is a serious offense."

Laura's heart was pounding so hard that it felt as if it might crack a rib. "But I've done nothing wrong."

"I know. And the police will figure that out soon." His grip tightened on her upper arms. "Ah, Laura. The security code used to enter the building was yours."

Laura's blood ran cold. "But I never even wrote it down! And I didn't tell anyone my numbers."

"Someone got their hands on it nevertheless." Isaiah kissed her forehead. "I have a copy of everyone's code in my files. So does Tucker. We both keep our file cabinets locked. But it's possible that one of us wasn't careful with our keys."

Laura made tight fists on the sleeves of his shirt. "Wh-what does this mean, Isaiah? You won't let them arrest me, right? You know I didn't do it."

"Of course I know you didn't do it, honey. But an offense involving controlled substances, especially in large amounts like this, is a felony. Class A or class B. Hell, I don't know. I don't keep up on that kind of stuff. I only know it's out of my hands. The stuff was found in your trunk, for God's sake. It stinks of a setup, but how the hell did someone get your trunk open without keys? There's no evidence of forced entry."

Laura could only shake her head.

"I'll get to the bottom of this, I swear it," he promised her. "And I've already called the best damned attorney in town. Zeke used him a while back. He looks like a warmed-up corpse, but he's sharp as a tack. They won't keep you at the jail, I promise."

"Keep me?" Laura's brain was short-circuiting. She could barely make sense of what he said. "Oh, Isaiah. Don't let them arrest me. I was with you. I didn't have a car. You *know* I didn't do it."

"I know it, Laura, but they don't. I told them you were with me, and they asked if I stayed awake all night and could swear you never left the house. I told them you had no vehicle, and they asked if I was absolutely certain you didn't use mine."

"Why would I use yours and leave the drugs in mine? It makes no sense."

"No, it doesn't, and once the cops have a chance to sift through all of this, I'm sure they'll realize that."

A police officer appeared behind Isaiah. He cleared his throat. "Ms. Townsend?" he said politely. "I'm afraid you'll have to come with me."

Isaiah kissed her forehead again. Then he stepped aside. Laura flashed him a frantic look. "Trust me," he said.

And then the policeman pulled a pair of handcuffs from his belt. As he snapped them on Laura's wrists, he read her her rights.

Being arrested wasn't quite as frightening as Laura expected; nothing like what she saw on television, anyway. The police officers were polite. They didn't shove her around or jerk her arms high behind her back to inflict pain. Except for being in handcuffs and being put in the backseat of the squad car behind a screen, she might have been taking a Sunday ride.

Once at the police station, it got a little scarier. She was led to a desk and pressed down into a chair. The man asking questions was fond of using acronyms, and Laura understood only about half of what he said. Even worse, he asked essentially the same questions over and over, a clear sign to her that he believed none of her answers. In an hour Laura was numb. In two, she could barely say her own name.

"What are you on?" the man demanded.

Laura had no idea what he meant. "I'm s-sorry?"

"What are you taking?"

Laura realized that he thought she was under the influence of something and started to laugh. He didn't see the humor. The angrier he got, the funnier it seemed. Pretty soon she couldn't stop laughing.

The attorney Isaiah had called arrived to save the day. He was skeletal and old, with a name that didn't stick in Laura's mind, but he seemed to know the ropes. He quickly explained the reason for Laura's halting speech, and the cop got over his huff. About an hour later Laura was informed that she could leave. She was helped up from the chair, the cuffs were removed from her wrists, and the lawyer escorted her from the office.

Isaiah was pacing back and forth just inside the front doors. When he saw Laura, he came rushing to meet her. She was too numb to do anything but lean against him when he put his arm around her.

The two men carried on a conversation over the top of her head as they exited the building. Laura heard the words, but their meaning didn't penetrate. *Bail, charges, felony, controlled substances.* Her head hurt. She felt sick to her stomach. All she wanted was to crawl into bed, pull the covers over her head, and hear nothing but silence for a while.

At the curb, Isaiah stopped to shake the attorney's hand. "I appreciate your quick response."

The attorney patted Laura's shoulder. "Mr. Coulter's sister is married to Ryan Kendrick. Any friend of the Kendrick clan is a friend of mine. Not to worry, Ms. Townsend. We'll have this ironed out in no time."

Laura let Isaiah lead her to his Hummer. She was glad when he grasped her at the waist and swung her up onto the seat. Her legs felt like limp noodles. A few minutes later, as he drove through town, he reached over to squeeze her hand.

"We've rearranged the schedule, honey. Your shifts are covered indefinitely. Until this is resolved, you don't need to worry about anything."

Laura thought of the kennel dogs. She would miss being with them every day. "Am I still in trouble?" She knew she should ask more detailed questions. Had he figured out how someone had gotten into her trunk without keys? Had he figured out how someone had obtained her security code? Did the police have any other suspects? Was she out on bail? And if so, what exactly did that mean? But her brain had reached overload. "Is it likely that they'll take me back and put me in jail?"

"I hope not." He glanced over at her. "We've sent all our emergencies to another doctor, canceled all appointments, and closed the clinic for the day." He glanced at his watch and then at his side mirror. "Tucker's meeting with me at my place in about an hour. We'll get to the bottom of this, Laura. You have my word on it."

Laura trusted Isaiah Coulter more than

she'd ever trusted anyone. But she also realized that he couldn't pull answers out of a hat. In short, she was still in serious trouble, and unless something happened to cast suspicion on someone else, there was every possibility that she could go to jail.

Oddly, the prospect didn't completely terrify her. Maybe she couldn't talk very well under fire, but that didn't mean she was totally clueless about the law. A prosecutor had to prove guilt. When this case was reviewed, any lawyer worth his salt was bound to see that there were holes in it large enough to accommodate an eighteen-wheeler. She'd been with Isaiah. She'd had no car. She had no criminal record. The blood tests would show that she'd never used drugs. At the end of the day, Laura felt confident that she would prevail.

She just prayed she wouldn't be forced to prevail from a jail cell.

Once at the house, Laura allowed Isaiah to baby her. Physically she was fine, but her damaged brain needed a rest. He pushed her down on the edge of her bed and removed her shoes. Then he drew back the covers so she might lie down. A few minutes later he brought in the portable stereo, plugged in a Christmas CD, set it at a low, soothing volume, and served her a piping-hot cup of herbal tea.

"Thank you, Isaiah. I'm sorry for going brain-dead. I'll feel better in a bit."

He leaned down to kiss her cheek. "Hey, no apologies. Getting arrested is scary as hell."

She gave him a questioning look. "You've been arrested?"

"Once in college. The charges didn't stick."

As he fed the puppies, he gave her what she suspected was a slightly fictionalized account of the incident. "I was with Tucker in a university bar, just standing there, minding my own business." He grinned and winked at her. "There was this trellis thing that divided the room. Anyway, a couple of guys Tucker and I knew were pretty lit, and God only knows why, but they decided to rip the trellis apart."

Laura took a sip of tea. "You weren't involved?"

"Hell, no." He went to the cage for another puppy. As he sat back down on the foot of the bed, he added, "Neither was Tucker. Problem: When you're close to six feet, five inches tall, you stand out in a crowd. We were near the guys who did the

497

dirty. One of us — I can't remember now if it was Tucker or me — tried to make them stop. From across the room the bouncer and bartender thought we were the ones who did it." He finished with the last puppy. "My one experience with getting stuffed and cuffed. Not something I'd like to repeat."

Laura was starting to feel a little better and managed a smile. "Me, neither."

"You won't," he assured her. The doorbell rang just then. He straightened from the puppy cage. "There's Tucker now." He leveled a finger at her. "You rest. Understand? At least an hour. Let your brain defrag."

"Yes, sir."

Laura had just drifted off to sleep when she heard voices lifted in anger. Her first thought was that the police had come for her. Isaiah was cursing. Over the soft Christmas music playing on the stereo, he sounded very upset. As much as Laura appreciated his loyal defense of her, she didn't want him to get in trouble with the law.

She swung out of bed and padded barefoot from her room. To her surprise, no one was in the living area. Following the sound of voices, she moved hesitantly toward the kitchen. As she came around the rock fireplace that divided the living and formal dining rooms, she realized that it wasn't Isaiah talking so loudly, after all, but Tucker. She froze in her tracks. An instant later she had firsthand knowledge that the old adage was true: Eavesdroppers never hear anything good about themselves.

"Are you out of your mind, Isaiah?" Tucker demanded in a hushed yell, clearly pitched low so he wouldn't be overheard. "Surely you don't intend to actually marry the woman. Be smart. Have a fling, wait for the newness to wear off, and then get the hell out."

"Tucker, for once would you just butt out? It's my life. What I choose to do with it is my business."

"Not when you're about to flush your future down the john. Laura is sweet. I'll be the first person to admit that. And there's no denying that she's pretty. But, for God's sake, Isaiah, use your head. She's also a brain-damaged misfit who can't pronounce three-syllable words or dole out dog food without messing up."

"She didn't mess up with the dog food."

"Would you listen to yourself?" Tucker

asked more calmly. "I don't have it in for Laura. You know that. I like her very much. But she isn't the woman for you."

"Excuse me, but isn't that for me to decide?"

Laura pressed a hand to her waist, feeling as if she might be sick.

"Everything may seem hunky-dory now," Tucker retorted, "but if you marry the lady, the day will come when you'll regret that you ever met her. She can't stimulate you intellectually, Isaiah. And she sure as hell isn't capable of being your helpmate at the clinic."

Isaiah tried to interject something, but Tucker cut him off. "Would you just hear me out?"

Isaiah muttered a sentence, but Laura didn't catch what he said. She had no problem hearing Tucker.

"If you marry her and are dumb enough to have kids," he rushed on, "who'll help them with their reading and math? You, that's who. Laura can't even write a damned grocery list. You'll be bringing in all the bacon and cooking it as well."

"Laura is a wonderful cook."

"Damn it, you know that isn't what I mean. Married to someone like her, you'll constantly have to compensate for all her failings."

"We'll iron out the wrinkles," Isaiah said.

"Wrinkles? Isaiah, you've got a brilliant future as a vet. With the right woman at your side, the sky's the limit. Laura isn't that woman. When the attraction wears off, what will you talk to her about? You sure as hell won't be able to have an intellectual conversation with her. When there are public functions you have to attend, what're you going to do, dress her up like a pretty little doll and tell her to smile and keep her mouth shut all evening?"

Laura winced.

"It's not like I'm climbing a corporate ladder," Isaiah countered.

"Yeah, you say that, and for right now it's true enough. But what if you decide later to enter the research field or want to teach? You want to get a taste of vicious politics, brother? Just visit any university or research center in the country. A beautiful, intelligent, accomplished, and entertaining wife will be a huge asset, and trust me, Laura will never cut the mustard."

Laura felt as if her heart were breaking. *Oh, God.* As a child she'd sung, "Sticks and stones may break my bones, but words will never hurt me." Not true. Words could inflict wounds that ran deeper than the flesh. The worst part was, she could refute nothing of what Tucker said. She *was* a brain-damaged misfit, a woman who'd been doomed to scrub toilets and walk dogs for a living until she met Isaiah.

And the rest was true as well. Isaiah did have a brilliant future ahead of him, and he needed a smart, charming wife who could complement him and help him accomplish all his goals. Laura remembered the night that he'd talked with her about the Chesapeake with autoimmune disease, and how respectfully he'd spoken of his colleague who had devoted his career to research. Isaiah hadn't told her that he wanted to follow in that colleague's footsteps, but in retrospect, when she remembered the look in his eyes, she knew the longing had been there. She'd just failed to see it, maybe because she hadn't wanted to.

Fearful that Isaiah or Tucker would turn and see her in the dining area, Laura retreated to her room and quietly closed the door. Dry eyed, she sank onto the edge of the bed and stared blankly at the floor. Before her accident she could have been the wife Isaiah needed. But, in all honesty, she knew she wasn't capable of that now. She loved him, yes, and she wished with all her heart that she had more to offer him. But she didn't.

Isaiah would marry her. Laura knew that. He was a kind, caring, and wonderful man, and in his heart he believed they could make a marriage work. But at what cost to him? She didn't want to be an anchor that held him back from pursuing his dreams.

Sometimes a woman had to love a man enough to walk away.

Isaiah refused to let Tucker piss him off. He knew his brother meant well. The way Tucker saw it, Isaiah would be making a disastrous mistake if he married Laura. Out of love, he was trying to make Isaiah see that.

"Okay," Isaiah said evenly, "I've let you have your say. Now will you let me have mine?"

Tucker waved his hand and leaned his hips against the counter. "Sure."

Isaiah positioned himself across from his brother, his hips resting against the work island. "I love Laura Townsend."

"That's your dick talking."

"Would you just shut up and listen? All my life everybody's harped at me to stop and smell the goddamned roses. 'Don't take life so seriously, Isaiah.' 'Get your nose out of that book, Isaiah.' 'There's more to life than work, Isaiah.' 'You need to find yourself a wife, Isaiah.' Yadda, yadda, yadda. Only me and my dick never ran into a woman we both wanted to stay with."

Tucker tugged on his ear. "Okay, I hear you."

"No, you don't hear me. You've never been in love. I may as well be talking Greek." He swung his hand toward the living room. "That girl in there has changed my whole life. The sex is great. I don't deny it. But I only discovered that just recently, and as wonderful as the physical aspects are, that isn't what I love about her. It was never about that."

"What is it about then?"

"It's about watching the snowflakes come down, damn it! It's about sitting by the fire at night to read a novel to her instead of poring over a medical tome. It's about having someone who listens to me. You say Laura and I can't have an intellectual conversation? *Wrong.* Her intelligence hasn't been affected by the aphasia. She's probably smarter than you are. And it goes without saying that her education is equal to yours. I don't give a shit if she talks to me using two-syllable words. It's what she's got to say that counts."

Tucker nodded, his brow furrowing in a thoughtful frown.

"It's about me getting a puppy of my own, and having him greet me at the door each night as if I single-handedly hung the moon. It's about laughing until my sides hurt. It's about having a life, Tucker — a life apart from my work that really matters to me and makes me feel complete. It's about having someone here who makes coming home seem worthwhile. When that girl in there smiles, I feel like the sun just came out on a cloudy day."

Tucker wandered over to the table and sank onto a chair. "Shit."

"That's right. *Shit.* I thought you were coming over here to help me make sense of the mess at the clinic. Instead you start in about my life choices. Well, hello? Like yours are so great? You're only three minutes older than me. I think I know my own mind." Isaiah gestured toward the living room. "If she heard you — if you've made her cry — I'll take every single tear she sheds out of your goddamned hide."

"I'm sorry," Tucker said gruffly. "I had no idea you loved her so much — or that she made you so happy." He rubbed a hand over his face. "Maybe she's exactly what you need in a wife, after all."

"Amen." Isaiah gave his brother a burning look. "Now, unless you want your future sister-in-law to serve time in the joint, you'd better put your mind to other concerns. Laura was with me last night — in my bed, in my arms. I slept, yes, but I know she never left my side. Someone at that clinic is trying to frame her. We need to find out who the hell it is and how the hell they did it."

An hour and a half later Isaiah sat hunched over a list at the kitchen table. *Possibilities.* He and Tucker had racked their brains, trying to come up with suspects, anyone at the clinic who might want to get rid of Laura, for whatever reason. So far James was their most likely candidate. But Isaiah's gut told him to look elsewhere. According to Laura, the kid was harmless. He needed to trust her instincts.

Isaiah was going over the list of employees again when the doorbell rang. He wasn't expecting anyone. He wondered if Tucker had come back. As he strode into the living room, Laura emerged from her bedroom. He'd thought she was asleep, so it was with no small surprise that he saw she was wearing her parka.

"Going somewhere?" he asked with a laugh.

"Yes," she said hollowly. "That's Gram. I called her to come get me."

It was then that Isaiah noticed her satchel set just outside the bedroom door. His stomach took a dive. Her eyes. Never had he seen such pain. *Tucker.* Isaiah knew then that Laura had overheard their conversation.

"Laura, don't pay any mind to my brother. He said his piece. I set him straight. It's all settled now."

Avoiding his gaze, she moved past him to answer the door. Etta stood on the porch. She looked beautiful for a woman her age, smartly turned out in a brown suede jacket over a camel pantsuit, her silver hair swept into a pile of curls atop her head. She flashed Isaiah a sad look, and then she smiled at her granddaughter.

"Hello, honey," she said as she gave Laura a hug. "I got here as fast as I could."

Isaiah advanced on the women. "Etta, this is all a big misunderstanding." He gave Laura a meaningful look. "We just need to talk it out — like two *mature* adults."

Laura didn't take the bait. In fact, Isaiah

got the awful feeling that she didn't even hear him. "Just let me get my things, Gram. I'll only be a minute."

True to her word, Laura returned seconds later with her purse strap over one shoulder, a bundle of clothes under one arm, and the satchel in her other hand. Before stepping out onto the porch with her grandmother, she turned to Isaiah.

"I phoned Trish. She says she'll come get the puppies. In about two weeks they'll be ready to go, and they don't have to be fed as often now. She can use the money that they'll bring in."

Isaiah's mouth had gone as dry as dirt. She honestly meant to leave him. "What about Frown Face?"

Hapless bounded up onto the porch, giving a happy bark. Laura didn't even look at the pup. "Things have changed. I can't keep Frown Face after all. I'm sure Trish will find him a good home."

"Laura." Isaiah followed her out onto the porch. He gave Etta a pleading look that sent the older woman hurrying down the steps to her car, which she'd left still running in the circular drive. "Please don't do this, Laura. I love you."

She shrugged and attempted to smile. "It'll wear off."

"No, damn it, it won't wear off. Tucker is an idiot. Don't let what he said ruin things for us."

A shimmer of brightness in her eyes told Isaiah that she was battling tears. He wanted to grab her up into his arms, but he had an awful feeling that she would fight him if he tried. If his father had taught him anything, it was never to use his strength against a woman. The only resolution to this problem was for them to sit down and talk.

"It never would have worked," she said shakily. "I'm glad it's ending this way. We can still be friends. Neither of us is angry. It's a good time for me to go."

"And I'm supposed to just let you? I don't think so."

"It's my choice." She blinked away the sheen of tears and met his gaze with a directness that told him she meant it with all her heart. "Don't call. Don't come around. It's over."

"And I don't have any say in it?"

"No."

She turned and hurried down the steps. As a teenager Isaiah had gotten his heart broken a few times. Back then he'd thought it was the end of his life. Now he realized he hadn't understood what real pain was.

Tears sprang to his eyes. That made him furious. He would never go crawling after a woman. If she was willing to throw everything away over some misguided comments made by his brother, he'd be damned if he'd beg her to stay.

"Fine, then!" he yelled. "You want to go? Go! Just don't kid yourself, sweetheart. I won't be sitting here twiddling my thumbs, waiting for you to get your head on straight! You're not the only woman on earth."

She never looked back. She just tossed her stuff into her grandmother's car, climbed in, and slammed the door. The Chrysler crunched over frozen snow to the road. Isaiah stared with burning eyes at the taillights. When the white car had disappeared from sight, he sank numbly onto the steps. Hapless crawled halfway into his lap and whined, almost as if he sensed that something was horribly wrong.

Isaiah grabbed Hapless up in his arms, buried his face in the puppy's fur, and wept like a baby.

Chapter Fifteen

"Come to my place tonight," Etta coaxed as they pulled into town.

Laura just wanted to go home so she could cry her eyes out without an audience. "No, thanks, Gram. I need to be by myself for a while."

"Pooh." Etta passed the turnoff to Laura's apartment. "You have no food there."

"I have stuff in the freezer." Laura couldn't imagine eating anything. "I'll shop for milk and eggs in the morning."

"Yes, perhaps you will. But for tonight you'll humor an old lady. I want to talk to you."

Laura heard it coming. "If you're hoping to convince me that this is a mistake, save your breath."

When they reached the house, Etta pushed Laura down onto a chair at the kitchen table, made a pot of tea, and arranged cookies on a plate. "You'll feel better with a little something in your stomach," she insisted.

Laura dutifully nibbled on a cookie. Normally she loved Gram's baked goods, but her taste buds felt anesthetized.

"Now," Etta said, cupping her dainty, rose-trimmed teacup in her gnarled hands, "talk to me. You were happy as a clam, and now you're devastated. There must be a reason."

Laura's cell phone rang just then. She fished in her purse, found the apparatus, and gazed glumly at the balloon displayed in the window.

"Isaiah?" Gram asked when Laura dropped the phone back into her purse without taking the call.

"I don't want to talk to him." Laura was afraid she might lose her resolve if she did. "It's better this way. Quick and clean."

Etta sighed and took a sip of tea. "You're probably right. *Men.* In the end they're all bastards."

Laura couldn't quite believe her grandmother had said such a thing. "Isaiah isn't a bastard."

Etta lowered her cup onto the saucer. "Well," she conceded, "there are a few exceptions. My Jim was one." She gave Laura a sidelong look. "And maybe your Isaiah is as well. If so, why are you leaving him?"

Laura recounted the conversation that

512

she'd overheard between Isaiah and his brother. "Tucker made some very good points."

"Such as?"

Laura's throat went tight. "I can't hobnob at classy dinners and fund-raisers, Gram. Isaiah may want to teach someday — or do research. He'll need to get grants for that. It's all a poli-tical game, and the best players get the goodies. You have to walk the walk and talk the talk."

Etta nodded. "I imagine so. But what's to say you can't? You're a lovely person, Laura."

"I can't speak very well."

"You're talking quite well right now. Slowly, I admit, with a little hesitation be-tween each word, but it's barely notice-able."

Laura recalled Rosie's candid question: *Do you have a speech impediment?* The people in Laura's family loved her. She was glad of that, and she appreciated it. But they overlooked a lot that other people couldn't or wouldn't.

"I don't want to hold Isaiah back." Laura met her grandmother's gaze. "Tell me I won't, Gram. Tell me that I can hold my own with the wives of professors at big, important colleges where politics are the name of the game. You tell me that, and I'll call Isaiah right now and tell him I've made a mistake."

Etta sat there for a long moment, staring at Laura. Then her rheumy eyes filled with tears, and she shook her head.

It was all the answer Laura needed.

Laura called her parents. Her father answered. Fighting to keep her voice steady, Laura said, "Hi, Daddy."

"Laurie? How's my little girl?"

Laura smiled through tears, glad to hear her father's deep voice. "I've been better."

"Uh-oh. That doesn't sound good. Something go haywire with the job?"

As briefly as possible, Laura told her father about all that had happened. Mike Townsend was silent for a beat when Laura stopped talking.

"If he loves you, Laura, none of that university and research business will matter a damn to him."

It mattered to Laura, and she feared that someday it might matter a great deal to Isaiah as well. "That isn't really why I called. I'm in a spot of trouble, like I said. Can you send me some money to pay for a lawyer? I'll pay you back. I just can't right now."

"How much do you need?" Mike asked.

Laura sighed. "I don't know. A couple of thousand will do for a start."

"I'll wire it tomorrow."

Laura squeezed her eyes closed. "When this mess is cleared up, I'd like to move down there, Daddy."

"To Florida, you mean?"

"There should be lots of housework," she said with a tremulous laugh. "All those retired women wanting to go to potlucks and parties."

"There is that," her father agreed. "And lots of dogs to walk as well."

"I'm tired of all this snow," Laura lied. "Down there I'll be able to soak up some rays. Maybe I'll even try swimming again."

Laura didn't tell her father that there was another very good reason for her move to Florida. It was almost four thousand miles from Isaiah Coulter. She couldn't bear the thought of running into him in town. Just seeing him from a distance would break her heart. Better that she make a clean break and never look back.

"You know we'd love to have you with us, sweetheart."

Laura thought of all the brain supplements her mother would force upon her and almost cringed. She loved her parents.

But a little distance as a buffer zone had been awfully nice.

Isaiah barely slept that night. Even though Trish had come to get the puppies, he woke up every three hours, on the dot, and then just lay there, listening to the awful silence. He'd tried to phone Laura several times before coming to bed. She wasn't taking his calls.

The following morning he was gritty-eyed and exhausted when he got to the clinic at six. Susan had already opened, which was normal on a weekday. Isaiah grunted a greeting to her as he passed through the kennels. When he entered the surgery, he was surprised to see Belinda.

"You're here bright and early," he said as he slung his coat over a hook and swept off his new Stetson.

"I thought I'd come in and make sure everything was okay to roll," she said. "Robberies don't happen every day, after all."

Isaiah stepped to the sink to scrub his hands. Then he checked his appointment roster. The world hadn't stopped turning. He had three surgeries scheduled for late morning, an afternoon that was booked back-to-back with appointments, and another two surgeries in the late afternoon. He went to check on the guide dog. The shepherd looked perky and happy to see him.

"Hey, buddy." Isaiah crouched down to examine the dog's gums. "Looking good," he said, trying to be his usual cheerful self, but somehow he couldn't quite muster a smile. He missed Laura so much. It had been only a little over twelve hours since he'd seen her, but he felt as if it had been a year. "You'll be getting your walking papers soon."

The shepherd whined and nudged Isaiah's hand for petting. Isaiah obliged for a moment and then pushed to his feet. No matter what happened in his personal life, he still had a job to do. First thing in the morning he always made rounds to check on his patients. He wouldn't neglect his responsibilities simply because things weren't going well for him privately. These animals were counting on him.

"What's the news on Laura?" Belinda asked.

"No news at all yet."

Belinda leaned her shoulder against the cages, standing so close that the back of Isaiah's wrist grazed her breast as he reached in to examine a cat that had been declawed and neutered two days earlier. "This guy should have gone home yesterday," Isaiah observed.

Belinda grabbed his wrist and drew it back to her chest. "Yum. That felt good."

Isaiah had been taken by surprise a few times, but her behavior totally sideswiped him. As he closed the cage, he tried to withdraw his arm. Belinda toppled against him if he'd pulled her toward him. Her breasts smashed against his chest. She gyrated her hips seductively against his pelvis. He stared stupidly into her brown eyes and wondered what the hell he'd done to bring this on.

"Laura's not here. I am," she said huskily. "Chances are she'll go to jail. Drug offense." She clucked her tongue. "Serious business, that. A felony, isn't it? If you plan to marry her, you may have a very long wait." She pushed her hips against him again. "A man has needs. I'd love to take care of yours."

Isaiah's body wasn't connected to his brain. When she rubbed against him, things happened. It wasn't about desire. It wasn't about emotion. Heck, he woke up with a hard-on when he needed to take a leak.

"Belinda, I —"

"You talk too much," she whispered.

Before Isaiah guessed what she meant to do, she locked her arms around his neck. The next instant her tongue was in his mouth. He tried to set her away from him. She clung like a leech. He finally managed to wrench his face to one side.

"This isn't happening," he ground out.

She rubbed her breasts against him. "You want me. I can feel it. You're hard as a rock and throbbing for me."

He was semihard, an anatomical reaction to uninvited stimulus. "No, Belinda. I'm sorry." He pried her arms loose and firmly set her away from him. "You're a pretty lady, but —"

She was wearing a tight zip-up sweater. She grabbed the tab. With a downward tug she bared her breasts. She wore no bra. Toying with her nipples to make them hard, she smiled. "Imagine your mouth on them, Isaiah. Imagine burying yourself in me. I'm already hot — and wet. We could do it on a table, or on the boxes in one of the storage rooms."

He couldn't believe this was happening. "Cover yourself. Susan could walk in."

"Do you think she's never seen two people getting it on?" She rolled her eyes. "Hmm, maybe not. She's built like a block."

Isaiah moved away. "Zip up. I'm not interested."

Silence. He stepped over to the counter. His hands were shaking as he flipped through the patient charts to update his notes. He couldn't make sense of the entries.

"You son of a bitch!" she cried. "You're a limp-dicked excuse for a man."

Throbbing for her one second and limp the next? That was interesting. Isaiah tossed down the pen and turned to face her.

Red-faced and trembling with rage, she jutted her chin at him. "I *love* you!" she cried, the impassioned declaration making her naked breasts jiggle. "I'm the one who's right for you. Why can't you see that? Instead you ignore me and pant after that stupid, moronic kennel keeper."

Isaiah's mind went cold with realization. "Oh, my God," he whispered. "It was you."

Belinda strode angrily across the room, doubled her fist, and swung. Isaiah caught both her wrists just before she planted her knuckles on his mouth. "It was you all along," he said, still incredulous. "You imagined we might get together. When Laura came along, you got jealous and started trying to get rid of her."

Belinda drew her head back and spat in his face. Isaiah blinked. Never in all his life had he been so tempted to hit a woman. But that wasn't the Coulter way, and he wasn't about to compromise his standards for the likes of her.

"You stole the drugs and planted them in Laura's car," he accused. "Somehow you got your hands on her security code. All you cared about was getting her out of here."

"Prove it, asshole."

She wrenched her wrists free and whirled to leave the room, bare breasts swinging. Isaiah was right on her heels. "Not so fast, sweet cheeks. You've got some questions to answer and a small matter with the police to settle."

"Fuck you!"

Isaiah followed her up the hall. He was tempted to grab her arm, but if he did that she'd undoubtedly start swinging. She was a sturdy woman. Being a man, he was at a disadvantage because he couldn't fight back. He figured he could probably subdue her, but in the doing he might hurt her. Better to let the cops handle her.

They reached the lobby. Val, the only office employee who came in early, was standing over the fax machine. She whirled around when Belinda skirted the counter and entered the workstation. Belinda promptly burst into tears, which took Isaiah totally by surprise.

"Help me!" she shrieked, and ducked behind Val as if for protection. "Oh, God, Val. Don't let him near me. H-he tried t-to r-rape me. We were in the s-surgery, and all of a s-sudden he jumped m-me. Look, just look. His fly is still bulging."

Isaiah almost clamped a hand over his crotch. *Oh, shit.* It would be his word against hers. Who the hell would ever believe him?

Val gave Isaiah a long look. Then she ran her gaze over Belinda's denuded breasts. "Bullshit," the office manager said. "I've been here since this place opened. A lot of good-looking babes have come and gone, honey. None of them ever had a problem."

"It happened!" Belinda cried.

"In your dreams, maybe."

Belinda made a bestial sound low in her throat, and the next instant the fax machine went crashing to the floor.

"Hey!" Isaiah yelled when the crazed woman headed for the office files. "Stop it, Belinda. What the hell are you doing? That's vital information on hundreds of animals!"

When he grabbed her arm to stop her from tearing folders from the shelf and throwing them to the floor, she whirled and attacked with fists, fingernails, teeth. Isaiah didn't want to smack her, but, oh, man, he was tempted.

"Belinda, stop it!" he cried.

She just kept swinging. He took a right hook to the eye, a left to his nose. The blows didn't really hurt, but Isaiah crossed his arms over his head and doubled over at the waist to protect his face anyway.

The woman had gone clear over the edge. Isaiah had never seen anyone lose it so completely.

"Val, call the cops!" Instead of racing for the phone, Val stepped in close and said, "Belinda?"

When Belinda stopped pounding on Isaiah long enough to glance over her shoulder, the wiry office manager smiled sweetly, and then she swung, nailing Belinda squarely in the face with a knotted fist. The tech dropped to her knees like a bag of wet cement.

"My nose! My nose!" Belinda cried.

Val stood at the ready to hit her again. "He can't fight back, you vicious little tramp, but I'm more than willing. You want to go a round or two with me, honey? Please, make my day."

Belinda scrambled to get away. Isaiah was already diving for the phone when the tech gained her feet and dashed from the building. Val started after her. Isaiah caught the office manager's arm.

"Let her go," he said. "The police can deal with her."

Val sighed and dusted her hands on her slacks. "What a pity. I was just getting warmed up."

An hour later Isaiah sat in his office with a grandfatherly police officer who'd asked him dozens of questions and been taking copious notes. Isaiah liked the fellow. He had gray hair, a ruddy complexion, and intelligent blue eyes.

"This isn't a mere fixation," Isaiah encapsulated, "but a sick obsession. I never encouraged Belinda. She just somehow got it into her head that we had a future together."

"It happens," Officer Keenan said. "People think it's always men. How wrong they are." He closed his tablet and put the pen in his pocket. "Your theories on the drug theft make sense to me. If you and Ms. Townsend forgot to lock her car the afternoon before last when you were trying to deal with the puppies, it would have been easy enough for Ms. Baxter to get inside the car, pull the trunk lever on the dash, stash the drugs, and then lock all the doors. As for Ms. Townsend's security code, if you or your brother is in the habit of leaving your clinic keys in a coat pocket or desk drawer, anyone could have grabbed them and gone through your files."

"Is Laura in the clear, then?"

Keenan smiled. "I sense you're fond of the lady."

Isaiah nodded. "You could say that."

The officer pushed to his feet. "She's not entirely off the hook, but I'm leaning very strongly in that direction. Let me run a background check on Ms. Baxter. Men and women who become obsessive about members of the opposite sex usually have a history of such behavior."

"How long do you think that will take?"

"With the information you've given me, I may be able to come up with something by tomorrow. The background check itself will take much longer."

"You're going to call the college she attended?"

"And all the employers she listed on her job application." Keenan settled his billed hat on his head. "Next time around you might be wise to check out all the references yourself before you hire someone, Dr. Coulter. These days you just never know about people."

Isaiah couldn't argue the point. He'd been shorthanded when Belinda had applied for a job. She'd been well qualified. He'd bypassed all the preliminaries and hired her on the spot. "I'll be more careful from now on — I guarantee that."

After Officer Keenan left, Isaiah tried once again to call Laura. The phone rang and rang. Finally her recorded message clicked on. Hearing her voice, so halting and sweet, almost brought tears to his eyes. He wished she would at least talk to him. Evidently she was screening her calls, and when a balloon came up in the window, she knew not to answer.

He thought about going to her apartment, but a quick glance at his watch had him springing to his feet instead. He had surgery in ten minutes. Love would have to wait.

At about four thirty that afternoon, Isaiah had just finished spaying a young Lab when Val popped into the surgery. "Officer Keenan is on the phone," she said.

Isaiah angled his bent arms backward to relieve a kink between his shoulder blades. "I'm done here. I'll take it in my office." He glanced at Susan, who'd been filling in all afternoon for Belinda. "Can you take it from here for me?"

The stout blonde nodded. Isaiah tugged off the surgical gloves, dropped them into a receptacle, and peeled off his lab coat, tossing it into a laundry basket as he pushed out the door.

Keenan got right to the point when Isaiah picked up the phone. "Bingo," he said. "Belinda Baxter has a nasty history."

Tugging a stethoscope from around his neck and tossing it on his desk, Isaiah said, "After what I saw this morning, I'm not surprised. What's the scoop?"

"University of Colorado, 1993. Ms. Baxter accused a male athlete of date rape. At the preliminary hearing, her version of the story was contradicted by several credible eyewitnesses, both male and female. They claimed she had a crush on the guy and retaliated when he told her he wasn't interested."

"Shit."

"The following year, she fancied herself in love with a professor. When he spurned her advances, she grew furious and accused him of coercing her into giving him sex in exchange for passing grades. Again, her story didn't hold together."

"I can't believe this," Isaiah said wearily.

"In short," Keenan went on, "the lady has a screw loose. We're trying to locate her for questioning. Unfortunately she seems to have vacated her apartment. We think she's left town."

Isaiah hoped she'd left and would never come back. If he never saw Belinda again, it would be too soon. "Does this mean Laura is no longer a suspect?"

"Going on what little I've already learned, I'm convinced that Ms. Townsend was set up. I'll call her the moment we hang up and give her the news."

"If it's not against procedure, can you postpone that call?" Isaiah asked. "I'd like to deliver the news to her myself, if that's all right."

Keenan laughed. "I'll give you a couple of hours."

"I appreciate it," Isaiah said. "And Officer Keenan? Thank you for all you've done."

"Just doing my job, son."

Because Laura's Mazda was impounded, her grandmother had driven her to a grocery store, and Laura was restocking her refrigerator with perishables when a knock came on her door. She froze with a jug of milk in her hand. Since early morning she'd been expecting Isaiah to show up. How like him to wait until he was finished at the clinic for the day.

The thought made Laura's heart hurt. Some women might be offended when they played second fiddle to a bunch of dogs and cats, but she wasn't one of them. One of the first things she'd come to love about Isaiah was his devotion to the animals in his care.

Laura shoved the milk in the refrigerator and headed for the front door. She couldn't avoid him forever. He'd called at least ten times. Knowing Isaiah, he wasn't likely to stop until she talked to him. She felt stronger today, less likely to fold under pressure. No matter how many times he said he loved her, she would stick to her guns, not because this was easy for her to do, but because her decision to end the relationship would be better for him in the long run.

Before opening the door, she took one last breath for courage. She was surprised to see Belinda standing on the landing. Laura was about to say hello and invite the technician in when she noticed the wild look in Belinda's eyes and the dried blood under her nose. A heartbeat later she saw the butcher knife clutched in the technician's hand.

Laura reacted quickly, throwing her weight against the door to slam it closed, but Belinda was faster and had the advantage of greater weight. Laura was thrown off balance as Belinda shoved her way inside. Before Laura could regain her footing, the brunette was upon her.

During rehab Laura had studied tai chi to help her stay calm, improve her equilibrium, and strengthen the right side of her body, which had been weakened. One particular technique called Push Hands had taught her how to defend herself nonaggressively, using her weight and balance to overset an opponent.

When Belinda stabbed downward with the butcher knife, that Push Hands training saved Laura's life. She caught Belinda's wrist, shifted her weight, and threw the other woman off her feet. Belinda hit the floor. Laura tried to run outside to scream for help, but to her horror Belinda sprang upright, lunged into her path, and came at her again.

"Bitch!" Belinda snarled. "He won't think you're pretty when I get done with you."

Laura bent her knees and bounced on her toes, doing a macabre dance with the knife blade in Belinda's hand, darting to one side, leaping backward, sometimes evading a lethal stab by mere inches.

"Don't — do — this," she managed to push out. "Please — don't."

Belinda only laughed crazily and came at Laura again. Laura jerked away, but this time she wasn't quite fast enough. Belinda grunted and stabbed downward viciously. Laura met the swing with a hard upward shove that knocked the other woman's aim off. Before Belinda could regroup and stab at her again, Laura propelled herself forward, hitting the tech in the midriff with her shoulder.

Belinda whooshed in startled dismay, staggering backward and losing her balance. The backward stumble carried her out the open doorway. Laura didn't wait to see where or how the woman landed. She threw herself against the door to slam it closed, shoved the dead bolt home, and then raced for her purse to get her cell phone.

For a horrible moment she couldn't remember the symbol Gram had programmed in for the police. Panicked, expecting Belinda to break through one of the windows at any moment, she scrolled down with frenzied urgency. Balloon, horse, cake, cat, dog. *Oh, God.* And then she saw it. *Star, to represent a badge.*

Hands shaking so violently that she could barely control her fingers, she punched the little green phone on the console to place the call.

Isaiah brought his Hummer to a fishtailing halt when he saw the police cars nosed in to the curb in front of Laura's garage apartment. Lights were flashing. Uniformed men were racing back and forth across the yard. For a terrible moment he thought the crumpled form of a woman lying on the snow was Laura.

"Holy Mother." Isaiah left the Hummer in the middle of the street. "Laura?"

He leaped over the curb and the snow-covered median to land on the icy sidewalk. He was still running when he saw that the woman had dark hair. He slowed his pace, his gaze fixed incredulously on her limp body. *Belinda?* He looked up and saw the broken railing.

"What happened?" he asked a police officer in a heavy blue bomber jacket and a hat with lined earflaps. "Is the lady who lives here all right?"

"She's fine. I think she's upstairs."

Isaiah took the steps three at a time. When he reached the landing he saw Laura standing in the open doorway, speaking to a police officer. She looked a little shaken up, but fine otherwise, except that she shivered from the cold.

"An ambulance is on the way," the policeman was saying.

"I — didn't — mean — to — hurt — her." Laura glanced past the policeman and saw Isaiah standing there. Her eyes told him everything he needed to know. "Isaiah?" she cried.

He pushed past the cop to pull her into his arms. "What the hell happened?"

Laura clung to his neck. She was shaking so violently that the tremors ran clear through him. Haltingly she recounted the incident. The cop filled in the blanks. Isaiah glanced over the edge of the landing. All he could see of Belinda now was her dark hair spread over the snow, because she'd been covered with a blanket. He knew it was bad of him, but he felt that she deserved whatever she got.

"Is she dead?" he asked the policeman.

"No. Neck injury, we think. The paramedics are on their way."

Isaiah tightened his arm around Laura's waist and led her back into the apartment.

All his rehearsed speeches would have to wait.

An hour later Laura was curled up at one end of the love seat, sipping a second cup of tea. Isaiah sat across from her on an easy chair. Belinda had long since been transported to the hospital by ambulance, and only a few minutes ago the police had called to report that her injuries were minimal. The snow had cushioned her fall. She'd only been knocked out. As soon as the doctors released her, she would be taken to the police station and booked on a number of charges, not the least of which was attempted murder.

Laura had had time to sort it all out now. Her hands were no longer shaking. Her thoughts had cleared. It was time for Isaiah to leave, but he sat on her chair as if he'd put down roots, looking so handsome it made her ache.

Laura knew she should tell him to go. Only it was much harder to do than she'd ever thought it would be. "I'm fine now, Isaiah."

He smiled slightly and nodded. "That's good."

Laura set her teacup aside and unfolded her legs to sit forward on the cushion. "I'd like you to go now."

"Don't lie to me, Laura. You're lousy at it." He sat forward, too, which made her want to retreat. "You love me. I'm the guy you were waiting for. Remember? You're thirty-one years old, and you'd never slept with another man. That's pretty telling, in and of itself. How can you expect me to walk away from that?"

Laura passed a hand over her eyes. She would do this, she told herself. For him, she would say the words that would drive him from her life forever.

"It was about time I had sex, don't you think?" She pushed to her feet. For an awful instant she felt a little dizzy. But her head soon cleared. She went into the kitchen to resume putting away her groceries. "I have things to do, Isaiah. It's over. Both of us need to move on."

"You're absolutely right." He stood up and sauntered slowly toward her. "We need to move on — together. The Christmas party is tonight. I won't go without you. And what about Christmas Eve and Christmas day? Without you to share it with none of it will have meaning for me."

Laura's chest felt as if a vise were tightening around it. "Go away. Please. I don't want you here."

"I can't do that. I love you, Laura."

She chanced a glance at him. Bad mistake. He was so beautiful — tall and dark, his hair tousled from the wind. He wore a green shirt with a button-down collar. The sleeves were rolled back to reveal his tanned, corded forearms. His Western belt buckle flashed at his lean waist, a preface to his long, powerfully muscled legs and a masculine stance to make any woman's heart skip beats.

"I know you overheard Tucker's tirade yesterday," he said softly. "But you obviously didn't listen long enough to hear what I had to say. I love you so much, Laura. I honestly don't think I can face life without you. Tucker left the house understanding that, glad to know that you'd soon be his sister-in-law."

Laura shook her head. "He was right at the start. You need someone smart and charming and accomplished. Someone who can help you re-alize your poten-tial. If you go into research, you'll need a wife who can charm people into giving you grants." She lost her grip on the eggs. The Styrofoam carton hit the floor with a loud report. Laura knew without looking that she'd just broken every shell, and she closed her eyes in frustration. When she bent to collect the container, egg yolks and whites streamed to the floor, forming slimy puddles. "I'm none of those things anymore."

"Forget research. I'm interested in that end of veterinary medicine. I won't deny it. But what really vitalizes me, what makes it all worthwhile, is actually working with the animals and making them well. I'd never be happy in a lab, and I'll never want to teach at a university for precisely the same reason."

Laura's heart surged with hope.

"As for my potential, I'm perfectly capable of realizing that by myself, without the help of a wife. That isn't to say I'd turn down some help. Only it would have to come from the right woman, someone who loves animals as much as I do, someone who can still smile while she's getting her hands dirty, someone who'll understand when I come home worried about a patient, and will worry about that patient with me."

Laura gulped and struggled to breathe, blindly smearing the broken eggs around on the floor with paper towels. Finally she gave up on it and tossed the slimy wad in the trash. "Sooner or later I'm afraid I'd ruin your life."

"What life? You're the woman I just described, Laura. You love those damn puppies so much, I'm afraid you'll want to keep all thirteen, and I love you so much, I'll let you."

That brought her head around.

"Remember me, the guy who never remembered to eat? You keep me centered." He took a step toward her. "Do you have any idea how long I went without reading a novel or watching a movie before you came along? Years!"

"Then you need to change that."

"I'm trying, but I need your help."

The sincerity in his voice had her searching his eyes.

"With you," he went on, "I notice things I'd never notice otherwise — how the air smells after it snows, and that no two snowflakes are alike, and how sweet the breath of a puppy is." Tears sparkled in his eyes. "Do you really want me to revert to my old habits? I'll forget to eat. My socks will never match. I'll go to work with a fabric-softener sheet stuck to the back of my collar and wear a purple polka-dot tie with a red striped shirt to receive the Vet of the Year award."

Tears sprang to Laura's eyes, too, even as a smile touched her lips. It would happen, she knew. Isaiah was nothing if not preoccupied and distracted.

Isaiah glimpsed the slight smile that touched her mouth. That was all he needed to see. He was across the kitchen and gathering her into his arms before she could protest.

"I love you. I need you in my life. What must I say, what must I do, to make you realize that?"

Laura leaned her head back to search his dark face, and in that moment she needed no more convincing. She saw his love for her in his eyes.

"You said you'd marry me," he said fiercely. "I'm holding you to it. I want you to have my babies. I want to grow old with you. You talk about my potential and my realizing my dreams? What's it about if all I do is work and never enjoy the everyday business of just being alive?"

"Oh, Isaiah," she said shakily. "I love you, too."

"I know you do," he whispered.

And then he kissed her. A sweet, tentative kiss that soon turned deep and hungry. Laura was incapable of resisting the delicious draw of his mouth. She curled her arms around his neck and went up on her tiptoes, accepting what she should have known all along — that she belonged exactly where she was, in his arms.

Epilogue

January 8, 2005

The cork shot from the bottle, and French champagne spewed like a geyser, drenching the sleeve of Jake's dark suit jacket. He laughed and reached across Isaiah's dining room table to fill the crystal flutes of the bride and groom.

Laura and Isaiah intertwined their arms, gazed deeply into each other's eyes, and took their first sip of champagne together as husband and wife. Laura was almost giddy with happiness. Everything in her world was exactly right. After her accident, she'd believed that her life had been destroyed. Now, lost in her husband's shimmering blue eyes, she realized that she'd had to lose her life in order to find it. And perhaps, in a much different way, he had as well.

Over the last couple of weeks, they had both come to understand so many things, namely that happiness wasn't about success or money or a brilliant future. It was about right now, today, and how well they lived each moment.

Bearing that in mind, they had chosen not to waste any of their moments together and had planned a quick wedding at a small church with only the people they loved present to witness their vows. Because Laura's parents were retired and living on a fixed income, she had handled all the details herself — making her own dress, doing her own flower arrangements, and simply phoning everyone to invite them. Natalie, Zeke's wife, had provided the music, and, best of all, had composed a song especially for Isaiah and Laura that they would cherish all their lives. The wedding feast had been potluck, with everyone bringing dishes, so there had been plenty of food, served family style, with very little fuss.

"Toast!" Hank yelled.

Laura's father raised his glass and turned toward her and Isaiah. Laura expected him to say the usual sappy stuff about losing his little girl and gaining a son. Instead he winked at her and said, "To the bride and groom. May they live happily in peaceful harmony until death do they part. If by chance, however, all doesn't go well, I have one important request, Laura. If you ever come running home to your mother, don't bring all fourteen dogs."

As if on cue, Hapless came bounding into the room and gave a happy bark. All thirteen rottweiler puppies wobbled in behind him. Everyone in the room burst out laughing. Laura had no intention of keeping all the dogs, of course, only Frown Face, but she was still glad to have puppies darting every which way at her wedding reception. Frown Face latched onto her father's pant leg, gave a gleeful growl, and braced his stout little legs to tug with all his might. Why not begin the first day of their life together the way they meant to continue, with animals playing a major role?

"Who let them loose?" Isaiah asked.

Jake's son, Garrett, skidded to a stop on the hardwood floor, glanced guiltily at his mother, Molly, and said, "Sly did it."

Isaiah chuckled and hooked an arm around Laura's waist. "Now, there's a chip off the old Coulter block. Blame it on the other guy."

Molly and Carly began trying to catch the puppies. Bethany followed behind in her wheelchair, ready to hold the furry little captives on her lap while her sisters-in-law captured the rest. Tucker and Ryan went to lend their assistance.

"Now you know why they held the reception at their house, Mom." Tucker glanced back over his shoulder to wink at Mary. "Leaky puppies and your carpet wouldn't go well together. You can thank your lucky stars."

Mary glanced over at Laura's grandmother, Etta, and smiled. Mary was indeed thanking her lucky stars, but for an entirely different reason than Tucker thought. Seeing the happiness in Laura's and Isaiah's eyes when they looked at each other was enough to warm any mother's heart, especially when she knew it had been partly her matchmaking scheme that had gotten them together. Isaiah was relaxed. Laura fairly glowed. They were perfect for each other.

But, then, hadn't Mary known that all along?

Smiling with smug satisfaction, Mary returned her gaze to Tucker. It occurred to her in that moment that he was her only son who still wasn't married. She sighed. He always had been her most difficult child, doing just the opposite of what she wanted or expected him to. '

Mary frowned slightly. Tucker's cavalier attitude toward women would make it tricky to find him a wife, but she felt equal to the challenge. He needed a young lady with plenty of spunk — that would be an absolute must — someone as beautiful as he was handsome, with enough steel in her backbone to go toe-to-toe with him and give back as good as she got.

Luckily Mary just happened to know a young lady with four older brothers who might be a perfect match for her willful, stubborn son.

Ah, yes, she thought as she sipped champagne. There might be some very interesting possibilities there.